CW01336535

The Life and Complete Works in Prose and Verse of Robert Greene ... - Primary Source Edition

Alexander Balloch Grosart, Robert Greene

THE HUTH LIBRARY.

LIFE AND WORKS

OF

ROBERT GREENE, M.A.

VOL. I.

STOROJENKO'S LIFE OF ROBERT GREENE:

WITH

INTRODUCTION AND NOTES.

"All the world's a stage,
And all the men and women merely players;
They have their exits and their entrances;
And one man in his time plays many parts."

As You Like It, ii. 7.

Augusti meditatio. Cap. 1

O Domine Jesu, da cordi meo te desiderare
desiderando quaerere, quaerendo invenire,
inveniendo amare, amando mala mea redimere, redempta
non iterare. Da domine deus meus
cordi meo penitentiam, spiritui contritionem,
oculis lachrymarum fontem, ori custodiam,
manibus eleemosinarum largitatem, ut tuus figaris
in me, qui tuus crucifixus pro me. Amen

Robert Greene

The Huth Library

OR

ELIZABETHAN-JACOBEAN

Unique or Very Rare

BOOKS

IN

VERSE AND PROSE

LARGELY

From the Library of

Henry Huth, Esqr.

(Engraved by C. H. Jeens from a Photograph)

Edited with Introductions, Notes and Illustrations, etc.

BY THE

Rev. Alexander B. Grosart, LL.D., F.S.A.

FOR PRIVATE CIRCULATION ONLY

The Huth Library.

THE

LIFE AND COMPLETE WORKS

IN

PROSE AND VERSE

OF

ROBERT GREENE, M.A.

CAMBRIDGE AND OXFORD.

IN FIFTEEN VOLUMES.

FOR THE FIRST TIME COLLECTED AND EDITED,
WITH NOTES AND ILLUSTRATIONS, ETC.,

BY THE REV.
ALEXANDER B. GROSART, D.D., LL.D. (EDIN.), F.S.A. (SCOT.),
St. George's, Blackburn, Lancashire.

VOL. I.

STOROJENKO'S LIFE OF ROBERT GREENE,
TRANSLATED BY E. A. B. HODGETTS, ESQ., LONDON,
WITH
INTRODUCTION AND NOTES BY THE EDITOR.

PRINTED FOR PRIVATE CIRCULATION ONLY.
1881-86.

50 *copies*.]

76345

Printed by Hazell, Watson, & Viney, Ld., London and Aylesbury.

CONTENTS.

	PAGE
NOTE	vii
INTRODUCTION	ix
LIFE	1
APPENDIX A AND B	257
FACSIMILE OF GREENE'S HANDWRITING.	*To face title-page*

„Bei aller verschmaechten Liebe! beim hoellischen Elemente!
Ich wollt', ich wuesst' was aerger's dass ich's fluchen Koennte!"

GOETHE.

NOTE.

I wish to record my right hearty thanks to E. A. B. Hodgetts, Esq., for his translation of Professor Storojenko's Life of Greene. It has been to him no perfunctory work, but a task of love and sympathy. I would emphasize my deep indebtedness to "mine ancient friend," Dr. Brinsley Nicholson, of Surrenden Lodge, for continuous and much prized help and suggestions. Anything more requiring to be said will be found in our Introduction and Notes throughout. It is no common satisfaction thus to have completed (for the first time) the Works of Robert Greene along with those of his associates, Thomas Nashe (6 vols.), and Dr. Gabriel Harvey (3 vols.). To students of Elizabethan-Jacobean literature it is believed the service thus rendered will be increasingly and wideningly appreciated.

Whilst I write these words, an examination of Bp. Grindal's Register (fol. 213), which was Newcourt's authority, shows that Robertus Grene was admitted to Tollesbury on 19th June, 1584, on the death of ffrancis Searle; and that fol. 225, in recording the succession of Moody, spells the name Greene, and adds—"per liberam et spontaneam resignationem Roberti Greene clerici ultimi"—the latter circumstance to be noted as inferentially telling us there had been no misconduct to lead to the resignation. The absence of the M.A. of Cambridge after the name introduces an element of doubt, but like absence in other entries prevents our rejecting this Robert Greene as the dramatist. R. W.'s 'red-nosed minister' in Martin Mar-Sixtus, and the Pinner noting 'minister,' seem to make it indubitable that whether he were vicar of Tollesbury or no, or whether he ever held a benefice or no, the dramatist was a cleric. Besides, let the dates and facts be kept in recollection as fitting in with the incumbency at Tollesbury: (1) In 1584 he published the 'Mirrour of Modestie,' also 'Arbasto'—the Vicar being appointed 19th June, 1584; (2) In 1585 he only published 'Planetomachia'—Vicar resigned 17th Feb. 1585, *i.e.* 1586; (3) In 1586 Greene published nothing, this being the year of his marriage.

For the original of our fac-simile of Greene's handwriting (as it is believed), I am indebted to a private collector in London.

A. B. G.

"This strange eventful history."

As You Like It, ii. 7.

INTRODUCTION

TO

PROFESSOR STOROJENKO'S LIFE OF GREENE.

BY THE EDITOR.

WHILST it is a pleasant proof—among many—of the breadth of interest modernly taken in our great English Literature, that it has been deemed expedient to furnish a new Life of ROBERT GREENE mainly in a translation of that in Russian by Professor Storojenko of Moscow, and whilst I give ungrudging recognition to this Life (as well as to his "Predshestveniky Shakspeara"), three matters-of-fact nevertheless demand statement, toward modifying the apparent blame of our own countrymen for leaving it to a Stranger to fulfil this task of love.

(*a*) That DYCE, in his matterful and careful "Account of Robert Greene and his Writings," prefixed to both his editions of his Dramatic Works and minor Poems, long since laid a "good foundation" for his successor, and on which that successor has necessarily built his own superstructure, without such definite and detailed and generous acknowledgment of indebtedness as it had been a pleasure to English scholars to have found.

(*b*) That besides his obligations throughout to Dyce, Professor Storojenko, in his most distinctive conclusions and critical results, had been anticipated by a good year by Professor J. M. BROWN, of Canterbury College, Christchurch, New Zealand; who in 1877 published his brilliant and penetrative literary Study entitled "An Early Rival of Shakespere" in the *New Zealand Magazine, a Quarterly Journal of General Literature*, No. 6, April 1877 (pp. 97-133).

(*c*) That it will be seen that, with all its painstaking and insight, this Life has had to be read somewhat vigilantly, and to be frequently and fully annotated, with corrective and supplemental additions. O' times, because of this, one was tempted to give an original Life and utilise Professor Storojenko's criticisms and comments. But it was felt that the announcement of a translation of Storojenko's Life required redemption.

With reference to Professor J. M. Brown's Paper, I mean in the outset, and as the first half of this Introduction, to reproduce it substantially, and thus reclaim for a "brither Scot" things that otherwise might seem to belong exclusively to the Foreigner. If Professor Storojenko worked out his problems independently (and *certes* he gives no faintest intimation of acquaintance with the Essay in question, although it is well known in Germany), the twofold agreement on the main points will be mutually confirmatory. And after every abatement, (*meo judicio*) this Russian Life of Robert Greene is noticeably well-informed, thoughtful, and fresh in substance; sound and sober, not speculative; practical and intelligible, not misty or super-ingenious; in style, lucid, and luminous; and as such deserving of translation. Compared with German investigators—*e.g.*, Bernhardi and Bodenstadt—it has exceptional merits.

Turning now to the Paper of Professor J. M. Brown, it thus opens:—

"'There is an upstart Crowe beautified with our feathers, that with his "Tygers heart wrapt in a Players hide," supposes he is as well able to bumbast out a blanke verse as the best of you: and being an absolute *Iohannes factotum*, is in his owne conceit the onely Shake-scene in a countrie.' Unconditional admiration has become so prevailingly the mood of nineteenth-century criticism of Shakespere, that to speak of the possibility of rivalry, or to question his supremacy, is to raise a contemptuous smile. To such a mood the sentence quoted seems little more than envious folly and untruth. But the circumstances in which it was written, if nothing else, demand for it serious consideration. The writer, Robert Greene, saw death close upon him when he wrote it; he was driven before the wildest of his repentant moods; and his repentances were ever whirlwinds of self-accusation, fiery, brief, and ruthlessly candid. Doubt has been thrown on the sincerity of his written repentances; and it must be granted that Greene was capable in his more Bohemian moods of the most hideous jests. But any one who studies the broken glimpses of his life, indistinct though it is as the very 'dream of a shadow,' sees its uncontrollable fits of dissipation and its equally uncontrollable fits of remorse, and then reads the passionate fervour of his last appeal to his brother dramatists, in which this attack on Shakespere occurs, will not hesitate to accept it as a genuine utterance of Greene's last thoughts. Else it is the weakest jest ever was perpetrated" (pp. 97-8).

Only the ghoul-like heart of Dr. Gabriel Harvey could have doubted, much less made mock of the final "Repentance" of Robert Greene, and my friend pays too much heed to suspectors of this ignoble type by spending a line upon them. Sincerity and reality pulsate in every word of these ultimate utterances, and I for one do not envy the man who can read them with dry eyes even at this late day. He proceeds:—

"If the sentence be accepted as genuine and serious, the charge must have had some foundation. The real question, therefore, is how far Greene was justified by his facts in the attack. Allowance must be made for the exaggeration of passion; so also for the unwholesome state of the author's mind at the time. But when all allowance is made, a kernel of truth remains worthy investigation, corroborated, as it is, by the author of 'Greene's Funeralls' (1594), who says:—

> "Nay more, the men that so eclipst his fame,
> Purloynde his plumes; can they deny the same?"

The most noticeable point is that the line 'Tygers heart wrapt in a Player's hide' parodies a line in *Henry VI.* (Pt. III., Act i., sc. 4), 'O tiger's heart wrapt in a woman's hide,' which also occurs in *The True Tragedie of Richard Duke of York.* It has been inferred from this, and confirmed by other trustworthy evidence, that Shakespere's *Henry VI.* (Parts II. and III.) is a recomposition of this old play along with another, *The First Part of the Contention betwixt the Two Famous Houses of York and Lancaster*, and that Greene had a hand in the composition of these. Our old dramatists, divided though they often were by personal quarrel or the rancour of artists, were as often united in mutual admiration and mutual help. A large number of the plays that have come down to us from their age bear the names of two, and frequently of three authors; and it is not unlikely that more than this number have contributed to dramas that have been published without name. How they apportioned their work it is impossible to say: most probably, one wrote the original draught, which they severally revised and added to, so that every part was the joint production of all" (p. 98).

En passant, I venture to remark that it has not been sufficiently noted that we are repeatedly told by Greene himself—*e.g.*, as 'Roberto' and 'Francesco'—that when in sorest straits he fell among 'actors,' and thereafter earned a good living by his part as a Playwright. This involves that the extant plays are a mere *flotsam* of his dramatic productions. The pity is that we have no such source as Henslowe's "Note-book" to shed light on his distinctive work. But the fact is to be accentuated that at this period Robert Greene was a principal writer of plays, and as such earned a continuous living. I must also at this point doubt of Simpson's interpretation of Greene's phrase "beautified with our feathers" meaning actors and so speakers of others' words. The allusion in "Greene's Funeralls" seems to point to something deeper and harder than this—if one may think of hardship at all in the mere speaking of their parts by the actors—to wit, actual appropriation of early forms of specific plays, and such revises and alterations as eclipsed these earlier forms—of which more hereafter. It is the more needful to emphasize this as our Essayist next puts his finger on the secret of Shakspeare's offence to Greene, thus:—

"A tacit code of honour seems to have held amongst them, and of this one of the chief articles was, that however much those wreckers the 'brachygraphy men' might pirate their unpublished dramas, no dramatist should remodel or put upon the stage another's work without due acknowledgment. Shakespere's name is almost the only one of the well-known playwrights which is not found with some other on the title-page of any extant play that has his hand clearly in it; and it is acknowledged on all sides, that at first he did little else than tinker the plays of others, and more than one of his dramas are reproductions of old plays which still exist. The conclusion is obvious, that Shakespere violated this unwritten law, whether from modesty, or from the calm audacity of genius, or from the very natural feeling of pique which he must have felt at the condescension of those who spread their University feathers towards this 'upstart crow' from Stratford. It is to this code that Greene appeals in his last indignant repudiation of 'those puppets that speak from our mouths, those anticks garnisht in our colours'; it is this which leads virtuous gall to his death-bed reflections, and affords a certain plea for epithets like 'apes,' 'rude grooms,' 'buckram gentlemen,' 'peasants,' 'painted monsters.' Shakespere did all his best work after Greene's death, and had excellent reason for refusing acknowledgment of any co-operation in his work: *Henry VI.* and *The Taming of the Shrew* are the only ones of his *rifacimenti* which contain recognisable features of the old originals; all the rest were so perfected by revision and re-revision as to make the models from which they started unreadable by comparison" (pp. 98, 99).

Two remarks are suggested by the last quotation. (*a*) That in the recollection that "Shakespere did all his best work after Greene's death" it might have been well to have headed the Paper, "An Early Rival of *young* Shakespere," so saving the grotesqueness of any 'rival' when he had produced *Hamlet*, *Lear*, *Macbeth*, *Othello*. (*b*) That the deftness with which Shakspeare (like Milton) availed himself of others' images and fancies, and more, without laying himself open to a charge of actual spoliation, could not but be exasperating to one like Greene. And

I question if ever he at any rate wrote anything that would or could be called "unreadable by comparison." What indeed would we not give for the plays of Greene and others from whom Shakspeare "purloynde plumes"! More on this also onward.

On the unassigned plays that have come down to us, Professor Brown continues trenchantly and suggestively:—

"If style and dramatic purpose are to be taken as any guide, many of the anonymous plays that have come down to our time were written by two or more of the comrades in art—Kyd, Marlowe, Greene, Peele and Lodge. In the old play *The Taming of a Shrew* there is evident the hand of Marlowe, in a weak, self-repeating humour, or else that of an audacious plagiarist of Marlowe; but over and above this, the comic parts smack of Greene. Sander is a combination of Greene's Jenkin and Adam; though even in the humorous parts one or two sentences are direct from Marlowe's *Faustus*. "The True Chronicle History of King Leir and his Three Daughters," from which Shakespere started with his greatest drama, has a close resemblance in tone and design to Greene and Lodge's *Looking-glass for London and England*. Both are religious and passionately moral in their tone, and their main design is to exhibit various forms of injustice and ingratitude, and especially the ingratitude of a child. Regan, in *King Lear*, though a woman, has distinct points of likeness to Radagon of the latter play, in character as well as name. But, besides this, there are, in the serious parts, echoes of Kyd's versification and metaphors, especially of his *First Part of Jeronimo*, and in the humour, echoes of *Solyman and Perseda*, which, from parallelisms, must be attributed to Kyd. There is little trace, it is true, of the epic tone of the old play remaining in Shakespere's masterpiece, as we have it; but it is only fair to assume—as of *Hamlet* there does exist an earlier and cruder form—that it did not spring into being and perfection at once, that there were earlier acting versions of it, which were improved from time to time. If such an assumption be correct, the debt must have seemed to the elder dramatist still greater than it does to us. *The Troublesome Raigne of King John*, which Shakespere abridges and strengthens into his own play bearing the name of that king, has no traces of Greene's hand in it, but is a product of the school of Marlowe, with pre-Marlowean versification (rhyming couplet and blank verse intermixed), and with occasional touches of the style of Kyd and Peele. To the objection that most of these were not published till after Greene's death, and some not till after the publication of Shakespere's plays of similar purport, the reply is that Shakespere, as an actor and manager, had always easy access to unpublished plays" (pp. 99-100).

One must interpose to say, Shakspeare could not have had access to those of rival companies.

Coming to details, the Essayist proceeds on lines thus occupied before Professor Storojenko :—

"But Shakespere's debts to his predecessors, and especially to Greene, were, of course, not confined to whole plays; he was not above borrowing their plots and characters. His *Winter's Tale* follows Greene's prose novel of 'Pandosto' in plot and character, all except Antigonus, Paulina, Autolycus, and the Young Shepherd. Launce, in *The Two Gentlemen of Verona*, has clear marks of the humour, and even of the sayings, of Greene's 'Slipper.' In Greene, too, are dramatic hints which might, without injustice, be deemed the source of the greater dramatist's best work. *Orlando Furioso* (along with Kyd's *Spanish Tragedy*) pointed the way to *Lear* and *Hamlet*; *Friar Bacon and Friar Bungay* (with Marlowe's *Faustus*), preceded Shakespere's use of the supernatural; the fairy framework of *James IV.* is followed by the *Midsummer Night's Dream*. The defence of Shakespere in this respect is, that he was doing just what other playwrights did—what Greene himself did. Had the dramatists been under the necessity of thinking out their plots, it is not improbable that their energy would have been exhausted in the effort, and that they would have been novelists instead of play-writers. But perhaps the nice conscience of the author of 'The Repentance' saw marked distinction between poaching from old and foreign writers, and poaching from living ones. Greene and the University men dramatised from the old chroniclers—as Shakespere often did too—and from Italian, Latin, and Greek authors. Shakespere generally preferred to take what was readiest to hand" (pp. 100-1).

It is to be noted that *Winter's Tale* came after Greene's death. Piercing still deeper—far deeper than Professor Storojenko's criticisms at best—we have next this:—

"In style, again, Greene is father of Shakespere—as far, at least, as an ordinary man may be said to be father of a giant. When matured, their plays have none of the 'thundering eloquence' or unrelieved passion of Marlowe's best work, nor of the delicate sweetness of Peele's. They have the irregular strength, the granite of Teutonic art. The gloom of gathering passion in them does not break in shower of tears and sorrow alone, but with lightning of laughter. They have as strong guiding intellects as they have emotions, and their emotions are therefore anything but one-sided. In the midst of some great passion, the thought turns upon itself, and a passing smile saves it from turgidity or paroxysm. Their humour ever dashes in, and makes softer as well as grander the storm of their tragedy. Contrast, relief, marks off their dramatic style; little touches of pathos breathe across their comedies; humorous passages chequer their serious plays as gratefully as clouds the midsummer sunlight. That humour of theirs, too, is, more frequently than other dramatists', of that wise, refreshing sort, which has the fear of fate before its eyes. The rollicking, reckless kinds—farce, burlesque, wit—have their place, but it is a subordinate one" (p. 101).

Here is the judicial summing-up of the whole thus far, with continuous depth:—

"It may seem strange that this kinship in genius did not destroy their antagonism; but likeness, when it does not reconcile, produces the most perfect of hatreds. And the enmity was not all on one side. Greene's has been attacked as envy and malice; but our supreme dramatist, as we can see from contemporary accounts, was on somewhat the same level of fame as his enemy when the latter wrote his 'Repentance'; and the faculty of generously recognising a new superior in a man's own department of work is so rare as to be almost godlike. But it is as rare and happy a faculty in men of character to see in weak spite the involuntary recognition of their power. Shakespere, with all his tolerance, was unable to refrain from retaliation; but it is with no venomous pen he retaliates. *Love's Labour's Lost* includes in its sweeping burlesque not merely Greene, but the whole early school of dramatists, and its enemy, Gabriel Harvey, too. He has, however, the vile trick of modern warfare, of supplying himself with his deadliest war-materials from his enemy's armoury. He borrows from his predecessors the very characters he uses to ridicule them. Pistol, into whose delightfully braggart mouth he puts some of the stagiest phrases from Kyd, Marlowe, Greene, and Peele, is borrowed in all his essential features from Piston in Kyd's *Solyman and Perseda*; Bardisco, in the same play, combines all the lineaments which Shakespere divided up into Falstaff, Bardolph, Nym, and Peto, and these are broad burlesques of the life which his predecessors led. Falstaff has no resemblance whatever to Sir John Oldcastle, in the old play of *Henry V.* (Dericke of the same play is more a prototype); and, in his death as well as his life, is a caricature of Greene. Shakespere, however, draws it with a broad and merciful hand—unlike Ben Jonson and the other authors of *Eastward Hoe*, who put into Quicksilver's mouth Greene's own phrases, and refer to his 'Repentance.' In the *Midsummer Night's Dream*, again, he takes this early school of amateur player-poets, and pillories them in Bottom, Quince, Snug, Flute, Snout, and Starveling; and with the elfin machinery he borrows from Greene, turns his caricature, Bottom, into everlasting ridicule. If *Henry IV.* and *Midsummer Night's Dream* existed in earlier form—as it is just to assume, from Shakespere's practice—it is easy to understand the impotent fury that could lead Greene to intrude a note sounding like envy and malice into his death-bed warning and prophecy.

It would take the meekest man to bear with patience such benignant ridicule, produced with weapons filched from himself, by a rival who is rising at his own and his comrades' expense into the throne of dramatic art" (pp. 101-2).

I felt disposed—yet most reluctantly—to acquiesce in Professor Brown's idea that in Falstaff Shakspeare had a tacit reference to Greene's death-bed. But on exchanging views with my good friend Dr. Brinsley Nicholson, I find myself willingly persuaded that it is most unlikely. He has pointed out that there is no "repentance" evident in Falstaff, though a charitably disposed person might hope that his "God, God" was some evidence of an unexpressed repentance. Neither is there, he argues, anything of the nature of travesty in it. Contrariwise, it is one of the strongest proofs we have of a deep, abiding moral sense in Shakspeare, even at this date, and is, when taken with the rest of Falstaff's life as depicted, one of the most pathetic passages in Shakspeare. Here is a man of great intelligence, humour and wit, who, after the rollicking, dissipated life which he has chosen for himself, dies like a brute beast, and impenitent, drawing from every beholder, or rather hearer, the reflection, "And this is the human end of such, and afterwards——" It revolts one to think of the "gentle" Shakspeare associating himself with the base Gabriel Harvey in travestying so tragical a death-bed as was Greene's. The same observation must be made of the alleged caricature of Greene in Bottom, of *Midsummer Night's Dream.* I must take this fresh opportunity of recalling that, as the converse of Herrick's famous (or infamous) pleading that if his verse was impure his life was chaste,

Greene's writings are exceptionally clean. Nor must he be refused the benefit of this in any judicial estimate of him. It is equally harsh and uncritical to say that this confessedly dissolute-living man wrote purely because it paid to do so. It did no such thing. It would have paid, and did pay, to write impurely, and as ministering to the insatiate appetite of readers for garbage. To his undying honour, Robert Greene, equally with James Thomson, left scarce a line that dying he need have wished "to blot." I can't understand the nature of any one who can think hardly of Greene in the light of his ultimate penitence and absolute confession. It is (if the comparison be not over-bold) as though one had taunted David with his sin after the fifty-first Psalm.

Mr. F. G. Fleay, in his new book of the "Life and Work" of Shakspeare (1 vol. 8vo, Nimmo, 1886), only beats out the bullion of Professor Brown's notices of *Love's Labour's Lost* and *Midsummer Night's Dream*, save when he interweaves (after the manner of Simpson) crotchets of paradox and misinterpretation.

Having completed his exposition of the "Repentance" words, our Essayist addresses himself next to a statement and illustration of a characteristic and merit (if the word be not too frigid) of Greene, that strikes every thoughtful reader of his works, and especially his plays. Professor Storojenko merely touches on it, though effectively; and from the close of his Preface it is perhaps to be concluded that he was not left free to say all he might have done on such a subject. Be this as it may, to Professor Brown belongs the distinction of having first put and urged it. Most noteworthy is every sentence of the following:—

"But surpassed as Greene was by his enemy in style, power, imagination, and everything that contributes to dramatic success, he remained in advance of all his contemporaries in prophetic sympathy. It is sometimes stated that the dramatists had no prescience of the coming storm—of the rise of the peasants for their rights, and of the Puritans for freedom of worship. And to compare the more enduring literature of our own day with that of Elizabethan times, brings out the truth with greater force. The modern stage is crowded with thinking artisans, inspired ploughmen, heroic women with no pretensions to birth. In the old drama, the hero must be a king, or at least an 'earl or belted knight,' and women beneath the *rôle* of queens are anything but heroic. To see the greatness of the contrast, it is only necessary to place side by side the work of Marlowe, the shoemaker's son, with that of Burns, the ploughman, each of whom opened his age. Marlowe revels in great names and titles, and has no ear for 'the still sad music of humanity' apart from adventitious ornament. To Burns, the essential principle of his art as well as of his life is, 'A man's a man for a' that.' The dictum is true of the majority of the dramatists, and certainly of Shakespere. But in Greene we have an exception. In his *Pinner of Wakefield* there is the most distinct recognition of popular rights, and of popular power to assert them; and in the *Looking-glass for London and England* there is so clear a prophecy of revolution, so unhesitating a threat of poverty and wrong rising in judgment against the tyrannously great, so decided a Puritan vein, that it might be taken as a dramatised chapter of a sixteenth-century Dr. Cumming. It is filled with passages such as this:—

'Oh London, maiden of the mistress isle,
Wrapt in the folds and swathing-clouts of shame,
In thee more sins than Nineveh contains!

* * * * *

Swoln are thy brows with impudence and shame,
Oh proud, adulterous glory of the west!'

"The voice of the peasant is rarely heard in Marlowe;

and then only when he can vaunt like a king, or talk like an ignorant buffoon. In Greene's dramas there mingles with the loud clash of armies and rulers, the wise and searching humour of the low-born clown—a key-note caught by Shakespere; but Greene in this direction surpassed the mightier son of his genius. He gives to his peasants the pathos and lovely emotions which in Shakespere belong only to kings and queens, lords and ladies. There rise from his pages the whisper of lowly lovers as pure and noble as one hears only in courts and on thrones in his great successor. The weary toil of artisan life, the wrongs of oppression, the sorrows of the poor, are not laughed at or forgotten; the romance which the nineteenth century has found in 'vile mechanicals' was long before painted in the neglected pages of Greene; Adam Bede and Felix Holt might find a worthy ancestor in George-a-Green, the Pinner of Wakefield; he has the same sturdy independence, the same determination to stick to his humble work, the same fearlessness of nobility and wealth, combined with a rational respect for law and equity; there is no more exalted picture of the muscular English working man to be found in English literature. In the first scene of the play, when Sir Nicholas Mannering appears in Wakefield with his commission from the rebel Earl of Kendal, and demands victuals for the rebel army, the stalwart pound-keeper steps forward, makes the knight eat his words, and then his seals:—

> 'What, are you in choler? I will give you pills
> To cool your stomach. Seest thou these seals?
> Now, by my father's soul,
> Which was a yeoman when he was alive,
> Eat them, or eat my dagger's point, proud squire.'

The Earl of Kendal and other noblemen next appear in disguise, and send their horses into the Pinner's corn to brave him; George approaches, and after altercation strikes the Earl, and to Lord Bonfield's 'Villain, what hast thou done? thou hast struck an earl,' answers such 'flat blasphemy' as might make the hair of the good old fox-hunting, radical-hating, pauper-driving squire of the present day stand on end:—

> 'Why, what care I? a poor man that is true,
> Is better than an earl if he be false.'

"Overpowered by numbers, he resorts to stratagem, and gets the three leaders to consult alone an old magician in a wood. George himself is the magician, and when he has them alone, slays one, and takes the other two prisoners. Yet he sits down and meditates—

> 'Here sit thou, George, wearing a willow wreath,
> As one despairing of thy beauteous love.'

He cannot get his 'Bettris' from her miserly father, Grime; but love is kind, and Jenkin, his man, walks in with his betrothed, rescued by a ruse. The rebellion is quelled, and King Edward offers him any reward he may choose. The poor pound-keeper replies that his only wish is to marry his 'lovely Leman, as bright of blee as is the silver moon.' To the offer of knighthood he begs,

> 'Then let me live and die a yeoman still;
> So was my father, so must live his son.'

"It is delightfully fresh to find a yeoman boxing the ears of an earl; fresh enough to have a queen doing so; but in a time when feudalism had left a loathsome sediment in social manners, when the drama rings with lordly arrogance, it satisfies our sense of justice to see a hind turn the tables on a noble. The play is founded on an old ballad, and has all the breezy freshness of the old ballads; but the subordinate scenes, such as that in which the shoemakers of Bradford make the Kings of England and Scotland yield to their ancient custom of 'Vail staff,' prove that it is to Greene, and not to the old ballad alone, that this democratic tone is owing.

"The play is redolent of the brighter side of English humble life. Across the three centuries come the scent of the new-mown hay and the rustle of the ripening cornfields; we can see the healthy open-air life of the yeoman, his rude practical justice, his rough honest jest; we can hear the ringing buffet in return for tyranny or insult, and the strong hearty laughter that saves from cringing insincerity or sullen rebellion; we can see the 'merry shoemakers' at work in the open air; at slight to their craft, they fling their awl and lapstone aside, and attack the slighter, be he king or earl or yeoman. Only the soft influence of rustic love can unnerve the brawny limbs; the invincible Pinner defeats his three—and sits down to wail his luckless love for churl-fathered Bettris.

"And what is really wonderful in this picture of rustic life is that there is no Corydon or Alexis or Tityrus, or even Corin or Sylvia; here no shepherds tune their oaten pipes; no maidens with crooks and sun-hats talk in stilted couplets; only shoemakers and rude yeomen, who use the roughest Saxon and the stoutest blows; there is not a classical quotation or reference from beginning to end; simple, strong, pure is the English of it as any homebred dialect. Even Shakespere, with all his genius for the natural and the true, did not escape the unreality of the pastoral in describing rural life; his *As you Like it* and *Winter's Tale*, instinct as they are with the breath of field and forest, are tainted by that classical tradition which would produce Elysium by a mixture of city craft and country homeliness. All honour to the poet who, with the temptation of a University training, was able to rise above its absurd traditions! It is more than probable that the play is the product of one of his periods of purity and repentance, when he forsook his evil companions; perhaps at these times he left London too, and returned to the natural life of the country, its fresh breezes and sweet-smelling clover fields; of such surroundings this drama savours" (pp. 102-6).

Turning back on our last long quotation, two remarks must be made: (*a*) That the adjectives applied to the Squire of "the present day" seem over-strong, and not characteristic of the class; (*b*) That Professor Ward accentuated, before Professors Brown and Storojenko, the country freshness of Greene. See quotation onward.

Another point made by Professor Brown is his examination of the chronology of the composition of the plays of Greene in so far as we have them. Professor Storojenko has taken much pains on this, but again was forestalled by this Paper. Few will greatly differ from the conclusions arrived at, as follows :—

"If conjecture were of any value, the absence of classical reference, and the interest in his country's history [shown in the *Pinner of Wakefield*] point to a time close to the production of *James IV.*, and the *Looking-glass for London and England*, the finest and last of his plays *; the latter was written when Lodge returned from Cavendish's expedition in 1591; it is more than likely that *The Pinner of Wakefield* was composed in Lodge's absence, during the publication of that remarkable series of repentant pamphlets which begins with his 'Never Too Late' and ends with his 'Notable Discovery of Coosnage'; its verse has more of the ring of simple prose diction than either *James IV.* or the *Looking-glass* (Ulrici conjectures that it was originally written in prose); these show traces of the classical tradition, and probably lie, one immediately before, the other immediately after, this most English drama. The style of these three plays is certainly the later style of the dramatist; it is not likely that he would recede from a taste for pure melodious Saxon to a love of those crude embellishments from the classics with which it is the pride of the youthful University man to lard his English. *Alphonsus, King of Arragon*, *Orlando Furioso*, and *Friar Bacon and Friar*

* I cannot agree with Professor Brown here. Looking to Lodge's verses (1589), in which he forswears writing dramas, the *Looking-glass* could not well be Greene's "last play." See Simpson in "Shakspere-Allusion Books," Part I., p. xxxviii. We find the *Looking-glass* acted early in 1591 by Henslowe, and not marked as a new play, and only very occasionally acted, as an old one would be, while its non-appearance before in Henslowe is accounted for by 1591 having been the first year's entries that we have of his, it having been the year he opened his new theatre. Nor was it possible that the *Looking-glass* could have been written "when Lodge returned from Cavendish's expedition in 1591." They started 26th August, 1591, and the first vessel that returned was 11th June, 1593. Fleay claims the most and best of the *Looking-glass* for Lodge—one of various preposterous claims for him—and one can simply ask for proof. Internal evidence would rather give the main portions to Greene.

Bungay, the three other extant plays of Greene, are distinctly marked by this alluring pedantry. The two former are the result of his Continental travels, and emulation of the sudden fame of Marlowe's *Tamburlaine*. *Orlando* is a free dramatisation of Ariosto's poem, for which he must have acquired a taste in Italy, as Sir John Harington's translation was not published till 1592. *Alphonsus* is a dull imitation of Marlowe's braggart play, remarkable only as one of the half-dozen plays which Shakespere burlesques in Pistol's speeches. Three other characteristics mark this earlier style, and distinguish these three plays from the later: (1) He crowds his stage with kings, emperors, and princes; (2) He is as fond of what may be called the poetry of geography as Milton in his 'Paradise Lost' and 'Paradise Regained': the names of countries which may be woven into a line have a strange fascination for his ear; (3) He displays an inartistic weakness for euphuism and alliteration. A comparison of the plays in these three respects clearly marks out their order of production. *Alphonsus* is earliest and *Friar Bacon* last of the three. The last characteristic relegates their production to the period when he published his pamphlets that avowedly imitate Lyly's 'Euphues' (1584-87). Even if the decreasing puerility and imitativeness of style did not fix the order, the advance in dramatic purpose and power should be enough to point it out. *Alphonsus* has no higher purpose than stage display, and 'great and thundering speech.' Such a close echo is it of *Tamburlaine*, without half its *motif*, that a little more exaggeration would produce the impression of burlesque. Moreover, its published title, *The Comical Historie of Alphonsus, King of Arragon*, whilst it is the only one of Greene's that has no humorous character in it, and is crowded with battle-scenes, has still no satisfactory explanation. It is easy to say with Professor Ward, in his excellent account of Greene ('English Dramatic Literature,' vol. i., p. 219), that it 'is apparently only called comical because its ending is not tragical'; but even if 'comical' were used as the mere negative of 'tragical,' it is not so easy to see how the poet of *George-a-Greene* and *James IV.* would have risked the laugh of his critics by such an ambiguous phrase, when he was content to call much more humorous and less bloody dramas merely histories. And it is no less difficult to believe that a man of Greene's sense of humour would write with serious purpose a play crowded wih Pistolic lines like these:—

> '"Villain," sayst thou? nay "villain" in thy throat!
> What, knowst thou, skipjack, whom thou villain call'st?'
>
> 'What, is he gone? the devil break his neck,
> The fiends of hell torment his traitorous corpse!'
>
> 'Slash off his head! as though Albinius' head
> Were then so easy to be slashèd off.'
>
> 'I conjure thee, by Pluto's loathsome lake,
> By all the hags which harbour in the same,
> By stinking Styx and filthy Phlegethon,
> To come with speed.'
>
> '"Villain," say'st thou? "traitor" and "dunghill knight"?
> Now by the heavens, etc.'

These, and such stage directions as 'Exit Venus, or if you can conveniently, let a chair down from the top of the stage and draw her up'; 'Calchas rises up in a white surplice and a cardinal's mitre'; 'Enter Alphonsus with a canopy carried over him by three lords, having over each corner a king's head crowned,' smack distinctly of burlesque. Whatever be the purpose of the play, whether serious or comic, it is not a high one" (pp. 106-7).

I pause a moment to intercalate that surely there can be no doubt that the placing of "Comical" in the title-page was a tacit intimation to spectators or readers that the whole thing was designed for a hit at the solemnities and tragic mouthings of the *Tamburlaine* type of play, inevitably perpetrated during Greene's quarrel-period with Marlowe. I do not forget that, as *Alphonsus* was not published until 1599, the word 'Comical' might have been inserted by the Players. Even so, they would hardly have so done unless they had knowledge of the *motif* of the Play. Greene was too astute to openly burlesque the 'mighty line' of Marlowe, but he could and did echo or imitate *Tamburlaine*; and in my judgment his imitations are all the more sarcastically effective in that they are unobtrusive and indirect—*i.e.* not put into the mouths of humorous characters introduced for the purpose. To take *Alphonsus* without a tacit reference to *Tamburlaine* seems to me to miss the entire impulse of its writer; and the same holds in part of *Orlando Furioso.* Professor Brown continues:—

"The art of *Orlando Furioso*, though more irregular, is, perhaps, more elevated. Its intention is, of course, to dramatise madness—a task incomparably more difficult than to describe it in Epic—perhaps, indeed, the most difficult of all dramatic tasks. It is scarcely necessary to say that Greene failed in it. The occasion of the madness is ridiculously inadequate: the hero reads love ditties that seem to have passed between his Angelica and some other lover called Medor, and on the spot, young and successful warrior and wooer though he was, turns incontinently mad. Compared with Lear's slow drifting from reason under the cruel buffets of ingratitude, and his seeming desertion by the whole world, this seems almost unmotived. It may be urged that Ophelia has as little occasion to go mad;* but there is no comparison in this respect between a warrior who had made his prowess felt throughout the world, and a weak-headed, soft-hearted, characterless girl, whose only claim on our interest is Hamlet's love, and the perennial pathos of her madness. The *dénouement* is no less sudden. The sight of Angelica does not restore him, nor does that of his old comrades in arms; it is the potion and wand of the enchantress, Melissa—as futile a conclusion, as Lear's return to reason under the influence of Cordelia's love is effective. A still greater error is committed by Greene in letting his Orlando 'live happy ever after' with Angelica.

* Surely this would be a superficial 'urging' in relation to one so finely-strung, and certainly in love with Hamlet, and on whom came such pressure of circumstance and events.—G.

To paint in his picture with such a sombre colour as madness, and then to let the tragic hold he has on his spectators pass away purposeless, is to trifle with art. A tragedy should be tragic to its close. Lear recovers from madness only to die. It may be well in real life to recover reason, and follow the common pursuits of life; but it completely strips off the romance madness throws round the commonplace; and in a drama, not the welfare of the puppets, but the continuity of the romance, is everything. The conception of Orlando's madness itself fails through a certain hesitation in the author's mind; he seems unable to decide whether pathos or humour should predominate. In Lear, these effects are as exquisitely mingled as an April shower with its sunshine; tears and laughter come together. In Greene, they stand side by side, the moving and amusing scenes alternate; and a want of the dignity which clings to Lear through all his madness is the result. The stage directions, 'Re-enter Orlando with a leg,' 'beateth them all before him'; 'Enter Orlando with a drum; Orgalio and Tom, Ralph, and other clowns as soldiers, with spits and dripping pans'; 'Orlando breaks the fiddle about the fiddler's head,' show clearly enough the tendency to farce, to which Greene has given way in this drama. But, after all is said against it, there remains the solid merit that it was a stepping-stone to *Lear* and *Hamlet*. Of course it is not a question to be answered whether Shakespere would have risked the introduction of such a strange subject as madness on the stage, had there been no predecessor to venture it. But there can be little doubt that Shakespere, actively connected as he was with the stage at its first appearance, marked with eager eye the merits and failings of the new performance. The old play on which *Lear* is founded has no mad scenes, and *Hamlet* was not an enticing subject to one who had not seen in actual working the powerful effect which madness could produce upon the stage. Greene's *Orlando* and Kyd's *Spanish Tragedy* are the models which the greater dramatist improved upon; and of the two Greene's is the pioneer" (pp. 107-9).

It must, however, be borne in mind that there was a pre-Hamlet to Shakspeare's *Hamlet*, as I have had occasion to annotate on Storojenko. Further: I must again differ from Professor Brown in his conception of Ophelia. There is not a trace of weak-headedness in her, and the only excuse for calling her 'characterless' is that she too pliantly obeyed her father—conduct more common then than now.

Professor Brown pursuing his keen-eyed inquiry into the characteristics of Greene, we have next a new element of indebtedness on Shakspeare's part admirably worked out, and which has quite escaped Professor Storojenko, as follows:—

"Another theme which Greene helped to prepare for the hand of Shakespere was the treatment of the supernatural. *Friar Bacon and Friar Bungay* deals with the difficult subject,—a play in style and dramatic interest showing a great advance on *Alphonsus* and *Orlando*, but considerably below Marlowe's *Faustus*, which probably suggested it. Unlike madness, magic and its cognates needed no apology or adventitious aid to recommend it in a century so close to the Middle Ages, whose superstitions, grown almost into instincts, it had not been able to discard with the outer robe of ceremonials and manners. The miracle plays had revelled in the supernatural: 'Payd for kepying of fyer at hell mothe, 4*d.*,' was not an uncommon item at their exhibitions; and had no Milton intervened between them and our own age, the devil might still have been the clown of our pantomimes. But there was also an aspect of terror and wonder to these mediæval fancies; and round the names of Faustus and Roger Bacon had clotted all the strange legends of supernatural power. Marlowe chose one and Greene the other; that Shakespere handled neither is sufficient to show that either the public or he was satisfied with what had been done. Of the two results, Greene's is naturally the more English; he cannot keep his gravity to the close, but breaks into a hearty guffaw almost before the agony has reached its crisis; and with the tale of wonder he mingles a tale of love.

Marlowe, on the other hand, precipitates the sombre elements of the legend; and though again and again he tries to snatch at the humour of it, his tale relapses into its unearthly gloom, and closes with one of the most harrowing scenes in English tragedy. Greene's play has all the leisurely beauty of an English summer day: we can see the lazy nodding of the wheatfield as it brushes the sky, and watch the waywardness of the silvery thistledown; we can hear the drowsy hum of the happy insect-world lulled by the fitful hush of the corn-bells; the mower quaffs his ale behind the haycock; the farmyard is silent; Isis sleeps in broken curves of molten silver from Godstow to Iffley; lazy scout-life crawls lazier still; while big Osney Tom tells noon from its tower as soft and mellow as for a city of the dead. Marlowe's play is like a tropical thunderstorm, intense, brief, and unrelieved. One rises from it as from a ghost story at midnight; there is scarcely a character in it one would care to meet after dark; and Mephistopheles had not developed that gentlemanly bearing which makes him such a Chesterfield in Goethe. Greene's characters, on the contrary, look as comfortable and sleek as kine in a rich meadow; his friars, with all their magic, would be no more uncanny to meet than any twopenny juggler in a strolling booth. His very devil is as accommodating a devil as one could wish—as, *e.g.*, when he appears for Bacon's man, Miles, at the end of the play:—

Miles. 'Faith, 'tis a place I have desired long to see: have you not good tippling-houses there? May not a man have a lusty fire there, a pot of good ale, a pair of cards, a swinging piece of chalk, and a brown toast that will clap a white waistcoat on a cup of good drink?'

Devil. 'All this you may have there.'

Miles. 'You are for me, friend, and I am for you. But I pray you, may I not have an office there?'

Devil. 'Yes, a thousand! What wouldst thou be?'

Miles. 'By my troth, sir, in a place where I may profit myself. I know hell is a hot place, and men are marvellous dry, and much drink is spent there: I would be a tapster.'

Devil. 'Thou shalt.'

"The only supernatural thing about this devil is perhaps his fine hospitality—the more marvellous when we consider what a tedious fool Miles proves himself throughout the play" (pp. 109-11).

The preceding must be read *cum grano*; for it is to be remembered that the supernatural power of witches was all but universally believed in. Then, specifically, as *Friar Bacon* was admittedly an imitation of *Faustus*, the credit—such as it is—belongs mainly to Marlowe. But Shakspeare only used witchcraft where it was given him by history, until James came to the throne; and then he applied it in *Macbeth*, where he would show that James was the rightful heir. We must add that the witchcraft of *Macbeth* has a weird grandeur, utterly in contrast with Greene's.

I omit an analysis of the plot and development of *Friar Bacon and Friar Bungay*, intended to show that "however genial the atmosphere of the drama is, the art is far from perfect," and especially wherein the author "attempts to mingle a love tale with the tale of magic, and succeeds only in making a clumsy mechanical mixture, seeming still more clumsy if compared with Goethe's subtle amalgamation of the same elements in *Faust*" (p. 111).* I must glean,

* Personally I differ from my friend's verdict here on the love tale carried on in *Friar Bacon and Friar Bungay*, and rather agree with Mr. J. A. Symonds, who in his "Shakespere's Predecessors in the English Drama" (1884) thus writes: "The conjuring tricks and incantations of the friar are cleverly interwoven with a romantic tale of Edward Prince of Wales's love for Margaret, the fair maid of Fresingfield; the Earl of Lincoln's honest treachery, who woos her for his lord and wins her for himself; and the history of her two suitors, Lambert and Serlsby, who, together with their sons, are parenthetically killed upon the stage." The remainder of the criticism may find place also: "A double comic interest is sustained by Edward's court fool Ralph, and Miles the

however, these incidental critical remarks on the Play.

"Its representation of rustic character is as unreal as that in *George-a-Green* is true. Margaret, the peasant girl, talks like a blue-stocking. The following specimens of her conversation show a queer bookishness in the 'country slut,' as she calls herself:—

'Phœbus is blithe, and frolic looks from heaven,
As when he courted lovely Semele.'

'Proportion'd as was Paris, when in grey
He courted Œnon in the vale by Troy.'

'His wit is quick and ready in conceit,
As Greece afforded in her chiefest prime.'

This is the character whose 'idyllic beauty' Professor Ward especially commends.* And her father is not far

---

servant of Bacon. Written by a clever story-teller, who, without a high ideal of art or deep insight into character, could piece a tale together with variety of incidents, this play is decidedly interesting. The action never flags. Pretty scenes succeed each other: now pastoral at Fresingfield, now grave at Oxford, now terrible in Bacon's cell, now splendid at the Court, now humorous with Miles, the friar's man. A jocund freshness of blithe country air blows through the piece, and its two threads of interest are properly combined in the conclusion. Edward pardons the Earl of Lincoln by giving him Margaret in marriage on the same day that he weds Eleanor of Castile. Friar Bacon foregoes his magic arts; and Miles, who is a lineal descendant of the Vice, dances off the stage upon a merry devil's back, promising to play the tapster in a certain thirsty place where 'men are marvellous dry.'" (p. 561).

* It is due to Professor Ward to give what he really says, thus:—"The more attractive part of the action, however, is concerned with the love of Prince Edward (I.) for a keeper's daughter, the fair Margaret of Fresingham [Fresingfield]. The scenes in the Suffolk village are written with a loving hand; there is a delightful air of country freshness about them, superior to any of Greene's contemporaries or successors, save one, and much idyllic beauty in the character of Margaret." (As before, I. 218.)

behind her. Greene had not yet thrown off the trammels of his University training. For Miles, who, like Wagner of the Faust legend, picks up the scraps of learning from his master's table, there is more excuse. But he too overdoes it. His conversation is as absurdly and tediously mongrel as if he had had the usual smattering of classics at a public school and University. The very shade of Hercules, when he appears 'in his lion skin,' announces himself in the shadiest of Latin. But, with all its pedantry, the play has many touches of Greene's later style. Such verses as—

> 'For timely ripe is rotten too too soon,'

are not uncommon; nor are such passages as this:—

> 'Apollo's heliotropion then shall stoop,
> And Venus' hyacinthe shall veil her top;
> Juno shall shut her gilliflowers up,
> And Pallas' bay shall 'bash her brightest green;
> Ceres' carnation, in consòrt with those
> Shall stoop and wonder at Diana's rose.'" (p. 112.)

The Essayist now turns to *James IV.*, and whoever critically studies it will not seek to abate from his very high estimate of this play; all the more that, like the others, it is left us in a corrupt state. He thus gives his estimate:—

"When Greene next resumes his dramatic pursuits, it is to pen the most perfect of his plays. By a course of prose pamphlets he has purified his style of all its questionable embellishments; the euphuism is almost gone, the weakness for classical quotations and references; his knowledge of character has widened, and its representation has grown simpler and more intense; he has acquired the faculty of reserve, of sacrificing extraneous ornaments to the growth or relief of character, passion and plot; his humour has gained body and purity. *James IV.* is the finest Elizabethan historical play outside of Shakespere, and is worthy to be placed on a level with Shakespere's earlier style. It has not, of course, the exuberance that marks even the first plays of Shakespere; and in this it is artistically higher;

it has an even flow, unbroken by bursts of imagination or flower-thickets of words; there is none of that tropical prodigality which impedes the way of the superficial reader, and proves Shakespere the worse artist, the greater genius. It is to other historical plays what Thackeray's 'Esmond' is to historical novels. Both have a simplicity of diction, a soft-featured lucidity, which commonly comes from age and distance, a quaint pathos, a mellow humour, a dim intensity, as of those pools of azure light that swim in the hollows of the noonday hills. One feature more than all others helps to add this twilight mellowness of atmosphere; it is the gentle beauty of the female characters. In Queen Dorothea, as in Lady Castlewood, there is a patient tenderness, with its sister, meek silence, which, when it does occur, is so lovely a thing in woman. But, like certain fragrant shrubs, it yields its perfume only under crushing pressure.

"*James IV.*, then, is a tale of neglected love and cruel wrong. For Dorothea is the heroine: she sees the king misled by flatterers; she sees the light of love die out of his eyes, and kindle for another, yet she utters not a murmur; nay, when the nobles exclaim against his inconstancy, she defends him on the plea of youth. Ateukin, a fawning villain, spurs him on to the love of Ida, daughter of the Countess of Arran, and acts as go-between. Ida has all the modest firmness of Shakespere's Imogen, and turns aside the prayers, flatteries and threats of the villain with admirable dignity. Thinking the queen the only bar to Ida's love, Ateukin offers the king to have her assassinated; Jacques, a Frenchman, who speaks the most tedious broken English, undertakes the task. Only now, and at the entreaty of the nobles, is she persuaded reluctantly to fly. To the suggestion of one, that her father will revenge her, she replies with indignant tenderness:—

> 'As if they kill not me, who with him fight!
> As if his breast be touched, I am not wounded!
> We are one heart, though rent by hate in twain:
> One soul, one essence doth our weal contain.'

"In male attire, accompanied by a faithful dwarf, Nano, she escapes. Her wanderings are represented with considerable pathos:—

'Ah Nano, I am weary of these weeds,
Weary to wield this weapon that I bear,
Weary of love from whom my woe proceeds,
Weary of toil, since I have lost my dear!
A weary life, where wanteth no distress,
But every thought is paid with heaviness!'

"Overtaken by the assassin, she fights, is wounded, and left for dead. She is rescued by a knight, and cured of her wound by his wife, who falls in love with her disguised patient, only to be rudely awakened. Meanwhile, James, driven by remorse at the supposed murder, but still more powerfully by Ida's marriage and the appearance of the King of England with an army, repents, and discards the flattering vipers; finds to his delight that Dorothea still lives; obtains her forgiveness, and 'lives happy ever after.'

"Throughout the play there runs a quaint vein of humour in the mouths of two as original characters as exist in the Elizabethan drama. These are Slipper and Andrew Snoord: Slipper, a combination of Launce and Autolycus; Andrew, a lineal ancestor of Scott's Andrew Fairservice in 'Rob Roy.' They appear in the first act, posting advertisements of their services, evidently in the market-place, and have a wit-combat, in which Andrew has the worst of it, through his inquisitiveness, cautious though it is. To his inquiries as to Slipper's trade, he gets reply: 'Marry, I'll tell you,—I have many trades: the honest trade when I needs must; the filching trade when time serves; the cozening trade as I find occasion. And I have more qualities: I cannot abide a full cup unkissed, a fat capon uncarved, a full purse unpicked, nor a fool to prove a justice as you do.' Ateukin appears in search of servants to aid him in pandering to the king, and reads Slipper's advertisement—'If any gentleman, spiritual or temporal, will entertain out of his service a young stripling of the age of thirty years, that can sleep with the soundest, eat with the hungriest, work with the sickest, lie with the loudest, face with the proudest, etc., that can wait in a gentleman's chamber when his master is a mile off, keep his stable when 'tis empty and his purse when 'tis full, and hath many qualities worse than all these, let him write his name and go his way, and attendance shall be given;' and the brave little dwarf Nano's—'Pleaseth it any gentleman to entertain a servant of more wit than stature, let them subscribe, and attendance shall be given;' and hires them both. Andrew, too, is added to his retinue. Nano is assigned to the queen, and proves himself warm-hearted and true, clinging to Dorothea through all her misfortunes—a truthful tribute to deformity of body which is not often paid by fiction-writers. Even Scott and Victor Hugo have helped to perpetuate the fallacy that a great or good spirit cannot dwell in a distorted frame. Slipper and Andrew both act the part of parasite's parasite, and by their witty licence of speech give the play half its liveliness. Between them, they contrive to check their own and their master's villainy. They hate dishonesty—in other people; and have the profoundest satisfaction in outwitting birds of their own feather. Andrew, for instance, sends Jacques off after the queen, on the road to that 'place of great promotion,' the gallows, and relapses into soliloquy: 'Go! and the rot consume thee! O what a trim world this is! My master lives by cozening the king; I by flattering him; Slipper, my fellow, by stealing, and I by lying. Is not this a wily accord, gentlemen?' Slipper enters with the produce of his knavery and bargaining with tradesmen. Dismissing them, he speaks with himself: 'Now what remains? There's twenty crowns for a house, three crowns for household stuff, sixpence to buy a constable's staff; nay, I will be the chief of my parish. There wants nothing but a wench, a cat, a dog, a wife, and a servant, to make a whole family. Shall I marry with Alice, Goodman Grimshaw's daughter? She is fair, but, indeed, her tongue is like clocks on Shrovetuesday, always out of temper. Shall I wed Sisley of the Whighton? O no; she is like a frog in a parsley bed: as skittish as an eel.' Andrew sends in 'three antics, who dance round, and take Slipper with them.' 'Whilst they are dancing, Andrew takes away Slipper's money, and then he and the antics depart.'

"The play is still more remarkable for its being amongst the first to have an acted prologue and interplay. Shakespere followed Greene's example in *The Taming of the Shrew* and the *Midsummer Night's Dream*, and the fashion became almost universal in the post-Shakesperean drama. Marston and Ben Jonson are especially fond of the practice.

But scarcely any of them surpass Greene in this acted induction. Its fairy framework is to the play like the garden perfume that preludes and closes a shower,—it is dainty, sweet, and subtle. In it appears Bohan, a character more grotesquely original than even Slipper and Andrew—just such a character as Sir Walter Scott delighted to depict—a Scotch Timon, who has become disgusted with the world, and has retired into a tomb to spend the remainder of his life. Oberon, King of the Fairies, 'with antics,' dances round the tomb till Bohan appears. The fairy tries to be friendly with the hermit, but gets rebuff after rebuff—'The de'il a whit reck I thy love'; and is even threatened with 'this whinyard.' But the weapon, by fairy influence, refuses to leave its sheath. The 'stoical Scot' cannot understand it. 'What de'il is in me? Whay, tell me, thou skipjack, what art thou?' Oberon asks him first why he has left the world to dwell in a tomb. Compelled by the little king, he answers he 'was born a gentleman of the best blood in all Scotland, except the king'; tried the life of a courtier, but found that 'flattering knaves that can cog and prate fastest, speed best in the Court'; then escaped to the country and married a wife, but he found 'the craft of swains more vile than the knavery of courtiers,' and 'wives' tongues worse than the wars itself.' 'In good time, my wife died—ay [= I] would she had died twenty winter sooner, by the mass!' 'Leaving my two sons to the world, and shutting myself into this tomb, where, if I die I am sure I am safe from wild beasts, but, whilst I live, I cannot be free from ill company. Besides, now I am sure, gif all my friends fail me, I sall have a grave of mine own providing. This is all. Now, what art thou?' To this he gets reply: 'Oberon, King of the Fairies, that loves thee because thou hatest the world; and, to gratulate thee, I brought those antics to show thee some sport in dancing, which thou hast loved well.' Bohan boasts of his boys, Slipper and Nano, and, making them dance, gets a blessing for them from the fairies before they go out into the world—Nano, 'a quick wit,' and Slipper, 'a wandering life.' The reintroduction of his acting chorus at the end of each act had, evidently, as its chief aim, the dancing of the 'antics'—in fact, was anticipatory of the ballet, to relieve the strain both on actors and audience. The main facts of the drama are not historical; only the main characters and the atmosphere are so. The interest seems to be rather autobiographical. . . ."

There are one or two points in the above that require brief notice. (1) Professor Brown forgets that *The Taming of the Shrew* followed *The Taming of a Shrew.* (2) He forgets that it is unknown which was first, *James IV.* or *Midsummer Night's Dream.* (3) He somewhat exaggerates the value of the 'fairy framework' of *James IV.* Sooth to say, it has little to do with the Play except to introduce Nano and his brother, and to make Oberon interfere when the Author was at a loss. Nor is it without elements of absurdity. It is quite possible that, as Greene had copied Marlowe because he was 'the rage,' so, *James IV.* being of his latest plays, he may have imitated Shakespere. (4) He further forgets that the Clown's jig was then in use.

And now, in continuing our quotation, I accentuate how again Professor Storojenko is anticipated:—

"It was, doubtless, written during one of those strange fits of repentance which chequer the life of Greene, and seems a tribute of remorse to the character of his deserted wife. James the Fourth's queen was named Margaret, whereas Greene's wife was a Dorothea, or Doll as he calls her in his last pathetic appeal to her. In the king, Greene figures himself surrounded by flattering knaves, 'burrs that cleave to him,' and led by them to desert his wife and take to evil ways. In Bohan, too, it is more than likely he depicts either his own aim or his actual life during the periods of remorse. Several of his pamphlets, and the scene before his death, show him during such a reaction against society and its wicked ways. Bohan invites the king of the fairies 'to the gallery,' to 'show him why I hate the world, by demonstration,' to see 'a king overruled with parasites, misled by lust—much like our Court of

Scotland this day,' and then, 'when thou seest that, judge if any wise man would not leave the world, if he could.' Bohan is Greene, in one of his Timon moods. If this theory is the correct one, it will explain why the play is by far his most successful. Whether the theory be correct or not, the piece certainly adds its quota to that great body of proof, in Elizabethan literature, how deep flattery and fawning had eaten into the vitals of Court life and all the life which came within its influence" (pp. 113-17).

I gladly add here Mr. J. A. Symonds' fine recognition of Greene's genius in its portraiture of Woman, suggested by the Ida and Dorothea of *James IV.*:—

"The drama illustrates the miseries of States, when flatterers rule the Court, and kings yield to lawless vice. In the portrait of the Lady Ida, for whose love James deserts his wife and plots her murder, Greene conceived and half expressed a true woman's character. There is a simplicity, and perfume of purity, in Ida, which proceeds from the poet's highest source of inspiration. Nor do the romantic adventures and pathetic trials of the queen fall far short of a melodramatic success. That this man, dissolute and vicious as he was, should have been the first of our playwrights to feel and represent the charm of maiden modesty upon the public stage, is not a little singular. Perhaps it was, in part, to this that Greene owed his popularity. Fawnia in 'Pandosto,' Margaret in *Friar Bacon*, Sephestia in 'Menaphon,' Ida and Dorothea in *James the Fourth*, Philomela and the Shepherd's wife in the 'Mourning Garment,' belong to one sisterhood, in whom the innocence of country life, unselfish love, and maternity are sketched with delicate and feeling touches."—"Shakespere's Predecessors in the English Drama" (1884), p. 560.

Professor Brown—like Dyce and Storojenko and all—thought that *James IV.* was simply imaginative on Greene's part,—*i.e.*, that Greene had no authority for his 'story.' This has been shown to be incorrect

In the *Athenæum* (October 8th, 1881), Mr. P. A. Daniel, London, supplied the needed authority. He writes as follows :—

"Greene's play is founded on the first story of the third decade of Cinthio's collection of tales. Except that Greene changes a Scottish king into a king of England, and an Irish king into James IV. of Scotland, there is very slight difference between the play and the novella. Cinthio himself dramatised the story in his *Arenopia*—the name of the chief heroine; but Greene's play must have been taken from the *tale*, not from Cinthio's *play*. The Oberon-Bohan Induction, I suppose, was of Greene's own invention; there is no hint for it in Cinthio."

Of course this does not make *James IV.* historical; yet does it give us Greene's source.

The *Looking-glass for London and England* our Essayist next places alongside of *James IV.*, alike in its quality and purpose; but see our note earlier (p. xxv) on his misdate of 1592. He thus reviews it :—

"The same lesson is taught by *The Looking-glass for London and England*, which Greene wrote about 1592, along with Lodge—a composition didactic enough for the pulpit. It consists of a series of graphic pictures of life in Nineveh, to each of which is attached its moral, in the shape of a prophetic chorus by Oseas and Jonas. The title alone, even without the numerous references to English life, is enough to show that Nineveh is London, and Oseas and Jonas, Lodge and Greene. They paint out newly pictures of the Court; high life and peasant life alternate; so that the result as a whole is as complete a representation of the worse side of contemporary English life as any historian might wish. But the desire to be didactic, and the Scriptural framework on which it is built, seriously vitiate its authority. Making allowance for this, there still remains sufficient to form a companion picture to *George-a-Greene*. In it there is a queen (Remilia), who is vain enough, not merely to swallow the openest flattery, but to utter 'flat blasphemy':—

'For I am beauty's phœnix in this world.'

'Shut close these curtains straight, and shadow me,
For fear Apollo spy me in his walks.'

'For were a goddess fairer than am I,
Ile scale the heavens to pull her from the place.'

The sternest moraller's model Providence could not give swifter or more satisfactory answer: the conceited beauty is 'strooken with thunder black,' and leaves King Rasni an astonished widower. On the spot, he sets a-wooing Alvida, the wife of the Paphlagonian king; Radagon, his prime minister, a fawning villain, spurs them on:

'The king is sad, and must be gladded straight;
Let Paphlagonian King go mourn meanwhile.'

"Alvida proves herself a worthy successor to Remilia, and in professing to return to her angry lord, poisons him. Her husband thus disposed of, and secure of her paramour's love, she begins to woo the King of Cilicia, in a scene which Charles Lamb thought worthy of selection; he resists her blandishments, and only Nineveh's terror at its threatening doom saves him from Joseph's fate. She repents comfortably in sackcloth and ashes, enjoys the ripe fruit of her sins, and is raised to the throne of Nineveh.

"The low life of the piece, though represented in less poetical language, looks more like a photograph of contemporary life. The characters are: Thrasybulus, a young man who has squandered most of his property; Alcon, a peasant, and his wife, Samia; a smith, his wife, and Adam, his man; a judge, a usurer, a lawyer, and a devil. The usurer lends small sums to the prodigal and the poor peasant, and unjustly cheats them out of their all; he bribes their lawyer and the judge, and they lose their case. Appealing to the King and his prime minister Radagon (Alcon's son), they are rudely ordered out of the way in such terms by Radagon:—

'Hence, begging scold! hence, caitiff clogg'd with years! . . .
Was I conceived by such a scurvy troll,
Or brought to light by such a lump of dirt?
Go, losel, trot it to the cart and spade!'

It is scarcely necessary to say that the same satisfactory Providence that dealt with the blasphemous beauty disposes of the disobedient child: 'a flame of fire appears from beneath, and Radagon is swallowed.' The unjust lawyer, usurer, and judge are left us in life to repent, for some mysterious reason. Towards the end, the usurer 'appears with a halter in one hand, and a dagger in the other,' 'the evil angel tempts him, offering the knife and rope,' but he only 'sits down in sackcloth, his hands and eyes reared to heaven.' Adam, who was more sinned against than sinning, and deserves forgiveness 'to seventy times seventy,' were it for his humour alone, after being threatened unsuccessfully by the devil, is carried off to be hanged, for not keeping the fast ordained in Nineveh. There is a curious fidelity to life in many of the scenes.

"A drama written by Greene in his healthier mood could scarcely fail to break into loud and hearty laughter, however serious the general purpose. The humour of the *Looking-glass* bears clear marks of Greene's earlier vein, but broadened and strengthened. There is less in it of that straining which makes so much of Elizabethan wit tedious. Humour, like beauty and virtue, must have an air of repose; the struggle of thought before its birth must be all concealed. The Elizabethan dramatists are too much children of nature to remember this, and the result is the toiling, floundering wit which disfigures many of their pages. Greene's, in this play, is more than ordinarily successful. Its fault is not so much effort as a tendency to farce. Adam, the smith's man, is own brother to Slipper and Autolycus—a roguish Bohemian, ready for any jest or any knavery, and generally coming off best in both; like genuine laughter, no respecter of persons—as ready to jest with a king as with a peasant. His encounter with the devil is of the same type as that of Miles in *Friar Bacon*, only broader and more farcical. The following will convey some idea of his humour:—

Adam. 'Well, Goodman Jonas, I would you had never come from Jewry to this country; you have made me look like a lean rib of roast beef, or like the picture of Lent painted upon a red-herring's cob. Alas, masters, we are commanded by the proclamation to fast and pray! by my troth I could prettily so, so away with praying; but for fasting, why, 'tis so contrary to my nature, that I had rather suffer a short hanging than a long fasting. Mark me, the words be these, "Thou shalt take no manner of food for so many days." I had as lief he should have said, "Thou shalt hang thyself for so many days." And yet, in faith, I need not find fault with the proclamation, for I have a buttery and a pantry and a kitchen about me; for proof, *ecce signum!* This right slop is my pantry, behold a manchet *(Draws it out)*; this place is my kitchen, for, lo, a piece of beef *(Draws it out)*,—oh let me repeat that sweet word again! for, lo, a piece of beef. This is my buttery, for, see, see, my friends, to my great joy, a bottle of beer *(Draws it out)*. Thus, alas, I make shift to wear out this fasting; I drive away the time.'

"But two searchers approach, and he resumes his prayers; they address him, and he replies, 'Trouble me not: "Thou shalt take no manner of food, but fast and pray."'

First Searcher. 'How devoutly he sits at his orisons! but, stay, methinks I feel a smell of some meat or bread about him.'

Second S. 'So thinks me too. You, sirrah, what victuals have you about you?'

Adam. 'Victuals! O horrible blasphemy! Hinder me not of my prayer, nor drive me not into a choler. Victuals! why, heardest thou not the sentence, "Thou shalt take no food, but fast and pray"?'

Second S. 'Truth, so it should be; but methinks I smell meat about thee.'

Adam. 'About me, my friends! these words are actions in the case. About me! no, no, hang those gluttons that cannot fast and pray.'

First S. 'Well, for all your words, we must search you.'

Adam. 'Search me! take heed what you do; my hose are my castles, 'tis burglary if you break ope a slop.'

"Poor Adam is searched in spite of his principles, and when he finds that the fast is to continue five days more, cheerfully agrees to be hanged at once.

"Alcon, the injured peasant, is also a humorous character, and contrives to burst in with his coarsest jokes in the midst of his heaviest misfortunes. This seems to have been a feature in Greene's own character—a sort of extreme reaction against extreme misery; when the bow is most bent, it breaks. In his hardest times, Greene strikes in with some jest; he is now preaching the most pathetic sermons to his reader, and the next moment is laughing at him round the corner. The stage directions often savour of this—such as 'Jonah is cast out of the whale's belly upon the stage,' between a solemn warning and a solemn prayer" (pp. 117-20).

With reference to the last remark, it was simply an effective stage action.

We have now reached Professor Brown's final verdict on Greene, which for thoroughness and sympathy leaves not Storojenko only, but Professor WARD and Mr. J. A. SYMONDS and every other, far behind.* It is as follows:—

"If Greene's dramas are any guide to his character, his is one of great attractiveness. He has a genuine Saxon nature, full of strange contradictions that to the common mind are irreconcilable. He has none of the gin-horse precision of motion which attracts as it soothes the conventional nature. His is a character as restless and unexpected in its movements as a child. There is in it none of that

---

* It may be permitted me to express my regret that Mr. J. A. Symonds ("Shakespere's Predecessors," p. 544) takes so harsh a view of Greene's *motif* in his exposure of "Conny-catching," etc. In disregard of his pathetic protestation that he made these revelations for the good of the commonwealth, and his courageous facing of all risks in so doing, it is painful to find it lightly turned into this—"Greene exposed the tricks of their trade in a series of pamphlets with startling titles . . . . proving himself vile enough to turn informer for the sake of a profitable literary venture." Doubtless there is added this saving clause—"We must, however, bear in mind that to earn money by his pen was an absolute necessity"; but the whole tone is unfeeling. Surely the recognised 'absolute necessity,' and the equally recognised sincerity of 'repentance,' might have modified if not cancelled such unforgiving words?

smooth obedience to rule which is the great bulwark of so-called society in its narrower sense—none of that motion within prescribed limits which is almost as good as sleep. He is the exact opposite of that oily adaptability, that sickening perfection, which alone wins the infamy of universal approval. He has the sweet fallibility of the Bohemian—by whom to be loved is truer testimony to character than the admiration of a whole commonplace world—the unconscious generosity, the recklessness of material and conventional interests, which is the unpardonable sin to the mass of Englishmen. The nomad instinct which brought our Asiatic ancestors to Europe, and survived in the roving spirit of our sea-king forefathers, lives again in him and his comrades—a fearless, heroic spirit, that is killed by the rampant consciousness of debit and credit. It breaks out ever and again in every manly nature and age—especially where the sea has influence: the sailor instinct of English boys, even when born far inland, is one of its manifestations; colonisation is another. But these, through their persistence and pecuniary results, have become recognised channels of respectability. So would piracy still be, if, like the 'rigs' of the stock exchange and the floating of bubble companies, it implied sudden elevation to the throne of 'the influential.' But to manifest this ancestral vagabondry in ways that show no balance to our credit—is it not shameful?

"Greene, like most of the dramatists of his time, was a born Bohemian; a lover of nature and the children of nature; keen to discern and admire sincerity and beauty of character, though wrapped in a 'beggar's gaberdine,' and shrinking instinctively from the smooth-tongued falsehood and shallow duplicity that wear so well in the world. The ruin that overtakes men like Greene is an everlasting wonder to the unthinking man. But given such a nature, and the ordinary surroundings of the routine commercial life, and the result is not difficult to see. The lives of Marlowe, Peele, Chatterton, Keats, Burns, Byron, Poe, Mürger, De Musset, Heine, and a hundred others, have stated the solution of the problem over and over again. Convention hedges them in from childhood upwards, galling them like chains that cut into the flesh, and when at last freedom comes with manhood, they know not how to use it; their nomad passion leads them to woeful excess, and tears their sensitive frames like an imprisoned whirlwind. Debauchery, madness, or suicide completes the story. It is easy to say it was their own fault, they should have exercised control, as other men do; but are other men any more truly master of themselves than they? On the contrary, it is other men's faculty of letting themselves drift, of acquiescing in the order of things, however foul, that makes them seem more self-controlling; passing over the fact that the difficulty of self-control depends on the quality and quantity of the self that is to be controlled, is it any nobler to become the slave of one's conditions than to rise in wild rage against their unfitness, and die in the attempt?

"Little is known of Greene's life, and that little we know only through his enemies and his own too candid confessions. It has been the fashion to accept these without reserve; and it looks reasonable to say that we must take a man at his own word: but if that word is uttered during wild fits of remorse, surely it needs qualification. Translate it into conventional phrase, and it would sound no worse than an account of those wild oats which the world permits its favourites to sow. The repentant's view of the past from which he repents is the gloomiest that can be taken; still worse is it when he is anxious to point a moral by it. If we were to believe some of the confessions made by revival converts of often blameless-seeming antecedents, we should take them to be the most atrocious villains that ever walked the earth. The closest analogy to Greene's position, in fact, is that of the revival preacher, who, to make the picture of the present as telling as possible, sees and paints his past in its very blackest colours.

"In his plays there has been already noticed a certain fondness for pulpiteering. It is still more decided in the pamphlets that cover the last three or four years of his life. Such sentences as the following from the 'Repentance' are exceedingly frequent: 'After I had wholly betaken me to the penning of plaies (which was my continual exercise), I was so far from calling upon God, that I sildome thought on God, but tooke such delight in swearing and blaspheming the name of God, that none could thinke otherwise of mee than that I was the child of perdition.' And it is from these later pamphlets that conjectures regarding his life have been made, aided by Gabriel Harvey's attack, although the testimony of this is vitiated by the writer's own statement, that he was cheated out of an action for libel against Greene by his death. It must also be remembered that he served the next two generations of preachers and tract writers as a 'frightful example.' Testimonies are not wanting on the opposite side; as, for instance, that by the unknown author of 'Greene's Funeralls':—

'For curtesie suppose him Guy, or Guyons somewhat less.
His life and manners, though I would, I cannot halfe expresse:
Nor mouth, nor mind, nor muse can halfe declare
His life, his love, his laude, so excellent they were.'

But these could not be allowed to dash so perfect a picture of a villain repentant; to condition, is to interfere unpleasantly with effective eloquence. And so the name of Robert Greene has passed down through the centuries as a synonym for literary gallows-bird" (pp. 120-3).

I fear it must be conceded that the laudation of "Greene's Funerals" cannot stand as a *per contra*, knowing his actual life and loves. But none the less is Professor Brown sound in his arguing for redeeming elements in Greene, and emphatically true-hearted in pleading for silence, not taunt, forgiveness, not accusation, in presence of his tragical penitence and burning tears. I join in denouncing the heartlessness that forgets Robert Burns' great words—

"What's done we partly may compute;
But know not what's resisted."

There succeeds this a summary-recapitulation of the main facts of Greene's life, which does not call for reproduction; but the 'end of the story,' as vividly and searchingly put, cannot be withheld; nor the eloquent final estimate, as thus :—

"Then begins the tragic struggle, in which relapse and repentance follow so close upon each other as to outwit record. Now he frequents taverns, till he 'has nothing to pay but chalk' [= go on score or into debt]; he hurries off a novel or a drama to save himself from prison. Now he 'falls amongst thieves,' and again, in the teeth of threats against his life, he unmasks their 'coosnage,' and warns young men against their 'connycatching' arts. Now he writes a pasquinade against some enemy (for he was hated as heartily as he was loved—two correlatives). Again he sits down to pen its palinode. Now plunged in debauchery, and again writing in bitter tears such admonitions as his 'Groatsworth of Wit.' Now weeping over his sins, and stirred to the heart by the thought of his weakness; again bursting out into such wild laughter as 'Greene's Newes, both from Heaven and Hell, prohibited the first for writing of bookes, and banished out of the last for displaying of connycatchers.' Revelling in the low haunts of London, yet able to write lyrics so redolent of rural life as the Odes in 'Philomela.' Wild with the feverish life of an actor, yet penning songs that breathe in every line of rest, like that beautiful one in his 'Farewell to Folly,' beginning—

> 'Sweet are the thoughts that savour of content;
> The quiet mind is richer than a crown.'

Oblivious to the graces of his most virtuous wife for the blandishments of 'a sorry ragged quean,' and yet capable of uttering that most lyrical eulogy of rustic married life, the Shepherd's Wife's Song, in 'The Mourning Garment, beginning :—

> 'Ah, what is love? it is a pretty thing,
> As sweet unto a shepherd as a king;
> And sweeter too,
> For kings have cares that wait upon a crown,
> And cares can make the sweetest love to frown:
> Ah then, ah then,
> If country loves such sweet desires do gain,
> What lady would not love a shepherd swain?'

In beggary and want, yet able to express his sorrows in that mournful song of a wasted life in the 'Groatsworth of Wit,' beginning—

'Deceiving world, that with alluring toys,
Hast made my life the subject of thy scorn;'

in which occur such passionate regrets and sorrows:—

'How well are they that die ere they be born!'
'Witness my want, the murderer of my wit;'

And saddest of all, to those who have looked on the unequal combat:—

'Oh, that a year were granted me to live,
And for that year my former wits restored!
What rules of life, what counsel would I give!
How should my sin with sorrow be deplored!'

Surely there could be no truer product of this terrible period of his life than his *Looking-glass for London and England*, with its wonderful contrasts of pride and downfall, tyranny and peasant life, blasphemy and religion, prophecy and laughter, feasting and fast, warning and jest."

I again intercalate that we must qualify this brilliant antithetic passage. It leads one to suppose that Greene wrote his "Groatsworth," then returned to his debauchery and wrote "Greene's News," then "Philomela," etc., until at last came his last repentance. This is taking "Greene's News" as Greene's own work, and forgetting that the "Groatsworth" was penned by him during his last illness. He proceeds:—

"At last came the last repentance. A surfeit of Rhenish and pickled herring was the cause. Much has been made of this by his enemies and editors, for no very evident reason. Why a surfeit of Rhenish and herring should bring forth a month's penitence and then death in Greene, and a surfeit of pippins half a century's pitiless satire and then madness in Swift, is a theme they might have enlarged on. The one is as reprehensible as the other, and for moral effect the Rhenish and herring is to be preferred. It is true, it led to that 'lamentable begging of a penny-pott of Malmsey,' which Gabriel Harvey makes the most of; but these 'penny-potts' were perhaps the very backbone of those doleful tracts of repentance he wrote on his death-bed. Deserted after his 'fatall banquet' by that judicious flattery which is commonly called friendship, thrust out of the tavern, he would have died, had not a kindly shoemaker 'neere Dowgate' given him shelter. In the poor man's house he lay dying, attended by his host's wife, who 'joyde to hear her nightingale's sweete layes' and the 'sorry ragged quean,' who, with all her sorriness and rags, retained a robe more precious than her scholarly critic's 'velvet breeches' and Venetian costume--the fine spirit of humanity. -The Puritan editor of his 'Repentance' is more worthy than his enemy to tell the rest. 'After that he had pend the former discourse (then lying sore sicke of a surfet which hee had taken with drinking), hee continued most patient and penitent; yea he did with teares forsake the world, renounced swearing, and desired forgivenes of God and the worlde for all his offences: so that during all the time of his sicknesse (which was about a moneths space) hee was never heard to sweare, rave, or blaspheme the name of God as he was accustomed to do before that time; which greatly comforted his wel willers, to see how mightily the grace of God did worke in him.' . . . 'And this is to bee noted, that his sicknesse did not so greatly weaken him, but that he walked to his chaire and backe againe the night before he departed, and then (being feeble), laying him downe on his bed, about nine of the clocke at night, a friende of his tolde him, that his Wife had sent him commendations, and that shee was in good health: whereat hee greatly rejoiced, confessed that hee had mightily wronged her, and wished that he might see her before he departed. Whereupon (feeling his time was but short), hee tooke pen and inke and wrote her a Letter to this effect: 'Sweet wife, as ever there was any good will or friendship betweene thee and mee, see this bearer (my Host) satisfied of his debt: I owe him tenne pound; and but for him I had perished in the streetes. Forget and forgive my wronges done unto thee; and Almighty God have mercie on my soule. Farewell till we meet in heaven; for on earth thou shalt never see me more. This 2 of September, 1592. Written by thy dying husband.

'ROBERT GREENE.'

"Harvey is not able to rob this letter of its pathos. In his harsh attack upon Greene, his version of it is: 'Doll, I charge thee by the love of our youth and by my soule's rest, that thou wilte see this man paide; for if hee and his wife had not succoured me, I had died in the streetes.

'ROBERT GREENE.'

"With this missive, summing up the faults of his life, he died; and as he lay with his 'amible face, his body well-proportioned, his attire after the habit of a scholar-like gentleman, only his hair somewhat long,' with 'a jolly long red peake, like the spire of a steeple, cherisht continually without cutting, whereat a man might hang a jewell, it was so sharpe and pendent,' his kind-hearted hostess, in her simple wonder and affection for the genius of the poet, placed around the 'ruffianly haire' a crown of bays.

"A picture follows that outvies for unholiness any the vilest that could be painted of Greene's life. The poet's funeral scarcely over, down sneaks to the Dowgate the courtly Cambridge hexameter-stringer whom Greene had stung by referring to his parentage (meanly enough, but harmlessly to any but unmanly coxcombs), in his 'Quip for an Upstart Courtier; or, A Quaint Dispute between Velvet Breeches and Cloth Breeches.' He had come to rake the filth with his fine-gentleman fingers from the poet's grave. He finds the good Amazon-armed housewife in a tearful mood, and she pours forth, as if to a friendly ear, the whole sad story of Greene's death. Storing up in his memory all he can gather, he gives it forth to the public in his 'Foure Letters concerning "the wretched fellow," or, shall I say, "the Prince of Beggars."' A most ghoul-like revenge! One can quite believe Nashe, when he tells this 'puissant epitapher' that the shoemaker's wife would scratch out his eyes 'for deriding her so dunstically.' 'A bigge, fat, lusty wench it is, that hath an arme like an Amazon, and will bang thee abhominationly, if ever shee catch thee in her quarters.' The tone of Nashe in this pamphlet reveals a certain under-current of humour attaching to the tale of Greene's death. The tongues which used to drive poor Greene back into debauchery, by calling him 'puritane and presizean,' were not likely to rest at such an excellent opportunity. Marston, Chapman, and Ben Jonson, in *Eastward Hoe*, caricature him in Quicksilver; and it is far from improbable that Mrs. Quickly's description of Falstaff's death is founded on some such version of the shoemaker's wife's story, current at the Mermaid or in the green-room. They have many features in common; and Shakespere does not shrink from burlesquing the most sacred things—as witness his parodies of Scripture in the *Tempest*—not to mention that whilst writing his *Henry IV.* and *Henry V.* he had Greene's plays always in his eye."

I must again interpose. I cannot admit, after re-reading *Eastward Hoe*, that Marston, Chapman, and Ben Jonson caricatured Greene in Quicksilver. So, as earlier I have shown, Quickly's description of Falstaff's death cannot be paralleled with Greene's, nor Greene's be accredited as having furnished materials for it. And where does Shakspeare burlesque Holy Scripture,'in the *Tempest*' or anywhere else? He continues:—

"Thus, in a whirlwind of remorse and contumely, affection and hatred, tears and flashes of humour, there passed away a son of storm and passion. By nature a nomad, his place was with Drake and Hawkins and Raleigh, who loved the restless element with hearts as restless, not on the dull earth, that needs plodding industry and wise patience. Else he should have been born in one of those wandering dwellings which we come across in the green lanes of England, planted in a shady nook by a brawling streamlet, that lends the dark-skinned dwellers round brook stones and pure brook water. There, with the minimum of convention and clothing, and a reduced list of commandments, he might have dwelt with the heart of summer, and sorrowed with the cruel grief of winter, knowing no limit to passion. He might have read the drama of men's lives in their hearts if not in their palms, and stirred strange perturbations in neighbouring poultry yards till he grew to be a patriarch, and not a hand raised to throw a stone at him. In fact, it was just such a gipsy life he did lead within the stiff pales and limits of society; and havoc was the result—he died ere summer came.

"But in him, as in his brethren, Burns, Byron, Poe, and Heine, there lived and struggled with his gipsy nature an element which, if it had gained the mastery, would have made him a stoic, a Puritan as true and noble in feeling as Milton. The world-sadness which goes to make the highest kind of poets, and wails through the crevices of their life like a winter-wind, cannot exist without this masterful element, with its intermittent godlike belief and remorse. Out of it rise Greene's frequent prophetic tone, and that pure morality which breathes through all his written work. From its fiery combats with the nomad instinct come those sudden and mysterious conversions of his, and that candidness which has injured him so much. And from their reconciliation arise the democratic sympathies and those pure idyllic pictures of rustic life which are the best product of his genius.

"After the tradition of his life has been purged of its grosser features, there still remain, therefore, the faults of a generous and weak-willed nature—such faults as become patent in their results to the whole world. Of virtues, the loudest are certainly the least amiable. Of vices, on the contrary, the silentest are the most hateful: those sly, crawling, serpentish vices, like religious hypocrisy, which seldom or never stir the surface of life; their possessors can wear sleek smiles and 'fox-furde' robes, and die amid glowing public panegyrics, and lie under a fulsome epitaph. So much for a good supply to life's end of 'the oyle of angels.' The poor sinner who sinks beneath vices that have material mark and issue must die in obloquy and neglect. If he be literary, he has a still more cruel doom; his open faults are raked out of his grave, and spattered across his memory like a lying epitaph. A poet's grave should be as holy as a child's, however blurred the life. The opposite is the case. Poor Greene's last cup of Rhenish, in an age from which the clink of the ale-can sounds loud across three centuries, has almost drowned for posterity the subtle flavour of his genius. It is true that every man ought to know the conditions of the life he chooses—ought to know that in the eyes of the world, poetry, like revolution, is a thing 'countenanced by boys and beggary'; that if he chooses the path of blunt unflattering truthfulness, he has the alternative before him of Bohemianism or complete loneliness, of being a Prince Hal or a Hamlet. But it is equally a fact, that few poetic natures do start with such a knowledge of the world, and still fewer have such manly consciousness of their power as to take the shallow criticisms and sneers and neglect of the world as the truest compliment it can pay them. They might then have the privilege that common humanity has after death, of having the evil in their lives forgotten. By their works ought they, like Christians, to be known.

"If Greene is to be known by his works, there are not many blots on his escutcheon; compared with the play-writers who follow him, he is purity itself; in many of these, a pure page is like one of those rare moments of exhilaration that make us fear some stroke of fate; it is but the prelude to surpassing impurity. In Greene's work there is a sound as of the sweet laughter of children that rises on the calm evening air; there is no mockery in it, no hollowness, no self-consciousness, no cruel exultation; it is soft and 'musical as is Apollo's lute.' Nor is it childish or insipid: the creation of such a character as Ateukin, that takes his place beside Shakspeare's Iago, Webster's Vittoria Corrombona, Balzac's Madame Marneffe, and Emily Brontë's Heathfield, is sufficient guarantee for that. All his characters, in fact, are drawn with bold, clear outline; we should know even his heroes and heroines if we met them 'in the flesh'—a thing not frequent in fiction—the injured Dorothea, the firm Ida, the sweet though learned 'slut' Margaret, Lacy, Orlando, George-a-Green. Still more memorable are his humourists: the keen Ralph Simnel (Prince Henry's clown in *Friar Bacon*); Miles, garrulous as the ticking of a clock; the roguish Slipper, the boisterous Adam, the cheerful Alcon, and the foolish, wily Jenkin, have all kinship with Shakespere's clowns, though coming before Shakespere; Bohan and Andrew in *James IV.* are distinct types, without any close kin in Elizabethan literature. Had this man lived to Shakespere's age, and gained mastery of himself as Shakespere did, what a gallery of characters we might have had from him! For he was of Shakespere's race, not Marlowe's or Peele's. Even with his demon dragging him down, and 'dead ere his prime,' he has a place in English literature that no other could fill. The wonder is, that with the life he led, he kept throughout a purer moral tone and a simpler style than any of his contemporaries. His style grows in purity and simplicity as he proceeds. And this simplicity is no mere barrenness of thought or fancy; it is the simplicity which has depth of clear, reflective power: we can see the whole sky, with its fleet of white clouds, mirrored in the shallowest little pool, when the ocean can show us only its turbid surface, or at best the floating tangle and creeping things that make the depths strange or hideous. Shakespere's diction has never-ending wonders to reveal in its heart; Greene's has a sweet attractiveness of its own; it has 'the pure serenity of perfect light.' But there moves through it all, like the funeral of a little child trailing through May cornfields, the beautiful sadness which comes as a prophecy of early death, a mournful feature in the style of all those poets of tainted heart, great mind, and weak will; they have the mark of eternal youth upon them, though their steps totter and their hair grows gray as with age. This alone should turn the gall of pharisaic criticism into tears of pity. It is a sight to move the gods—this strong intellect and fiery fancy, chained to a frame that is only hurrying to the grave. It is sad enough to see autumn dying into bleak winter, or day getting woven down like a Samson below the close and closer-moving meshes of night; sadder still to see the pallid artist Consumption paint in and out the preternatural rose upon the cheek of youth; but saddest of all is it to find this taint creep into the poet's soul, and give his fancy unearthly brilliance. Surely Robert Greene deserves our sympathy and gratitude, even if he were the criminal he has at times been painted" (pp. 126-33).

Having thus reproduced gratefully the very able Paper of Professor J. M. Brown, with running comments, I have now to consider various controversial points in the Life and Writings of Greene. By the necessities of the case, these partake of a miscellaneous nature ; yet one purpose—viz., to bring out the truth—will bind them together. The following group seem to require examination in the first instance :—

(*a*) Who was meant by "Young Iuvenall, that byting Satyrist," in Greene's dying appeal to his three friends ('consorts') ?

(*b*) Is Professor Storojenko's assumption that Robert Wilson, the Playwright, wrote "Martin Mar Sixtus," and his conclusion therefrom, warranted ?

(*c*) Is Professor Storojenko's theory of Greene's original "failure" as a playwright well grounded ?

(*d*) Was Robert Greene ever a clergyman ?

(*e*) Is our inclusion of *Selimus* among Greene's Plays justifiable ?

I wish to try to return answers to these successive questions.

(*a*) *Who was meant by "Young Iuvenall, that byting Satyrist" in Greene's dying appeal to his three friends ('consorts') ?*—This demands more thorough treatment than Storojenko has given it. The chief passage thus runs: "With thee ["a famous gracer of Tragedians"=Marlowe] I ioyne young Iuuenall, that byting Satyrist, that lastlie with mee together writ a Comedie. Sweete boy, might I aduise thee, be aduised, and get not many enemies by bitter words: inueigh against vaine men, for thou canst do it, no man better, no man so wel ; thou hast a libertie to reprooue all, and none more ; for one being spoken to, all are offended, none being blamed no man is iniured. Stop shallow water still running, it will rage, tread on a worme and it will turne: then blame not schollers vexed with sharp lines, if they reproue thy too much libertie of reproofe" ("Groatsworth of Wit": Works, Vol. XII., p. 143). With the Works of Nashe before me from day to day as I prepared them contemporaneously with Greene's, I arrived at the inevitable conclusion, in utter ignorance of what others had said, that "young Juvenall" could only have been THOMAS NASHE. Later I found that I had been long anticipated, as will immediately appear. The whole thing has been handled by Richard Simpson in a very able paper which appeared in the *Academy* of April 11th, 1874 (p. 400), and which was reprinted by C. M. Ingleby, LL.D., in "Shakspere Allusion Books," Part I., 1592-8 (1874), of the "New Shakspere Society,"—the fresh discussion of the points in hand having sprung out of a recent letter by Howard Staunton to the *Athenæum*, wherein he challenged the "Shake-scene" passage as applying to Shakspeare, and vindicated Farmer's interpretation of "young Juvenall" as = Nashe. I know not that I can do better than in the outset leave Simpson to state the case, as thus:—

"With regard to the question whether the 'young Juvenal' of Greene's letter was Lodge or Nashe, Dr. Farmer first said it was Nashe" [I intercalate, to be found in the Variorum Shakespeare, ed. 1821: vol. ii. p. 207.—G.]; "but Malone denied it on two grounds: that we know that Greene and Lodge wrote a comedy together, *The Looking-Glass for London*, but we know of no comedy written by Greene and Nash; and that Nash was pointed at as the real author of Greene's posthumous letter, which would not be natural if he was one of those to whom it was addressed. Therefore Malone concluded 'young Juvenal' was Lodge, and not Nash. And Shaksperian scholars have generally followed Malone's lead, till Mr. Howard Staunton.

"But 'young Juvenal' cannot be Lodge. The chief point which Greene dwells upon is the age of the man he addresses. He is 'young' and 'boy.' Now Lodge was three years older than Greene. In 1592 Lodge was 35 and Greene was 32; neither of them 'boys.' Lodge was born probably in 1557; he was B.A. July 8th, 1577. In 1592 he was a weather-beaten sailor. Greene was born in 1560, and became B.A. at an earlier age in 1578.

"Again, Lodge was absent from England at the date of Greene's letter. He sailed in Cavendish's second expedition; the ships left Plymouth August 26th, 1591, reached Brazil December 15th, and remained at Santos till January 22nd, 1592, when they sailed for the Straits of Magellan. On September 13th, 1592, the South Sea was sighted, but the ships were driven back into the straits. October 2nd they fetched the South Sea again, where they were cruelly buffeted, but recovered the straits a third time. February 6th, 1593, they were at Placentia. One of the ships, without victuals, sails, and almost without men, came to land at Bearhaven, in Ireland, June 11th, 1593. It is not to be supposed that the absent Lodge was one of those to whom Greene addressed his letter, as if they were all present in London at the time.

"Again, it is generally thought that Lodge had forsworn writing for the theatre in 1589. The last stanza of his *Scillaes Metamorphosis* of that date contains the lines :—

> . . . 'And then by oath he [Glaucus] bound me
> To write no more of that whence shame doth grow,
> Or tie my pen to Pennie Knaves delight,
> But live with fame, and so for fame to write.'

"If he kept this vow, it is clear that his two plays must be dated before 1589. And *The Looking-glass for London*, in which Greene was parcel author with him, seems to have been written early in 1589, for Greene, in the dedication of his "Mourning Garment" (1589) to the Earl of Cumberland, has some allusions to the matter of the play, as if it was then fresh in his memory. Thus Lodge and Greene had written a comedy together early in 1589. Is this any proof that Lodge must have been the person whom Greene, three and a half years later, addressed as having 'lastly with me together writ[ten] a comedy'? Lastly means 'quite lately.' It would be absurd to torture the meaning of the word to prop up so weak a conclusion as this, that Lodge must have been the man, because a comedy written by Lodge and Greene nearly four years before happens to have survived, whereas in the general shipwreck of Greene's dramatic works, no comedy avowedly written by him with any one else has been preserved.

"Again, Lodge could not with propriety be called a Juvenal in 1592. 'A Fig for Momus,' his only satirical work, was not published till 1595. And when he there states that the present instalment was only a trial, and that he had in his hands a whole centon more satires, which should suddenly be published if those passed, he implies that those printed were the only ones that had seen the light, or had been submitted to men's judgment. But the satirist whom Greene mentions had already 'vexed scholars with his sharp and bitter lines,' and they had 'reproved his too much liberty of speech.' 'Young Juvenall' had attacked individuals, and Greene advises him to do so no more. Lodge had never done so. Even after 1595 Lodge was never called 'Juvenal.' His satires fell flat, and the world never asked him to publish the store which he had in reserve, or to print a new edition of those he had given forth. Two years after 'A Fig for Momus,' Hall published the first three books of his Satires, and in his prologue, oblivious of Lodge, claimed to be the first writer of this kind:—

'I first adventure, follow me who list,
And be the second English satirist.'

"In the controversy about priority between Hall and Marston [and Donne—G.] no one ever thought of pleading Lodge's indubitable first claim. Perhaps the title of Juvenal, except in irony, would have been the last to be conceded by his contemporaries to this sweet pastoral poet, indifferent satirist, and still less commendable play-writer.

"'Young Juvenall,' then, is not Lodge. Is he Nash?

"Nash's age and appearance fit well. He was born in

November 1567. He was seven years younger than Greene, and wanted some two months of twenty-five years when Greene's letter was written. He was a beardless youth, with a shaggy head of hair, if we may credit his portrait in the 'Trimming of Thomas Nash,' where, however, his open mouth and 'lips ugly wrested' might, on a too slight inspection, be mistaken for a hungry beard.

"Nash also was a 'biting satirist,' who since 1589 had been sowing his pasquinades broadcast, and had already 'vexed scholars with his sharp and bitter lines.' He had begun writing as Greene's coadjutor, with a preface to 'Menaphon,' in which whole classes of the writers of the time were treated with much disdain. The attack was followed up the same year in his 'Anatomy of Absurdity.' The Puritans, their favourers, and all who wished to give them a fair hearing, were attacked with wit, malice, buffoonery, and venom in 'The Countercuffe,' 1589, 'The Return of the Renowned Cavaliero, Pasquil of England,' 1589, 'Martin's Month's Mind,' 1589, 'Pasquil's Apology,' 1590, 'An Almond for a Parrott,' 1590. The personal war with the Harveys was already begun in the 'Wonderful Strange Astrological Prognostication,' 1591. 'Pierce Penniless,' 1592, is subsequent to Greene's death, for Nash tells us that he had intended to print an epistle 'to the ghost of Robert Greene' in the first edition of it, had not the fear of infection detained him with his Lord (Whitgift) in the country (at Croydon) Here was abundant material for calling Nash 'young Juvenal.' He had already christened himself the Pasquil of England; and 'Juvenal,' if I remember rightly, was the name given him by Meres, in 1598."

I pause a moment to accentuate the last fact about Meres. It is of the last importance to recall that he in his "Palladis Tamia," in pleasantly noticing Nashe's luckless play of the *Isle of Dogs*, addresses him directly and identically as Greene did—"Dogs were the death of Euripides; but be not disconsolate gallant *young Juvenal*." Besides, as Mr. J. A. Symonds has emphasized in characterising Nashe's "coarse vigour and grotesque humour," "his lampoons attracted immediate attention. Their style was imitated but not equalled by Lodge, Lylly, and others. Nash acquired a sudden and a lasting reputation as *the first and most formidable satirist of his epoch.* His name is always coupled with some epithet like 'gallant [young] Juvenal,' the 'English Aretine,' and 'railing Nash'" ("Shakespere's Predecessors," p. 574).

Simpson proceeds next "to show that Nashe and Greene had probably written a comedy together, shortly before September 1592." I do not quote his paradoxical argument, for it involves (1) that Greene took part in the Anti-martinist controversy; (2) that *A Knack to know a Knave*, which was brought out in 1592, was not improbably the 'comedy'; and there is not 'jot or tittle' of the former, whilst no one who reads *A Knack* can possibly find in it one line from either Greene or Nashe. There is no call to find the 'Comedy.' In the knowledge that we have of Greene's habitual writing of plays over many years, with the meagre number surviving, it is easy to understand how either such 'comedy' has perished, or remains anonymous. Simpson concludes:—

"There is only one other point to notice: it is Malone's argument, that because some contemporaries supposed the letter to be Nash's and not Greene's, therefore Nash could not be one of the persons to whom it was addressed. But surely these readers may have been either careless readers, who had failed to notice the two short sentences in which Nash is described, or wary readers who thought that Nash, when he wrote in Greene's name, not impoliticly addressed the letter to himself, in order to put guessers off the true scent, and to suggest to them the very same false argument which took in so good a critic as Malone. . . . What I have adduced convinces me that Lodge certainly was not, and Nash almost as certainly was, the person addressed by Greene as 'young Juvenal.'"

I add three additional elements of proof:—

(*a*) Thomas Nashe boasts throughout his writings of the Juvenal-like pen he held. He is never weary of proclaiming how terrible resources of lash and gall and wormwood and gunpowder and other vengeful materials were at his disposal, and with what a will he should employ them all against any who dared to assail or challenge him. It was to this fierce and haughty, defiant and provocative spirit and temperament, the dying Greene addressed himself. Nothing of this is found in Thomas Lodge.

(*b*) It is also to be remembered that though most probably Nashe's 'Plays' were never so numerous as Greene's, yet he must have written far more than *Summer's Last Will and Testament*—his one surviving play—and *The Isle of Dogs*, that has perished. For Meres expressly names him as "known for Comedy." So that there is here another reasonable ground for co-operation in a 'comedy' with Greene, precisely as Greene tells us "young Juvenal" did 'lastly' = quite lately.

(*c*) It is vital to keep in recollection—as Simpson has proved and Fleay leaves untouched by his array of comparative year-dates (p. 261)

—that Nashe was "young," and that a difference of seven years made him a "sweete boy" in Greene's regard. Lodge was older than Greene by three years. In connection with this point it is fitting to note Slipper's ironical "*young stripling* of the age of thirty-six or thirty-seven years" of *James IV.* (Works, Vol. XIII., p. 226) as going strongly to prove that "young Juvenal" could not have been Lodge, aged thirty-three.

It is perhaps due to so laborious a Shakspeare student as Mr. Fleay to mention that in his new book on Shakspeare ("Life and Work of Shakspeare," 1886), he claims "young Juvenal" as Thomas Lodge, but without adducing one scintilla of proof, and either ignoring, or betraying utter unawareness of, Simpson's *Academy* paper. This is only one of a number of preposterous claims made by Mr. Fleay for Lodge on his own *ipse dixit.* How purblind he is let this quotation prove:—

"In December Chettle issued his *Kindhearts Dream*, in which he apologises to Marlowe in the *Groatsworth of Wit*, 'because myself have seen his demeanour no less civil than he excellent in the quality he professes; besides divers of worship have reported his uprightness of dealing, which argues his honesty, and his facetious grace in writing which approves his art.' . . . . Shakespeare was not one of those who took offence" (p. 111).

This, after Chettle's damning renunciation of any wish to know Marlowe, and after Greene's 'Shake-scene.' Yet even this could be equalled over and over. Half a dozen leaves, and not a thick octavo, would have been ample for any contribution to sound Shakspearean criticism or fact in this new venture.

It pricks one as with pins to come on trivial biographic facts and occurrences inserted in the midst of critical discussions and narratives; whilst the repetitions are tedious as needless; nor less to be reprobated is the ingratitude with which he names Dr. J. O. Halliwell-Phillipps, contemporaneously with flagrant appropriation and scarcely any acknowledgment of his labours.

(*b*) *Is Professor Storojenko's assumption that Robert Wilson the Playwright wrote "Martin Mar-Sixtus," and his conclusion therefrom, warranted?*—I have no idea of allowing myself to be tempted into 'intermeddling' with the late Mr. Richard Simpson's many addled eggs in that huge mare's nest yclept "The School of Shakspeare" (2 vols., cr. 8vo). He has brought in Robert Greene by head and shoulders, and in such paradoxical fashion as would demand a volume for the confutation of his theories and (mis)interpretations. Neither does it seem to be obligatory upon me to discuss here the authorship of *Fair Emm*. But Professor Storojenko having—and perhaps legitimately—accepted *Fair Emm* as the production of Robert Wilson, and regarded "Martin Mar-Sixtus" as also his composition, and containing a defence of *Fair Emm*, it is necessary to state that in my judgment, whoever R. W. may have been, there is no evidence that he was Robert Wilson the playwright, or that in the passage quoted by Storojenko he had any reference to *Fair Emm*. I ask the reader to turn to the quotation (pp. 235-7) and judge for himself whether it can be applied to *Fair Emm*? Further—It would appear that the playwright Robert Wilson was known as a

Puritan. But the author of "Martin Mar-Sixtus" is no Puritan. Storojenko held the R. W. of "Mar-Sixtus" to be Puritan doubtless from his adoption of the name Martin added to Mar—like Martin Mar-prelate. But there is another explanation of it, in that he might well have utilised the name to make a telling title. He indeed explains that he chose "Martin" because it is *Mar* plus *tine*, the murthering end of a fork [= agricultural or any fork.] "But," he continues, "there is this difference between the great Martine and myself, that whereas he most unnaturally laid siege against his native soyle and spent his powder upon his owne countrey walles, I have picked me out a forreine adversary." In accordance with this, my friend Dr. Brinsley Nicholson, after reading the booklet, writes me as follows:— "That though he [R. W.] was a stout Protestant, there is not a sign in style or anything else that he was a Puritan. His style, on the contrary, is against this view. He says: 'Methinks I heare the ghost of Aquinas very scholastically,' and he uses quotations from the Latin poets not infrequently. Thus he says, 'A poet can teach thee wit Etsi ego indignus,' etc. That from these things, from Robert Wilson being a Puritan player, and from the style of the writer, which besides being good and vigorous, is that of a literate and close-reasoning and intellectual man, R. W. was not Robert Wilson the player."

With respect to Greene's assailants and quarrellers as illustrated by Robert Wilson, never let it be forgotten that, twice-over, a march (so to say) had been stolen upon him. (1) By Marlowe, when with his "mighty line" and blank verse he depreciated the rhymed and classical style hitherto cultivated by him. (2) By Shakspeare's star rising in splendour above the horizon. Most distressing is it to have such an one as Mr. J. A. Symonds making no allowance for all this, and solving the complex problem by "envious hatred of a rival, wiser in his deportment, and more fortunate in his ascendant star." The grace of the tribute to Greene is marred by its wretched opening—"Despicable as were the passions which inspired it, we cannot withhold a degree of pity for the dying Titan, discomfited, undone and superseded, who beheld the young Apollo issue in splendour, and awake the world to a new day" ("Shakspeare's Predecessors," p. 551).

(*c*) *Is Professor Storojenko's theory of Greene's original 'failure' as a playwright well grounded?*—As I state in addition to note [136], the usually accurate biographer and critic seems to me to have singularly missed Greene's meaning in the words upon which he rests his "theory." When we turn to the Epistle to "Penelope's Web" (Works, Vol. V., p. 144) we thus read continously, and not brokenly as in his quotation—"for they which smiled in the *Theatre* in Rome, might assoone scoffe at the rudenesse of the *scœne*, as giue a Plaudite at the perfection of the action, and they which passe ouer my toyes with silence, may perhappes shrowde a mislike in such patience: if they doe, yet soothing myselfe in the hope of their courtesies, I sleepe content like Phidias in myne owne follies, thinking all is well, till proofe telles me the contrarie." Surely it is clear,—

(1) That as the Epistle is addressed to the Gentlemen Readers of "Penelope's Web," it alone

was the 'toy,' or, regarded in its parts, 'toyes,' referred to.

(2) That the closing words "if they doe" point to a hypothetical condemnation, not a past one, and again could only refer to the present book.

(3) That there is not the shadow of authority for assuming that the 'toyes' were Plays or 'toys' of the theatre. The mere illustration from the 'Theatre' in Rome can't be so 'tortured.'

(4) That this passage is illegitimately put against those in "Never Too Late" and "Groatsworth of Wit." The one does not contradict the other two at all at all. Storojenko's 'theory' of 'failure' is in my judgment a fundamental mistake, and worse.

(*d*) *Was Robert Greene ever a clergyman?*—Professor Storojenko rightly sets aside Dyce's quotation from Lansdowne MSS. 982, art. 102, fol. 187, under the head of "Additions to Mr. Wood's Report of Mr. Robert Green, an eminent poet who died about 1592." By this it appears from a reference to a document given in Rymer's *Fœdera* (reprinted by Dyce) that a "Robert Grene" was in 1576 one of the Queen's Chaplains, and that he was presented by Her Majesty to the rectory of Walkington in the diocese of York. But in 1576—whether 1550 or 1560 was his birth year—this could not have been our Robert Greene, seeing that he was then pursuing his education (1575-78) and 1583-88). But this is not the only ground on which Robert Greene has been held to have been a clergyman at one time.

Octavius Gilchrist (in his "Examination of Ben Jonson's Enmity towards Shakspeare," p. 22) states that a Robert Greene was presented, 19th June, 1584, to the vicarage of Tollesbury, in Essex, and that he resigned it the next year. Gilchrist gives no authority; but on consulting Newcourt's *Repertorium* (ii. 602), that is found to have been his authority. The entry thus reads:—

"Tollesbury (Vicarage).
"Rob. Grene, cl. 19 Jun. 1584. per mort. Searle.
"Barth. Moody cl. 17 Feb. 1585. per resign. Grene."

This makes Greene incumbent for a year and a half,—February 1585 being an ecclesiastical date equivalent to our 1586. The spelling "Grene" is of no moment, as we all know the orthography of proper names (like all orthography) was arbitrary. Moreover, as our facsimile of Robert Greene's writing and autograph in the present volume shows, he himself used 'Grene.' The present vicar of Tollesbury has done his best to help me, but unfortunately the registers of the period have disappeared, and his only authority is Dyce. But the dates so corresponding, it seems safe to assume that this "Rob. Grene, cl." was Robert Greene the dramatist. Further—We have the inscriptions on the title-page of the *Pinner of Wakefield*, which expressly states on the authority of Shakspeare that its author was a "minister"; also the "red-nosed minister in Artibus Magister" of Martin Mar-Sixtus. I must ask the student-reader to turn to our facsimile (in Works, Vol. XIV.) of that title-page, seeing that Professor Storojenko in note [153] has strangely blundered and misargued. My readers will agree with me, I think, (1) That there being two handwritings, and at different times, gives two informants and witnesses; (2) That the dotted space thus . . . .

"Written by . . . . a minister"

is not a name 'worn away by time,' or ever has had a name written, but is so jotted down because the writer had momentarily forgotten the name given him by Shakspeare, who by the way could not fail to know well about Robert Greene; (3) That the second entry, on the authority of Juby, is no supercession of but a confirmation of the other—*i.e.*, that 'Robert Greene' is now filled in as having been the 'minister' originally named by Shakspeare. Thus regarded, each entry is corroborated by the other. My answer, accordingly, to our fourth question, "Was Robert Greene ever a clergyman?" must be —Yes. And hence I give here a renewed quotation from Professor J. M. Brown (as before):—

"The year of his taking M.A. at Clarehall (1583) probably marks one of his more effectual repentances; and at this period would best be placed that year or so of clerical life which one or two notices attribute to him with great likelihood. Even his dramas bear the traces of clerical occupation; and his pamphlet published in 1584 has a clearly religious purpose and tone; its title is 'The Myrrour of Modestie. . . . . . .' It is noticeable that in this he gives only his initials—perhaps exhibiting a desire to retire from notoriety: on all others, except the Connycatching scenes, does he give his name in full" (p. 125).

Mr. F. G. Fleay (as before) speaks of Greene as the "drunken parson." I am aware that "once a parson always a parson." Still, this is uncritical and uncharitable language. Having entered the Church, it may surely be assumed that he ministered at her altars worthily. His renunciation of "love pamphlets" and steadfast continuance as an ethical-didactic writer assure us that he could and did will and abide by his resolves.

(*e*) *Is our inclusion of "Selimus" among Greene's Plays justifiable?*—As having been the first (so far as I am aware) to reclaim *Selimus* for Greene, and the first to place it among his Works, I must now state the external and internal grounds on which I have acted.

(1) *External.*—This evidence is found in the well-known early collection of quotations from the then extant poetical literature of England, entitled "England's Parnassus: or, the Choysest Flowers of our Moderne Poets, with their Poeticall Comparisons; Descriptions of Bewties, Personages, Pallaces, Mountaines, Groves, Seas, Springs, Rivers, etc. Whereunto are annexed other various discourses, both pleasaunt and profitable. . . . 1600." The Dedication and Address to the Reader—in verse—are signed "R. A." These initials have been varyingly assigned to Robert Allott and Robert Armin—the latter in one of too many somewhat unintelligent fillings-in of names in the otherwise excellent catalogue of the British Museum. Dr. Farmer's copy of the book is in the British Museum, and he distinctly records that he had seen a copy with the initials filled up contemporarily 'R[obert] A[llott].' No one could have been better-advantaged to know his authors and authorities than this fine old English publisher.

The important fact, then, is, that in "England's Parnassus" there are no fewer than thirty-five quotations as from Greene. Mr. J. Payne Collier, in his reprint of it, has traced and recorded the sources of most of these, including a well-known one from the "Faerie Queene," and another from "Mother Hubbard's Tale,"—two remarkable slips of Allott; but No. 4 (page 55 of "England's Parnassus," 1600, on "Delaie," No. 6 (*ibid.* pp. 89-90), on "Feare," No. 11 (*ibid.* p. 158), on "Dionysus," No. 13 (*ibid.* p. 219), on "The Rose," No. 15 (*ibid.* p. 244), on "Prayer," No. 21 (*ibid.* pp. 326-7), on "Lycaon's Sin," No. 24 (*ibid.* p. 364), "Tempest," and No. 26 (*ibid.* p. 377). "Disquiet Thoughts," he left untraced, and they never hitherto have been traced. But spite of Mr. Collier's note on No. 4 as "only found in 'England's Parnassus,' it and No. 11 are found in *Selimus*, and Nos. 13 and 21 in respectively *James IV.* iii. 3 (Works, Vol. XIII., p. 273), and *Orlando Furioso* (*Ibid.* p. 134). *En passant*, Nos. 6, 15, 24 and 26, being still untraced, enables me to cherish the "Pleasures of Hope" that by them some other anonymous play (or it may be others) may yet be found to belong to Robert Greene. May I invite fellow-students to co-operate with me herein?

The following are the two quotations in "England's Parnassus":—

1. "No. 4. Delaie.

"He that will stop the brooke, must then begin
When sommers heat hath dried vp the spring;
And when his pittering streams are low and thin:
For let the winter aid vnto them bring,
He growes to be of watry flouds the king:
And though you damme him vp with loftie rankes,
Yet will he quickly overflow his bankes.

"*R. Greene.*"

2. "No. 11. Damocles.

"Too true that Tyrant *Dyonisyus*
Did picture out the image of a king,
When *Damocles* was placed on his throne,
And ore his head a threatning sword did hang,
Fastened vp only by a horse's haire.
"*R. Greene.*"

(See Works, Vol. XIV., pp. 211, 224.) These quotations from *Selimus*, having the name "R. Greene" attached to them exactly as in the others, must assure us that Robert Allott had good authority, if not personal knowledge, for assigning them to Greene. But this involves that Greene was the known author of *Selimus*. It must be added that no other claimant ever has been brought forward for *Selimus*. For Langbaine's extension of the initials stupidly put ('T. G.') on the title-page of the edition of 1638 was a mere guess on the part alike of him and of the 1638 publisher, in each case fetched doubtless from Thomas Goffe's other tragedies—viz., *The Raging Turk, or Bajazet the Second*, and *The Courageous Turke, or Amurath the First.* Of course, as *Selimus* appeared in 1594, it is impossible that Thomas Goffe could have been its author. He was not born until "about 1592," so that in 1594 he was still in the first of the seven famous stages. Further—It is to be noted as a subsidiary 'external' element, that *Selimus* was published by Thomas Creede, who published *James IV.* and *Alphonsus, King of Arragon.*

(2) *Internal.*—One specific passage by itself would have determined my assigning *Selimus* to Greene. Thus we read (Works, Vol. XIV., p. 270) :—

"The sweet content that country life affoords,
Passeth the royall pleasures of a king;
For there our ioyes are interlaced with feares,
But here no feare nor care is harboured,
But a sweete calme of a most quiet state."

Place beside this the song of 'Sweet Content' in the "Farewell to Follie":—

"Sweet are the thoughts that savour of content,
the quiet mind is richer then a crowne:
Sweet are the nights in carelesse slumber spent,
the poore estate scornes fortunes angrie frowne:
Such sweet content, such mindes, such sleep, such blis,
Beggers inioy, when Princes oft do mis.

The homely house that harbors quiet rest,
the cottage that affoords no pride, nor care;
The meane that grees with Countrie musick best,
the sweet consort of mirth and musicks fare;
Obscured life sets downe a type of blis,
a minde content both crowne and kingdome is." *

More widely I would accentuate that at the close of *Alphonsus, King of Arragon* (Works, Vol. XIII., p. 414), Greene prepares us for a second play on the same or a selected subject, *e.g.*—

"Meane time, deare *Muses*, wander you not farre
Foorth of the path of high *Pernassus* hill,
That, when I come to finish vp his life,
You may be readie for to succour me:
Adieu, deare dames; farwell Calliope."

Dyce annotates—"This proves that Greene intended to write a Second Part of *Alphonsus.* Perhaps, indeed, he did write one: 'possibly,' observes Mr. Collier ("Hist. of *Engl.* Dram. Poet." iii. 171), 'the continuation has perished.'" Granted that, literally interpreted, the words intimate a 'finishing

* Works, Vol. IX., pp. 279-80.

up' of the 'life' of Alphonsus; granted, further, that that may have been the intention of Greene at the moment, I can perfectly understand that with one so impulsive and volatile it is extremely likely that, on finding *Alphonsus* did not furnish materials for a 'Second Part,' he selected a subject kindred with his former, and so produced *Selimus.* It is no objection to this that *Alphonsus* was not published until 1599 (so far as we know), whereas *Selimus* had appeared in 1594. Both having been posthumously printed, their issue was very much accidental, and does not determine their chronology of composition. If he ever wrote a 'Second Part' of *Selimus*, which itself is named 'First Part,' it has disappeared in the general loss. I would add that as *Alphonsus*—as we have seen in this Introduction—had tacit girds at Marlowe, he may have been very willing to rid himself of the necessity of continuing those by surceasing production of a 'second part.'

Further—It is to be noted that not only does *Selimus*, like *Alphonsus*, develop itself on Eastern (Asiatic) and Turkish ground, and by Eastern and Turkish 'characters,' but that the character-names of *Alphonsus* are echoed in *Selimus.* I go no further than the names; for the 'characters' are quite different, save superficially and in subordinate points. Nevertheless, if in *Alphonsus* we have 'Amurack, the Great Turk,' in *Selimus* we have 'Bajazet, Emperour of Turkie,' and 'Selimus' himself 'Emperour of the Turkes, youngest son of Bajazet'; in *Alphonsus* 'Arcastus, King of the Moors,' and 'Claramont, King of Barbary,' and in *Selimus* 'Acomat, Corcut, sons of Bajazet'—'Mustaffa, high official of Bajazet'; in

Alphonsus 'Crocon, King of Arabia,' and 'Faustus, King of Babylon'; and in *Selimus*, besides 'Mustaffa, high official of Bajazet,' are 'Aladin, Amurath, sons of Acomat'; in *Alphonsus* 'Fausta, wife of Amurack,' and in *Selimus* 'Zonara, sister to Mahomet,' and 'Solyma, sister to Selimus, wife to Mustaffa,' and 'Queene Amasia, wife of Acomat'; in *Alphonsus* 'Two priests of Mahomet,' and 'Provost, soldiers, janissaries, etc.'; and in *Selimus* 'Janissaries, souldiers, messengers, page.'"

It will be recognised that the whole of these names and characters in *Selimus* might have gone into *Alphonsus*, and so have figured in the 'Second Part,' and to a large extent conversely.

Still further—the treatment of the subject is similar. The 'plot' unfolds itself in both along the same lines, and the successive 'characters' deliver themselves of the same sentiments; and more than that, in *Selimus* peculiarly and noticeably we find those autobiographic touches that were inevitable to Greene. As examples, I ask the critical student to read deliberatively ll. 231—314. Unless I very much mistake, there we have the very substance of these 'opinions' and sentiments that so stung him with remorse in his final 'Repentance.'

Then, more specifically—*Selimus* (like *Alphonsus*) belongs to Greene's first period, when he had not yet surceased his love of rhymed lines or fully acquiesced in Marlowe's blank verse. The opening scene of *Selimus* (pp. 195—201) presents a crucial example of his odd and quaint blending of rhyme and blank verse, couplet and alternate rhyming, albeit there is far more of the latter in *Selimus* than in *Alphonsus*.

Compare with this 'opening'—among various—the interview between 'Carinus the Father and Alphonsus his sonne' in *Alphonsus* (Works, Vol. XIII., pp. 336-38), where rhyme and blank verse are intermittent. So throughout in both. But it demands painstaking study and comparisons (not 'odious') to feel the full force of this evidence.

Further—As in *Alphonsus* and *Orlando Furioso* and *Friar Bacon*, there occur in *Selimus* these semi-parodyings of Marlowe. Let the reader pause over ll. 349-68, ll. 1244-51, ll. 1257-62, ll. 1400-15, and ll. 1950-62. Similarly his 'humorous vein' in the *Looking-glass* and elsewhere breaks out in *Selimus*: *e.g.*, ll. 1876—1926 (note 'conicatching crosbiter.') Yet again,—With our restoration of Greene's own descriptions of the movements and arrangements on the stage (so mutilated and smothered by Dyce), it will be seen how in *Selimus* there are exactly such descriptive *bits* as in the other plays. I note the following: pp. 214, 217, 225, 228, 233, 241, 263, etc.

Finally,—The critical reader of *Selimus* will discover Greene's words, epithets, occasional looseness of syntax, phrases, turns of expression, false quantities—*e.g.*, Ixion (l. 355). Our 'General Index' will guide readily to these (Vol. XV.). I dare not enter into details with my waning space. I trust no reader will now hesitate to accept our assignation of *Selimus* to Robert Greene; and it is something, I dare to say, to have thus restored to him a hitherto unassigned play.

I have now to bring together a number of minor things referred to in Notes and Illustrations, and in the General Index, etc., in Vol. XV., and reserved for this Introduction. It will be self-evident that I must be as brief as I possibly can; and if any little promises elsewhere given—*i.e.*, beyond those notified as above (Vol. XV., pp. 239-44), remain unredeemed, I plead for excuse. I shall follow the order of the record mentioned.

Vol. II., pp. 6, 97, 284; iii. 209; iv. 75; v. 280, *et freq.*, '*cooling card.*' Mr. Fleay, in his new book on Shakspeare, argues for the Lodge authorship on the ground that 'cooling card' does not occur in Greene. These references show he is mistaken. 'Cooling card' was an ordinary gaming term. One with excitement and triumph puts down a card, which in all likelihood will win; an after player puts down a better. This is to the former player a '*cooling* card.'

" " pp. 12, 306—'*His filed phrase deserves in learnings throne to sit.*' With respect to 'filed phrase' Dr. Dowden, in his Sonnet notes on Shakspeare's use of the word 'filed,' thus writes:—"lxxxv. 4, '*Filed*,' polished, refined (as if rubbed with a file). *L. L. Lost*, v. 1, l. 11, 'his tongue *filed*.'" See note on Sonnet lxxxvi. 13. "lxxxvi. 13, '*Fill'd up his line.*' Malone, Steevens, Dyce, read *fil'd*—*i.e.* polished . . . But 'fill'd up his line' is opposed to 'then lacked I matter.'" Dyce had anticipated Dr. Dowden's opposition of 'fill'd . . .' to 'then lacked . . .' but none the less he argued for and retained 'fil'd' as = filed. Surely the thought rather is that his Patron-friend's patronage ('countenance') of his (Shakspeare's) rival—whoever he was—had given such lustre to his line = lines or verse, that it silenced him ('Then lack'd I matter')? In 'countenance' and context, there is (*meo judicio*) a remembrance of Psalm iv. 6, "Lord, lift Thou up *the light of Thy countenance* upon us." *Certes* the Patron-friend's 'countenance,' whilst it might be said to make lustrous, as a thing polished with a file, could scarcely 'fill up' the Poet's verse.

Vol. II., p. 14, *'fourme of her feature.'* The Glossarial Index, *s.v.*, supplies other uses of 'feature.' It is a tempting word for detailed examination and illustration from Elizabethan to Victorian times. I must content myself by a reference to Schmidt's 'Shakspeare Lexicon,' *s.v.*, as = shape, make, exterior, the whole turn or cast of the body; also Dyce's 'Shakspeare Glossary,' *s.v.* The origin of its present limited application to the 'face' has not been carefully traced or accounted for. Most of my various Glossaries supply examples of the word.

" " p. 15, *'made stealth'* = taken stolen possession of [the heart of Florion].

" " p. 21, '*traine.*' As explained and illustrated, the word is here = stratagem, artifice, as in Shakespeare and Spenser. So the verb is used as = to draw or allure or entice—*e.g.*, "*train* me not with thy note to drown me" (*Comedy of Errors* III. ii. 45), *et freq.* But it is found in its present-day sense of educate or bring up—*e.g.*, "you have *trained* me like a peasant" (*As you Like it*, I. i. 72). Our Glossarial Index, *s.v.* 'trayned' (ii. 106), gives a curious example of the former = caused his hook to allure by baiting it; also as noun 'traynes' in vi. 196 *et freq.* = laid to allure birds. In xii. 121, l. 2, 'trained' is = traced or tracked; in xiv. 102 'traine' is = guide, or perhaps, as before, 'allure' (l. 2358). For other occurrences of the word as verb and noun, see our Glossarial Indices to Dr. Gabriel Harvey, i. 166, 209; ii. 172; and 'trainement,' i. 277, 279; and to Nashe, i. 83, 105; ii. 10; iv. 24. As with 'feature,' this word in its varying shades of meaning deserves more thorough treatment than hitherto.

" " p. 27, '*curious*' = scrupulous. Our Glossarial Index, under 'curioser,' 'curiositie,' 'curious,' 'curiously,' and 'curiousnesse,' supplies various uses of the word. Ordinarily it is = careful or over-careful. Its modern sense of 'inquisitive' has not been sufficiently dealt with, or the gradual limitation illustrated. Schmidt, *s.v.*, as before, furnishes abundant examples in Shakespeare; so too Dyce, *s.v.*, as before. It were a worthy thing to follow up the earlier and later meanings.

Vol. II., p. 29, '*tryed*' = proved. See 'tryed,' ii. 27; iii. 51, 113; iv. 14; 'trie,' iv. 120, 131, etc., etc. Skeat (Etymological Dictionary, *s.v.* 'try'), has excellent examples of the primary and later senses. These supersede those I had collected. Schmidt, *s.v.*, exhaustively records the Shakespearean uses; *ibid.*, '*for her honestie shee might haue tryed the daunger of Diana's caue.*' See Ovid, "Metam." iii. 156-9—fable of Actæon.

" " pp. 30, 311, '*diamond* v. *magnet*.' Our Glossarial Index references, *s.v.*, sufficiently illustrate this. More especially see vi. 234, 'dress set with *adamants*,' and xiii. 256, 'The *adamant*, o King, will not be filde.' So too in Glossarial Index to Dr. Gabriel Harvey, *s.v.* (ii. 236); *ibid.*, '*goats blood*.' Greene was apt to jump at such folk-lore as this. In his time jewels had each special virtues, or rather powers for good or evil and counteractives were associated with them: specifically, goat's blood, new and warm, was fabulously believed to soften the diamond; and the diamond to cause the magnet not to draw iron. See Pliny, 20. c. 1—37, c. 15: and Barth. 16. c. 9.

" " p. 32, '*Calicut*' = capital city and port of Malabar; *ibid.*, '*Orme*'—can hardly be = Ormus of Persia. Query the French river Orne?

" " pp. 35, 312, '*vaded* v. *faded*.' I must rest satisfied here by a reference to my very full and fully illustrated discussion in F. W. edition of Marvell's Works, vol. i., pp. 126-7, which I gratefully see is referred to by Dr. Ingleby in his *Love's Labour's Lost* as 'an able note.'

Vol. II., pp. 38, 313, '*reclaimeth*' = recalleth. Shakespeare's use is only = subdue, tame, make gentle. Greene's approaches the present-day use. *Reclamare* gives us *re* = back again; *clamare* = cry.

" " pp. 54, 315, '*crost*.' In x. 101, l. 6, 'crost' is = marked off with a bad mark as a fool.

" " pp. 63, 317, '*labour lost*.' More frequently than many think, Shakspeare used proverbial phrases, and this is one of the latter very often met with contemporarily.

" " pp. 106, 322, '*grauelled*' = being thrown on the gravel in wrestling.

" " pp. 114, 323, '*golden boxe*.' I must refer students to the commentators on the 'casket' in the *Merchant of Venice*.

" " pp. 276, 337, '*Algorisme*' = arithmetic.

" " pp. 75, 342, '*misse the cushion*.' I suppose the reference is to the old English game (not obsolete) of hunting the cushion, like hunting the slipper.

" " pp. 85, 342, '*fish*' = something to occupy and detain him, as one would have if fish and fish scales, sticking to his fingers, had to be picked off.

" " pp. 94, 343, '*two faces*.' It reminds one of the little girl who, having heard her mother speak of a certain lady-guest as 'two-faced,' walked round and round her, and on being asked why she did so, replied—to the horror of mother and visitor—"I'm looking for your other face, for mother said you were two-faced."

" " pp. 99, 343, '*fool's paradise*.' I have mislaid my intended reference to Lylly; but it is found in *Romeo and Juliet*, II. iv. 176—"if ye should lead her in a fool's paradise." Schmidt makes it = make an April fool of; but I can't accept this. Dyce has wholly overlooked it.

" " pp. 285, 343, '*rule the rost*.' Like 'traine' and 'feature' and many other words, this phrase has not been carefully or adequately elucidated. I regret that my preoccupied space does not admit of various quotations that I had meant to record.

The thing demands investigation. See also iv. 133. In both cases a woman is spoken of, and she naturally managed household affairs and 'ruled the rost.' The cook in a book of 1641 is named of 'Rulerost.'

Vol. III., pp. 153, 269, '*bee*.' The elder and later Puritans delight in the contrast between the 'bee' and the 'spider,' in so far as the former is represented by them as sucking only 'honey' from the flowers, whilst the latter is alleged to suck 'poison' (which it never does or in any way touches flowers).

" " pp. 203, 272, '*harte at grace*,' and 'hart at grasse.' The latter corruption is to be put alongside 'hocus-pocus' for 'hoc est corpus,' and the like.

" " pp. 209, 272, '*toades*.' It is curious to observe the present-day shrinking from the 'toad' as still "ugly and venemous," while the 'frog' is freely handled.

" " pp. 247, 277, '*castles in the air*.' This phrase abounds contemporarily and later, as many of my Glossaries show. It has been turned to beautiful and pathetic account in the sweet Scottish lyric of 'Castles in the Air,' by James Ballantyne—one of the gems of a casket of gems, "Songs for the Nursery" (1844).

" " pp. 251, 277, '*Catherismes*.' From 'eies' and 'cockatrice' immediately after, it looks like the name of some animal—one of the Lylly and Greene fabrications, perhaps. καθαρισμος = a cleansing from pollution or sin, and thence the means of cleansing or atonement or expiation only suggests that there may possibly be some Talmudic superstition about the eyes of the scape-goat. But it will be noticed that Greene's word is Cath*e*, not Cath*a*, whence there may be a reference to καθερμα, given as necklace by some, but by Jones, in his Lexicon, as "a necklace with an image of Mercury," whence possibly the 'eies.'

" IV., pp. 75, 328, '*cooling Card*.' See note above on ii. 6, etc.; also ii. 304. It were easy to multiply examples of the term, for it was very common. Shakspeare has it in 1 *Henry VI.*, V. iii. 84, "there all is marred; there lies a cooling card," which Schmidt explains as = "one which dashes hopes." But he adds, whimsically and wrongly, "perhaps not the same word, but derived from Carduus benedictus." See also Dyce, *s.v.*, as before. It is palpable that Greene uses it as a 'card' in the games of card-playing.

Vol. IV., pp. 100, 330, '*camisados.*' See iii. 275-6.

" " pp. 130, 333, '*retrive.*' Skeat, *s.v.*, as before, gives numerous examples, which the student will do well to consult. Modernly = recover or 'retrieve' a blunder or error, fault or game (*i.e.* sporting); like 'curious,' bewrays its transitional meaning.

" " pp. 156, 337, '*doubteth.*' Schmidt, *s.v.* 'doubt' = fear, *a* 3, gives the Shakspeare references, and also all the other uses of the word. See Dyce's quotation, *s.v.*, from Dr. Johnson.

" V., '*Patron names.*' Storojenko has noticed these well in his 'Life.' Some of them tempt to enlargement; but I dare not.

" VI., pp. 78, 300, '*Marte.*' See v. 197. 'Marque,' *Marc*, Sax. = *signum*, corrupted into 'Marte,' reminds us of 'Martinmas' corrupted into 'Martlemas,' and many other similar.

" " pp. 104, 302, '*holiday oath.*' I suppose = sportive. See xiv. 35. So Shakspeare, 'holiday terms.'

" " pp. 156, 306, '*canuisadoes.*' See ii. 175, 270.

" " pp. 189, 308, '*cock-boate.*' See ii. 179; iv. 295, 297, etc., etc. Still in use.

" " pp. 77, 314, '*nose.*' I have mislaid reference to an earlier use of the phrase. It is a common one = ridiculed her.

" VII., pp. 107, 329, '*marble.*' The 'weeping' of marble, or the growing 'wet' or 'damp' before a storm, has a very mundane and simple explanation—viz., the moisture in the air that inevitably damps a polished surface. But as in Greene, I've met with it (unless I mistake) in George Herbert and elsewhere.

" IX., p. 224. Though 'Farewell to Follie' only survives in 1591 edition, it is entered in Stat. Reg. 11 June, 1587.

Vol. IX., pp. 294, 375, '*knee-stead*' = place. I must refer to my edition of Richard Barnfield's collected Poems for the Roxburghe Club, *s.v.*, on 'girdle'-steed.

" " pp. 293, 375, '*pensicke*.' Dyce reads (that is, misreads), and prints, '*pensive*,' which I for one can't accept, deeming 'pensicke' = writing-sick, as poor hack Greene must often have been: much more characteristic and expressive, albeit 'pensive' gloses well enough. See iv. 115; xii. 26.

" " pp. 310, 376, '*call*.' This hawking term is found in *The Taming of the Shrew* (IV. i. 178)—"Another way I have to man my haggard, To make her come and know her keeper's *call*"; also *King John* III. iv. 174—"as a *call* to train ten thousand English to their side": = summons (not 'instrument,' as Schmidt doubtfully).

" " pp. 338, 377, '*fact*.' See ii. 151, 167; iii. 14; vi. 167 *et freq*.

" X., pp. 17, 284, '*browne study*.' Whilst the term occurs very frequently, I have failed to devise or find an origin or explanation of it = unsatisfied.

" " pp. 37, 288, '*thieves words*.' With the full, perhaps over-full collection of these—for a number included are not distinctively 'thieves' words'—for text, I felt inclined to enter into a critical examination of the many singular and racy terms and phrases. In denying myself, I venture to remark that it is surely about time this were done by competent English scholars; for just now this strong factor in our language has been uncritically and superficially dealt with, and even recorded.

" " pp. 62, 291, '*Iack Drum*' = a proverbial phrase that was taken by Marston for title of his Play.

" " 113, 299, '*small beere*.' Let this word and reference be filled in in the 'General Index.' See also Dyce, *s. v.* Single (tennis) ale and double or strong ale, are similar terms. 'Beere' is a very ancient English home-brewed drink. 'Small beere' occurs in 2 *Henry IV.*, II. ii. 8, 13; 2 *Henry VI.*, IV. ii. 63; *Othello*, II. i. 161; and it lives in the famous phrase 'chronicle small beer' of Byron, quoting *Othello*.

Vol. X., pp. 223, 310, '*masse priest*.' The *morale* of the R. C. 'priests' is an old matter of accusation. 'Morrow,' 'morwe,' 'morwening,' all signified morning, just as *Morgen* in German is both morning and morrow. Hence 'a morrow masse priest' was a hit at the R. C. priests, since by comparatively late edicts (1550-8) the celebration of mass was forbidden after midday.

„ XI., pp. 49, 303, '*Deloney*.' It is of our *desiderata* to have brought together the many waifs and strays of this maligned ballader. Some of his most hastily 'packed up' things have the true ring, if all too many are somewhat formless.

„ „ pp. 62, 306, '*gilden Thombe*.' I can only again refer to Nares, *s.v.* It is of the many gibes against the Miller tribe.

„ XII., pp. 104, 297, '*nouerint*' = 'know all men by these presents,' and thence used for a scrivener. See "The Mistery and Misery of Lending and Borrowing," by Th. Powell, 1636, p. 138, or its quotation in *Gentleman's Magazine*, 1829.

„ XIII., p. 22, '*cope*' = chop or exchange (Halliwell-Phillipps, *s.v.*).

„ „ p. 119, '*statues* v. *statutes*.' As noted *in loco*, Dyce corrects into 'statues,' but the spelling was then frequently interchanged, and still is.

„ „ p. 122, 'Or.' I changed 'Who' into 'Or' because two are necessary if the context is not to be confused. The 'Nimphe of Mercurie' is one and 'Phœbus' the other, and what applies to the one would not to the other.

„ „ p. 128, '*smother*.' I query 'smoulder,' but feel now doubtful of the word.

„ „ p. 129, '*friends* v. *friend*.' I re-note that Dyce is much too finical in his corrections and emendations. I suppose that,—Scot though he was,—

Hogg's 'When the kye comes hame' would have been similarly refined into 'come.'

Vol. XIII., p. 162, '*Brandemart.*' Rodamant is spoken of as dead, p. 169, and Brandemart is not killed afterwards. But some one is killed here (see ll. 992-5). Therefore Orlando kills Brandemart now, while Rodamant must fall in some unrecorded skirmish. The note [1] on p. 162 is wrong. I had confused *Brandemart* with *Mandrecart*, who alone appears afterwards.

" " p. 170, '*Marsilius.*' As this 'character' (like all) occurs so frequently in the play, it has not been recorded in the Index of Names. An examination of its occurrences and recurrences will show that 'Marsilius' and not 'Marsillus' is the proper spelling.

" " p. 178, '*Else, etc.*' Cf. the Alleyn MS. reading, which confirms Dyce's note *in loco*; and perhaps I ought to have worked in 'Some drynke, some drink, . . . my lord,' into the text.

" " p. 179, '*What sights, etc.*' So the Alleyn MS. reading might be utilised to improve the text.

" " p. 186, '*schedules.*' I have failed to come on 'sedulet' elsewhere; and yet I have a dim remembrance of meeting it.

" " p. 205, '*Ridsdale.*' One queries where was this 'dale'?

" " p. 207, '*threap*' = contradict argumentatively.

" " p. 218, '*Linke.*' It is a meditative introspective appeal to himself in his 'better part' to re-link himself to his pure and true and dishonoured queen.

" " p. 234, '*doubts*' = fears. See note above on Vol. IV., pp. 156, 337.

" " p. 238, '*warpe*' = go awry [*i.e.* spoilt].

" " p. 243. The prefix 'Ateu.' is rightly taken away from "Come, etc.," l. 856; but it ought to have been inserted before l. 858, "Stay, etc." The old copy had 'Ateu.' too high.

" " p. 250, '*raine.*' Evidently poor Greene knew little of horses. He had better have used 'bridle,' or bit.

Vol. XIII., p. 281, '*Storris.*' I can't yet shed more light on this term.

" " p. 322, '*aldertruest.*' Mr. Fleay makes too much of the occurrence of this word here. See his "Life and Work of Shakespeare," p. 269.

" XIV., p. 9, '*Mars*' and 'Mavors' were interchanged frequently.

" " p. 16, '*Autem glorificam*' = a pseudo-legal phrase, I suppose.

" " p. 20, [1]. See Glossarial Index, *s.v.*, for other references and notes from Dyce. See Thomas Dekker, *s.v.*

" " p. 27, '*ciuill*' = polite, refined, fair-spoken.

" " p. 29, '*Knancks.*' I have not met with this word as = eunuchs; but Dyce's reading seems right.

" " p. 30, '*I will*' = I'll, as *freq.*; and so had better be read as in the 4tos, after all.

" " p. 69, '*Bisas bitter blast.*' Cotgrave, 'Bise' = north wind. Boyet translates it 'A north-east wind,' but Cotgrave gives 'Bise transverse' as a N.W. or N.E. wind.

" " p. 70, '*gassampine*' = cotton cloth (?); 'gosampine' (Cotgrave) and 'gossampino' (Florio) = the cotton plant. Davies, *s.v.*, as before.

" " p. 89, '*sober to bed*' = without full carouse and drink enjoyment!

" " p. 147, '*considering*'—the preferable word, but = consid'ring.

" " p. 153, '*perseuerance.*' This accentuation is frequent, and so in the verb 'persever.'

" " p. 260, '*thrillant.*' To Dyce belongs this excellent emendation.

And so the Life and Works of Robert Greene are completed worthily. "Hail and farewell" all!

Alexander B. Grosart.

ROBERT GREENE:

HIS LIFE AND WORKS.

A Critical Investigation

BY

NICHOLAS STOROJENKO.

Translated from the Russian by E. A. Brayley Hodgetts, *London. With Introduction and Additional Notes by the* Rev. Alexander B. Grosart, D.D., LL.D., F.S.A. (*Scot.*)]

He was of singuler pleasaunce, the verye supporter, and, to no man's disgrace be this intended, the only Comedian of a vulgar writer, in this country."
Chettle, "*Kind-Hartes Dreame*" London, 1593].

MOSCOW
1878

TO THE MEMORY OF

JOSEPH MAXIMOVITCH BODYANSKI

THE AUTHOR

REVERENTLY DEDICATES

THIS WORK.

PREFACE.

IN the Preface to my first Work,* devoted to a review of the Dramatic Works of Lylly and Marlowe, I expressed a hope to be able soon to publish a continuation, which was to contain an account of the Dramatists of second rank that sprang up under the influence of these writers, especially the latter, and formed, as it were, a connecting link between them and Shakspeare. When, however, I applied myself to the study of the most important of these, —ROBERT GREENE,—I discovered that a full delineation of his character and literary labours would entail a consideration of his numerous Prose Works, which, from their peculiar character, are strongly allied to his Dramas. During my two sojourns in England I had the opportunity of studying in chronological order all GREENE'S pamphlets. If the result of this study has not fully realised my hopes, the

* "Predshestveniky Shakspeara" (the Predecessors of Shakspeare): St. Petersburg, 1872.

pamphlets have at any rate given me a firm basis from whence to pursue further investigations.

A careful study of GREENE'S Prose Works has led me to the conclusion that most of the erroneous views frequently met with in the works of German and even English critics have originated in their insufficient acquaintance with them. As I have been compelled during my work constantly to investigate and question these views, my book has necessarily assumed a critical character.

In submitting the following researches—really a part of the second volume of my "Predecessors of Shakspeare"—to the judgment of my readers, I consider it my duty to confess that I have treated my subject unequally in some of its aspects, and that, owing to circumstances unconnected with it, I am prevented from publishing my book in the form I had originally proposed.

*** Storojenko's own notes are referred to by the numerals [1], [2], onward; mine by [a], [b], [c], onward. Additions and corrections of the former are placed within [ ] at close of the several notes, and bear my initial.* *G.*

CHAPTER I.

BIOGRAPHICAL SKETCH.[1]

Greene's birth and education.—Cambridge University.—Journey abroad.—Return home and first literary works ("Love-Pamphlets").—Greene commences to write for the stage.—His marriage and subsequent separation from his wife.—Return to London.—New productions and growing popularity of Greene.—His literary patrons.—Friends and enemies.—Sudden change in his literary labours.—Exposure of sharpers.—Last years of Greene's life.—His association with Marlowe.—Greene in the society of sceptics and freethinkers.—Greene as a moral character.

ROBERT GREENE was a native of the town of Norwich, in the county of Norfolk, and was descended from a very old and respectable family. The exact year of his birth is not known. From his entering the University in 1575, however, and leaving the same,

---

[1] The sources to which I am indebted for my biography of Greene are of a twofold character: namely, official documents, and the works of Greene and his contemporaries. With the first category may be classed Cooper's *Athenæ Cantabrigienses* (2 vols., London, 1860-61), and the "Registers of the Stationers' Company," edited by Arber. In consulting

with the degree of B.A., in 1578,[3] it may be supposed, with some degree of certainty, that he was born about

---

the latter authority, however, it must be borne in mind (1) that it is not always the first edition that is entered in the "Registers," and (2) that some of Greene's well-known pamphlets are not found entered here at all, owing to the carelessness of the clerks and officials of those days. This last circumstance considerably lessens the value of an authority which is, in many respects, unreplaceable. In the second category the works of Nashe, Chettle, Harvey, and others, may be classed, together with Greene's own "Groatsworth of Wit" and the "Repentance of Robert Greene." The greater part of this widely diffused material may be found systematically arranged in Dyce's "Account of R. Greene and his Writings," with the exception of the "Repentance," from which there are only sparing quotations. [If the clerks were careless they must have been worse—*i.e.*, misappropriated the money; but there is not a tittle of proof that they did. Many books, we know not why, never were entered. Further, it seems doubtful, except in cases of transfer, that the first edition was not, as a rule, entered.—G.]

[3] In the "Repentance of R. Greene" Greene thus speaks of his parents:—"I neede not make long discourse of my parentes, who, for their grauitie and honest life [were] well knowne and esteemed among tneir neighbors namely in the Cittie of Norwitch, where I was bred and borne" [Works, Vol. XII., p. 171.—G.] That they were well circumstanced

1560. He was therefore several years older than both Marlowe and Shakspeare.[4] It is equally un-

---

may be inferred from their being able to send their son abroad—an undertaking involving considerable expense in those days. Although Greene never signed himself "gentleman," as Nashe did, preferring his university degree to any distinction of birth, yet we may conclude that he belonged to the landed gentry, from Elliot's French sonnet written in his honour, and inscribed "Au R. Greene, Gentilhomme." [This sonnet was prefixed to Greene's "Perimides the Blacksmith" (London, 1588). Works, Vol. VII., p. 10. There is no evidence that the family was what we call "an old family," much less "very old"; and no proof whatever that he was a 'gentleman' by law and heraldry. On his birthplace, etc., it is to be noted that he signs his Epistle to Lady Elizabeth Hatton before his "Maidens Dreame" (Works, Vol. XIV., p. 300), "R. Greene *Nordouicensis*," and in that to Viscount Fitzwaters before Lodge's "Euphues' Shadow," "Robt. Greene Norfolciensis."—G.]

[3] Cooper, "Athenæ Cantabrigienses," vol. ii., pp. 127-8. ['Leaving' is inaccurate: he remained, and in 1583 took his M.A. degree, as onward.—G.]

[4] Dyce, in his "Account," p. 3, is for fixing the date at 1550, because he wishes to identify R. Greene the dramatist with the court chaplain of Elizabeth, R. Greene, of whom mention is made in Rymer's "Fœdera Conventiones," t. xv., p. 765 (1576). We shall see further on why Dyce wishes to make this

known where he received his elementary education, but it is more than probable that he attended the grammar school of his native town;[a] from whence, on the 15th of November, 1575, he was entered as a student at the college of St. John's, Cambridge. The English universities in the time of Elizabeth were far from being in a brilliant condition. Externally magnificent, furnished with all the indispensables for the prosecution of scientific studies, there still lurked within them traces of recent troubles and moral degeneration. A theological spirit, routine in teaching, a want of moral discipline: such were the more prominent features of the internal life at Oxford and Cambridge in the time of Elizabeth. A Historian of the English universities—Huber—says that the young men studying at Oxford were distinguished for their immorality, impiety, dissipation and disreputable conduct.[6] Cambridge was very little behind Oxford in these respects. If we are to believe Greene, his stay at Cambridge had a most baleful effect on his character. "I light amongst wags as

---

identification, which we are unable to recognise, if only for the reason that in 1575 Greene the dramatist first entered Cambridge as a student. [See on this our Introduction.—G.]

[6] See the description of English university life in his "Die Englischen Universitäten," Band II., s. 58 *et seq.*

[a] See "Repentance" (Works, Vol. XII., p. 171): "My Father had care to haue mee in my Non-age brought vp at Schoole, etc."—G

lewd as my selfe," Greene wrote, in his "Repentance" (p. 172, as before), "with whome I consumed the flower of my youth." These same jolly boon companions persuaded Greene to go abroad to Italy and Spain, on leaving the university, under the plausible pretext of finishing his education,—in reality, to see the world and enjoy life. There is reason to believe that this project did not meet with any special sympathy on the part of Greene's father, otherwise there would have been no necessity for Greene to have recourse to various "cunning sleights" to obtain the necessary means.[b] In those days a tour on the Continent, especially in Italy, besides entailing considerable expense, alarmed parents; who regarded the Continent as an abyss of dissipation and vice, in which, they opined, the inexperienced hearts of youth were sure to perish. The reaction against Italian culture had already begun in English society. Every one remembered the words of the venerable old pedagogue, Roger Ascham, who warned his countrymen as early as 1570 against the enchantments of this new Circe, and cited, in confirmation of his warning, examples from the lives of his friends, who went to Italy pious and God-fearing young men, and returned from thence more metamorphosed than they would have been had they fallen into the hands of the real Circe.[a]

---

[a] "The Scholemaster," by Roger Ascham. New edition by Mayor (London, 1863), p. 74. Lord Burghley, in his "Ten Precepts," which he left his son for

[b] It is to be noted that Greene tells us his mother had been specially indulgent (Works, Vol. XII., p. 172).—G.

Greene's life abroad, as far as we can tell from his confessions, seemed fully to justify the fears of his father. The inexperienced young man, still probably under twenty,[7] was not long in succumbing to the influence of his travelling companions. These were men of jovial temperament, frightful debauchees, but "good fellows" nevertheless; who undertook to enlighten him after their own fashion, and whose example he strove to follow. The dissipated life he led in the society of such companions Greene used

---

guidance (they are printed in the third volume of Nares' "Memoirs of the Life and Administration of W. Cecil, Lord Burghley," London, 1828-31), says:—"Suffer not thy sons to pass the Alps, for they shall learn nothing there but pride, blasphemy and atheism." *Vide* also the author's work, "Predshestveniky Shakspeara," Notes 156 and 157, where there are several quotations from other contemporaries bearing on Italy and the Italians.

[7] On this subject there is a considerable difference of opinion. Dyce assigns the period between the obtaining of Greene's B.A. and M.A. degrees (1578-83) for his tour. Bernhardi ("R. Greene's Leben und Schriften," p. 13), from the fact that the first part of "Mamillia" was published October 3rd, 1580, and the second entered in the "Registers" under the 6th September, 1583, and from his not being able to discover any publication of Greene's to have appeared in the interval, supposes Greene to have been abroad during that period. Bernhardi is refuted by Greene's

to recall with shame. In his "Repentance" he confesses, with a contrite heart, that abroad he was given to vices which it was "abhominable to declare" (p. 172, as before). The natural results of so mad a life were temporary satiety and disenchantment. Towards the close of the sixteenth century there were not a few Englishmen who, having tasted abroad the fruits of a refined Epicurean life, and having been gorged with its enjoyments, on their

---

own words in his "Repentance," from which we conclude that Greene's tour took place immediately after his leaving the university. Here are his words:—"For being at the Vniuersitie of Cambridge, I light amongst wags as lewd as myselfe, with whome I consumed the flower of my youth, who drew mee to travell into Italy, and Spaine, etc." Besides, we find in the "Registers" an entry on the 20th March, 1581, of a ballad, which has not come down to us, by Greene, entitled,—"Youthe, seing all his Wais so troublesome, abandoning Virtue and Learning to Vice, recalleth his Former Follies with an Inward Repentance." As we know, from his own confessions, that Greene led the most dissipated life abroad, we may assume with some degree of certainty that this ballad was written by Greene shortly after his return home. In view of the above facts, we think that in all probability Greene began his tour in 1578 and returned home about 1580; for in the autumn of that year he had already published his first work. [Cf. "Discovery of Coosnage," Works, Vol. X., pp. 6-7.—G.]

return affected to be disappointed in life, found everything English bad and coarse, and absolutely did not know what to do with themselves. A type of this kind was represented by Shakspeare in his *As you Like it*, in the character of the "melancholy Jaques."[c] Greene returned from his travels tainted with the same moral disease. In his "Repentance" we read, "At my return into England I ruffeled out in my silks in the habit of Malcontent, and seemed so discontent that no place would please me to abide in, nor no vocation cause mee to stay my selfe in," etc. (p. 172, as before).

But such a miserable, and we may add, partly affected state of mind, could not long have possession of one so lively as Greene, to whom activity and change of impressions were indispensable. Instead of confirming himself in his disgust and apathy, Greene went to Cambridge, wrote there his first pamphlet, "Mamillia" (in two parts), and prepared for his M.A. degree. It is not known why Greene was unsuccessful in finding a publisher for his first literary production; the first part of which only saw the light in 1583—*i.e.*, three years subsequent to its entry in the "Registers of the Stationers' Company of London." On the other hand, Greene's scholastic studies were crowned with eminent success. On the 1st of July, 1583, he was admitted[d] by the Cambridge

[c] See *As you Like it*, ii. 7, 64-9; yet one feels inclined to protest against Jaques being classed as above.—G.

[d] Storojenko says 'honoured,' but that suggests *honori causâ*. He had passed A.B. at St. John's in 1578; his M.A. degree was taken at Clare Hall, *ut supra*. His

University to the learned degree of Master of Arts. Having received a degree which gave him, in a measure, a right to an honourable position in society, Greene set out for London to devote himself entirely to literary work. At first he worked hard and zealously. From his prolific pen flowed with astonishing rapidity a series of stories which he has himself entitled "Love-Pamphlets," because they treat almost exclusively of love, its pleasures and sufferings. Such are—"The Mirror of Modestie," "Morando," "Arbasto, the Anatomie of Fortune," "[Gwidonius or] The Card of Fancie," all written between 1583 and 1584. In the following year Greene had added to his literary work the profession of medicine; for at the end of a very extensive pamphlet published in 1585, we find the signature—"*R. Greene, Master of Arts and Student in Phisicke.*"* But even such feverish activity could not fully satisfy Greene's energetic nature. His evil spirit—a restless imagination—frequently turned him from the path of work and science to the wild career of debauchery

---

"Second Part of Mamillia" was dated in its dedication "From my Studie in Clarehall" (Works, Vol. II., p. 143). He was incorporated 'M.A.' at Oxford in July 1588 (Wood's *Fasti*, by Bliss, Part I., p. 245). The loss of the early editions of his books makes one uncertain as to his use of both degrees; but apparently he first used both in the title-page of his "Mourning Garment" (1590-1), which has "Utriusq[ue] Academiæ in Artibus Magister" (Works, Vol. IX., p. 117).—G.

* Read rather "On the title-page of his unusually large booklet, 'Planetomachia,' but on no other, we find, etc."—G.

and orgies, in which he was joined by his professional comrades, who were engaged likewise in literary labour and in "burning the candle at both ends" as he did. However much Greene earned by his pamphlets, the dissolute life he led rendered his earnings inadequate, and obliged him to seek fresh sources of income. Accident brought him into contact with actors, who at once saw what profit they could derive from Greene's gifts, and asked him to write for the stage, promising him large rewards.[8] Greene accepted the offer, and we must suppose that from this time his worldly condition slightly improved. His purse still reminded him, according to his own expression, of the sea with its ebb and flood; but still he was less frequently in want, receiving good remuneration for his work. But if Greene's exchequer was more flourishing, his morality suffered. Moving in the loose society of actors, he got deeper and deeper into dissolute ways. It is with difficulty we can believe that such a life could satisfy Greene; that the fumes of sensuality could completely choke the ideal aspirations of his soul. His works testify that now and then he was seized with sad reflection and

[8] See the account of his meeting with actors, in "Groatsworth of Wit," where he represents himself in the character of "Roberto." According to the testimony of Harvey, which Dyce credits ("Account of R. Greene," p. 35), Greene was for a short time himself an actor. [Having performed the part of the "Pinner" in *George a-Greene*. See our Introduction.—G.]

was not far from repentance; but these good intentions, with Greene's weakness of will and the ruinous influence of the set he was in, were never realised. In his "Repentance" Greene gives us an episode which well illustrates his character, and shows us the society in which he mixed. In one of his journeys home to Norwich, Greene entered St. Andrew's Church, to hear a local preacher whom he respected. The impassioned words of the Heaven-inspired orator, calling people to a purer life, and representing in vivid colours the fate of unrepenting sinners, made a deep impression on Greene. His conscience awakened in him, and a fear of the judgment of God seized his soul. He was disgusted with his dissolute life, and he determined to have done with the past for ever and to turn to the path of righteousness. "Lord," he prayed, "haue mercie upon me; and send me grace to amend and become a new man" ("Repentance," p. 176, as before). In such pious mood he returned to London, and astonished his friends by the melancholy expression of his face.[1] On being asked the reason for such an incomprehensible change, Greene frankly told them his resolve. Of course they derided him, called him a puritan, and said they "wished I might haue a pulpit, with . . . other scoffing tearmes." Weak-willed Greene was led away by the gibes of his

[1] This may have been; but he only says, "This good motion lasted not long in mee; for no sooner had I met with my copesmates, etc." ("Repentance," Vol. XII., p. 176). He may have had 'copesmates' in Norwich as well. Indeed, they most probably were of his native town in the present instance.—G.

friends, his good intentions were cast to the winds, and everything went on as before.

At one time, however, it seemed that this dissolute life was to come to an end. Greene fell in love with a beautiful girl, the daughter of a squire[2] in Lincolnshire, Dorothy by name, who reciprocated the feeling. Their marriage took place towards the close of 1585 or in the beginning of 1586. The new style of life, a journey with his wife to his native county, where they most probably spent their short period of conjugal happiness,[1] drew Greene away, for a time, from his literary occupations. At all events, during the whole of 1586 Greene only had one novel printed—the second part of "Morando." In the following year the newly married couple parted, never to meet again. She went off to Lincolnshire, and Greene to London.

[1] There is no doubt that they parted in 1586. In his "Repentance" Greene says, addressing his wife: "But oh my deare Wife, whose company and sight I haue refrained these *sixe* years: etc." Greene died on the 3rd September, 1592, consequently he must have deserted his wife in 1586. The supposition that they spent the short period of their married life at Greene's native place is based on Greene's own words, when, speaking of his separation, he says of her, "who went into Lincolnshire and I to London." They must, therefore, have lived at some third place, most probably at Norwich. [Storojenko inadvertently gives 1587.—G.]

[2] Greene only says "a Gentleman's daughter of good account" ("Repentance," as before, p. 177).—G.

What, then, could have been the cause of so sudden a rupture between Greene and his beloved wife, the union with whom seemed to have promised him a peaceful haven and lasting family happiness? On this subject Greene gives a short but very important explanation in his "Repentance."[10] In our opinion his own statements, slightly developed, are sufficient to clear the mist that hangs round this distressing incident. To begin with, we may observe that such impetuous, energetic natures as Greene's are seldom fitted, especially in youth, for quiet family life. Not that such natures are incapable of understanding the poetry of family love,—the lyrical productions of Greene go to prove the contrary,[11]—but their restless

---

[10] "Neverthelesse, soone after I married a Gentleman's daughter of good account, with whom I liued for a while: but for as much as she would perswade me from my wilful wickednes, after I had a child by her, I cast her off, hauing spent vp the marriage-money which I had obtained by her." [Works, Vol. XII., p. 177. But the quotation ought to have been continued, thus—"Then left I her at sixe or seuen, who went into Lincolneshire, and I to London." This "sixe or seuen" reads somewhat indefinitely. Probably it is merely a variant of our "at sixes and sevens." But it is to be recalled that Francesco (=Greene) in "Neuer Too Late" represents himself as bidding "farewell to his wife" after "they were married seuen years" (Works, Vol. VIII., p. 66).—G.]

[11] As an instance, let us remind the reader of Greene's highly poetical song in "Menaphon," "Weep

imagination, accustomed to strong and passionate excitements, cannot content itself with the monotonous flow of family life. The air gets too close for them, and they tear themselves away to breathe freely, mercilessly sacrificing the happiness of others in the act. However Greene tried to overcome his restless imagination—doubtless his rupture with his wife cost him a struggle, though he does not say so—he was obliged to succumb in the end. His former wild instincts, temporarily suppressed, raged in his soul with new strength; to satisfy the impassioned and excited condition of his mind became an indispensable necessity, and the voice of duty and reason was choked. Greene began to absent himself from home, and to live his old life. It is extremely probable that, as soon as the paroxysm had passed, Greene would himself have returned to his wife for pardon, endeavouring to live down his offence by loving attention. Thus such passionate and excitable natures generally act, not unfrequently combining wild and untamable passions with the most devoted love and tenderness. A wise woman wed to such a man would know how to act towards him without lowering or irritating him. Unfortunately Greene's wife did not understand her husband's character. She was revolted by his conduct, and reproached him for it with all the indignation of an honest heart. Greene could not endure these continual family scenes, and forsook his wife and newly born child

---

not my wanton, smile upon my knee, etc." [Works, Vol. VI., pp. 43-4—G.]

for ever, having previously squandered his wife's dower.[h] [i]

When Greene returned to London he was not the unknown author he had been when he arrived there three years before from Cambridge. Now he had a name in literature. His books were the fashion, and bought up with avidity. Booksellers and publishers vied with each other to secure his work for themselves. Wishing to satisfy them, Greene wrote much, although the rapidity of his labour prevented his carefully finishing his productions. Thomas Nashe—an intimate friend of Greene's, and an eye-witness of his life in London—thus describes the fecundity and rapidity of his work: "In a night and a day would he haue yarked vp a Pamphlet as well as in seuen yeare, and glad was that Printer that might bee so blest to pay him deare for the very dregs of his wit."[12]

---

[12] "Strange News, of intercepting certain Letters" (London, 1592). This pamphlet of Nashe's was reprinted by Collier in his "Miscellaneous Tracts *temp.* Eliz. and Jacob." (London, 1870). Part I. [See our

[h] Not a shadow of ground for this harsh judgment on his wife. His words are simply "as she would perswade me from my wilful wickednes" ("Repentance," as before, p. 177).—G.

[i] Is it worth while noticing Collier's egregious suggestion that an entry discovered by him at St. Bartholomew the Less [London] referred to Greene—viz., "The xvj[th] day of Februarie 1586, was maryed Wilde, otherwise —— Greene, unto Elizabeth Taylor"? ("Memoirs of the Principal Actors in the Plays of Shakespeare," Introd., p. xxi). Whoever heard of Greene being 'Wilde *alias* —— Greene'? and we know that Robert Greene's wife was called Dorothy, not Elizabeth. Nor is it at all likely that he was married in London.—G.

It was owing to the extraordinary rapidity with which he worked that he was able to write nine long love-pamphlets in the three years of his sojourn in London (1586-9); not to speak of his theatrical plays, the writing of which became, during the latter part of his London life, his constant occupation. He led, as before, the most dissolute life. His admirers, belonging, as Greene himself expresses it, to the most dissipated class of people, were his constant companions, and, not content with ordinary tavern orgies, would carouse in his own rooms for days and days together.

Owing to the usage, then customary among authors, to dedicate their works to the nobles that favoured and helped them, we are able to name nearly all those persons who gave Greene their patronage. At the head of these we must place the family of Lord Derby, which was one of the foremost to assist him when he first came to London to seek work. It was to Lady Margaret Derby that Greene dedicated one of his earlier works, the "Mirror of Modesty" (1584). To another member of this family who did him so much good service in his literary career, Ferdinand Stanley—subsequently fifth Earl of Derby—Greene dedicated his well-known pamphlet "Ciceronis Amor, Tullie's Love" (1589).[13] Besides the family of Derby, Greene

collective edition of Nashe's Works in "THE HUTH LIBRARY," Vol. II.—G.]

[13] Ferdinand Stanley was himself a poet, and was known in literary circles under the pastoral pseudonym of "Amyntas." Several eminent poets, such

was patronised by the Earl and Countess of Cumberland[14]; Robert Carey, the Earl of Monmouth[15]; Lord and Lady Fitzwater, who came from the same neighbourhood as Greene, and had been the patrons of his family for years[16]; Earls Leicester, Arundel,

---

as Spenser, Harington, Marston, and others, were among his friends. Spenser, in his "Colin Clout's come Home Again," weeps over the death of his friend Amyntas. Spenser also celebrated his wife, Alice Stanley, as "Amarilla." ("The Stanley Papers." Manchester, 1853. Part I., p. 32. Chetham Society.) *Vide* also "Royal and Noble Authors," vol. ii. (Walpole—Park), pp. 45-51, [and our Works of Spenser, Vol. I. *et alibi*: in large-paper copies for the first time an original portrait of the "fair lady," imperishably associated with Spenser, Shakspeare, and Milton, is given.—G.]

[14] To the former Greene dedicated two productions: "Pandosto," and "Mourning Garment," and to the latter, who was an authoress herself—*vide* "Royal and Noble Authors," vol. ii. (Walpole—Park), pp. 168-9—"Penelope's Web."

[15] To him Greene dedicated his "Farewell to Follie," and "Orpharion." R. Carey's memoirs were published at Edinburgh in 1809.

[16] In his dedication of "Philomela" to Lady Fitzwater, Greene speaks thus of his devotion to her husband: "finding my self humbly deuoted to the Right honourable the Lord Fitzwaters, your husband, not onely that I am *borne his*, etc." These words have a deeper meaning than mere superficial polite-

Essex,[17] and others. Supported by the assistance and sympathy of such prominent personages, another in the place of Greene would have benefited by the advantages of his situation, and have made a brilliant career, or at all events secured a fair independence. But the careless Greene was positively incapable of deriving any profit from his acquaintance with the mighty of the land. "His only care," according to Nashe, "was to have a spel in his purse to conjure up a good cuppe of wine with at all times."[18]

To go by the laudatory verses, prefatory to nearly every one of Greene's pamphlets, written by friends and admirers, we may conclude that the following were the more particularly intimate friends of Greene:—

1. Roger Portington, Esquier, a countryman of Norfolk,[19] and an enthusiastic admirer of Greene's. He wrote a prefatory poem to the first part of

---

ness; they have reference to some feudal relations of Greene's family towards Lord Fitzwater. It is very probable that the Greenes, although belonging to the landed gentry, tenanted one of Lord Fitzwater's farms near Norwich.

[17] To Leicester he dedicated "Planetomachia," to Arundel "Morando," to Essex "Euphues his Censure of Philautus."

[18] "Strange News." "He (Greene) made no account of winning credite by his workes as thou dost" (Nashe says, referring to Harvey); "his only care was to have a spel in his purse, etc."

[19] Bloomfield makes frequent mention of the family

"Mamillia," "in comendation of this booke," in which he compared Greene to Cicero, and declared that "Mamillia" had completely eclipsed the diction of the French. He was also the author of a Latin poem prefixed to Greene's "The Carde of Fancie," and entitled "In Laudem Authoris." [But this is signed *Richardus* Portington: Works, Vol. IV., p. 9.] Greene repaid the debt by dedicating the second part of "Mamillia" to Robert Lee[20] and Roger Portington, calling them in his dedication his "especiall friends."

2. G. B. Cantabrigiensis, as he signed himself at the foot of his works, one of the friends of Greene's youth, and a fellow-student at Cambridge. The first part of "Mamillia," published in 1583—though written two years earlier—was prefaced by a poem written by him and entitled "In praise of the Author and his Booke." We are induced to believe that their friendly relations lasted many years, for we find his signature under two other poems in praise of Greene. One of these was prefixed to "Alcida," written in 1588, and the other to "Ciceronis Amor," which appeared in 1589.[j]

---

of Portington in his "History of Norfolk," vol. ix., pp. 271, 273, and vol. xi. p. 198.

[20] Robert Lee was an actor and dramatist, and was author of a play acted in 1598, which has not been preserved, entitled *The Miller* (Halliwell,

[j] See G. B.'s poem in "Mamillia," Vol. II., pp. 249-50, not *ut supra*. It is before "The Anatomie of Lovers Flatteries," which had no separate title-page, but followed Part II. as Part III. of "Mamillia."—G.

3. JOHN ELIOT, the author of a French sonnet in honour of Greene prefixed to "Perimides the Blacksmith" (1588), in which he calls himself the friend of Greene. He was known to fame for his work entitled "Orthoepia Gallica" (London, 1593), and for his translation of a thesis by De Loque, "Discourses of War and Single Combat."[21]

4. THOMAS BURNABY (or BARNABIE, Esq.), was one of Greene's most devoted friends, who more than once got him out of difficulties.[22] To him Greene dedicated his "Never too Late" (Works, Vol. VIII., p. 5) and "A Quip for an Upstart Courtier" (Works, Vol. XI., p. 209). In the dedication [of the latter] he signs himself "Your duetifull adopted sonne." He wrote two poems in honour of Greene. The first,

---

"Dictionary of Old English Plays," London, 1860, p. 170).

[21] *Vide* Hazlitt, "Handbook to Early English Literature" (London, 1867), *sub nom.* [The signature is 'I. Eliote' (Works, Vol. VII., p. 10). The translation of Bertrand De Loque's little treatise is dated 1591.—G.]

[22] In his dedication of "Never too Late," printed with Burnaby's assistance, Greene says, "I have for sundry favors been affected by your worship"; and in his dedication of "A Quip for an Upstart Courtier," Greene calls Burnaby the father of the poor, etc. Probably this was the same Burnaby of whom the celebrated actor Edward Alleyn bought a Bear Garden in 1594 for £200. ("The Alleyn Papers," ed. by Collier. London, 1843. Introduction, p. xiii.)

prefixed to "Menaphon," he signed [heads] with the anagram "Thomas *Brabine*, Gent.," the second—"Thomas Burnaby, Esq."

5. THOMAS NASHE, an eminent satirical writer, began his literary career by the well known preface to Greene's "Menaphon" (1589). Nashe, who made the acquaintance of Greene at Cambridge, was an intimate friend of Greene's to his death, and, after that event, defended his friend's memory from the attacks and slanders of Harvey.

6. THOMAS WATSON, who wrote a Latin poem in praise of Greene in "Ciceronis Amor" (1589), was one of the most celebrated lyric poets of his time. He was called the English Petrarch. A collection of sonnets of his, "The Passionate Centurie of Love," written in imitation of the style of Petrarch, and published in 1582, was specially valued.

7. THOMAS LODGE, the author of "Rosalinda," from which Shakspeare borrowed the plot for his *As you Like it*, was for many years a sincere friend of Greene's. In 1589 he prefaced Greene's "Spanish Masquerado" with a charming French sonnet, in which he calls Greene "*mon doux ami*" [Works, Vol. V., p. 240.] He and Greene wrote a play together, entitled *A Looking-Glasse for London and England*, which was acted on the 9th of March, 1591, by Lord Strange's company.[23] When Lodge had to leave for the West Indies, in the same year, he intrusted to Greene the publication of his

[23] "The Diary of Phillip Henslowe," ed. by Collier (London, 1845), p. 23. [See our Introduction on this.—G.]

pamphlet, "Euphues' Shadow," which the latter duly edited in 1592.[k]

8. GEORGE PEELE, a poet and dramatist, seems to have been one of Greene's most intimate friends, although the particulars of their relations are not known. Greene did not forget him during the last moments of his life, and called on him to leave off blaspheming, drinking, and play-writing.

9. CHRISTOPHER MARLOWE, the greatest dramatist that preceded Shakspeare, made Greene's acquaintance only during the last years of his life. It is more than probable that they were on extremely bad terms with each other previous to that period, and that Greene was envious of Marlowe's success as a dramatist. At all events, in his preface to "Perimides the Blacksmith" (1588), Greene has inserted a few very transparent, and, we may add, perfectly undeserved innuendoes regarding Marlowe.[l] He laughed at Marlowe's introduction of blank verse; and his friend Thomas Nashe, in writing, the following year, a preface to Greene's "Menaphon," did not allow the opportunity to escape for attacking his friend's fortunate rival, of course with a view to flattering

---

[k] See Appendix A for Greene's Epistles from "Euphues' Shadow."—G.

[l] **One must demur to this statement. Marlowe had attacked Greene, and he must not reply! In his reply he calls him "blaspheming Tamburlan," etc. Was that underserved? or was it 'innuendo'? "I but answere in print, what they haue offered on the stage" are Greene's words (Works, Vol. VII., p. 8). See our Introduction on Greene's alleged 'envy.'—G.**

Greene.[34] When Greene and Marlowe were afterwards reconciled we do not know, but it is beyond a doubt that, during the last years of his life, Greene was one of those intimate friends to whom Marlowe confided his rationalistic views.[m] In his "Confession," being after-words to the "Groatsworth of Wit," Greene entreats him to discard the soul-destroying theories he had adopted.

Besides the above-mentioned persons, whose friendship is testified by the evidence of contemporaries and Greene's own works, we have the signatures of several other more or less intimate friends of his attached to poems in his praise: such as Richard Hake; a certain Bubb, gentleman; Henry Gale, M.A.; Henry Upchear, gentleman; Edward Rainsford, Esquire; Ralph Sidley; Edward Percy, gentleman; George Meares, gentleman; and Stapleton,—the names of all of whom, with the exception of the last,[35] are unknown

---

[34] Nashe evidently aims at Marlowe when he talks of the alchimists of eloquence, "who, mounted on the stage of arrogance, think to outbrave better pens with the swelling bombast of bragging blank verse."

[35] There were two literary Stapletons at that period: Richard, whom Chapman praises in his preface to his translation of the "Iliad" (*vide* Warton, "History of English Poetry," new edition by W. C. Hazlitt, vol. iv., p. 318); and Thomas, the author of three poems in praise of T. More and his family (1588), entitled "Tres Thomæ" (Hazlitt, "Handbook

[m] 'Confided' is inexact. Every one knew Marlowe's 'views'; nor is rationalistic = atheistic.—G.

to fame. So respectable a number of friends and acquaintances testifies, of course, to the sympathetic character and communicativeness of Greene, and suggests how fascinating he must have been in society. Chettle calls him, with reason, "the verye supporter" of society.[n] But it makes us suspect that he was incapable of concentrating his affection on a limited, "chosen few." We shall see in the end how dearly Greene had to pay for this defect in his character. We shall see how, seemingly loved by all, possessed of such a large number of friends and acquaintances, he was left, at the fatal hour of his life, alone and homeless.

A prominent, self-reliant and witty man, insolent in the use of his tongue, Greene had naturally many literary enemies and enviers, who, in their mention of him, frequently passed the barriers of literary propriety, circulating various ugly slanders about him. It is at this kind of people, most likely, that Eliote's French poem is aimed, for in it he advises Greene to pay no attention to what Zoiluses and Momuses may say of him, assuring him that no calumnies invented by them could do his good name harm.[30] Whom Eliote

---

to Early English Literature," *sub voce*). The latter was a zealous Catholic. We are therefore inclined to believe that the former, who had taken his B.A. degree in 1591, was Greene's friend.

[30] "Courage, donc," etc. [Works, Vol. VII., p. 10.—G.]

[n] Chettle does no such thing. He calls him "the very supporter [of the stage]," as quoted in Storojenko's own title-page. At least, so I read it, punctuating (,) after 'pleasaunce.'—G.

means here it is hard to determine; but it is not difficult to name several persons who played the parts of Momus and Zoilus towards Greene, and whom he repaid honestly with the same coin.° In his preface to the "Mourning Garment" (1590), Greene hints at one of these enviers and sneerers, capable, as he expresses it, rather of *μωμησέται* than *μιμησέται*. When, in the course of the next year, Greene published his pamphlet "Farewell to Follie," wherein, as well as in the preceding one, he repents bitterly of his former literary works, and assures his readers that from henceforth he will devote himself to the promotion of morality, his literary enemies doubted the sincerity of his professions. One of these, in a pamphlet entitled "Martine Mar-Sextus," which appeared soon after the "Farewell to Follie," did not refrain from classing Greene with the herd of contemporary pharisees, proclaiming aloud their repentance *ut ab hominibus audiantur*. In 1591-92 Greene published a series of satirical pamphlets descriptive of the tricks of the knights of the order of industry of those days, the so-called "Conny-catchers." This exposure was of no small service to the public, coming as it did from a man who, during the many years of his dissolute life, had abundant opportunities for meeting conny-catchers in the dirty dens of London, and of hearing from their own lips stories of their exploits. Greene had, evidently, a right to expect the gratitude of every honest man. It turned out very differently.

° Except Marlowe and R. W. of "Martine Mar-Sextus," unknown; later came Harvey.—G.

The literary enemies of Greene took advantage of this opportunity to blacken his good name. One of them, under the pseudonym of "A Conny-catcher," wrote a naïvely-sly pamphlet, in which he related one of the ugly actions of the exposer of conny-catching. It seems that Greene sold his play *Orlando Furioso* first to one company of actors and then to another.[27] One of the most malicious and bitterest of Greene's literary enemies was the well-known pedant and poetaster, Gabriel Harvey, cruelly satirised by Greene in his witty pamphlet "A Quip for an Upstart Courtier" (1592). Even after Greene's death Harvey continued to persecute him with his hatred, and blackened his memory in every way; for which he was condemned even by his contemporaries, who

---

[27] "The Defence of Connycatching, or a Confutation of those two infamous Pamphlets published by R. G. against the practitioners of many Nimble-witted and mysticall Sciences, by Cuthbert Connycatcher" (London, 1592). This pamphlet is very rare: it is not even at the British Museum. The author made use of a reprint by Halliwell, the whole edition of which consisted of twenty-six copies. [After all, judging from the title and style, one cannot help a shrewd suspicion that Greene himself may have had a hand in the production of this "Defence." He was capable (I fear) of resorting to such an expedient in order to call the more attention to his "Conny-catching" pamphlets. See the "Defence" in full in Works, Vol. XI., pp. 39—104.—G.]

compared his cruelty to that of Achilles, trailing the lifeless corpse of Hector round the walls of Troy.[38]

We have stated above that Greene was at the height of his literary fame at about 1589. Thomas Nashe bears witness that his pamphlets fetched a great price in the literary market; and another friend of his (Chettle) avers that he was "the only comedian of a vulgar writer in this country." But as soon as Greene attained so privileged a position (a position which he hardly dared to dream of during the early part of his London life), a torturing doubt on the usefulness of his literary work crept into his soul. His literary fame, the favour of influential people, the admiration of his friends, and his material profits,—all these would have been more than sufficient for any other man; but Greene was dissatisfied. It seems that this literary hack, this debauchee, saturated in the mire of a dissolute life, took an exalted view of the aim of literature. In his eyes a true author was a good teacher of the people, who helped them to understand the deep and important meaning of life. When Greene looked at his love-pamphlets, written solely to amuse, from this exalted point of view, they appeared

---

[38] The critic Meres, in his "Palladis Tamia, Wit's Treasury" (London, 1598), says: "As *Achilles* tortured the deade bodie of *Hector*, and as *Antonius* and his wife *Fulvia* tormented the livelesse corps of *Cicero*: so *Gabriel Harvey* hath shewed the same inhumanitie to *Greene*, that lies full low in his grave."

to him, not only useless, but positively hurtful and iniquitous.[a]

From henceforth he determined to change his style and not to write anything that did not expound and inculcate moral and edifying precepts. His pamphlet the "Mourning Garment," published in 1590, he himself considered the "fruit of my new labours," as he says. This was closely followed by his "Farewell to Follie," which, though written earlier, was first published in 1591. In his preface to this latter, Greene styles it the "ultimum vale" to the errors of his youth. "Sweete companions and lovemates of learning," he says, "looke into my Farewell . . . . *Felix, quem faciunt aliena pericula cautum*" (Works, Vol. IX., p. 231).

Greene's conversion was more thorough than might have been expected, considering his erratic disposition. He kept his promise, and from the time of the publication of his "Mourning Garment" he wrote nothing in the style of his former love-pamphlets, and became exclusively a serious writer.[29] His labours as a dramatist, however, he continued—a circumstance of which he latterly deeply repented. During Greene's

---

[29] "Philomela, the Lady Fitzwaters Nightingale," published in 1592, was written much earlier, as Greene himself says in the preface.

[a] Perhaps Storojenko does not sufficiently realise the inordinate vanity and the Reuben-like instability of Greene. Nevertheless, his spasms of remorse and penitence were genuine and torturous. It was the old, old story of seeing the right way and going the wrong; but no one of the make of Greene could do so without misery.—G.

dissolute life he was often thrown among the lowest layers of London society, and associated with people of most suspicious character. It is a known fact that Greene was intimate with, and had a child by, a woman, the sister of one famous "Cutting Ball," the captain of a gang of thieves, who eventually met his death on the gallows.[30] Having decided on becoming an instructive and edifying writer, Greene resolved to turn his acquaintance with the manners and customs of this suspicious class of society to account. He therefore wrote a whole series of pamphlets in which he exposed all the traps and snares that swindlers and every description of knave laid for inexperienced people, especially those "up from the country." These pamphlets of Greene's, attracting, as they did, the attention of society and the authorities, to one of the most dangerous plagues of London life, tended materially to reduce the practice of the "conny-catchers," and we may well imagine what indignation they awakened among them. In his preface to his

[30] "Although we have this information from Greene's bitterest enemy, Gabriel Harvey ('Foure Letters and certain Sonnets, etc.,' London, 1592), yet its truth is confirmed by the parish registers of St. Leonards, where, under the 12th August, 1593, we find an entry of the burial of Fortunatus, Greene's illegitimate son" (Dyce, "Account of R. Greene," p. 22 [from Collier's "Lives of Orig. Actors," p. xx]). In the "Groats-worth of Wit" Greene says that Roberto lived with a courtesan, whose brother met with his death on the gallows. [The 'captainship' is an over-statement.—G.]

first pamphlet of this kind, "A Notable Discovery of Coosnage" (1591), Greene informs us, no sooner had they heard he was preparing a printed exposure of their practices, than they begged him to desist from his purpose, assuring him that they would cut off his hand in the event of his not complying (Vol. X., p. *ut inf.*) When Greene, notwithstanding their threats, published his book, they made an attempt on his life, as related in his "Disputation betweene a Hee Conny-catcher and a Shee Conny-catcher"[n] (Vol. X., p. 236).

The above quotation shows that the post of a public Exposer was not without its dangers in those rude times, and that it required much courage on Greene's part to continue in his line of action in spite of threats that had been already partly carried out.

The decided change in the tone of Greene's literary labours was unfortunately not accompanied by a corresponding change in his mode of life.[q] Notwithstanding his stepping forward as an exposer of the plagues of society, he continued his wild career of carouse and revelry with consistent weakness, giving hereby to his numerous literary adversaries a powerful weapon against him. Intemperance, licentiousness, an irreverence for religion, sometimes finding vent in coarse and revolting blasphemies : these were the sins

---

[n] "A Disputation betweene a Hee Connycatcher and a Shee Connycatcher" (London, 1592). This pamphlet is a still greater rarity than the "Defence of Connycatching." The author saw a copy in the Bodleian Library. [See Works, Vol. X., pp. 192—278.—G.]

[q] See note [p] on this.—G.

with which he was charged by his enemies, and to which he has himself pleaded guilty. We shall perhaps be not far wrong if we attribute some of these misdeeds (as for instance his blasphemies) to the influence of Marlowe, with whom Greene was on the most intimate terms during the latter years of his life. Marlowe passed for a man of extremely rationalistic views, who, according to the testimony of his contemporaries, was not content with spreading his doctrines by word of mouth, but wrote whole disquisitions against religion.[32] Marlowe's propaganda was not a solitary phenomenon of the kind. We have information, coming from various sources, unanimously speaking to the fact that not only individuals, but whole cliques, devoted themselves to the diffusion of sceptical doctrines, which had lately been imported from the Continent.[33] Such, for instance, was the

[32] Thos. Beard, "The Theater of God's Judgment," London, 1597. (*Vide* Dyce, "Some Account of Marlowe and his Writings," p. xxi). [Sir William] Vaughan, "The Golden Grove" (London, 1600), confirms Beard's testimony, and says that Marlowe's essay against the doctrine of the Holy Trinity was written "about fourteen years ago,"—*i.e.* in 1586. Collier has found similar testimony in a copy of Marlowe's *Hero and Leander* (London, 1640), written evidently by one who was personally acquainted with Marlowe (*vide* Collier, "Bibliographical Catalogue," vol. i., p. 520). ["Repentance" (p. 174) dates his 'blasphemy' early, and so before he knew Marlowe.—G.]

[33] The principal source of these doctrines was the

circle that used to assemble at Sir Walter Raleigh's house. At the head of this clique, called by a contemporary writer "the public school of Atheism,"[34] was

celebrated work "De Tribus Impostoribus Mundi," which first appeared in the latter half of the sixteenth century, and was well known in England. Harvey, in his "New Letter of Notable Contents" (London, 1593), ascribes it to Pietro Aretino. Thomas Nashe, in his "Unfortunate Traveller" (London, 1594), defending Aretino's memory, informs us of a rumour that this dreadful book was written by a disciple of Macchiavelli. There is not the slightest doubt that Marlowe was well acquainted with "De Tribus Impostoribus" (*vide* Dyce, "The Works of Christopher Marlowe," London, 1865, Appendix II., and compare with "De Tribus Impostoribus," ed. Brunet, Paris, 1867, pp. 14, 24).

[34] The Jesuit Parsons, writing under the pseudonym of Andrew Philopater, in his "Elizabethæ Angliæ Reginæ Hær. Calvinianum propugnantis sævissimum in catholicos sui regni Edictum cum responsione ad singula capita. Per Andream Philopatrem" (Romæ 1593), says: "Et certe si Gualteri quoque Raulei scholæ frequens de Atheismo paulo longius processerit, quam modo ita notam et publicam suis in ædibus habere dicitur, astronomo quodam necromantico præceptore." The astronomer and magician is evidently Harriot. All London knew that Raleigh was a sceptic in religious matters, and that in his house persons having the reputation of freethinkers were in the habit of assembling—such as the Earl of

the famous mathematician and astronomer, Thomas Harriot, who was far in advance of his times.[86] The

---

Northumberland, Thomas Harriot, Edward Vere, Earl of Oxford, and others. Many years later, during his trial, Sir Walter was called a "damnable atheist" by the Chief Justice, and his friend Harriot was spoken of as a devil (Edwards, "The Life of Sir Walter Raleigh," vol. i., pp. 432, 436). It is, however, necessary to add, that in the sixteenth and seventeenth centuries the term "atheist" had a broader meaning than it has now. In those days this term was not confined to absolute unbelievers in any deity whatever—of which there were comparatively very few then—but to sceptics, rationalists, theists, deists, philosophers, and all those who did not cherish a dogmatic fanaticism towards people that held another belief from their own. Thomas Nashe, in his "Strange News" (London, 1592), calls Martin Marprelate (a puritanical agitator) a "mighty platformer of atheism"; and Gabriel Harvey, in the heat of polemical rage, calls Nashe an atheist (*vide* his "Pierce's Supererogation," ed. by Collier, p. 85, and in Harvey's Works in HUTH LIBRARY, Vol. II.). [By Burton ("Melancholy") and nearly all his contemporaries Mahomet is always denounced as an 'atheist.' No one to-day will admit the monstrous calumny against Raleigh. Our own recent Bradlaugh controversy shows how Church-fanatics and bigots still charge their opponents as 'atheists,' and the like.—G.]

[86] Thomas Harriot (1568—1621) was the friend of Raleigh, and his companion in the American expe-

celebrated opponent of theatres, the puritan Gosson,[38] speaks of another circle of the same kind, which he calls "the damned crew." A friend of Greene's, Thomas Nashe, advises ecclesiastics to lay aside for

---

dition. The map of Virginia was executed by him. He was considered one of the most illustrious English mathematicians of his day (*vide* Hoeffer, "Histoire des Mathématiques," Paris, 1874, pp. 366-7); and his knowledge of physics, chemistry and astronomy caused him to be regarded as a magician by his contemporaries. Harriot corresponded with most of the celebrated foreign mathematicians of his day, and Kepler always styled him "Harriote celeberrime." From the Earl of Northumberland's letters we learn that many of the discoveries in astronomy and physics that have been ascribed to the seventeenth century were, as it were, foreseen by Harriot (*vide* his "Correspondance Astronomique," Génès, 1822, vol. vii., p. 105 *et seq.*). We find an account of Harriot's religious opinions in Wood's "Athenæ Oxonienses," vol. ii., *sub voce.* Wood's testimony as regards Harriot's freethinking views is supported by a letter of the latter to Kepler, dated 13th July, 1609, in which Harriot deplores his having to live at a period at which it was impossible to express one's views freely: "Ita se res habent apud nos ut non liceat mihi adhuc libere philosophari." [An adequate Life of Harriot is a *desideratum.* He was a prescient thinker and observer.—G.]

[38] Gosson, "The Trumpet of Warre" (London, 1598). *Vide* Collier's "Bibliographical Catalogue," vol. i.,

a time all disputes with heretics and sectarians, and to turn their attention to the propaganda of atheism, as there was no sect in England more widely spread than the sect of atheists.[37] Nashe's advice was most appropriate, as the new-fashioned sceptical writings had penetrated into the midst of the very clergy.[38] Into which of these cliques of freethinkers Marlowe introduced his friend, we are unable to say. It is very probable that he took him to Sir Walter Raleigh's,[39]

---

p. 324, where Gosson's account of the miserable fate awaiting the "damned crew" is cited.

[37] "Christ's Tears over Jerusalem," ed. 1592, pp. 62, 63. [See Nashe's Works, as before, Vol. IV.—G.]

[38] The following is an extract from a MS. at the British Museum (Lansd. MSS., No. 982, fol. 46.):— "The Form of Adjuration of Heretics and Errors made before the Archbishop and Bishops in Convocation, by John Hilton, clerk, who having been imprisoned by the High Commission, dide appear before the Upper House on Dec. 22nd, 1584, and confessed his accusation, saying that he had said in a sermon at St. Martin's-in-the-Fields that the Old and New Testaments are but fables, etc."

[39] According to tradition, Raleigh was a friend of Marlowe's (*vide* Dyce, "Some Account of Marlowe," p. xlv, note). Once Marlowe sent him his newly written poem "The Passionate Shepherd to his Love," beginning with the words "Come, live with me and be my love," to which Raleigh wrote a witty reply entitled "The Nymph's Reply to the Shepherd." Both poems are printed in "England's Helicon"

where Harriot presided, whom Marlowe venerated.[40] From Greene's works it does not appear that his conversations with Marlowe and his partisans left any very deep impressions on his mind, or that he worked out, —like Marlowe,—a whole system of atheistic philosophy. The preponderance of the mystical element in Greene over the analytical was a great safeguard against the extremes of a sceptical tendency. All the free-thinking that he acquired, by associating with the *esprits forts* of London, was limited to irreverent scoffing against religion, against eternal rewards and punishments, and a future life, a specimen of which he gives us in his "Repentance."[41] We shall see

(London, 1600). [See Dyce's Marlowe, p. xlv, which shows that this is a "three black crows" version.—G.]

[40] Bame says: "He (Marlowe) affirmeth that Moyses was but a Juggler, and that one Heriots can do more, than hee."

[41] On his being entreated by his friends to leave his dissolute way of living, that could only lead to ruin, Greene answered as follows: "Tush, what better is he that dies in his bed, than he that endes his life at Tyburne: all owe God a death: if I may have my desire while I live, I am satisfied, let me shift after death as I may." When his friends reminded him of hell he laughed in their faces: "Hell (quoth I) what talke you of hell to me? I know if I once come there, I shall have the company of better men than my selfe; I shal also meete with some madde knaves in that place, and so long as I shall not sit there alone, my care is the lesse, etc."

later on that Greene was more guilty after another kind—namely, a rejection of the principles of morality and virtuous living.

The dissipated life which Greene led for many years gradually undermined his constitution; and at last the prophecies of his friends, who had entreated him to leave off his carouses and orgies, which would sooner or later work his ruin, were fulfilled. After one of his drunken orgies, of which the leading features were pickled herrings and Rhenish wine, Greene was seized with indigestion and took to his bed. His broken down constitution was incapable of coping with sickness. Bad medical aid, the absence of attendance, and his extreme poverty, completed the rest. Deserted by his friends and boon companions, who were either in ignorance of his condition, or else with unpardonable levity neglected to visit him, Greene expired, alone in a poverty-stricken room rented on credit of a shoe-maker. But his landlord and landlady proved themselves kind-hearted people, and showed a sincere interest in him. They and the woman with whom he had been living, were the only people that did not desert him during his illness. Lying on his death-bed, during the long and sleepless nights, Greene reflected much over his fate, and he was seized with sincere penitence for the wasted time of his youth and his misused life. In these moments of mental anguish he threw off his last two pamphlets, "A Groatsworth of Wit," and "Repentance." The former of these is an autobiography in the form of a novel, in which Greene has depicted himself under the name of Roberto. The other is a sort of short autobiography. Leaving the minute criticism of these works for the next chapter, we will here content ourselves by referring to the after-words to "A Groatsworth of Wit," containing, in the form of a letter to his friends and companions, Greene's confessions: "To those Gentlemen his Quondam acquaintance, that spend their wits in making Plaies," etc.[1]

All are agreed that the "famous favourite of tragedians" was Marlowe, who was then considered the first of tragic writers in England. With regard to Greene and Marlowe's instructor in atheism, the majority of critics, with Dyce at their head, have accepted Malone's conjecture, that Greene means Francis Kett, a Master of Arts at Cambridge University, who was burnt for heresy in 1589. Greene's latest biographer, Bernhardi, also accepting Malone's supposition, finds a confirmation of it in Greene's own words, "by him persuaded,"[42] which, according to him,

[42] In the original "by him persuaded to that liberty." Simpson (*vide* his article on the "Groatsworth of Wit," reprinted by Ingleby in his preface to his edition of the "Shakespeare Allusion Books," London, 1874) thinks that the word "liberty" is here used in the sense of religious tolerance. We believe that it means "self-will"—*i.e.* an absence of all moral restraint—of which Greene also accuses himself in his "Repentance." Greene's pamphlet "The Spanish Masquerado" proves conclusively that Greene was not in favour of tolerance [= the supposed 'liberty' Atheism gives.—G.]

[1] See Works, Vol. XII., pp. 141-6, for this infinitely pathetic and interesting "appeal"; and our Introduction on it.—G.

point towards Kett's personal influence.[43] In 1874 an English scholar, Simpson,[44] first, so far as we are aware, expressed a doubt whether Greene could justly call Kett a "broacher of atheism," as Kett was a zealous Unitarian, and suffered for his heresies and not for atheism. Simpson believes, that Greene meant by the above phrase no other than Macchiavelli, of whom it was rumoured in England at that time that he died by his own hand, like Judas. Simpson's view, expressed parenthetically in a newspaper article, and unaccompanied by a proper amount of evidence, was allowed to pass unobserved by literary authorities; but nevertheless he was nearest the truth of all. In the face of such difference of opinion, on a subject of such utmost importance not only to the biography of Greene, but also to the whole circle of English freethinkers of the sixteenth century, it becomes incumbent on every new biographer of Greene to take on himself the *onus probandi*, whether he likes it or not.

First of all, it is necessary to do away at once and for ever with the assumption about the unfortunate Kett, whose religious views were as far removed from rationalism as from the 39th Article of the orthodox creed.[45] We have been fortunate enough to find several

---

[43] "Robert Greene's Leben und Schriften" (Leipzig, 1874), p. 9.

[44] *Academy*, 21st March, 1874.

[45] The only point on which Kett and Marlowe agreed was one at which they had arrived by opposite ways, and this was a rejection of the Divinity of Our Lord

documents bearing on Kett's trial (printed in the Appendix)[a]: they leave no doubt behind them that Kett was—as Simpson justly remarked—a Unitarian, the missionaries of which sect penetrated into England from Holland in the beginning of the sixteenth century.[46] Although Kett was a native of Norfolk, the county which was considered the principal nest of Unitarianism,[47] yet up to 1585, while he lived at Cambridge and in London, we find no clear traces of the Arian heresy in his religious views.[48] It was not till after he had returned to his native place that Kett succumbed to the influence of Haworth

---

Jesus Christ. This was probably the reason why Myles Davies, a writer in the eighteenth century, in his "Athenæ Britannicæ," vol. ii., pp. 376-7, speaking of the Arianism of Lewes, Hamont, and Kett, mentions Marlowe as one of the sect. Davies' opinion was unknown to Dyce, though it was probably this that suggested to Malone's mind the idea of the intimacy of Kett and Marlowe.

[46] Wallace, "Antitrinitarian Biography," vol. i., p. 3, etc.

[47] Bloomfield's "History of Norfolk," vol. iii., p. 290. The first Unitarian martyr in England was the Dutchman Georg van Parr, burnt at Norwich 1542. At the same place were burnt: Mathew Hamont (1579), John Lewes (1583), and Francis Kett (1589).

[48] In 1585 Francis Kett published a work "The Glorious and beautifull Garland of Man's Glorification," which he dedicated to Elizabeth. The dedica-

[a] See Appendix B. in this volume.—G.

and Lewes, accepted their doctrines, and preached them,—for which latter offence he was condemned. Malone and Dyce supposed Marlowe to be a disciple of Kett's on the ground of Kett's having been a fellow of Benet College (otherwise called Corpus Christi College) at the time that Marlowe was studying there; but even this assertion, though rather a weak argument, it must be confessed, is contradicted by a modern historian of Cambridge. He has proved that Kett, who was really a fellow of Corpus Christi College from 1573, left Cambridge for good in 1580—*i.e.*, in the same year in which Marlowe first entered the university.[49] There are also no proofs of Kett's having ever been a friend of Greene's; and even if such evidence existed, it would be positively of no value, seeing what a wide difference there was between the religion of Kett, and Marlowe and Greene's free-thinking views.

---

tion was accepted, which of course would not have been the case had the book contained any heretical doctrine. [See our Introduction on this book.—G.]

[49] "Francis Kett, *alias* Knight, was born in Norfolk, probably at Wymondham. In 1566 he was admitted of Corpus Christi College, and proceeded B.A. in 1569 and M.A. in 1573. In the latter year he was elected a fellow of his college. He retained his fellowship till 1580, when he left the university, but on what account is unknown," etc. (Cooper, "Athenæ Cantabrigienses," vol. ii., p. 38). "Marlowe matriculated at Cambridge, 17th March, 1580" (Dyce, "Some Account of Marlowe," p. xiii).

With the removal of the hypothesis regarding Francis Kett, the credit of Simpson's hypothesis in reference to Macchiavelli rises, especially as this latter flows naturally out of Greene's own words. We know that in the sixteenth and seventeenth centuries Macchiavelli was considered almost the leader of atheism and immorality. Cardinal POLE [50] was the first to declare in print "Il Principe" to be so full of every kind of irreligion that it might have been written by the devil himself (*Satanæ digitis*). The historian Paolo Giovio, enraptured through he was with Macchiavelli's genius, nevertheless stigmatises him as "*irrisor et atheos.*" [51]

A few years later the well known French humanitarian Louis Lerois (Regius), calls Macchiavelli an author without either conscience or religion.[52] Towards the close of the sixteenth century a Spanish Jesuit, Ribadeneira, in his refutation of "Il Principe" of Macchiavelli, assures us that the followers of the latter acknowledge no religion whatever.[53] In 1594 an

[50] "Machiavel," par Nourisson (Paris, 1875), p. 4.

[51] "Elogia doctorum Virorum" (1557), p. 192.

[52] *Vide* chapter xlvii of Artaud's work, "Machiavel, son Génie et ses Erreurs" (Paris, 1833). [Villari's recent full Life, which has been translated into English, supersedes all others.—G.]

[53] This work appeared in Spanish in 1595, and was translated into Latin in 1603, under the following title, "Princeps Christianus, adversus Machiavellum" (Moguntiæ, 1603). In his preface ("Ad lectorem") the learned Jesuit says, "*Politici et Machiavelli sectatores*

English translation appeared of the second volume of La Primaudaye, *L'Académie Française*, containing a refutation of atheistic doctrines. In his dedication to John Pickering, Lord Keeper of the Great Seal of England, the translator, a certain "T. B.," speaking of the strong growth of atheism in England, sees the source of these ruinous doctrines in the works of that "monster" Macchiavelli.[54]

At a first glance it seems rather strange that an author like Macchiavelli, who in his works only touches on religion in passing, and then always speaks of it with the greatest respect, as the great pillar of the state,[55]

---

nullam religionem agnoscunt, veræ falsæque delectum ac discrimen tollunt; religionem igitur heretici ex parte, politici omnino respuunt, etc."

[54] "Let Florence testifie this to all posteritie succeeding, when *that Monster Machiavell, first began to budde, who hath now spredde abroad his deadly branches of Atheisme over the most countries of Christendome*, insomuch as fewe places but are well acquainted with his doctrine, that the whole course of men's lives almost everywhere is nothing else but a continuall practice of his precepts, etc." The French theologian Marin Mersenne, the friend of Descartes, in his work on "Questiones celeberrimæ in Genesim" (Lutetiæ, Parisiorum, 1623, folio), is of the same opinion, and speaks thus of Macchiavelli: "Nicolaus Machiavellus atheorum hujus sæculi facile princeps, etc."

[55] Take the following passage, for instance, from his "Discorsi": "Considerato adunque tutto, conciudo che la religione introdotta da Numa fu tra le prime

should be accused of atheism. But we have only to transfer ourselves mentally into the sixteenth century, and to take the point of view of his contemporaries, and then this accusation will appear to us as natural as possible. The fact is, Macchiavelli's contemporaries must have been extremely indignant that the great politician, looking at religion from a political standpoint, should have given his unhesitating preference to heathenism rather than Christianity,[56] and that he should have set aside all considerations of conscience and morality in his system, and advised people to be guided solely by their interests. If Dolet, Rabelais, L'Hôpital and others, were stigmatised as atheists by their contemporaries from a want of dogmatic intolerance in their views, how much more, from their

---

cagioni della felicità di quella citta, perche quella causò buoni ordini, i buoni ordini fanno buona fortuna, e dalla buona fortuna nacquero i felici successi delle impresse. E come la osservanza del culto Divino e cagione della grandezza delle republiche, così il dispregio di quello e cagione della rovina di esse" (lib. i., cap. 11); or, "Quelli principi o quelle republiche, le quali si vogliono mantenere incorrote, hanno sopra ogni altra cosa a mantenere incorrote le ceremonie della religione, e tener le sempre nulla loro venerazione. Perche nissuno maggiore indizio si puore avere della rovina d'una provincia, che vedere dispregiato il culto Divino, etc." (*Ibid.* cap. 12).

[56] The comparison between heathenism and Christianity is made by Macchiavelli in the second book of his "Discorsi."

point of view, did heathen Macchiavelli deserve such a title! The above considerations, strengthened by evidence, make it extremely probable that Greene's instructor in atheism was no other than Macchiavelli. An attentive perusal of Greene's works will transform this probability into a complete scientific fact. Indeed, where could Greene have got those principles from, but from the works of the Florentine historian? Who but he boldly proclaimed the principle of self-interest to be the sole foundation on which politics and government could be built? Greene was not wrong in connecting Marlowe's atheism with his study of Macchiavellian politics, which are nothing else than a rejection of the divine principle in life. Does not the life of Macchiavelli bear a strong resemblance in its general features to that of the unknown atheistic leader described by Greene? Was not Macchiavelli, like the latter, continually aiming at the attainment of a happiness, wealth and position, which seemed to be continually eluding his grasp? Did he not live in fear and die in despair? It remains for us to explain another expression of Greene's—"by him persuaded" —in which the supporters of the personal-influence hypothesis (Bernhardi, for instance) see a strong confirmation of their argument. Certainly, in simply conversational language, the term "by him persuaded" would be used to imply personal influence rather than literary; but to measure the figurative language of Greene's style by the standard of ordinary conversation would be as unreasonable as to apply analytical criticism to those effusions written with a trembling hand in moments of agony of soul. Greene, always fond of inaccurate, figurative expressions, was of course all the less able carefully to weigh his words on his death-bed. Taking advantage of his moments of relaxation from suffering to pour out his heart, he used the expressions that first came to hand. Previous to the passage containing the expression "by him persuaded," Greene speaks of the instructor of atheism as a dead man, and adds, turning to Marlowe, "and wilt thou, my friend, be his Disciple?" To be the disciple of a dead man is impossible. It is evident that no personal, but literary influence is meant; and the word disciple is used in the sense of partisan. In the same figurative sense Greene uses the expression "by him persuaded." That Greene in his turn was not free from Macchiavelli's influence is proved by the testimony of a contemporary, as well as by Greene's own confessions. The translator of "L'Académie Française," above mentioned, speaking of the adherents to the atheist doctrines of Macchiavelli in England, counts Greene among the number,[67]

[67] "That there are such (*i.e.* atheists) amongst us, even in these times wherein we live, let [speak] the testimonie which *one of that crew gave lately of himself, when the heavy hand of God by sickness summoned him to give an accompt of his dissolute life.*" Here he quotes an anecdote from Greene's "Repentance," and concludes with the following words: "The vayn of a meere atheist; and so afterwards he pronounced himself, when he was checked in conscience by the mightie hand of God. And yet this fellowe in his lifetime and in the middest of his greatest ruffe, had

although he does not call him by name. Greene in his "Repentance," telling of the first years of his London life, expresses himself in the following manner: "As I grew in yeares, so I waxed more ripe in ungodlines, and scoffed at . . . . . any wholesome or good admonition."[t]

From Marlowe Greene proceeds to address other friends of his. "With thee I joyne young Juvenall. . . . . thou art unworthie better hap, sith thou dependest on so meane a stay."[u]

The degrading trade that Peele followed was no other than that of Greene and Marlowe—*i.e.*, he wrote for the stage. Malone, Dyce, and all other critics (with the exception, however, of Farmer), believe that by the young Juvenal Greene means Thomas Lodge, who certainly wrote jointly with Greene the comedy entitled *A Looking-glasse for London and England.* It is only recently that Staunton and Simpson have returned to Farmer's hypothesis, and considerably turned the scales in favour of Thomas Nashe.[58][v] With

---

the presse at commandement to publish his lascivious pamphlets, when he infected the hearts of many young gentlemen and others with his poisonfull platforms of love and divillish discourses of fancies, etc." [As with Harvey, this assailant had not read the books.—G.]

[58] *Vide* Staunton's letter to the *Athenæum*, 7th February, 1874, and Simpson's article "Greene on

[t] Works, Vol. XII., pp. 161-2.—G.

[u] *Ibid.*, p. 143.—G.

[v] See our Introduction to this Life on this.—G.

regard to the third stranger all are agreed. This is no other than Greene's old friend, the dramatist George Peele.

Having strongly urged his friends to desert the dramatic art, and to have nothing to do with vulgar-minded actors, Greene continues: "But now returne I againe to you three, knowing my miserie is to you no news . . . . . The fire of my light is now at the last snuffe, and the want of wherwith to sustaine it, there is no substance left for life to feede on." [w]

From his friends and fellow-authors the dying thoughts of Greene turned to his wife, whom he had so foolishly and cruelly deserted. Under the influence of the sincere repentance which had seized him, he wrote her a touching letter, which was found after his death among his papers, and was appended to the "Groatsworth of Wit."

Nashe," *Academy*, 11th April, 1874, reprinted in the "Shakspere Allusion Books." Part I. (London, 1874.) As additional evidence, we may state that the title of "Young Juvenal," thus given Nashe by Greene, stuck to him. In 1598, the critic Meres, speaking of Nashe's play *The Isle of Dogs*, says, "As *Actæon* was wooried of his owne hounds: so is Tom *Nash* of his *Isle of Dogs*. Dogges were the death of Euripides, but bee not disconsolate, gallant *young Juvenall*, Linus, the sonne of *Apollo*, died the same death, etc." [See our Introduction on this.—G.]

[w] Works, Vol. XII., p. 145.—G.

The devout state of mind, sincere contrition, and broken spirit of Greene, with which the "Groatsworth of Wit" is filled, stands out even more strongly in his "Repentance"—a small work written by him a very short time before his death. Here Greene recounts, for the benefit of others, his dissolute life, and, in a fit of self-accusation, endeavours to paint himself and all his actions in the worst of colours. The "Repentance," consisting altogether of a few pages, finishes with after-words by the editor, Cuthbert Burbie, which contain an interesting account of the last moments of Greene's life. Cuthbert Burbie had previously edited Greene's pamphlet entitled "The Third and Last Part of Conny-Catching," and was probably personally acquainted with Greene. He was kept informed of the progress of Greene's disease by the people who attended the latter, and for this reason the information he gives is certainly worthy of our attention. He affirms that Greene's repentance was sincere and thorough, and that during Greene's illness, which lasted a long time, he took leave of life with tears in his eyes, and prayed God and men to forgive him the many misdeeds and transgressions committed by him. He was continually exclaiming, "O God! have mercy on me! forgive me my sins!" On the eve of his death Greene was visited by one of his friends, who brought him a message from his wife and the news that she was well. Greene was much gratified, expressed his wish to see her once more before dying, and confessed he had greatly wronged her.

Feeling he had not long to live, he convulsively

seized pen and paper, and with a hand that was fast growing cold wrote off the following lines to his wife :—

"Sweet Wife, as euer there was any good will or friendship betweene thee and mee, see this bearer (my Host) satisfied of his debt: I owe him tenne pound, and but for him I had perished in the streetes. Forget and forgiue my wronges done vnto thee, and Almighty God haue mercie on my soule. Farewell till we meet in heauen, for on earth thou shalt neuer see me more.

"This 2 of September.
1592.
"Written by thy dying Husband.
Robert Greene."[59]

This letter is also appended to the "Repentance."[1] The next day Greene was no more.

Greene had hardly been buried before one of his bitterest literary enemies—Gabriel Harvey—who had been satirised by him in his witty pamphlet "A Quip for an Upstart Courtier," hurried to his lodgings to collect all the particulars he could of the last moments of his sworn foe.

Mistaking Harvey for a friend of the deceased, the

---

[59] Harvey's version, in his "Four Letters," is shorter (Dyce, "Account of R. Greene," p. 57), but this is explained by his quoting from memory. Both editions, however, bear on the whole a strong resemblance to each other.

[1] Works, Vol. XII., pp. 185-6. See our Introduction.—G.

landlady, with tears, told him of Greene's illness, of the extreme poverty he was in, and how she had put a wreath of bays on the head of the departed poet. On hearing all this the soulless and malignant pedant returned home to scratch off his "Four Letters." In these the author, taking advantage of the information he had received, slandered the memory of Greene in the most insolent manner possible, ridiculing, at the same time, his kind-hearted landlady, whom he ironically called the tenth muse, who had not refused Greene after his death what her sisters had never granted him while living.

Greene left two sons. The first, by his wife, lived with him in London, and was sent back to his mother by Greene only a short time before his death. What eventually became of him, as well as of his mother, is not known. His second son was the fruit of his *liaison* with the sister of "Cutting Ball"; his name was Fortunatus, and he died in 1593. (*Vide* Note No. [30].)

Although no portraits of Greene have been preserved, we are able to get a conception of his personal appearance from the descriptions of Chettle, Harvey and Nashe.[60] Chettle describes Greene as "a man of indifferent yeares, of face amible, of body well proportioned; his attire after the habite of a scholler-like Gentleman, onely his hair was somewhat long" ("Kind Hartes Dreame," ll. 22-24). Harvey says of Greene that he was vain of his Master of Arts robes, and wore such long hair as was only worn by

---

[60] *Vide* Dyce, "Account of R. Greene," p. 58.

thieves and cut-throats. Thomas Nashe [tells us that Greene "had a iolly long red peeke (=beard, probably) like the spire of a steeple," which shows that he was red-haired.—G.]

With regard to Greene's moral character and his merits as an author, the opinions of his contemporaries are divided. They either praise Greene indiscriminately, or else equally indiscriminately abuse him, according to the party to which they belonged. Greene's literary enemies, with Harvey at their head, could not find words to lower him sufficiently in the eyes of the public, not only as a man but also as an author. Harvey in his "Four Letters" (*vide* especially letters Nos. 2 and 3) calls Greene a base man, the king of paupers, an arch-atheist, a dishonour to the stage, and the ape of Lylly, etc. Another literary enemy of Greene's, the anonymous author of a pamphlet entitled "Martine Mar-Sextus," looking on Greene's works from his puritanical point of view, calls them fascinating, dishonourable love tracts.[y] On the other hand, a certain anonymous admirer of Greene's, calling himself "R. B.," the author of "Greene's Funeralls" (London, 1594),[61] bows down before his intellect, his learning and his eloquence,

---

[61] The only copy of this curious production is to be found in the Bodleian Library at Oxford. We owe the deepest gratitude to Mr. Frederick Harrison, of the *Fortnightly*, for a minutely accurate copy taken from it.

[y] See our Introduction on 'Martine Mar-Sextus.'—G.

compares him with Jupiter, Apollo and Mercury, and affirms that his pamphlets, although on the subject of love, are possessed of a high moral tendency. In his enthusiastic blindness he goes as far as to declare that Greene's life even was a pattern and a model for every one to follow.[a] Much more impartial are Chettle's and Nashe's accounts of him; for these, without hiding the faults of their friend, do full justice to his merits.

Chettle knew Greene's faults and his lawless life, but he likewise knew the nobler side of his nature and his sincere repentance. In view of the calumnies hurled at the memory of his untimely departed friend Chettle thought it his duty to raise his voice. In his "phantastical" pamphlet "Kind-hartes Dream" (an indirect answer to Harvey's "Four Letters," which had only just been published),[83] Chettle informs us that in a dream Greene's spirit appeared to him, and laid a

[83] Harvey's "Four Letters" are entered in the "Registers" under the 4th December, 1592, and on the 8th of December of the same year we find the entry of Chettle's pamphlet. Such rapidity of work can only be explained by the supposition that the printer of Harvey's pamphlet allowed Chettle to read the proofs.

[a] This must suffice for "Greene's Funerals." Had our space not been long exhausted, considerable quotations had been given. A copy is in the British Museum, and also in the Bodleian. With reference to the apology on pp. 49-50, it is very needless. One may be 'persuaded' by a book as well as by a man personally. We English do not think it necessary to see one, to be his disciple.—G.

manuscript on his breast. This manuscript was nothing else than a letter of Greene's to Nashe, in which the former begs Nashe to defend his memory and punish his calumniators, that gave him no peace in his grave. "Having with humble penitence," Chettle makes Greene say, "besought pardon for my infinite sinnes, and paid the due to death; euen in my graue was I scarse layde, when Enuie (no fit companion for Art) spit out her poyson, to disturbe my rest. *Aduersus mortuos bellum suscipere, inhumanum est.* There is no glory gained by breaking a deade mans skull. *Pascitur in vinis liuor, post fata quiescit.* Yet it appeares contrary in some, that inueighing against my workes, my pouertie, my life, my death, my burial, haue omitted nothing that may seeme malitious. For my Bookes, of what kind soeuer, I refer their commendation or dispraise to those that haue read them. Onely for my last labours affirming, my intent was to reproue vice, and lay open such villainies, as had been very necessary to be made knowne, wherof my *Blacke Booke*, if euer it see the light, can sufficiently witnesse." . . . . . "Awake (secure boy) reuenge thy wrongs, remember mine: thy aduersaries began the abuse, they continue it: if thou suffer it, let thy life be short in silence and obscuritie, and thy death hastie, hated, and miserable."[**]

By such exhortations, put in the mouth of the

[**] See the whole striking appeal to Nashe to defend his dead friend in "Kind Hartes Dreame," as found in Dr. Ingleby's "Shakspere Allusion Books": Part I., 1592-8, pp. 60-1 (New Shakspere Society).—G.

deceased poet, Chettle wanted to rouse Nashe to commence with all alacrity the defence of Greene's memory. As far as we know, Nashe was not one of those people who require long exhortation under such circumstances. From his early youth he had been in the habit of occupying the position of skirmishing free-lance in paper-wars, and had acquired the reputation of being a witty and bitter pasquinader, and utterly unscrupulous in the means he employed.[bb] We have already seen that Greene, before dying, entreated him to be more moderate in his attacks on persons. Nor was Nashe in the present instance long in coming to the front. Chettle's pamphlet, containing Greene's letter to Nashe, is mentioned in the "Registers of the Stationers' Company" among the books newly published on 8th December, 1592; and a month afterwards, on 12th January, 1593, we find Nashe's pamphlet, "Strange News," already entered there. In this pamphlet Nashe did not content himself with simply defending Greene from the attacks of Harvey, but, according to his custom, took the offensive. For us only those passages of his pamphlet are of interest which relate to Greene, and where Nashe endeavours to show the character of his friend in its true light. In refuting Harvey, Nashe says: "Greene inherited more virtues than vices . . . . his onely care was to have a spel in his purse to conjure up a good cup of wine with at all times."[cc]

[bb] This language is not justified by Nashe's writings up to that date.—G.

[cc] See Nashe's Works, Vol. II., pp. 220-21, in HUTH LIBRARY.—G.

Greene's moral character presents an interesting subject for psychological analysis. We can find no author whose writings and life are so opposed to each other, so decidedly contradictory, and seemingly so irreconcilable, as Greene's. A sensualist[dd] and a cynic in his life, Greene was ideally pure and edifying in his writings. Not only his dramas and lyrical works, but even his love-pamphlets,—of the composition of which he subsequently so bitterly repented,—are impressed with a moral tone, and are full of exalted flights in the domain of idealism. It is with difficulty we are brought to believe that a man possessing such exalted views on the destiny of mankind and moral duty, who had created such ideal female characters as Angelica (in *Orlando*), or Dorothea (in *James IV.*), could spend whole days in the filthy dens of vice, surrounded by half-drunken, admiring boon companions and courtesans. This contradiction between the life and writings of Greene, as also his periodical alternations of boisterous debauch with burning repentance, of which he speaks himself in his confessions, are only partially explained by his want of firmness of will and the weakness of his character. Such an explanation might be allowable in the case of a broken-down, worn-out constitution, deprived of all energy; but this cannot be said of Greene. We know that in several instances (as in the affair with the connycatchers, for example), Greene showed a

---

[dd] He gave way to thoughtless passion and immoral living and free speech; but his very remorse and penitence darkly witness to higher opinions and convictions.—G.

remarkable energy and even strength and perseverance of character, which inclines us to believe that his nature was not a worn-out and flaccid one. It seems to us, in explaining the contradictions and waverings of which Greene's life was made up, that a great deal of it ought to be put down to his passionate and hot-blooded temperament, which formed the physiological basis of his moral character. We are here involuntarily reminded of the first Napoleon's profound remark on the relation of a man's character to his actions: "On vous dit encore, que quand on connait le caractère d'un homme on a la clef de sa conduite; c'est faux: tel fait une mauvaise action, qui est foncièrement honnête homme; tel fait une méchanceté, sans être méchant. C'est que presque jamais l'homme n'agit pas par l'acte naturel de son caractère, mais par une passion secrète du moment, refugiée, cachée dans les derniers replis du cœur."[68] These few words of Napoleon's give us the key to the incomprehensible contradictions with which Greene's life is full. How often—led astray by the impetuousness of his passions, which he was powerless to control—he crossed the barrier of moral duty and gave himself up to vices and excesses against which his moral sense [afterwards] revolted. But the tempest spent itself and passed over; reason and conscience again assumed their rights; Greene became ashamed of his dissoluteness; he burned with contrite sorrow; he promised himself to reform and to walk in the

---

[68] These words occur in Las Casas' "Mémorial de Saint-Hélène."

path of order and duty; and he really kept his promise—till the next outbreak.

Evidently it was but for a time that his passions allowed him freedom of action, and then only to grasp him more firmly in their clutches afterwards. But we will not judge him too harshly. Carlyle says somewhere, that we should not endeavour to make man the expressionless embodiment of impossible virtues: which of us has not fallen and covered himself with mud in the act? The great object, he adds, is not to be always behaving properly, but to be always striving to attain excellence, and to be filled with an honest and insurmountable desire to do right. Greene seems certainly to have possessed this aspiration. His works testify how honestly he endeavoured to solve the problem of life. The mire into which he sank did not, however, soil his pure imagination, which so frequently depicted to him images distinguished by the stamp of high moral purity and human dignity. The discord between the passionate impulses of his inborn nature and the ideals ingrafted by education constitute, in our opinion, the tragedy of Greene's life. It is a known fact, that under the influence of temperament a man forms certain habits, which give a certain tone to his imagination, and forms certain views on the duty of life, personal happiness, etc. A man of a passionate temperament would hardly see any happiness in the mortification of the flesh and the subjection of the passions. On the contrary, it is more natural for him to represent happiness as sensual gratification, as a series of strong, passionate, and exciting sensations. Greene's life proves to us that in his youth he took this view of happiness, and greedily drained his cup of sensual enjoyments to the dregs. His acquaintance with Macchiavelli's system of philosophy, which he had studied in his youth, and of which, we may add, he took much too one-sided a view, applying its principles indifferently to private as well as political life, could only confirm him in this bias. The theory of self-interest, as the motive of human action, reconciled itself admirably with Greene's epicurean view of life, formed under the influence of his passionate temperament and restless imagination. But, sooner or later, this theory of egotistical epicureanism, forming at one time the essence of Greene's philosophy of life, would have to come into collision, in his mind, with another system, the principal component parts of which were religion and philosophy. The result of such a collision might be divined beforehand. All that was noble and exalted in Greene loudly told him on which side the truth lay. From this moment the tormenting discord in Greene's mind may be said to commence. His passionate instincts draw him one way; his principles another. Powerless to resist the attacks of his passions and the obscuring charms of his wild imagination, Greene often threw himself into the stream of dissolute life; but the delirium over, he did penance for yielding to these allurements by sincere contrition and moral self-flagellation—in which he seemed to indulge with a sort of morbid pleasure. This self-flagellation is strongly connected with a really attractive feature of Greene's character: we mean his sincerity,—a boundless sincerity, which never allowed him to spare himself, and which sometimes went to the extreme of cynicism in its manifestations. Greene was incapable of posing and pretending to be what he was not. If in his confessions he sometimes exaggerates, it is always to his own disadvantage. This is why we may fearlessly believe him when he speaks of the anguish of his soul and the sincerity of his repentance.

We have endeavoured to explain, as far as our sources would permit, the internal drama of Greene's life. An acquaintance with this is absolutely necessary in helping us to form an accurate opinion of his moral character. A man whose deflections from the path of virtue cost him so much moral suffering can of course not be measured by the same standard as the man who acts basely and remains at peace with himself, defending his faults by all kinds of sophistry. Although Greene did not survive the erratic period of life (he died in the thirty-second year of his age), his anguish and sincerity, the ideal tendency of his mind, and his works, serve as a guarantee that he was really becoming more strict towards himself and his literary work; and all this taken together inclines us to believe that the time was not far distant when he would definitely and irrevocably have gone forward on the path of moral regeneration.

CHAPTER II.

CRITICO-BIBLIOGRAPHICAL REVIEW OF GREENE'S PROSE WORKS.

Greene's love-pamphlets: their contents and peculiarities.—Greene's political pamphlets: "The Spanish Masquerado."—The pastoral novel, "Menaphon" or "Arcadia."—The pamphlets indicating a change in his literary labours: "Mourning Garment," "Farewell to Follie," and "Never too Late."—Greene as an exposer of public nuisances: a review of his works against the "Conny-catchers."—Specimen of the literary polemics of the sixteenth century: Greene's pamphlet in satire of Harvey, "A Quip for an Upstart Courtier."—The autobiographical pamphlets of Greene: "A Groatsworth of Wit," and "Repentance."—A general survey of Greene's literary labours.

THE earliest work of Greene's of which an entry has been preserved in the "Registers" is the first part of "Mamillia," entered among the books permitted to be printed, on the 3rd of October 1580, but not published [so far as known] till 1583.[64] The

[64] Bernhardi (in "Robert Greene's Leben und Schriften," p. 11) avers that the "Mirrour of Modestie" was written earlier than "Mamillia." In confirmation of this opinion he quotes the "Registers," in which

cause of this delay is not known. It was probably owing to the reminiscences still fresh in Greene's mind of Italy, from whence he must have returned in the spring or summer of 1580, that he laid the scene of his first story in Padua.[**] It is there that the beautiful Mamillia, daughter of the Paduan ruler Gonzago, blooms and flourishes. She falls in love with a volatile young man, Pharicles[65] by name. The latter has a tender feeling for Mamillia, and, as old Gonzago has nothing against the union of the two —on the contrary, thinks it a good match—we thus seem to be near the end of the romance. In reality, however, it is here that the plot begins to thicken. Mamillia has a charming relation, called Publia, a meeting with whom causes a change to take place in Pharicles' affections. He forgets all about

---

we find an entry under the 7th April, 1579, of a work entitled "Myrrour of Modestie," with no author's name given. But this is evidently a misunderstanding, arising from the similarity of the title. The "Mirror of Modestie" entered under the 7th of April was not written by Greene, but by a certain Thomas Colter (*vide* Collier, "Bibliographical Catalogue," vol. ii. p. 312).

[65] [See Vol. II., pp. 3 and 139.—G.]

** I visited the famous University of Padua expressly to see if Greene could be traced there. I found many English and Scotch names among the lists of the students, but nothing of Greene. It must be stated, however, that the records are fragmentary and loose.—G.

Mamillia, and falls madly in love with Publia, who in her turn is much interested in Pharicles, especially after the latter has made a learned and witty speech at supper on the theme "What is love?" But his passion for Publia proves as changeable as his love for Mamillia. A few days pass by, and the weak-minded youth comes to the conclusion that Publia is not such a prize as he at first supposed, and he begins again to think of Mamillia. Here Greene expresses himself pungently on the frivolity and fickleness of the youth of his day. These remarks may not be devoid of an autobiographical element; seeing that the frivolous character of Pharicles bears some resemblance to that of Greene. "Where by the way, Gentlemen," Greene says, "that Pharicles must needs be Carpet Knight: for they thinke it as hard to lyve without loue as without meat."[11] The hero of this novel belongs to this class of character, and his frivolous, peevish imagination is for ever tossing him from one side to the other. He had almost decided to go off to Mamillia and ask her pardon, but in the course of a few hours he changes his mind and writes a rapturous letter to Publia. The latter, however, begins to see what sort of a man Pharicles is, and offers him her friendship by letter. Pharicles has, therefore, nothing left but to return to Mamillia, who was languishing with grief. It is hardly necessary to add that she receives him with rapture and forgives his inconstancy. They both go to Mamillia's father, discover their regard for each other to

[11] See Works, Vol. II., pp. 19-21 *et alibi.*—G.

him, obtain his consent, and are immediately betrothed.

Having taken this decided step, Pharicles again begins to waver; on his return home he reads and re-reads Publia's letter, and at each perusal it seems less and less cruel. To make matters worse, his obedient imagination conjures up Publia's wicked eyes, which seem to peep almost out of every line; he forgets all about his promise to Mamillia, and determines again to throw himself at Publia's feet. For a time his conscience torments him; but what would have been the use of his classical learning, had it been unable to help him in this difficult moment of his life? He soothes himself with the recollection of the examples of Jason, Æneas and other heroes, who treated the women they loved as he was treating Mamillia; and he writes Publia a touching letter, in which he offers her his hand and his heart.

Although Publia is touched by the eloquence and learning of this letter, she is not sufficiently so to make her regardless of all precautions. Without refusing Pharicles, she promises to think over his offer. Pending her decision, Pharicles, in the garb of a pilgrim, goes forth to wander about the world. "Marrie whether *Pharicles* proued as inconstant a husband as a faithlesse wooer, I knowe not: but if it be my hap to heare, looke for newes speedilie as may be." Thus Greene finishes the first part of his novel.[22]

The second part of "Mamillia" was written by

---

[22] See Works, Vol. II., p. 248.—G.

Greene at Cambridge[66] also, and is entered in the "Registers" 6th September, 1583, but was not published till after his death, in 1593.[67] Here Greene finishes the history of Mamillia and Pharicles. The unexpected departure of Pharicles falls like a clap of thunder on poor deluded Mamillia. But the sorrow and despair that possess her are unable to eradicate the image of the faithless lover from her heart. Greene seizes this opportunity to draw a parallel between the incontinence of men and the faithfulness of women, and writes an enthusiastic panegyric in

---

[66] The poem in honour of the author, prefixed to it, contains the following lines:

"Greene is the plant, Mamillia the flower,
Cambridge the plot where plant and flower grows," etc.;

and the dedication is dated from Clare Hall (a college at Cambridge), 7th June, 1583. [See Vol. II., p. 249.—G.]

[67] The explanations given by Bernhardi to account for this delay are not uninteresting. (*Vide* "Robert Greene's Leben und Schriften," pp. 11—13.) [Not proven nor likely. That it was published before is not only probable from the non-ending of the story in the first part, and from Greene's consciousness of this as shown by his conclusion of it, but by its being by "Robert Greene, Maister of Arts *in Cambridge*," and not 'Utriusque Acad.' It is also most unlikely that when later than 1583 Greene's booklets were much looked for, Ponsonby should unprofitably keep it by him, especially as it was he who published "Gwydonius."—G.]

honour of the latter. Pharicles, in the meantime, goes to Saragossa, where a certain courtesan falls in love with him. Rejected by him, this woman accuses him falsely to the authorities, and Pharicles is thrown into prison. When the news of this event reaches Mamillia, she disguises herself, like Portia in the *Merchant of Venice*, as a man, and goes to Saragossa and effects Pharicles' escape; who, touched by her love for him, really marries her at last.

In this novel of Greene's the influence of Lylly's "Euphues" may be traced. This was a celebrated romance which appeared in 1579, and left its impression on the whole series of English works of fiction that succeeded it.[68] Greene not only appropriated the refined mannerism of style of his pattern, which is known by the name of Euphuism, but borrowed several of Lylly's dogmas and modes of treatment, of which he made a clever use. Take, for instance, the speech at supper on the subject "What is love?" where Pharicles had the opportunity of displaying his learning and his talents as an orator, and conquered the heart of Publia. This bears a strong resemblance to discussions of the same kind in Lylly's novel; Lylly himself having, in his turn, borrowed this effective mode of treatment from the Italian novelists. The very character of the hero is a copy of Lylly's "Euphues,"—and if Greene's frivolous and volatile lover is more lifelike,

---

[68] For an account of Lylly's novel, see our work entitled "Predshestveniky Shakspeara" ("The Predecessors of Shakespeare"), vol. i., note [164].

and stands out in greater relief than Lylly's, this may be accounted for by the internal affinity between the character of Pharicles and that of Greene himself.

The "Myrrour of Modesty," written probably immediately after "Mamillia," and appearing in 1584, was composed by Greene at the request of a lady (as he informs his readers in the preface), and does not afford any interest, either from a biographical or a literary point of view. The wish to imitate Lylly here approaches the ridiculous. Greene makes every effort to approximate to the style of his teacher, ignoring all rules of art, and even transgressing probability. It is impossible to read without a smile the long tirades which the old men exchange with Susanna, on penetrating into her bathing-house, where she is discovered robed in the classical costume of the Venus de' Medici. In none of his works does Greene show himself so slavish an imitator of Lylly's as in this; and we may add, nowhere does he prove himself so bad a story-teller.

In 1584 three love-pamphlets of Greene's appeared. We shall speak of them in the order in which they were entered in the "Registers."

1. "Gwydonius, the Card of Fancie," was entered in the "Registers" 11th April, 1584, and published in the same year by the bookseller Ponsonby. Greene dedicates it to Edward Vere, Earl of Oxford. Prefixed to this novel is a Latin poem "In laudem autoris," signed by Richard Portington. We are unable to state whence Greene borrowed the plot of his "Gwydonius," but it is extremely probable that he was indebted for it to the Italian novelists.

The Duke Clerophontes, ruler of Metelyne, had two children, a daughter Leucippa, distinguished for her personal and moral perfections; and a son, the handsome but dissolute Gwydonius. In consequence of various complaints made by the Duke's subjects of the profligacy of Gwydonius, it is decided to send him abroad on his travels. On arriving at the town of Barutta, Gwydonius collects a gang of ne'er-do-wells as bad as himself, and commences to play his old pranks. However, it is in this town that he gets his first lesson in experience of the world. The licentious and profligate life that Gwydonius leads excites the suspicion and displeasure of the town authorities, and he is thrown into prison. Here Gwydonius learns how far to rely on friends. As soon as he is arrested all his boon companions disappear, leaving him to the tender mercy of fate. But Gwydonius escapes from prison, and, leaving the ungrateful town, departs for Alexandria. At Alexandria Duke Orlanio was then reigning. He had two children—a son, Thersandro, and a daughter, Castania. The Duke was so enchanted by the wit, beauty, and fascinating manners of the young stranger, that he not only received him into his service, but made him the companion of his son. Attending at court, Gwydonius has the opportunity of meeting and falling in love with Castania, who reciprocates the feeling. The young people already dream of marriage, when an unexpected occurrence nearly destroys their hopes. It so happens that a quarrel arises between the ruler of Metelyne, Clerophontes, and his tributary and vassal Orlanio, in consequence of the latter's non-payment of his customary tribute. It was even rumoured that Clerophontes was collecting an army for the purpose of supporting his claims at the point of the sword. Orlanio, however, does not lose all hope of settling matters peaceably, and sends his son to Metelyne to negotiate with its ruler. Although Thersandro does not succeed in persuading Clerophontes to moderate his demands, he succeeds in stealing the heart of Leucippa. Thersandro has hardly time to return home to his father, when the legions of Clerophontes are already on the march. Orlanio prepares for the defence, and appoints Gwydonius commander-in-chief of his army. This latter, not wishing to fight against his countrymen, devises a plan of escape to join his father, with Castania. But this plan is discovered by a courtier, a certain Valerio, who loves Castania but has been rejected. By command of Orlanio Gwydonius is thrown into prison. In the meantime the army of Clerophontes is approaching the walls of Alexandria. Here a battle ensues, at which the Metelynes are victorious, but suffer severe losses. To avoid further bloodshed, it is decided to settle the question at issue by single combat. The champion of the Metelynes is Clerophontes himself. The Alexandrians send out Gwydonius disguised. Clerophontes is vanquished and taken prisoner into Alexandria. Here the opponents make a treaty, which is strengthened by the double union of Gwydonius with Castania and Leucippa with Thersandro. The story finishes with a description of the marriage festivities.

2. The next book of Greene's that we find entered

in the "Registers" (13th August, 1584) is "The Historie of Arbasto, King of Denmark."[*] This story is told in the first person by the author, who visits in his travels a hermit living in a cave near Sidon. This hermit informs Greene that he was called Arbasto, and had been the mighty ruler of Denmark; and that his love for Doralicia, the daughter of Pelorus, king of France, had proved his ruin. It happened in this wise: Arbasto was at war with France, his armies were everywhere victorious, and Pelorus at last became convinced it was impossible to defeat his enemy by sheer strength of arms. He therefore had recourse to artifice. He entreated Arbasto to make a truce for a month. Too chivalrous and noble-minded to believe even his enemy capable of treachery, Arbasto agreed. As customary on such occasions, the most magnificent festivities celebrated the armistice. Arbasto was frequently invited to the French camp, where he saw the daughters of the king, the eldest of whom, Doralicia, awakened in him a tender feeling. Without in the least suspecting it, he in his turn was beloved by the youngest daughter, Myrania. Arbasto's frequent visits to the French camp gave Pelorus a capital opportunity to get rid of his successful enemy. At

---

[*] The oldest edition of "Arbasto" that we know of is one of 1594 (*vide* W. C. Hazlitt, "Handbook to Early English Literature," p. 242). From the fact that it was published by the same bookseller (Hugh Jackson) who received permission to print it ten years earlier, this was probably not the first edition.

one of these visits the renowned Arbasto was seized, together with his friend Egerio, and thrown into prison. The day was already appointed for their death, when Myrania found the means of saving them. Touched by the love and self-denial of Myrania, Arbasto promised to marry her. This promise he was prompted to make by his gratitude and reason, but his heart was still Doralicia's. As soon as Myrania discovered that Arbasto was secretly paying attentions to her sister,—who, however, rejected him,—she died of grief. The Danish people, indignant at Arbasto's breach of faith, rose under the leadership of Egerio, and drove Arbasto out of Denmark.[hh] Turned out of his own kingdom, and reproaching himself with Myrania's death, Arbasto, broken-hearted, determined to leave the world for ever and to become a hermit; in which guise the author found him.

3. "Morando" Greene dedicated to Earl Arundel, the celebrated patron of letters.[70] We see from the very title that this latter is not a novel in the proper sense of the word, but rather, a series of moral

---

[70] This novel was published in 1584 by the bookseller, Edward White. The entry of it in the "Registers," 8th August, 1586, probably refers to a second edition, published in 1587 (with the addition of a second part) at the expense of the same bookseller. The dedication to the Earl of Arundel must have appeared in 1584, as the Earl was committed to the Tower for high treason in the following year.

[hh] Scarcely accurate account; besides, it was the 'peers' who rose.—G.

dissertations on love, clothed in a story.[n] These dissertations are supposed to occupy three evenings: hence the title "Morando the *Tritameron* of Love," evidently written by Greene as a *pendant* to Boccaccio's "Decameron." We shall give the contents in as condensed a form as possible. The widow of Signior Bonfadio, Panthia, and her three daughters, Lacena, Sostrata and Fioretta, are invited by an old companion in arms of the widow's late husband, Signior Morando, to his country seat. Here they meet a party consisting of Aretyno, Signior Peratio and Don Sylvestro. At supper a picture of the abduction of Europa gives rise to a discussion on love. Peratio, a decided woman-hater, takes upon himself to prove the dogma, certainly unflattering to the fair sex, that *Amor fa multo, ma argento fa tutto* ("love doth much, but money doth all.") At first Panthia enters into a dispute with him, but after a time she declines to argue any further on so frivolous a subject, and leaves her eldest daughter Lacena to defend the reputation of her sex. On the following day the host proposes a new theme for discussion—namely, "Whether it be good to love or no?" in the consideration of which the whole party join. On the third day a fresh love thesis is taken: "By natural constitution women are more subiect vnto loue then men?" On the part of the men the discussion is conducted by Signior Silvestro; whilst the lady champion is Panthia's youngest daughter, Fioretta. The disputants as-

---

[n] See, for this note, the full title of the novel in Vol. III., p. 45.—G.

tonish their hearers by the eloquence and adroitness of their arguments. The second part of the novel is properly the story of the loves of Silvestro and Lacena. The narrative, alternately prose and verse, is interspersed with illustrations, anecdotes and dogmas taken from classical writers, and testifies to Greene's high scholarly attainments. Disputes on happiness and love fill up no small portion of this second part also, which concludes with the happy union of Lacena and Silvestro.

Greene's first works had considerable success with the public; but, perhaps by reason of that success, were subjected to violent attacks from his literary contemporaries. In his address, before the second part of "Mamillia" (1583), Greene speaks thus of these attacks: "Let Momus mocke, and Zoilus enuie, let Parasites flatter, and Sicophants smile. . . . .[11] In his preface to "Morando," Greene, probably irritated by fresh attacks, refers again to furious satyres and flearing sycophants, who try to depreciate everything, although nobody believes them.[JJ]

In 1585 Greene published only one pamphlet, "Planetomachia," dedicating it to Elizabeth's all-powerful favourite, the Earl of Leicester.[n] This

---

[n] We hasten to correct a little inaccuracy which has crept into Simpson's excellent, though slightly paradoxical article on Greene, in the second volume of his posthumous work, "The School of Shake-

[11] See Works, Vol. II., p. 145. Storojenko misassigns the 'address' to Lee and Portington.—G.

[JJ] See Works, Vol. III., p. 50.

work is properly a dispute between the planets Saturn and Venus; each trying to prove that it has the greatest and best influence on men and their affairs. The dispute is settled by the Sun, which is called in by both parties as arbiter. Venus, having dilated at length on the bad influence exercised by Saturn on the fate of mankind, and having shown that people born under that planet were miserly, cowardly, hypocritical and morose, tells a story in confirmation of these assertions, entitled "Venus' Tragedie." Once upon a time there lived at Ferrara a certain Duke Valdracko, a covetous and revengeful man, and a great hypocrite and egotist into the bar-

---

speare" (London, 1878). On p. 342 Simpson states that Greene's "Planetomachia" "was both registered and published in 1585." In the "Registers" we have been unable to discover this entry, although there is no doubt that the work was published in 1585. Such small inaccuracies occur not unfrequently in Simpson. For instance, he says (p. 314), that the reprint of "Morando," with the additional second part, was licensed on 8th of August, 1587, whereas this was really done a year earlier. (*Vide* "A Transcript of Stationers' Registers," ed. by Arber vol. ii., p. 209, b.) On the same page, Simpson, relying on Herbert, asserts that "Perimides the Blacksmith" was licensed also in 1587, whereas it is entered in the "Registers," with a clearness admitting of no doubt: "Anno Domini 1588, 29 die Marcii, allowed unto him (*i.e.* the publisher, Edward White) for his copie a booke intituled 'Perimides the Blacksmith,' etc."

gain. He had an only daughter, Pasylla by name, who was clever and beautiful. With this lady a certain Count Rodento, the deadly enemy of her father, fell deeply in love. Love is deft at overcoming obstacles, and, notwithstanding all precautions taken by the suspicious Valdracko, Rodento succeeded in delivering, through the agency of a lady at court, a written declaration of love to the object of his passion. Aware of the revengeful disposition of her father's character, and knowing that his love could not come to any happy termination, Pasylla considered it wisest to reject Rodento's advances. After writing a refusal, Pasylla retired to rest, but somehow could not go to sleep. The fact was, that Venus, exasperated at her coldness and calculation, filled her mind with sweet dreams of happiness and love, and of Rodento. Not till morning did the poor girl find sleep; but when she awoke, she was already passionately in love with Rodento. The change that had taken place in her was so sudden and inexplicable, that she felt ashamed of herself. Under the influence of this feeling she received the lady-in-waiting, who came for an answer, rather unkindly, and sent her away without giving her any definite reply. The whole of that day Pasylla spent in her room reading and re-reading Rodento's letter, and unable to come to any decision. When her father, concerned at her absence, came to her room to see her, she was too much engrossed in her thoughts to put away Rodento's letter, which was lying open before her. On reading the letter the old Duke's rage was extreme, but, like a true son of Saturn, he knew how to hide his anger.

Meeting on the same day Rodento's father, Count Cœlio, in the senate, the Duke proposed a reconciliation, and, as an earnest of his good intentions, he offered to marry his daughter to the Count's son. Suspecting the Duke of no deceit, and knowing that his son loved Pasylla, old Cœlio accepted the offer with delight. The marriage was celebrated with all possible solemnity and magnificence; and the young couple were made happy. But soon the deceitful and vengeful character of the Duke began to show itself. He bribed a mercenary assassin to murder Cœlio and poison his son-in-law. On discovering the author of her husband's death, Pasylla murdered her father, and then, in despair, committed suicide. Saturn, having attentively listened to "Venus' Tragedie," remarks that the story does not support Venus' argument. For, he argues, had Rodento not fallen in love with Pasylla, and had Venus not co-operated with him, all this misfortune would never have taken place. Venus retorts that the cause of all unhappiness was not Rodento's love, but the deceitful wickedness of the old Duke. The Sun as arbiter decides for Venus. Saturn, disgusted with this verdict, tells a story in his turn, where love works the ruin of the actors and causes all their misery. The heroine, an Egyptian courtesan, Rhodope by name, succeeds in captivating old Psamnetichus; who makes her his queen. She then falls in love with his son Philarkes; and Psamnetichus, on discovering their intimacy, kills both his son and wife, and finishes by taking his own life.

Greene's marriage, and the journey to the country

which it involved, explain to us why[kk] the year 1586 presents a blank in his literary labours; for with the exception of the second part of "Morando," he published nothing during this year.[ll] On returning to London after his rupture with his wife, Greene re-commenced work with renewed activity, as if striving to silence thereby the gnawings of his conscience and the misery of his shame. His "Farewell to Follie" was the fruit of this state of mind. This pamphlet is entered in the "Registers" under 11th June, 1587, as one of the books that Edward Aggas was permitted to print. But, for some reason or other, Greene decided on not having it published, and, taking back his manuscript, gave the publisher in exchange —as Simpson ingeniously suggests—another tale, "Penelope's Web," which was duly entered in the "Registers" on the 26th June of the same year to the same.[73]

This pamphlet Greene dedicated to Lady Margaret,

[73] Dyce, who did not know of the edition of "Penelope's Web" of 1587, preserved at the Bodleian Library at Oxford (*vide* Hazlitt, "Handbook to Early English Literature," *sub voce*), considered the edition of 1601 to be the oldest. (*Vide* "List of Greene's Prose Works" in his edition of Greene's Dramatical Works.)

[kk] 1585 gave us but "Planetomachia": explained as having been vicar of Tollesbury.—G.

[ll] This is the more likely, inasmuch as it now bears "Utriusque Academiæ," and is not therefore likely to have been a reprint of a copy that could have but had "Master of Arts in Cambridge."—G.

Countess of Cumberland. The author puts us on the isle of Ithaca, in the bed-chamber of Ulysses' faithful wife, who is discovered sitting and weaving, surrounded by her attendants. The conversation is on love, and the attendants argue and reason like scholars and philosophers, interspersing their sentences with quotations from the ancient philosophers and poets. One of them expounds the Platonic theory of love, borrowed by Greene from the Italian Platonists, although considerably altered in appearance. "True and perfect love," says one, "hath his foundation vppon vertue onely."[mm] In illustration of such constant and ideal love, the orator takes her mistress for an example, who does not love her husband with the foolish, passionate love which is generally ascribed to the influence of Venus, but with a deep and lasting feeling that originates in a love of virtue. From love the conversation naturally turns to the married state, and the interlocutors treat of the qualities necessary in a wife to make her husband happy. According to Penelope, these qualities may be classed under three heads: obedience, chastity, and a modest reticence of speech. In confirmation of her opinion, Penelope tells three stories. The heroine of the first tale is Barmenissa, the wife of the Egyptian sultan Saladin. Saladin falls in love with a courtesan, Olynda, raises her to the throne; and sends his wife away to live in poverty. All this his obedient wife patiently endures, never bewailing her fate, and even endeavouring to defend her husband's conduct in the eyes of others.

[mm] See Works, Vol. V., pp. 156-7.—G.

In the meantime, Olynda, believing herself all-powerful, ruins the people, provokes the Sultan to commit acts of injustice and cruelty, and, to crown all, demands the complete banishment of the unfortunate Barmenissa from the kingdom. The last demands prove her ruin: the Sultan, exasperated at her extravagance and despotism, banishes her for life, and reinstates on the throne his modest and obedient wife, with whom he lives till his death in amity and love.

On the following evening, as soon as her suitors, of whom she is heartily tired, have left her, Penelope tells her "second tale," in which the chastity of a farmer's wife, Cratyna, is victorious over the sensuality of a nobleman, Calamus, who is so struck with her virtue that a moral change takes place in his character, and he becomes a better man. On the third evening, it is the question of modesty that has to be illustrated, and Penelope tells her third tale. A Delphic king has three sons. Feeling his death drawing near, he calls them to him, to inform them that, as he loves them all equally well, he is unable to leave his kingdom to the eldest. But to avoid offending any one of them, he promises to leave it to the son that has the best wife. The sons agree to this arrangement, and alternately extol the virtues of their wives. The king, however, gives his crown to his youngest son, whose wife was silent, whilst the wives of the other two sons kept wrangling for their rights. When Penelope has finished this tale, the news is brought that fate has rewarded her for her constancy and love, and that her longed-for Ulysses has landed on the shores of Ithaca.

A few months later Greene published another tale, entitled "Euphues, his Censure to Philautus."[74] As the title indicates, his work stands in close connection with Lylly's celebrated story. Lylly's story closes with the marriage of Philautus, and the retirement of Euphues from the world to the mountain of Silexedra, where, far from the busy haunts of men, he broods over his misfortunes. The popularity that Lylly's book had enjoyed induced Greene to write a continuation of it. In his dedication to Lord Essex Greene gives the imaginary history of his work, affirming that some part of Euphues' 'counsell,' written from Silexedra to Philautus, who had been made the commander-in-chief of some fictitious army, had accidentally fallen into his hands. "In these counsels Euphues, following in the footsteps of Tullies orator, Platoes cōmon wealth, and Baldessars courtier,[75] aymeth at the exquisite portraiture of a perfect martialist."[aa]

---

[74] In the "Registers" it is entered under 18th September, 1587, and the bookseller, Edward White, published it in the same year. We made use of a beautifully preserved copy of this edition, now in the British Museum.

[75] Here Greene means a work by Count Baldessaro Castiglione (1478—1529), "Il Libro del Cortegiano," which first appeared at Venice in 1528. In 1561 it was already translated into English by Thomas Hobby. [To be included (D.V.) in "THE HUTH LIBRARY.—G.]

[aa] See Works, Vol. VI., p. 152.—G.

The discussion arises in the following manner. Taking advantage of a short truce, the Trojan ladies, Andromache, Polixena, and others, pay a visit to the Grecian camp. Achilles and Ulysses receive the guests with knightly courtesy. The accomplished Ulysses pays the ladies compliments of which the most eminent courtiers of Elizabeth's reign might well have been proud; and expresses his surprise that Paris should have eloped with Helen from Greece, when Troy abounded in such unsurpassable beauties, etc., etc. The guests are then welcomed by the Grecian ladies, and a general conversation ensues, which is interlarded with antitheses, sophisms, and quotations. Iphigenia tackles Andromache, and Briseis argues with Cassandra. After supper, venerable old Nestor proposes, as a theme for discussion, the qualities which an ideal general should possess to live happily and die honoured, Hector maintains that the most important qualities for a general are fortitude or magnanimity. Achilles, on the contrary, stands up for liberality. Helenus thinks the most important are wisdom and knowledge. In agreement with Agamemnon's proposal, everybody is to support his argument by a story in illustration. It is Helenus' turn to speak first. He pronounces a long panegyric on wisdom and knowledge as the source of all success, and supports his position by a story in which wisdom (or rather deceit and cunning) triumphs over brute force.

On the following day the Greek ladies, attended by Achilles, Nestor, and the other Grecian heroes, visit Troy, and are received with all due politeness by old

Priam in his magnificent palace. After dinner the company resume the question they had considered the day before. It is Hector's turn to support by facts his opinion, that fortitude or magnanimity are indispensable qualities for war in general and for a leader in particular. Besides general arguments and historical examples, Hector tells a story, "Hector's Tragedie," borrowed from Egyptian history. After Hector Achilles' turn comes. He maintains that the greatest virtue in a general is liberality; and proves it by quoting an incident from Athenian history relating to a certain general called Roxander, who inspired his soldiers not so much by his own courageous example as by his liberality. Roxander's soldiers knew that all booty taken by them in war would belong to them, and for this reason they fought with the most unprecedented courage. Achilles having finished his story, Priam, who is chosen by the disputants, decides the question by saying that a good general should possess in an equal degree every one of these three qualities.

In 1588 three novels of Greene's appeared—"Perimides the Blacksmith," "Pandosto," and "Alcida." [76]

---

[76] "Perimides the Blacksmith" is entered in the "Registers" under 29th March, 1588. The first edition appeared in the same year. It was reprinted by Collier, who began his series of "Miscellaneous Tracts, *temp.* Eliz. and Jac. I." (London, 1870), with it. As to the celebrated "Pandosto," it is not entered in the "Registers," although it was published in 1588. "Alcida" met quite a different fate: it

The first of these has a most interesting preface; which throws a strong light on Greene's relations with some of his literary contemporaries—to wit, Marlowe, and another dramatist, whose name is not now known. To account for the irritable tone in which Greene writes, we must bear in mind that Marlowe had not long before—probably towards the end of 1586—got his *Tamberlain* acted: a piece that constitutes an epoch in the history of the English drama, as much for its dramatic qualities as for its beautiful blank verse, which from henceforth became an indispensable medium for histrionic rhetoric. The immense success of *Tamberlain* awakened the envy of Greene. He, who had until now confined himself to the writing of stories under the well known motto "*omne tulit punctum qui miscuit utile dulci*," and perhaps comedies now and then, determined to try his powers in the domain of the historical drama. It may be surmised that the experiment was not quite successful. Indeed, according to Greene, both his motto and his blank verse were severely satirised from the boards of the stage by two poets.[77] Which play of Greene's it

---

was entered in the "Registers" 9th December, 1588, but the oldest edition that we have any record of is dated 1617. There is no doubt, however, that there must have been a much earlier edition of "Alcida," for one of Greene's most enthusiastic admirers, one "R. B.," the author of "Greene's Funerals" (London, 1594), included "Alcida" among the most celebrated of Greene's works.

[77] In view of the importance of this passage, we give

was that met this fate we are unable to say. Simpson makes an extremely probable guess in supposing it to have been *Alphonsus King of Arragon* which bears strong traces of being an imitation of Marlowe's *Tamberlain*, and is also written in blank verse. We are equally unable to say who those two dramatists were that made it the butt of their sarcasm. We are of opinion that it is not unlikely one of the offenders was the author of *Tamberlain* himself. It is only after making this supposition that we are able to explain the unseemly spitefulness of Greene's attack on *Tamberlain*. Touched in a vulnerable point, Greene is not squeamish in the choice of his language. He calls "Tamberlain" an atheist, defying God Himself in the Heavens, and adds that he would rather live by stealing than thus frivolously expose to view such leaden specimens of intolerable doggrel, etc.[78]

---

it in full. "I keepe my old course," says Greene, "to palter up some thing in Prose, using mine old poesie still, *Omne tulit punctum*, although latelye two Gentlemen Poets, made two mad men of Rome beate it out of their paper bucklers: and had it in derision for that I could not make my verses jet upon the stage in tragicall buskins, everie worde filling the mouth like the faburden of Bo-Bell, daring God out of heaven with that Atheist *Tamburlan*, or blaspheming with the mad preest of the sonne." [Works, Vol. VII., pp. 7-8.—G.]

[78] "But let me rather," Greene continues, "pocket up the Asse at *Diogenes* hand: then wantonlye set

The sarcasms which Greene's enemies launched against him were warmly taken to heart by his friends and admirers. One of these, a certain Eliote, in a French sonnet prefixed to "Perimides," having sung of the services Greene had rendered the English language, begs him to treat the yelping of curs, the cawing of crows and the hooting of owls with the contempt they deserve, and patiently to ignore their attacks.

"Perimides" is written in Greene's usual love-pamphlet style, with which we are already familiar. As in the case of others, the plot serves as a framework for a series of tales and the morals deduced from them. Greene begins his story by painting an ideal picture of the life of the Memphian blacksmith Perimides and his wife Delia. Although they were both very poor, and lived by the sweat of their brow, they never complained of their fate. Working hard all day, they would meet in the evening in their home, and tell each other stories; which would afterwards be discussed. A few of these evenings the author wishes to describe. The first evening Perimides tells his wife the following tale:—Once upon a time, at Tyre, there lived a certain Prestines, one of the nobles of King Euribates, with his wife Mariana. They lived happily for a long time, until the king of Sidon

---

out such impious instances of intollerable poetrie." [Storojenko, it will be seen, mistakes. His memory was probably misled by remembrance of the phrase 'pocket vp.' See onward, where he says one was Marlowe.—G.]

invaded the country. After defeating Euribates' army and killing Euribates, the king of Sidon took into captivity all the nobles and generals of Tyre, and among others Prestines. As soon as Mariana heard of the invasion of the army of Sidon, she, being near her confinement, took her child, with its nurse, a few of her valuables, and fled. She embarked in a common fishing-boat, with the intention of joining her friends at Lipari. On the way the boat was wrecked in a storm, and Mariana was tossed ashore by the waves. In this condition she bore a son, whom she called Infortunio. But this was only the commencement of her misfortunes. Pirates carried away her children and nurse, and left her alone on a desert island. Three years she lived on this island, supporting herself on the fruits of the earth, and by that time she grew perfectly wild. At last Fate, seeing her resignation, took compassion on her. It so happened that the ruler of Decapolis, passing through the desert island, saw one day a beautiful and nearly naked woman, with her hair reaching to her feet, playing with a fawn. At the sight of a human being she immediately endeavoured to hide herself, and it cost the ruler of Decapolis and his wife no small pains to persuade her to come and settle with them. The atmosphere of love and tenderness with which she was surrounded by the ruler and his wife had so good an effect on Mariana, that she soon again got used to society, and told them her story. From that time forth they employed every means in their power to find Mariana's children. For a long time their endeavours were fruitless, until Fate herself assisted them. Through some fortunate accident the pirates had sold both Mariana's children and the nurse to a certain Lamoraque; the brother of the despot of Decapolis. The nurse gave out that the children were hers; they were educated as common labourers, and were employed in all kinds of work. When they grew up, however, the nurse told them the secret of their birth, but made them swear not to betray her. The children kept their oath, but day by day they felt more and more the narrowness of the sphere in which it had pleased Fate to place them. Consequently the eldest, Procidor, took the first convenient opportunity of effecting an escape into Egypt, to seek his fortune. Accidentally he found his way to Decapolis, the despot of which took him into his service. The mother and son were both living under the same roof for some time, without knowing each other. In the meanwhile, Marcella, the daughter of the despot, and Procidor, fell passionately in love with each other. Marcella told her father that she would marry no one else than Procidor. The enraged parent wanted to have them both put to death, but his milder consort persuaded him to limit their punishment to separate solitary confinement. Sitting in his prison, Procidor wiled away the hours by telling his gaoler the history of his life and noble origin. The latter communicated the story to Marcella's father, who, on learning who Procidor was, agreed gladly to his marriage with Marcella. Mariana's joy, on learning that Procidor was her son, and was going to marry the daughter of the despot of Decapolis, may easily be imagined. Messengers were at once despatched to learn what had become of Infortunio. The messengers returned with the news that Infortunio was still living at the court of Lamoraque; and was already affianced to his daughter. On hearing that his mother was still alive, Infortunio came with his affianced bride and future father-in-law to Decapolis. Here the two marriages were celebrated at one and the same time. During the marriage festivities news was brought that the son of Euribates had defeated the king of Sidon, and reigned in his father's place at Tyre, having duly restored Prestines to his former position. Thus sorrow was changed into joy, and Mariana, with her sons and daughters-in-law, departed for Tyre to join her husband. The story finishes with the happy meeting of husband and wife. Having heard her husband's tale to the end, Delia observed that such sudden changes of fortune were the lot of high-born people, and as the tempest shivered the tall cedars but did not hurt the bushes and underwood, the obscure and humble, like themselves, were safe from such vicissitudes.

The next evening it was Delia's turn to tell a story, the plot of which is as follows:—In the island of Lyparie there lived a youth Alcimedes, gifted with all possible perfections of mind and body. His only disadvantage was his extreme poverty. On attaining maturity he fell in love with Constance, a girl of noble birth, and very rich. Although Constance was equally fond of the handsome Alcimedes, her parents would not hear of the union, on account of the young man's want of means. Seeing that poverty was the only bar to his happiness, he determined at all hazards to make his fortune. He got together a band of smart young dare-devils, and constituted himself a pirate, causing no small consternation and terror to the merchants and inhabitants on the coast. Soon, however, he was himself made a prisoner, and taken by Saracens to Tunis, to be thrown into a dungeon. When the news of this catastrophe reached Constance, she, refusing to survive him, got into a boat, and gave herself up to the mercy of the winds. As chance would have it, a storm drove her frail bark to the very town in which her lover was imprisoned. In the meantime Tunis was attacked by enemies. Alcimides, as an experienced leader, was liberated, and the king not only promised to restore him to liberty, but even pledged himself to reward him, should he succeed in beating off the besiegers. Alcimedes defeated the enemy, was created Duke of Tunis, and, after numerous adventures, was at last united to Constance.[oo]

We shall not give an account of Greene's "Pandosto, or Dorastus and Faunia," for it is already well known,[79] and has served as the original for Shake-

[79] This pamphlet has been reprinted by Collier in the second volume of his "Shakspeare's Library" (London, 1843), and lately by Hazlitt in vol. iv. of

[oo] See Works, Vol. VII., pp. 23-42. By the kindness of a literary friend (Mr. W G. Stone) I find that "Perimedes" is a close copy of the story of Madonna Beritola Carraciola (Mariana) in the "Decamerone" Giorneta II., Novella VI. Greene has even made the nurse call the elder boy Procidor, doubtless because the nurse in Boccaccio's novel named her elder charge Gianotto di Procida.—G.

speare's *Winter's Tale*; we shall, moreover, have to allude to it in our last chapter. For the present we will merely draw attention to the preface and dedication. We can plainly hear the echoes of Greene's quarrels with contemporary authors. In the preface Greene points at certain "fond, curious, or rather currish backbiters," who "breathe out slaunderous speeches"; and in his dedication to the Earl of Cumberland he entreats the Earl to take his pamphlet under his protection thus: "I seeke to shroude this imperfect Pamphlet vnder your honours patronage, doubting the dint of such inuenomed vipers, as seeke with their slaunderous reproches to carpe at al, being oftentims, most vnlearned of all."[pp]

---

his "Shakspeare's Library" (London, 1875, 5 vols.). A minute account of it is given by Simrock in "Quellen des Shakspeares," and Fr. Hugo in vol. iv. of his "Œuvres Complètes de Shakspeare." Schack (in "Geschichte der dramatischen Literatur in Spanien," Band II., s. 338), in view of a strong similarity in many respects between Lope de Vega's "El Marmol de Felisardo" and Shakspeare's *Winter's Tale*, and also in view of the improbability that the former should have known Greene's pamphlet, suggests that De Vega and Greene were indebted to a common source. This guess has been confirmed more recently by Karo's investigations ("Ueber die eigentliche Quelle des Wintermärchens," in the *Magazin für die Literatur des Auslanaı*, 1863, No. 33), who has

[pp] See Works, Vol. IV., p. 231.—G.

On the 9th December, 1588, we find entered in the "Registers," among the books licensed to be printed, Greene's "Alcida," which was, however, not published until a little later.[80] We believe that it could hardly have been printed before the end of the following year, otherwise Nashe, in his "Anatomie of Absurditie," published in the autumn of 1589, could not have called Greene the "Homer of women." We are ignorant of the causes that could have influenced Greene to change his front so suddenly, and to send the shafts of his wit against the very sex which he had always so highly lauded. It is certain that all the tales of which "Alcida" is composed have a

---

very satisfactorily proved that Greene borrowed the plot of his pamphlet from some reproduction, which has not been preserved, of a Polish legend concerning the tragic fate of the wife of Duke Masovius Zemovitus. This legend was recorded by a contemporary, the Archbishop of Gnesen, Tcharikovski, in his chronicle, reprinted in the second volume of Sommersberg's "Rerum Silesiarum Scriptores" (Lipsiæ, 1729-32). From Tcharikovski's chronicle, or rather from the reproduction of the tale, Greene might have gleaned the interesting information made use of afterwards by Shakspeare in his drama, that Bohemia had a sea-coast.

[80] This is probably the reason why, under the entry in the "Registers" referring to it, the words "no sum stated" are put instead of the usual sixpence, the sum charged for every printing license. [No earlier edition known than 1617.—G.]

decided tendency, and were written for the purpose of exposing the want of character in women; their frivolity and love of gossip. For this tendency a friend of the author's, a certain Bubb, praises him in a laudatory poem prefixed to the work.[81]

The story is told by the author in the first person; who, having been shipwrecked, was thrown by a tempest on one of the islands on the African coast. He found refuge in the cottage of an old woman (Alcida), who took a great interest in him, and warmed and fed him. Noticing signs of internal sorrow on Alcida's countenance, the author asked the old woman to tell him her history. Instead of answering, the old woman led Greene to a marble pillar, which stood in the vicinity of the cottage, "fashioned and pourtraied like a woman." On approaching the pillar, the old woman clasped it in her arms and burst into tears. At last she composed herself, and told him the following story. Alcida was the daughter of a count, and in her youth she had been so beautiful that she was called the Venus of Taprobane. She married the ruling prince Cleomachus, by whom she had one son, who succeeded to the throne after her husband's death, and three daughters, the melancholy fate of whom caused her inconsolable grief. One Telegonus, the son of a count, fell in love with her eldest daughter, Fiordespine; but the proud beauty, mindful of her descent from a ruling prince, despised

[81] "Subtil are women, then it men behoves
To read, sweet friend, and over-read thy bookes,
To teach us ware of women's wanton lookes."

her suitor as beneath her in station. His passionate letters she answered by insulting messages, and his prayers and entreaties were met with coldness and contempt. The young man, unable to endure such cruelty, fell ill with grief, so that his life was despaired of. His parents appealed to Alcida to use her influence with her daughter, and to persuade her at least to look at the sufferer. Fiordespine, in obedience to her mother's wishes, went and visited Telegonus. Seeing him thin and suffering, without saying a word, she turned her back on him and smiled scornfully. For such cruelty Mercury turned her into a statue, and the young man died of grief on the spot.

After dinner Alcida led her guest into a thick forest. As soon as they had sat down in the shade of a magnificent cedar, a little bird flew up to them, and kept continually changing its colours. Alcida looked at it and sighed, and told her guest the story of her second daughter, Eriphila. Her second daughter was as clever and frivolous as her eldest was beautiful. After falling in love with the Duke of Meribates, she exchanged him for another lover, the latter for a third, and so on. When Meribates, who loved her passionately, remonstrated with her for her incontinence, she answered him very coolly: "*Si natura hominum sit novitatis avida*, giue women leaue to haue more fancies than one . . . *Venus* temple hath many entrances: Cupid hath more arrowes than one in his quiuer, and sundry strings to his bowe," etc. Meribates died of grief on hearing such arguments, and the gods, indignant at Eriphila's frivolity, changed her into a chameleon.

The next day Alcida led her guest to the sea-shore. Here Greene saw a stone slab, over which a rose-bush had spread out its branches. On asking her whose grave this was, Alcida told him the story of her third daughter, Marpesia. Grown wise by the melancholy example of her sisters, Marpesia endeavoured in every way to avoid the evil passions that had proved their ruin. But even she could not escape her fate. Venus, dissatisfied with her modesty and self-restraint, inspired her with a passion for one of her brother's attendants at court, the handsome young Eurimachus. Another courtier, Cleander by name, informed Marpesia's brother of her attachment, and Eurimachus was banished the country. Eurimachus knew whom he owed his banishment to, lay in wait for Cleander and killed him. In the meantime Marpesia fell ill with grief, and her brother, seeing her despair, permitted Eurimachus to return to court, and, with an aching heart, consented to his sister's marriage with a subject. But this marriage was not fated to take place, through Marpesia's fault. At one of their meetings she asked her lover what made him look so sad. Eurimachus confessed he had murdered Cleander, and that ever since his conscience gave him no peace. On the same day Marpesia confided Eurimachus' secret to a particular friend, this friend confided in another friend, etc., etc., and by the evening Marpesia's brother had heard of it. He immediately had Eurimachus arrested and tried. The court, founding its judgment on Eurimachus' own statements, condemned him to death. Standing on the scaffold, Eurimachus addressed a few parting words to the people, in which he told them he died a victim to a woman's love of gossip. Eurimachus was put to death and buried under the slab; and Marpesia came there so often to weep over his grave, that Venus took compassion on her, changed her into a rosebush, and placed her over his grave. When Alcida had finished her story a vessel neared the shore. The sailors recognised the author, and proposed to take him back to Alexandria. He bade farewell to Alcida, and went on board. But Alcida, on being left alone, wept so bitterly, that the gods in pity changed her into a well of tears.

The summer of 1588, which saw the threatened attack of the "Invincible Armada" of Philip II., was a critical moment in English history. It requires no profound knowledge of politics to understand that in this combat with Spain, England threw into the scale not only her own national independence, but the fate of Protestantism in Europe. Englishmen understood the momentousness of this crisis, influencing as it did the history of the world, and cheerfully contributed their last shilling towards the war expenditure. Success crowned the patriotic sacrifices of the English people; but the universal rejoicings that ensued at the destruction of the Spanish fleet were mixed with the dread of a new invasion, with which Catholic fanatics threatened England. In England people were convinced that matters would not end thus: that within a year or two Philip II. would risk a fresh attempt. These fears were very clearly expressed in the speech of the Lord Chancellor at the opening of Parliament in the February of the following year. The result was that Parliament immediately voted two subsidies for the war expenditure.[82] It is easy to imagine the excitement that reigned at the time, and the feelings cherished, not only against Spain, but against all Catholics in general, who were considered the chief cause of England's dangers. Under the influence of this feeling Greene's "Spanish Masquerado" was written, which appeared exactly at the time of the opening of Parliament.[83] In his preface Greene says that he had up to then written on love, but that now the time had come for him to disclose his religious opinions.[qq] The future rationalist appears here not only as a zealous Protestant, but also as a writer who takes his stand from a theological point of view. In the attempted invasion of the Spaniards he sees the hand of God, directed towards England for the purpose of awakening her religious enthusiasm; in Englishmen he sees God's weapons for the punishment of Spaniards for their pride and dishonesty. As a Protestant, Greene re-

[82] Knight, "The Popular History of England" (London, 1857), vol. ii., p. 238.

[83] In the Registers it is entered under 1st Feb., 1588.

[qq] I see no reason for this adjective; for there is every probability (and no proof to the contrary or shadow of proof) that Greene was as careless of religion and as given to all evil in 1588-9 as at any time of his life. Storojenko has spoken of the discrepancy between his life and his writings. But it may well be that the crisis awoke for the time, as it did in many, his better and more serious feelings; and it might also lead him to assimilate them in some degree to an accordance with the feelings of the times, to gain the more hearers and the more pence.—G.

peats what other Protestant writers had said at the time. He calls the Pope, Antichrist and Lucifer, and identifies the papal authority with that strange beast of which Ariosto speaks.[84] He thanks the Queen for the severe measures against the Catholics, and calls her the "glorious daughter of the illustrious Henry," who, treading in the steps of her father, had justly assumed to herself the right of supremacy in matters of faith, and had cleansed churches from absurd ideas and heresies. Greene praises Elizabeth especially for regarding the Pope as Antichrist, and seeing in the Catholic religion that Babylonian fornicatress of which mention is made in the Apocalypse. The fifth chapter is devoted to the consideration of the Catholic monks. Availing himself chiefly of Boccaccio's "Decameron," Greene cites many scandalous stories, calculated to lower the Catholic monastic system in his readers' eyes. The narrow Protestantism with which Greene's pamphlet is filled agrees but ill with his subsequent freethinking views; and we are involuntarily induced to believe that Greene's zeal against the Catholics was in a great measure the consequence of his indignation at the double-handed game they played during England's most critical year. Greene was in all probability acquainted with the Catholic plot to take advantage of the absence of troops from

---

[84] Greene here refers to the following lines of Ariosto:—

"Quisi una bestia uscir de la foresta
Parea di crudel vista, odiosa e belle
L'havea l'orechie d'Asino e la testa di Lupo," etc.

London, and, should the Spaniards effect a landing, to make a rising there, to release Arundel from the Tower, and, under his leadership, to join the Spaniards.[85]

Besides its historical and autobiographical value, Greene's pamphlet has no other; and at the present time it is difficult for us to understand how a production so very insignificant from a literary point of view could have called forth from his friends such enthusiastic praise. But the time was such, that every true patriot thought it his duty to welcome Greene as the champion of the honour and dignity of England, and to defend his name against the attacks "des gens séditieux," as Lodge expresses it in his French sonnet in honour of Greene—where, by-the-bye, he calls his friend the "compagnon des dieux."[86]

---

[85] Froude's "History of England from the Fall of Wolsey to the Defeat of the Spanish Armada" (Longman's edition, London, 1870), vol. xii., p. 355. [If the plot was known in 1589, of course Greene knew it; if it was not then publicly known, there is no probability that he knew it.—G.]

[86] "Ton nom, (mon Greene,) animé par mes vers,
Abaisse l'œil des gens séditieux
Tu de morteles compagnon des dieux, etc."

Simpson ("The School of Shakspeare," vol. ii., p. 364) thinks that by "gens séditieux" are meant Puritans, who commenced their attacks on the Church of England at that time in the person of John Penry ("Martin Marprelate"). But we think it more easy to suppose that Greene meant the Catholics, against whom the pamphlet was written.

The success of Sidney's "Arcadia," which appeared in the autumn of 1588,[87] [rr] moved Greene to try his hand at the pastoral style. In the August of 1589 he therefore published his pastoral tale entitled "Menaphon, or Arcadia,"[88] which was accompanied by Nashe's famous address to the students of Oxford and Cambridge. This address, as also a poem prefixed to "Menaphon," has only one object: the exaltation of Greene, and the complete discomfiture of those insolent dramatists who had not long before

---

[87] Although the oldest edition of Sidney's "Arcadia" that has come down to us is one of 1590, there is no doubt that this work was published two years earlier, as the following facts show: (1) Its entry in the "Registers," 23rd August, 1588; and (2) that Puttenham, in his "Arte of English Poesie," licensed to be printed 9th November, 1588, refers to the "Arcadia" as a universally known work. (Collier, "Bibliographical Catalogue," vol. ii., *sub voce*). [Not a tittle of evidence that Sidney's 'Arcadia' had been 'published' before 1590. Even then it was surreptitiously done, as every schoolboy knows. It was doubtless 'seen' privately.—G.]

[88] There exists a conviction even now, and shared by such authorities as Dyce and Collier, that Greene's "Menaphon" was first published in 1587, although no one has yet been able to discover the edition. Hazlitt, evidently also a believer in its existence, considered it necessary to add that he was unable to

[rr] The note of Professor Storojenko does not sustain the date of "1588." See our addition to note [87].—G.

satirised him from the stage boards. In the preface to his readers Greene gives us to understand that the whole tale bears reference to the disputes that had arisen.[89]

A friend of Greene's, Thomas Barnibe (the author of one of the poems prefixed to "Menaphon," who signs with the anagram Brabine), expresses himself more plainly, and, addressing Greene's censurers, ridicules their high-flown style, and challenges them to write anything that could equal "Menaphon."[90]

---

give any information with regard to this edition (*vide* "Handbook to the Early English Literature," p. 238). In our opinion, the belief in this early edition is founded on one of those misunderstandings which frequently occur in the chronicles of literature. My reasons for supposing that the edition of 1589 is the earliest have been given at length in *Notes and Queries*, 3rd December, 1873. [If "Menaphon" 1589 had been the first edition, it would have had "Utriusque Acad. in Art. Mag."—G.]

[89] An attempt to solve the problem has been made by Simpson (*vide* "School of Shakspeare," vol. ii., pp. 355-56, and 370-72), who is of opinion that Greene's "Doron" is a skit on Shakspeare.

[90] "Come forth you wits, that vaunt the pomp of speech,
And strive to thunder from a stageman's throat;
View Menaphon, a note beyond your reach,
Whose sight will make your drumming descant doat,
Players, avaunt! you know not to delight;
Welcome, sweet shepherd, worth a scholar's sight."

[**] The biographer assigns to Greene himself here what belongs to Nashe, and to him only indirectly.—G.

Besides, Nashe's Epistle leaves no doubt that this is the continuation of the affair we are already acquainted with. Addressing the students of Oxford and Cambridge, Nashe cautions them against an exaggerated, fashionable, high-flown style, the use of which can only be explained by a desire slavishly to imitate the grandiloquent diction of "vainglorious tragedians, who contend not so seriouslie to excell in action, as to embowell the clowdes, to outbrave better pens with the swelling bumbast of a bragging blanke verse." [tt] Comparing this passage with Greene's preface to "Perimides," we can easily conjecture whom Nashe is aiming at. But the success of Marlowe, who had taken his M.A. degree at Cambridge, could not hurt Greene's self-love to such an extent as that of dramatists who were not only without a university education, but had not even visited any respectable school; and who, following in the footsteps of Marlowe, and having acquired his high-flown dramatical diction and blank verse, had met with the sympathy and applause of the theatre-going public. It was against these half-educated writers—whom Nashe very characteristically calls "lacklatines" — who allowed themselves the liberty, into the bargain, of ironically sneering at former literary celebrities, that the most venomous sarcasms of Nashe are directed. That Nashe here hints at Shakspeare,—as Simpson supposes,—is not at all improbable,[uu] considering

[tt] See Works, Vol. VI., pp. 9-10.—G.

[uu] Most improbable; for none of Shakespeare's present plays were then written. He had in all probability been then less than three years an actor.—G.

that Shakspeare, who had then already commenced his dramatic career, might well be classed with the genus "lack-latin," who not unfrequently united in one person the qualities of actor and playwright, and were dangerous rivals of Greene's. From these ill-mannered phrase-mongers, "that feed on nought but the crummes that fal from the translators trencher,"[77] Nashe passes on to Greene's "Menaphon," and praises his friend for originality of thought, and that *temperatum dicendi modus* which Cicero considers the first condition of eloquence. With regard to the former it is difficult to give an opinion, as we do not know the original source of "Menaphon," but as for Greene's style Nashe's partial view may, in our opinion, be explained by his wish to contrast the less elaborate style of Greene with the figurative and extravagant diction of his literary opponents. It is certainly true that "Menaphon" is less euphuistical than those pamphlets of Greene's that had preceded it; and it is also true that Greene frequently ridicules the style of his master Lylly[91]; but nevertheless the

[91] When Samela answers Melicertus with Euphuisms in the style of Lylly, Greene adds humorously, "Samela made this replie, because she heard him so superfine, as if Ephæbus [one of the characters of Lylly's novel, a friend of Euphues] had learnd him to refine his mother tongue, wherefore thought he had done it of an inkhorne desire to be eloquent, and Melicertus thinking that Samela had learnd with Lucilla [the heroine of "Euphues"] . . . . . to anato-

[77] Works, Vol. VI., p. 10.—G.

language of "Menaphon" is far removed from the simplicity of Greene's later works, and if the author can be praised at all, it is perhaps for his endeavour to leave the tutelage of Lylly and to write less artificially and less gorgeously.

But the contents of "Menaphon" are very different from the love-pamphlets that we have reviewed. The plot, extremely complicated, and full of effective although improbable incidents, completely shuts out the didactic element. The tale opens thus:—Menaphon, the shepherd of King Democles, was sitting on the sea-shore, indulging in melancholy reflections on the vanity and insignificance of love, when he suddenly descried a wrecked vessel which the tempest had driven on shore. Out of this vessel two persons stepped, saved by a sort of miracle. These were—a dignified old man, and, leaning on him, a beautiful woman with a child in her arms. She was Sephestia, the daughter of King Democles, who had been banished by her father, and the old man was a relative of hers, Lamedon by name. One glance hurriedly

---

mize wite and speake none but *Similes*, imagined she smoothed her talke to be thought like Sapho, Phaon's Paramour. [Lylly wrote a comedy entitled *Sapho and Phaos*.] In another place he makes the following remark: "Thus ended this merrie eclogue betwixte Doron and Carmela: which, Gentlemen, if it be stufft with prettie Similies and farre-fetched Metaphors; thinke the poore Country-lovers knewe no further comparisons, then came within compasse of their Country Logicke."

thrown by Menaphon on Sephestia sufficed to prove to him the weakness and fallacy of his pessimist philosophy; and, after talking with her for a few minutes, Menaphon felt himself transported to the seventh heaven. In her conversation with Menaphon Sephestia did not give her real name, but called herself Samela, a native of Cipres, and the widow of a gentleman who had only lately died. Menaphon invited the travellers to take up their abode with him for the time being. On arriving at Menaphon's modest hut, both Samela and Lamedon, fatigued by the events of the preceding day, soon went to sleep; but Menaphon could for a long time find no rest,—the enchanting form of the stranger could not be banished from his mind. The next day, after breakfast, they all went out for a walk, and Menaphon, taking advantage of the opportunity, as soon as he was left alone with her, lost no time in discovering his feelings to Samela. The answer, however, was not very satisfactory. Samela, who had not yet become accustomed to her new rôle, began to say something to the effect that in love an equality of social status in both parties was indispensable. As Menaphon grew paler and paler at these words, she hastened to gild the pill by adding, that love does not enter a woman's heart suddenly, that it takes time, etc. Menaphon was too naïve to understand the bitter meaning of this polite refusal, and resolved to wait until she would learn to love him. He therefore entreated Samela and her companion to stay a little longer with him, to which these consented. Living thus in Menaphon's house, Samela gradually got accustomed to his surroundings, and began to take an interest in shepherd life; she even frequently drove his cattle out to graze. Menaphon, on his part, desirous of offering his beautiful guest some amusement, invited Samela to come to a pastoral fête; to which she went, previously disguising herself in the clothes of Carmela, Menaphon's sister.

Unfortunately for Menaphon, Samela met there a shepherd, Melicertus by name, whose amiable features strongly reminded her of her deceased husband. At the sight of Melicertus Samela was unable to hide her pleasure, and the joyous expression of her face was at once detected by Menaphon's jealous heart. From thenceforth Samela and Melicertus met frequently, and it may be imagined that each time a meeting was effected they could not part without paying each other elaborate compliments and making elegant speeches, in the style of Lylly's "Euphues." Parallel with the love-story of Melicertus and Samela, that of a certain shepherd Doron and the shepherdess Carmela developes. Thus days, and even years passed on, until an unsuspected and afflicting occurrence put an end to this idyl, which was growing more and more uncomfortable for poor Menaphon, who was still waiting and hoping, and loving Samela. It so happened that Samela's son, Pleusidippus, was carried off by pirates, who made a present of him to the king of Thessaly, Agenor. When she heard of this, Samela was inconsolable, and gave way to the wildest despair and grief. Menaphon, with a want of delicacy common to his class, tried to comfort her by saying that she should not kill herself over a lost son, as she had only to wish it and she could have another. Samela was indignant, said many unpleasant things, and finished by leaving him altogether. She took up her abode in the neighbourhood, in the cottage of another shepherd, which had been bought her by Lamedon.

There she lived many years, mourning over her son, and living in the hope of finding him again, sooner or later. In the meantime Pleusidippus grew up at the court of the wise king Agenor, who loved him as if he were his own son. On arriving at man's estate he fell in love with Agenor's daughter Olympia, was considered her intended husband, and would most likely have soon married her. But at a dinner at the king's, one of the guests, who had just returned from Arcadia, told the young man wonders of the beauty of the shepherdess Samela. The youth's heart was inflamed, he forgot the promises he had made to Olympia, the kindness shown him by her father, and started for Arcadia to find the incomparable shepherdess. Here Greene heaps one improbability on the other. Not content with making Pleusidippus fall in love with Samela, he makes the old king Democles appear on the scene among the number of suitors for her hand. When Samela, who had given her word to Melicertus, refuses both, old Democles, with the aid of Pleusidippus, seizes and carries her away to a castle (pp. 116-17). At last the appearance of an old prophetess, who discloses the real name of Samela, cuts this Gordian knot of complications and improbabilities. Melicertus discovers himself to Samela as her husband Maximian, whom she had believed dead. Old Democles, ashamed of his conduct, begs his daughter's pardon, and invites her to come and live with him, with her husband; while he makes Pleusidippus, who marries Olympia, the heir to his throne.

Among Greene's literary labours in 1589, his "Ciceronis Amor, Tullie's Love," which has been omitted in the "Registers," must not be forgotten.[92] This tale, together with "Dorastus and Faunia," belong to his most popular productions. Collier enumerates ten editions of it between 1589 and 1639. Greene himself, however, esteemed it much less than "Menaphon."[**] In the preface he excuses himself for having written his story in a worse style than usual, stating in extenuation that the endeavour to imitate Cicero entangled him in a labyrinth of affected and vague expressions, etc. After the preface follow several poems in praise of the author —one by the celebrated Petrarchist, Thomas Watson,

---

[92] The only copy extant of the first edition of this work is the property of a private gentleman in England. [Alfred H. Huth, Esq., London.—G.] We made use of a later edition (1605) at the British Museum.

[**] "Menaphon" is not named, and the Epistle "to the Gentle Readers" (Vol. VII., p. 102), merely shams self-depreciation. He does not hesitate to tell Lord Strange (p. 100) that "Tullie's Love" was "the fruite of well-intended thoughts." Compare "Conclusion" of one of the best and most finished of his later books, "The Mourning Garment" (Vol. VIII., pp. 220-22); and so *frequenter*.—G.

and another signed by an old friend and patron of Greene's, Thomas Burnaby.[11]

Here is a short abstract of the story. In Rome there lived a highly respected senator, Flaminius by name, with whose daughter, the proud and inaccessible Terentia, Lentulus, a young general who had only just returned to Rome from a victory over the Parthians, falls in love. The story opens with a feast given by Flaminius in honour of Lentulus. At table the conversation turns on love, jealousy, and questions of a similar character. Lentulus and Archias are the chief disputants. After dinner, during a walk, Lentulus has the opportunity of becoming better acquainted with Terentia, who has completely bewitched him. He, on the other hand, without in the least suspecting it, has made a deep impression on one of Terentia's friends, Flavia. On returning home, Lentulus finds, awaiting him at his house, a friend of his, who has not come alone, but has brought Cicero with him, then a youth of twenty, but already famous for his eloquence. Lentulus soon becomes intimate with Cicero, confides to him his secret, and, calculating on the eloquence of his friend, entreats him to dictate a letter to Terentia which she would be unable to resist. The poor fellow forgot that there was only one Cicero at Rome, and that his style was too well known to be adopted by another without detection. On receiving this elegant epistle from Lentulus, Terentia could not refrain from showing it to her friend Flavia, who immediately discovered who its real

[11] Another by Edward Rainsford, besides a Hexasticon by "G. B."—G.

author was. Terentia had already heard much of Cicero, and now began seriously to think of him. Mischievous Cupid took advantage of this opportunity, and shot off one of his arrows into her heart. Under the influence of feelings by which she was suddenly seized, she wrote Lentulus so harsh and hopeless a refusal, that he took to his bed from sheer grief. On his part, Cicero had soon an opportunity of meeting Terentia, and fell in love with her passionately; but, knowing she was loved by Lentulus, he resolved to subdue his feelings. He remained firm to his purpose, even when Terentia herself declared her love to him, and, regardless of his own personal happiness, he entreated her to forget him, and to give her heart to Lentulus; assuring her that Lentulus was more capable of rendering her happy.

The situation becomes still more complicated by the appearance of a third lover, in the person of Fabius, a youth whom Terentia has met in a forest, and who also falls in love with her. This youth, who has up to the present been a pattern of dissoluteness, and who had been banished to the country by his father for his extravagances, suddenly changes, under the influence of love, and becomes a model good young man. Greene explains this change very curiously, by saying, that the noble qualities which this youth had received from heaven were hidden by envious Fate in the remotest corners of his heart; but Love, being a stronger power than Fate, broke through the restraint, and nature asserted itself. Consequently, Greene adds, we should look on Love as one of the purest and noblest emotions that man is capable of. Returning to Terentia, we may state that she was as little moved by the love of Fabius as by that of Lentulus. Her heart belonged entirely to Cicero. In the meantime, the latter, seeing his friend was not getting better, carried his self-abnegation so far as to go to Terentia's father, and, after telling him the whole story, to ask him to exert his parental influence in favour of Lentulus. But this act cost Cicero dearly; and he was himself obliged to take to his bed. When Flaminius informed his daughter of the object of Cicero's visit, Terentia, especially indignant that Cicero, knowing her love for him, had resolved to sacrifice her to his friendship, wrote him a letter. In this she warned him that women go to extremes in their passions, and that their love, if refused, easily changes into deadly hate. This letter found Cicero already prostrate in bed. On reading it, he lost consciousness and fainted, whilst the letter dropped out of his hands. Just at this moment Lentulus entered the room, to visit his friend. Finding a letter lying on the floor, he picked it up and read it, as they had no secrets from each other. The discovery he made by the perusal sobered Lentulus at once. He saw what noble self-abnegation Cicero had exercised, and he resolved to be worthy of his friend, and to do all in his power to bring about the happy union of Terentia with the disinterested object of her affections. Not so thought hot-blooded young Fabius, the other competitor for Terentia's fair hand. Offended at the preference shown to Cicero, he assembled his followers and clients, and determined to kill his more fortunate rival. As soon as rumours of Fabius' plan reached Lentulus, he collected his friends and partisans, and stood guard over Cicero's house. This affair might have easily grown into a civil broil, as both parties had many friends in Rome. To prevent bloodshed, the senate took upon itself to settle the matter. While the question was being discussed in the senate, Cicero appeared, and in an eloquent speech declared himself ready to offer his love on the altar of public peace, as he had offered it up on that of friendship. This speech had such an effect on the hearers, that Fabius, thoroughly ashamed of himself, publicly resigned all claims on Terentia. The latter, at the advice of a senator, was there and then betrothed to Cicero, and Lentulus married Flavia, who had loved him so long.

The year 1590 signalises, as we have already stated in our previous chapter, the turning-point in Greene's literary labours, which from henceforth assumed a moral and edifying tendency, and were not infrequently devoted to the exposure of public scandals. Besides the story of "Orpharion," written much earlier (at least two years before), Greene published during this year two original pamphlets: "Mourning Garment" and "Never too Late," and a translation of a moral thesis entitled "The Royal Exchange." We shall speak of these works in the order of their entry in the "Registers."

The "Orpharion" was written by Greene in 1588, at the same time as "Perimides," or perhaps even earlier; at all events, in his 'Address to the Gentlemen Readers' in the latter Greene speaks of it as a work already completed.[98] The word "Orpharion" means a village musical instrument, like a lute, and is used by Greene to denote that his work is as inartistic and rough as a village lute.[77] There is no especially moral or edifying tendency discernible in this "Orpharion"; on the contrary, it resembles in character the former love-pamphlets of Greene. This

[98] This was first noticed by Hazlitt (*vide* "Collections and Notes," London, 1876, p. 192). The earliest edition that has come down to us of "Orpharion" is dated 1599; but that an earlier edition must have existed is proved by "Greene's Funeralls" (London, 1594), where this novel is mentioned together with other works of Greene's. In his preface Greene says that "Orpharion" lay with the publishers a whole year. In that case the entry of it in the "Registers" under 9th February, 1589-90, must refer to the first edition. We cannot understand how Collier could—keeping these facts in view—have raised the question of the authenticity of his pamphlet. [Collier had no insight or critical faculty. Greene does not say 'Orpharion' was "a work already completed." Here are his words—"which I promise to make you merry with next tearme." This is confirmed by the dates: "Perimides" 1588, "Orpharion" 1589. Therefore when "Perimides" was published he was probably engaged on "Orpharion"—*i.e.*, he was either writing it, or had planned it.—G.]

[77] Storojenko mistakes. See title and preface. He calls his work 'harsh' (with his usual sham depreciation), but he does not call the instrument, the Orpharion, 'harsh,' but the contrary. See text.—G.

fantastical story consists of the description of an imaginary dream, that the author had on the top of Mount Erecinus, during a sleep into which he is supposed to have been lulled by the sounds of a Pan's-pipe. The author dreamed he was carried away to Olympus, where he assisted at a feast given by Jupiter to the other gods and goddesses. To amuse the guests, Orpheus and Arion were summoned from the lower regions. The former told a story of the cruel daughter of Astolpho, King of Lydia, who treated a certain knight, called Acestes, who loved her sincerely, most inhumanly. To please her, Acestes conquered whole empires for her father, but neither his courage nor his devotion moved her hard heart. When, in despair, he went over to the side of the enemy, and defeated her father, she contrived, by her prayers and coquetry, to deprive him of the fruits of his victories. But this was not enough: some time afterwards Astolpho and his daughter succeeded in treacherously securing Acestes' person, and condemned him to the tortures of a death by starvation. Acestes died; but the people, enraged at such conduct, revolted, and killed the king, condemning his daughter to the same kind of death she had devised for Acestes.

Arion's story is less melancholy. One Philomenes, the ruling prince of Corinth, married Argentina, the daughter of one of his subjects. The fame of Argentina's wit and beauty extended so far, that one of the neighbouring kings, Marcion by name, was inflamed with the desire of carrying her off by force of arms. Under some frivolous pretext he declared war against Philomenes, defeated his army and drove him out of Corinth. But it was not so easy to conquer the virtue of Argentina, who continued faithful to her banished husband. Marcion employed all the means in his power to induce her to love him; and in these fruitless attempts whole years passed away. Either because she got tired of this persecution or wished to get rid of him, Argentina made Marcion the following proposal: she promised to give him her hand, but only on condition that after a three-days total abstinence from food, he would prefer her to any viands. If, however, he should break down, he was to promise to leave her alone for the future. Marcion accepted the challenge, was locked up in a tower and starved for three days. On the fourth day Argentina came to release him from his voluntary confinement; but she did not come alone,—she was attended by a servant carrying a dish full of steaming and savoury delicacies. At the sight of the welcome food, the ravenous Marcion forgot his promise, and Argentina, and fell on the viands to allay his hunger. Of course he had lost his wager, but, astonished at the virtue and wisdom of Argentina, he not only left off persecuting her, but restored her husband to the throne.

Two months later than the entry of "Orpharion" we find entered in the "Registers" a new work of Greene's entitled "The Royal Exchange," a collection of moral aphorisms, translated chiefly from the Italian.[94] From the fact of this work being dedicated

---

[94] Storojenko's note here is superseded by ours in

to the Lord Mayor and citizens of London, it is evident that Greene had already begun to tune his lyre to moral strains before he published his "Mourning Garment," as "The Royal Exchange" may be considered a kind of prologue to his subsequent ethical pamphlets.

"But nowe," he writes, "honourable Cittizens, looke not into my Exchange for any wealthy traffique of curious merchandize . . . onely thys Exchange is royall, and the Phylosophers sette abroche theyr principles."[22]

Under the 2nd of November, 1590, we find an entry in the "Registers" of Greene's "Mourning Garment," the herald to a series of moral tales of his. There is every reason to believe that this direction of his literary labours was the consequence of his own bitter experiences. For in both tales we find seductive courtesans, who catch inexperienced youths in their snares, and pick them clean; while the author, in describing their cunning devices, frequently interrupts the thread of his narrative with virulent invectives, which clearly bear the impress of personal anger. In the dedication to the Earl of Cumberland, Greene compares himself to Nineveh, suddenly awakened

Vol. VII., p. 218, and by the "Royal Exchange" itself. [Works, Vol. VII., pp. 217—326.] He adds, "It is my agreeable duty to testify my deep gratitude to Professor M. M. Kovaleffsky, my fellow-professor, for the copy he has taken of this great bibliographical curiosity."

[22] See Works, Vol. VII., p. 227.—G.

from a state of sinful forgetfulness of the future by the prophetic words of Jonah.[aaa] In conclusion, Greene flatters himself with the hope that his lordship will be pleased to hear of the repentance of a second Ovid.[bbb]

Well aware that people who had known anything of his former life would doubt the sincerity of his contrition, Greene, in his address to the students of Oxford and Cambridge, implores them to trust the sincerity of his work. "The Grecians," he says, "would not heare Antisthenes dispute of the immortality of the soule, because his former Philosophy was to the contrary. Sodain changes of mens affects crave great wonder, but little beliefe; and such as alter in a moment, win not credit in a moneth. These premisses (Gentlemen) drives me into a quandary, fearing I shall hardly insinuate into your favours, with changing the titles of my Pamphlets, or make you beleeve the inward metamorphosis of my minde, by the exterior shew of my workes, seeing I have ever professed myselfe Love's Philosopher."[ccc]

Let us now turn to the story itself. In the town of Callipolis, situated on the banks of the Euphrates, there lived a very worthy Jewish family; the father, a rabbi, distinguished for extraordinary kindness of heart and wisdom, and two sons. The elder of these, Sophonos by name, was of a quiet disposition, and used to help his father in looking after the house. The younger, however, Philador, who possessed a

---

[aaa] See Works, Vol. IX., pp. 119-20.—G.
[bbb] *Ibid.*, p. 121.—G. [ccc] *Ibid.*, p. 122.—G.

lively imagination and a passionate temperament, could find no satisfaction in quiet family life. He had hardly come of age when he besieged his father with entreaties to be allowed to go and see the world. It was in vain that his father, grown wise from experience, pleaded with him to remain at home, assuring him that he would learn no good abroad. In Spain he would be contaminated by pride, in Italy by dissoluteness, in England by gluttony, in Denmark by intemperance; and, the old man added, he would return home morally disfigured and mutilated. But the son obstinately persisted. Seeing that nothing but personal experience would convince the youth, the old man at last consented reluctantly. He gave him a good round sum of money, and let him go wherever he liked, having previously furnished him with all sorts of injunctions as to how he was to behave himself in foreign lands. Many wise counsels did the old rabbi give his son; and he especially advised him to avoid the society of women, for these "Adamants that drawe, Panthers that allure, and Syrens that entice," were the cause of the ruin of many youths. Philador listened to all his father's advice attentively, and started on his journey. At first he bore his father's injunctions in mind, behaved himself cautiously in relation to women, and, notwithstanding all sorts of temptation, remained invulnerable. After much travel he came to Thessaly, where he made the acquaintance of a shepherd and shepherdess, who led a blissful existence in a luxuriant valley watered by a sparkling stream. The description of their life is full of pastoral charm.

In a song which the shepherdess is made to sing to the accompaniment of her husband's pipe she praises the delights of a pastoral life, and shows its superiority over the restless and careworn life of kings.

Having passed the night with these happy shepherds, Philador left them for the neighbouring town. The shepherd, who volunteered to be his guide, warned him not to stop at the inn of the sign of the unicorn, kept by three beautiful sisters, seductive as syrens, and cruel and mischievous as Circes. But the shepherd's account of these young women only awakened our traveller's curiosity, and made him wish to make their acquaintance. When he entered the dreadful inn he certainly found that the sisters exceeded his expectations. Each of them was perfection in her style. Nevertheless, the youngest pleased Philador's fancy most; and she, noticing this, coquetted with him unconscionably. Philador put up at the sisters', who succeeded in robbing him so thoroughly that he was soon without a penny, when he was most unceremoniously turned out into the streets. Finding himself thus houseless, and without money or friends, Philador felt rather desperate. Fortunately he met a farmer, who took compassion on his youth and his misfortunes, and took him home with him to be his herdsman. The subsequent history of Philador strongly resembles that of the "Prodigal Son."[ddd] After going through all manner of miseries for some time, Philador penitently returned to his father, made a long speech,

[ddd] St. Luke xv.—G.

told him his adventures, and asked his forgiveness. The father, who had believed him lost, not only forgave him, but gave a grand feast in honour of his return. As in the parable, the eldest son was angry that his father should show such distinction to his dissolute brother. The story concludes with a shepherd's song in honour of Philador. In the afterwords Greene once more entreats his readers to forget the errors of his youth, and to receive cordially this the first fruit of his new resolutions.

"Never too Late," which appeared also in 1590,[96] bears still stronger traces of Greene's personal experience. The story is told in the first person. The author, in a journey to Italy, meets a compatriot of his, Francesco, near Bergamo, in Lombardy, attired in the garb of a pilgrim, and evidently smitten with grief and heartfelt contrition. In the first part of the story Francesco tells the author ("The Palmer's Tale") the adventures that had befallen him since the

[96] Owing probably to the carelessness of the clerk, we find no entry of this pamphlet in the "Registers," but a copy dated 1590 is in the library of the British Museum. The pamphlet consists of two parts, each of which has a separate dedication to Thomas Barneby, at whose expense it was printed. The motto of the first part is Greene's curious posy, "Omne tulit punctum"; the motto to the second is "Sero, sed serio," the same that is prefixed to the "Mourning Garment," to show that from henceforth his literary labours would enter a new field. [See our former note; also our Introduction on this.—G.]

day he left England. He gives a minute description of Paris, the French court and society, sketches refined life at Lyons, and severely condemns French women for their frivolity and coquetry. Germany he shows in its most unattractive light, as the country of gloom and savagery, devoted to drunkenness and religious controversies. The only exception is Vienna, which even then struck travellers as a second Paris. Francesco's story, and the views he expresses with regard to women and actors, are so like Greene's own, that we are involuntarily brought to believe that Greene represented himself under the garb of Francesco, as he afterwards did under the name of Roberto in the "Groatsworth of Wit." Francesco relates how he married the daughter of a gentleman, called Isabella; how he frivolously deserted her, and formed an intimacy with a courtesan, Infida, who robbed him; how he consequently fell into extreme poverty, from which he was rescued by accidentally meeting some actors, who recognised his talents and invited him to work for the theatre; how he soon rose to fame in this career, etc., etc. Although the story is told by Francesco,—reminding us in many instances of his own,—Greene does not infrequently make digressions that betray his own personal feelings. Thus, for instance, on the subject of Infida's deceitful conduct, he addresses the following words to his readers: "Where, by the way (gentlemen), let vs note," etc.***

*** See Works, Vol. VIII., p. 90.—G.

In another place Greene speaks even more cynically of women.[fff]

The first part concludes with the rupture between Francesco and Infida, his contrition and firm resolution to return to his deserted wife. In the second part the reconciliation between husband and wife takes place; the latter, seeing Francesco's sincere repentance, magnanimously forgiving him everything. The reconciliation scene between husband and wife, which unfortunately had no place in Greene's actual life, is described with such simplicity, and at the same time with such touching sincerity, because probably the feelings ascribed to Francesco were those of the author.

The last of the series of moral and partly autobiographical works of Greene's is his pamphlet "Farewell to Follie." This production, which was composed several years before (for it was mentioned in the "Registers" in 1587), did not appear till 1591; and then, there is not the least doubt, in a considerably different form from that wherein it had been previously written. To this tale are prefixed a dedication to Robert Cary, and an extremely interesting address of

---

[fff] See Works, Vol. VIII., pp. 107, 165. 'Cynically' is not the best word. I must doubt whether Greene in this tale, or elsewhere, ever speaks 'cynically' of woman generally. He speaks 'cynically' of "strange women"; but throughout differentiates them from true women, whom he contrasts with them, thus showing that the memory of Isabel [= Dorothy] was still pleasing to him, and thus refuting Storojenko's harsh misjudgment of Greene's wife (p. 19, [b]). The date 1587 below shows more than one fit of repentance and relapse.—G.

Greene's to the students of Oxford and Cambridge, throwing much light on his relations with a contemporary dramatist. In the preface to his "Mourning Garment," Greene already expressed the opinion that in all probability his literary enemies would doubt the sincerity of his repentance, which was so sudden as to astonish even his friends, and that they would lose no opportunity of ridiculing him.

From the poem of one of Greene's friends—Ralph Sedley—prefixed to the second part of "Never too Late," we can gather that there was no lack of attacks and jeers.[96] It is to these that Greene refers in his dedication of the "Farewell to Follie." Having stated that that pamphlet was written to justify the expectations of his friends, and to inform the public of his determination henceforward to tread the path of virtue and truth, Greene goes on to say: "But .... some are so peremptorie in their opinions, that if Diogenes stirre his stumpes, they will saie, it is to mocke dancers, not to be wanton, that if the fox preach, tis to spie which is the fattest goose, not to be a ghostly father," etc.[97] [sss]

---

[96] "The more it works the quicker is the wit,
The more it writes, the better to be 'steem'd;
By labour ought men's wills and wits be 'deem'd,
Though dreaming dunces do inveigh against it;
But write thou on, though Momus sit and frown,
A carter's jig is fittest for a clown."

[97] Greene refers to a contemporary puritanical agitator, known under the pseudonym of "Martin Marprelate," who attacked the Church of England

[sss] See Works, Vol. IX., p. 228.—G.

From this dedication we can gather that by "follie" Greene means his love-pamphlets, and that, consequently, by saying "Farewell to Follie," Greene says farewell to his former literary productions.[hhh] In his address to the students of Oxford and Cambridge Greene uses the word folly in a broader sense, and means by it all amorous distractions and vanities of life.[iii]

The German scholar, Bernhardi,[89] as far as we know, was the first to conjecture that Greene here hits at a contemporaneous play called *The Fair*

---

and her defenders most virulently, Lylly and Nashe among the number, and not improbably also Greene. [Not a shadow of evidence that Greene had aught to do with the Marprelate tractates.—G.]

[88] Battilus [Bathyllus], a Roman poet of no talent, who passed off several poems of Virgil for his own. [See ref. *infra.*—G.]

[89] "Robert Greene's Leben und Schriften," p. 40 *et seq.*

[hhh] To be taken *cum grano.* The life had been madly foolish, not the books, and his remorseful preface was to sunder himself from his past. It was a morbid misjudgment to equalize his (so-called) love-pamphlets with his evil life. In Henry Vaughan the Silurist we have another example of how a new-awakened nature regarded harshly quite innocent secular poems. See Works by me in "FULLER WORTHIES' LIBRARY," (4 vols.).—G.

[iii] Here (and throughout), instead of quoting with Storojenko, the reader will please turn and read the entire Epistle, in Works, Vol. IX., pp. 230-33. See also note [88] on Battillus.—G.

Emm, where the passages occur that Greene refers to. Who the author of this play was, and what roused Greene's indignation against him, Bernhardi does not say. But Simpson unhesitatingly declares the author of *Fair Emm* to be no other than Shakspeare. Leaving the question of the authorship of this play for our last chapter, we come to the contents of the "Farewell to Follie."

Greene's tale is properly speaking no tale at all, but a dispute (which takes place at a villa near Florence) on different vices and passions, such as pride, love, intemperance, etc. These discussions have interspersed—according to a custom inherited by Greene from the Italian novelists—tales, supposed to be told by the disputants in support of their arguments. Thus, in the first discussion, on Pride, one of the speakers, Peratio, expresses his opinion that this vice is peculiar to military men, who are always associating their actions with ideas of honour and glory; and in confirmation of his words he tells a story. His opponent, Bernardino, uses the same method in proving that pride is as much a scholarly as a military vice. In the next discussion, on Love and the follies it gives rise to, one of the disputants gives force to his arguments by telling the well-known story of Ninus and Semiramis. On the next day the conversation turns on Intemperance of every kind; which gives the speakers an opportunity of remembering the gluttons and drunkards of the world, and displaying a rare knowledge of anecdotes and personal history. In conclusion Bernardino tells a story of a certain Duke Antonio of Augsburg, who was fond of getting intoxicated, and in this condition committed various acts of injustice.

The construction of "Farewell to Follie" bears a strong resemblance to that of Greene's love-pamphlets. According to Greene's own statement it is the last debt he paid to his former frivolous literary tendencies. Indeed, soon after—as already seen—the publication in 1591 of his "Farewell to Follie," Greene published a whole series of works, having for their object the exposure of impostors and villains. The first of these is "The Notable Discovery of Coosnage," and is entered in the "Registers" under the 13th December, 1591. In the long preface to the reader, Greene avers that this production is an act of penitence on his part for his misspent youth. "Diogenes," he says, "from a counterfeit Coiner of money, became a currant corrector of manners, as absolute in the one, as dissolute in the other," and then he applies this and other classical things to his own case.[111]

The aim of this pamphlet is purely practical: to warn inexperienced country people, coming up to London, of the cunning snares laid for them by the London sharpers. For this purpose Greene minutely describes the favourite arts of these "connycatchers," and acquaints the reader with the cant terms of their thieves' language, etc. The most dangerous to the purse of the poor countryman are the card-sharpers and panders; the latter often possessing such gentlemanly manners, that they are capable of deceiving even more experienced people. Greene

[111] See Works, Vol. X., pp. 5—13.—G.

describes this peculiar branch of knavery, "the art of cross-biting," not without humour. Here cards are superseded by women, the wives, sisters and mistresses of the conycatchers, who are made to ensnare country folk in their toils, whilst the men afterwards adroitly play the part of jealous husbands and offended brothers, and not infrequently demand pretty round sums for the alleged insults offered to their family honour. In the same year (1591) Greene managed to get printed "The Second and Last Part of Connycatching," which contains a few more exposures of this art. On the 7th February of the following year we find an entry in the "Registers" of a licence granted to Cuthbert Burbie, to print "The Third and Last Part of Connycatching."[kkk] Greene says, at the beginning of this pamphlet, that he had intended to confine himself to two parts of "Connycatching," but having one day accidentally met a justice of the peace who had frequently examined conycatchers and taken down their evidence, he determined to make use of the information procured from so experienced a personage, and this had given occasion to the production of the third part of his work. These pamphlets of Greene's, though they raised him

---

[kkk] Storojenko has misread the entry. The booklet was published by Cuthbert Burbie, but printed by Th. Scarlet, and it was to this latter that it was entered in "Stat. Reg." It is doubtful why some books were entered to their publishers and some to their printers. The reason of the distinction must have been connected in some way with this other fact—viz., that a book is entered to a publisher with the proviso that a certain printer shall always print it.—G.

in his own self-respect, caused the greatest indignation in the conycatchers' camp. In the previous chapter we have shown, from Greene's own words, how these gentry concocted a plan to murder him, and how this plan miscarried, through a fortunate accident. Rage on the part of persons whose profession had been exposed to society and the authorities; whose income, owing to this exposure, had considerably diminished, and whose chances of getting hanged had as considerably increased, is comprehensible. But that Greene's comrades in letters not only gave him no credit for his noble aims and the fine courage he had displayed, but even took advantage of this circumstance to lower him in the eyes of the world, is incomprehensible. Greene had hardly published his first two pamphlets when some unknown writer,[100] hiding under the pseudonym of "A Connycatcher," printed "The Defence of Connycatching," which is full of furious abuse of the exposer.[111] On reading Greene's pamphlet, he says, he found his art was as faithfully and graphically described by the author as if he had himself practised it for a considerable period. Having heard that the author of this pamphlet was famed in literature, a master of arts, and himself a conycatcher in his way, and having carefully studied his works, the writer was astonished at the folly of a

[100] Nashe, in "Have with you to Saffron Walden" (1596), says that Harvey's "hang-by," one Valentine Bird, wrote against Greene. Might he not have been the author of "The Defence of Conny-catching"?

[111] See note [97] (p. 30).—G.

man who thus pursues a gnat but does not observe an elephant. Consequently the writer decided to compose an apology of his art, and to show that conycatchers were only so many insignificant flies, devouring perhaps one or two leaves at the utmost, and could not do much harm, but that there were other professions in England, the representatives of which were big conycatchers, enormous serpents, who destroyed whole cornfields.

Undeterred by the threats of conycatchers and the insinuations of his literary enemies, firmly convinced that the work he had undertaken to do was good, Greene continued his exposures. During the earlier portion of 1592 he prepared and produced two pamphlets—"A Disputation between a He Conny-Catcher and a She Conny-Catcher," and "The Blacke Booke's Messenger." The latter must not be confounded with the "Blacke Booke,"[101] a compendious work on conycatchers which Greene had long promised his readers, but which he was prevented from completing by his illness.[102] In the preface to the former of these works Greene informs his readers that he is going to acquaint them with the manners and customs of the London *demi-monde*. Having himself frequently fallen into the clutches of London

[101] As Rimbault does, for instance, who edited Chettle's "Kind-heart's Dream" for the Percy Society" (London, 1842), and Dyce (*vide* "Account of R. Greene, London, 1861, Routledge, p. 70, note).

[102] This note is also superseded by a reference to Works, Vol. XI., pp. 5-6.—G.

courtesans, Greene was an authority on this subject. He was therefore specially qualified to describe the cunning arts practised by these local syrens to fascinate the hearts of inexperienced youths.

After a description of the characteristics of the London *demi-monde*, comes the story. This is a tale of how a courtesan succeeded in duping and overreaching one of the sharpest and most experienced of conycatchers, who was obliged to confess himself vanquished. Hence the title, "A Disputation between a He Connycatcher and a She Connycatcher." Greene concludes with an account of the repentance and reformation of a prostitute, to which is added a postscript, wherein he assures his readers that this account had been taken down from the words of the woman herself, and was not fictitious. The history of her life is the usual story of a woman whose first false step has gradually led her on to complete ruin. Having been seduced and deceived by her first lover, she in her turn deceived and cheated others, and sank lower and lower until she became a regular registered prostitute.[***] An accidental meeting in a tavern with a young man, who expressed his sympathy for

[***] No rising in Prostitution. The height is occupied at first, and then down and down. By 'registered' Storojenko must mean simply 'notorious' or 'recognised.' *Certes* such women never have been 'registered' in England. Were it for the facts alone, Greene's Cony-catching books would be of permanent value and interest; but no books are more out-and-out sincere than these, and this gives them a unique power and pathos combined. One wishes Professor Storojenko had more recognised the moral value of Greene's writings, as distinct from their mere literary qualities.—G.

her, and modestly admired her beauty—who, in a word, treated her with some amount of humanity—produced a sudden change in her mind. Her former life seemed unbearably disgusting as she fully saw the loathsomeness of her position. With a contrite heart she fell on her knees before the stranger, and with tears entreated him to help her out of the abyss into which she had fallen. The young man listened to her with evident sympathy; and when, on leaving, he kissed her tenderly and respectfully, that kiss seemed to her the sweetest and most delightful she had ever received. He saw her frequently afterwards, and, on being convinced that her repentance was sincere, eventually married her. All this is told in simple and touching language, and full of a humane spirit that does Greene credit.

The other pamphlet, "The Blacke Booke's Messenger," is less interesting. It is an account of the life and achievements of a celebrated conycatcher of that period, one Ned Browne, containing the repentant speech pronounced by the criminal from the scaffold to the people assembled to witness his execution. This is most probably the reason why Greene's pamphlet is called in the "Registers" "The Repentance of a Connycatcher." [108]

On the whole, during the latter part of his life Greene worked with a feverish activity and haste.

---

[108] "21 Aug. 1592: entred for his (John Danter) copy a booke intituled 'The Repentance of a Conycatcher: with the life and death of [blank] Mourton and Ned Browne, two notable Conycatchers.'"

Besides his pamphlets against the conycatchers, he edited, in February 1592, "Euphues Shadow," a novel by his absent friend Lodge,[104] and added a preface of his own.[nnn] In the July following he published his long story entitled "Philomela," and a biting pamphlet in satire of Harvey. When, at last, he lay prostrate on his death-bed, as though he dreaded to die without having given utterance to all that was on his conscience, he wrote, with hands fast growing cold, his two autobiographical pamphlets,

[104] Collier ("Bibliographical Catalogue," vol. i., p. 264) is inclined to believe that "Euphues' Shadow" was written by Greene himself, who took advantage of Lodge's absence (Lodge left England 26th August, 1591, to sail round the world with Cavendish) to put the name of his friend under his own work. Greene's supposed motive for this innocent forgery was, in Collier's opinion, the idea that he would excite the interest of his readers by a comparatively new name, as his own had already been so often before the public. Collier bases his argument chiefly on the remarkable similarity of style between "Euphues' Shadow" and Greene's own pamphlets. Though we would not venture to argue with an English scholar on the delicate refinements of style, we think that evidence of style is always more or less subjective, and consequently partial, and when not supported by more weighty testimony can hardly be considered

[nnn] See our Introduction on this, and on Fleay's over-exaltation of Lodge at the expense of Greene and others, in his "Life and Works of Shakspeare" (1886).—G.

"A Groatsworth of Wit" and "Repentance." We shall treat of these productions in the order in which they are entered in the "Registers."

Foreseeing that the publication of a love-pamphlet might call down on him a just rebuke for inconsistency, Greene informs us, in his preface to "Philomela,"[105] that this novel had been written a long time ago, at the request of a certain lady of rank, and that it was only in compliance with the earnest entreaties of his publisher that he had consented to affix his name to it. A detailed review of this pamphlet has been already made by Dunlop.[106] It is

---

of scientific value. Collier's arguments in support of his hypothesis do not seem to us sufficiently convincing. Greene had no need to cover his goods under Lodge's flag, for his name was much more popular than that of Lodge, and a pamphlet with his signature had more chances of a good sale than with Lodge's, or indeed any other contemporary writer. [Both imitated Lylly; and therefore some similarity of style. See Appendix in this vol. for Epistles before 'Euphues' Shadow.'—G.]

[105] Although the earliest edition of "Philomela" that has come down to us is dated 1615, yet from the entry in the "Registers," 1st July, 1592, and from the fact that the author of "Greene's Funeralls" (London, 1594) mentions it in his list of the more important of Greene's works, we have every right to believe that it was published in Greene's lifetime.

[106] Dunlop's "Geschichte der Prosadichtungen," deutsch von Felix Liebrecht (Berlin, 1851), pp. 435-7.

therefore superfluous for us to describe it. Suffice it to say that "Philomela" is one of Greene's most finished tales, although we are of opinion that it does not deserve the high praises showered on it by Dunlop and Brydges,—the latter having reprinted it in the first part of "Archaica." Sir Egerton Brydges, especially, is enraptured with the character of the heroine, in which, woven, as it were, out of love and self-sacrifice, Greene has realised his ideal of woman. "This single work is sufficient," says he, "entirely to clear Greene's memory from the slander that he served immoral purposes. He who wrote a novel like that must have been gifted in the highest degree with the feeling of right and wrong. The character of Philomela is drawn in such perfection, full of such magnanimity, such purity, that the imagination which created it must, at times, have been illuminated by the purest ideas, the most exalted aspirations." [ooo]

In the London literary circles [ppp] of that time the brothers Harvey occupied an important position. They were the sons of a rope-maker, who had grown rich. The eldest of them, Gabriel, was Doctor of Laws; the next, Richard, consecrated himself to the ecclesiastical profession; and the youngest, John, was a physician. The most celebrated of these was

---

ooo See "Philomela," in Works, Vol. XI., pp. 105—204; also our Introduction on it. The 'slander' originated, doubtless, in Greene's own passionate expressions of repentance.—G.

ppp Scarcely the "literary circles," and only Gabriel, who had a mere scholarly repute in his university. See my Life before his collected Works.—G.

Gabriel Harvey, a profound scholar in classical literature and Roman law, who counted among his friends Spenser and Sidney. In the capacity of men of means and of society, the Harveys looked down with contempt on such poor literary hacks as Nashe, Greene, and Peele. In his treatise entitled "The Theological Discourse of the Lamb of God," Richard Harvey, who had old scores against Nashe, Tarlton, and others,[107] to settle, called the whole of their circle "piperly make-plaies and make-bates."

Insulted by this wholesale treatment of his professional comrades, and having reason to believe that the elder brother had a hand in the matter, Greene determined to attack the presumptuous upstart, and to remind him of his plebeian origin and his father's trade. It was this, if we are to believe Nashe,[108] that gave rise to Greene's "A Quip for an Upstart Courtier, or a Quaint Dispute between Velvet-breeches and

---

[107] Richard Harvey studied astrology, and predicted an earthquake, which was to bring much misery over England. Harvey's prophecy troubled all minds, and the superstitious people waited with aching hearts for the day of desolation. When, however, the appointed time came round and no earthquake took place, Harvey was ridiculed by every one. Nashe, in his "Anatomy of Absurditie," has a good skit on the charlatan-astrologer, and Tarlton satirised him from the stage. [See Gabriel Harvey's collected Works, 3 vols., and Nashe's, 6 vols., in the HUTH LIBRARY.—G.]

[108] "Not me alone did he (Richard Harvey) revile

Cloth-breeches," entered in the "Registers" under the 20th July, 1592.

This pamphlet was dedicated to the same Thomas Burnaby whose adopted son Greene calls himself in one of his former pamphlets ("Never Too Late"). From the preface we gather that Greene's object in writing this pamphlet was not solely to attack Gabriel Harvey, but was more general. –He wanted to show up, in the person of Gabriel Harvey, all upstarts and parvenu aristocrats, for whose ostentation and luxuriousness their tenants had to pay dearly.

The author narrates how, having one day fallen asleep on a hill in a forest, much frequented by the people of the neighbourhood, he dreamed a most wonderful dream. He dreamed that a strange headless being approached the hill. This creature marched proudly and not ungracefully along, drawing nearer and nearer to the hill. On looking at this strange creature more attentively, the author discovered that it was not only without a head, but

---

and dare to the combat. . . . He mistermed all our other poets and writers about London 'piperly makeplaies and make-bates.' Hence Greene, being chief agent of the companie (for he writ more than four other) took occasion to canvaze him a little in 'Cloth breeches and Velvet breeches,' and because by some probable collections he gest the elder brothers hand was in it, he coupled them both in one yoke." ("Strange News," London, 1592, ed. by Collier in his "Miscellaneous Tracts *temp.* Eliz. and Jac. I.," Part II.) [and in G. Harvey's Works, *ut supra.*—G.]

had also no body, and consisted of two long legs dressed in breeches of the best Neapolitan velvet, lined with expensive silk and embroidered with gold lace. He had hardly recovered from his astonishment when he discovered on the opposite side of the hill a similar being, only dressed in common cloth breeches. Modestly and quietly, but not without a certain sense of its own worth, it approached the top of the hill, where the other had stopped in a proud and defiant attitude. The author was still more astonished when he heard these strange beings enter into a violent dispute with each other, in good English, as to which of them deserved most respect of mankind. In reply to the boast of the velvet breeches, that they were better because they came from the land of chivalry and civilisation, the cloth breeches roughly answered, that this civilisation had for some time cost the English people dearly; that the introduction of foreign luxuries and fashions into England had resulted in a raising of the rents for farms, and that the poor tenants would soon have to pay for the very smoke that passed through their chimneys. Velvet-breeches was, however, not convinced by this argument, and produced fresh proofs of his superiority, while Cloth-breeches in his turn warmly refuted them. Seeing that their dispute might thus never come to an end, the author proposed they should put the affair before a jury to decide. At that moment a tailor, a broker, a barber, a surgeon, a watchman, an apothecary, and others opportunely approached the hill. But the breeches had, both of them, objections to raise against every one of these professions. Cloth-breeches objected against the tailor, as the impartiality of a man who earned his living by executing the orders of dandies could not be trusted. Velvet-breeches, on the other hand, objected against the pawnbroker, as he was always at war with him on account of his high rate of interest. Thus all trades and professions were shown to be biassed against either one or the other party. But in the distance there appeared a collier, as black as the devil, minus his ears, which had been cut off for some rascality or other, accompanied by a ropemaker.

"Sir," the collier complained to the author when he came up, "this Ropemaker hunteth [? haunteth] meeheere with his halters," etc.[qqq]

The coalheaver and his companion were followed by three other persons: a cooper, a bootmaker, and a porter, whom the parties declined, as cunning scamps. These are followed by a country gentleman (knight of the shire), attended by two esquires. The author does not hide his respect for this class of people, in which he sees the personification of old English valour. We quote his description of an honest and honourable gentleman: "Vox populi, vox Dei!" etc.[rrr]

This opinion of the author's was not shared by Velvet-breeches, who declined to have the representatives of the landed gentry as jury, wisely supposing that they would not look favourably on upstarts and parvenus. As, after the rejection of the knight and

---

[qqq] See Works, Vol. XI., p. 259.—G.

[rrr] See *Ibid.*, p. 267.—G.

squires, nobody was left, the disputants put it on the author to settle their quarrel. The latter at once invited the knight and squires to be members of the jury. To these he added a few others of various professions, against whom the disputants had no objections to offer; and thus the legal number of jurymen was obtained. Having taken the usual oath, they decided the case, after a short consultation, in favour of Cloth-breeches. Velvet-breeches had to withdraw ignominiously, pursued by cries of derision.

As far as we know, Collier was the first to point out[109] that Greene had borrowed the fundamental idea and plot of his pamphlet, together with several details, from an anonymous poem entitled "The Debate between Pride and Lowliness."[110] Although we fully agree with Collier's opinion, that Greene's

[109] *Vide* preface to his edition of that poem in "Shakspere Society's Publications" for 1841, and also his "Bibliographical Catalogue," vol. ii., pp. 427-32. Basing his arguments on the initial letters F. T., Collier thinks the author of the poem to be Francis Thynne; but it is not so long ago since Furnivall, the founder of the "New Shakspere Society," proved, in the preface to his edition of the "Animadversions" of Thynne, that the latter could not have been the author of the poem, and pointed out that the letters F. T. were put on the title-page for the purpose of baffling the curious.

[110] Lately it has been twice reprinted. First by Collier, in his "Miscellaneous Tracts *temp.* Eliz. and

pamphlet is not an entirely original work, yet we are not inclined to believe that Greene's work consisted solely in changing the measured stanzas of his original into good prose, as Collier suggests. A careful comparison of Greene's pamphlet with the poem has induced us to come to a different conclusion. Not only did Greene treat the original with little ceremony, adding much matter of his own, and omitting much that was there; but his story, with its typical peculiarities, wit, and vivacity, vastly surpasses the monotonous narrative of the poem. Owing to this independent position towards the original, and the talent of the author, who succeeded in changing mere abstracts into living characters, Greene's pamphlet, though not original in conception, became original in execution. Where, for instance, shall we find in the poem that love for the working-classes which Greene shows, and the fine indignation against their oppressors which he expresses? The democratic tendency which flows through the whole of Greene's pamphlet throws a new light on several of the characters and episodes. How well, for instance, Greene depicts the yeoman farmer, with his honest contempt for the Italianised gentleman, who annually raises the rents on his estates, that he may be able to flaunt in silks and velvets! Taking advantage of the idea of a jury, Greene introduces the reader to a whole series of representatives of various professions and classes of contemporary society, and gives us, in describing

---

Jac. I.," Part III.; and by Charles Hindley in his "Miscellanea Antiqua Anglicana" (London, 1871).

them, various hints and details, which make his humorous production a work of interest even from a historical point of view.[sss]

Greene's pamphlet had a great success, and went through several editions in a single year. Its fame soon spread into foreign countries. In 1601 it was translated into Dutch and published at Leyden, where it also went through several editions,[111] and a little later it was translated into French.[ttt] With this pamphlet of Greene's a paper-war of five years' duration commenced, which was carried on with equal obduracy, though with very unequal talent, between Harvey and Nashe. This war was of so scandalous and virulent a character, and excited public opinion so much at the time, that the authorities felt themselves called upon to interfere. In 1597 the Archbishop of Canterbury, who was at that time superintendent-in-chief over the press in England, prohibited any further pamphlets of Harvey's or

---

[111] An account of this translation will be found in *Notes and Queries*, 8th February, 1851.

[sss] Collier's pseudo-invalidation of Greene's originality was only one of many similar hasty and haphazard uncritical conclusions. Never was there a more sawdust-brained editor or reader of books than J. Payne Collier. His Shakspeare and other annotations and emendations are wooden. He had no insight. This is separate from his forgeries and deceptions.—G.

[ttt] The Dutch editions I have seen, but nowhere has a French version been traced. Mr. George Saintsbury tried in vain to discover an exemplar in Paris and elsewhere for me.—G.

Nashe's to be printed, and those already published were taken from the booksellers and destroyed.

We now come to the two autobiographical pamphlets which Greene wrote on his deathbed. The first of these bears the strange title "A Groatsworth of Wit, bought with a Million of Repentance," and was edited by Chettle from Greene's original manuscript.[113] At the first blush his work has the appearance of a moral pamphlet, like those before mentioned, and it is only at the conclusion that we recognise in Roberto the author himself. The following gives a short *précis* of the contents:— "Gorinius, an old usurer, had two sons. The eldest of these, Lucanio, was a man of business, and helped his father in his commercial transactions[113a]; the

[113] *Vide* his preface to "Kind-Heart's Dream" (London, 1593). Chettle's evidence is perfectly reliable, as he was biassed in favour of Greene, and therefore would not attribute to him a work which in any case reflected no credit either on Greene or his circle. Chettle's edition is entered in the "Registers" under 20th September, 1592, but no copy has been preserved. The earliest edition of the "Groatsworth of Wit" that has been preserved is one of 1596. It is in the possession of a private individual. [Alfred H. Huth, Esq., London, as before.—G.] An account of it is given by Corser in *Notes and Queries*, 14th July, 1851.

[113a] It is greatly to be wished that local antiquarians would address themselves to the elucidation of the facts concerning the Greene family. The descriptions in the "Groatsworth of

younger,[***] Roberto, left his home, devoted himself to learning, and did not conceal his disgust for his father's trade. Knowing the bent of mind of his sons, Gorinius, when he died, left all his property to business-like Lucanio, and gave Roberto, the idealist, a single groat, accompanying his present with the following speech: 'I reserve for Roberto . . . . an olde Groate (being the stocke I first began with), wherewith I wish him to buy a groatsworth of wit: for he in my life hath reprooved my maner of life, and therefore at my death, shall not be contaminated with corrupt gaine." Having said these words, the old usurer gave up the ghost. On their father's death the two brothers pursued diverse courses, and arrived at very different goals. Business-like Lucanio opened out his father's commercial enterprises and extended them, whereas the unpractical Roberto soon sank into the most abject poverty. Indignant at his father's injustice, and envious of his brother, who lived in the midst of plenty, Roberto considered himself justified in trying to obtain a part at least of his patrimony.

Wit" are evidently so true and realistic that the Greenes—father and sons—must have occupied a good social position and played a prominent part in their town and neighbourhood, It ought to be possible to find them out in town records. etc. Until such information is obtained, it must remain a question whether Greene's father was a usurer *pur et simple*, whether Greene had an elder brother, and whether he cozened him as Roberto did with Lamilia; especially in the recollection of the laudation of his parents in "Repentance" p. 171).—G.

[***] Works, Vol. XII., p. 106. See the whole tractate.—G.

With this view he introduced his simple-minded brother to a disreputable woman, an acquaintance ("a female Serpent") of his. This woman, Lamilia by name, was to exert all her arts on Lucanio, and get as much money out of him as she could, which she was afterwards to divide with Roberto. The first part of this plan succeeded admirably. Lucanio was charmed with Lamilia's beauty. He presented her with a magnificent diamond, and, besides, lost a large sum of money to her at dice. But when Roberto demanded his share of the booty, the artful woman not only refused to give him anything, but informed his brother of the affair, who broke off all connection with him. Left without the means of supporting life, and tormented by repentance and sorrow, Roberto had already contemplated suicide, when an accidental meeting with a troupe of strolling actors restored him again to the world and its pleasures. Judging by his conversation that they were dealing with a scholar and an author, the actors invited Roberto to write plays for their company, promising to pay well in the event of success. Roberto gladly accepted the offer, and set to work at once. The result of his dramatic experiment exceeded all expectation, and its success was accompanied by money. But this was not all. It seemed as though, in reward for the sufferings he had undergone, Fate wished to shower on Roberto all the blessings of life, and make him happier than others. His successes in the dramatic line obtained him the friendship of a worthy old gentleman, the father of a beautiful daughter, whom Roberto married. The result proved that the frivolous Roberto did not deserve the good fortune that had befallen him. Quiet home-life did not satisfy him. He absented himself from home, made friends with spendthrifts, gamblers, scamps and sharpers, and spent days together in the society of such suspicious characters, When his wife wrote despairing letters to him, entreating him to return, he showed these to his boon companions, who ridiculed her and laughed over them. Even the melancholy fate that overtook many of his companions, who were delivered over to justice for their numerous malpractices and dishonest proclivities, had no effect on him. It was only when intemperance and excess of every kind at last confined him to a sick-bed, and deprived him of every means of working, when of all the money he had possessed only (that one groat) remained which his father had bequeathed him, that he fully comprehended his situation. "Oh!" he cried out, looking at his father's present, "now it is too late!"

At this point Greene interrupts the story, and informs us, point-blank, that under the name of Roberto he has represented himself. "Heere (Gentlemen) breake I off Robertos speech; whose life in most parts agreeing with mine, found one selfe punishment as I have doone." ***

Although we have no reason to doubt the sincerity of such a heartrending confession, which Villemain very aptly calls "*la confession d'un enfant du XVIe siècle*," we think that Greene's testimony against his

*** See Works, Vol. XII., p. 137 onward.—G.

life and works should be received with great caution, in view of his exceptional state of mind. In another work of ours,[113] we said that Greene "wrote his confessions in the dreadful moments of his soul's agony, when his conscience, terrified by the nearness of death, represented his past life to him as a continuous series of infamous deeds. To prove that the mournful view Greene took of his literary labours was the result of an exceptional state of mind, brought on by severe illness, it is enough to quote a passage from "A Groatsworth of Wit,"[114] which was written at the beginning of his sickness, when Greene still hoped to recover, and in which he speaks less gloomily of his works. "Yet if I recover," he says to his readers, "you shall all see more fresh springs, then ever sprang from me, directing you how to live, yet not diswading you from love."[xxx]

But when he got worse, when his mental vision was dimmed, and the threatening phantom and the terrors of judgment haunted him, then he looked on his labours from a different standpoint. His poems, pamphlets, plays, and literary triumphs, not only seemed utterly vain and frivolous to him, but even

---

[113] "Predshestveniky Shakspeara" (St. Petersburg, 1872), p. 214.

[114] This interesting preface has only been preserved in the edition of 1596. It is unaccountable how it managed to elude Dyce's attention, for Corser has reprinted it in full in his article (note [113], above).

[xxx] See Works, Vol XII., p. 101.—G.

criminal, at the approach of death. His affected rationalism, which he flaunted in the literary circles of London, forsook him, and the bandage fell from his eyes. The "poor naked wretch" (as King Lear calls man), found himself confronted face to face with mysterious eternity, and from his breast there issued a groan, praying for mercy.

Greene's pamphlet closes with an appeal, to which we have already called the reader's attention, to his friends and literary companions. Standing on the edge of eternity, Greene only concerned himself with the salvation of the souls of those he loved on earth. He little thought that, in imploring his friend Marlowe to renounce the pernicious fallacies of atheism, he was betraying him to the authorities, who lost no time in setting a secret watch over his movements.[117] We are of opinion, however, that this imprudent act does not deserve the cruel censure to which Bodenstedt subjects it[116]; who avers that he would sooner forgive Greene all the sins of his former irregular life, than such open treachery towards his friends. We would at

---

[116] "Shakspeare's Zeitgenossen und ihre Werke," vol. iii., p. 67.

[117] This is one of those fiery glimpses that one gets of the monstrous way in which, in Elizabethan and even Jacobean and Carolian times OPINION was dealt with as if it had been ACT. Nor less noticeable is the then smallness of London, that made mere private and personal opinion of individuals known to the authorities; for it is to be remembered that Marlowe had never published his alleged atheistic ideas. But see our Introduction on mistakes above.—G.

once, and unhesitatingly, subscribe to this sentence, if it could be proved that Greene's betrayal of a sad secret was designed and intentional, and that he could have foreseen the consequences of his indiscretion. We are much more inclined to blame the editor of the "Groatsworth of Wit," Chettle, who, according to his own account, suppressed several passages bearing on Marlowe, but carelessly let this stand, without, of course, duly weighing all the risks to which he was subjecting the renowned dramatist.[222]

Before entering on a review of the last of Greene's productions, "Repentance," entered in the "Registers" under the 6th of October, 1592, we must touch on the question of its authenticity, which is doubted by several scholars of the present day. The famous editor of Greene's works, Dyce, according to his own words, was at one time himself suspicious of this pamphlet, but came to recognise its authenticity.[22]

To the best of our belief, Dyce's opinion is at present accepted, with a very few exceptions,[116] by all

---

[116] Collier has also suspected the authenticity of Greene's "Repentance." "This tract," he says, "is imputed by Dyce to Greene; but it appears to have been written by Luke Hutton, who was afterwards executed for robbery. He himself acknowledged the work in the dedication to a piece he published prior to 1600." (*Notes and Queries*, 26th April, 1862.) In deference to the opinion of an authority like Collier, W. C. Hazlitt (in his "Handbook to the

[222] See onward on this.—G.

[22] See Works of Greene (1861), pp. 58-9.

English scholars who have made Shakspeare and his predecessors their study. Ulrici is evidently inclined to consider the "Repentance" a forgery,[117] and Bodenstedt, in support of his doubts, adduces his proofs,[118] which, however, are unfortunately of no scientific value. The first of these is the personal judgment of the critic, that "Repentance" is written in a worse style than Greene's other works; and the second is rather of a psychological nature, consisting of Bodenstedt's opinion that the tone of the work is not that of a

---

Early English Literature," p. 289) ascribes the "Repentance" to Luke Hutton without further ado, adding that Hutton speaks of this work in the preface to his poem "The Blacke-Dogge of Newgate." Hutton certainly does mention a "Repentance" in the preface to this poem, but he means his own "Repentance," which he seems to wish to distinguish from any other work bearing the same title. "Gentle readers," he says, "for my *Repentance* was so welcome and so much the better because it was *mine*." Thus we are justified in forming a directly opposite conclusion from the perusal of Hutton's preface. Besides, if we turn to Cooper's account of Hutton's "Repentance" ("Athenæ Cantabrigienses," vol. ii., p. 540), we find that it is not a prose pamphlet, but a poem. [Collier and Hazlitt are alike uncritical and unreliable.—G.]

[117] "Shakspeares Dramatische Kunst," dritte Auflage (Leipzig, 1868, Part I., p. 166, note).

[118] "Shakspeares Zeitgenossen und ihre Werke," vol. iii., p. 59.

repentant sinner. Admitting Bodenstedt's argument, that "Repentance" is not so well written as the preceding works of Greene, we can only see in this imperfection a confirmatory proof of the authenticity of the pamphlet; for poor dying Greene had no time to carefully polish his style. Bodenstedt's second argument is weaker still, in our opinion. It is founded on a misconception. It is evident that Bodenstedt's acquaintance with the "Repentance" is limited to the extracts given by Dyce. He does not know that it consists of two parts; the first of which is written in that very spirit of a repentant sinner which the critic was unable to discover in the second, although its presence is plainly discernible even there. Here Greene, in a fit of repentance, goes so far as to accuse himself of crimes which, in all probability, he never committed.[119] The proofs in favour of the authenticity of "Repentance" are very weighty, and gain much by comparison with the weakness of the arguments against it.

---

[119] The following is an extract from the copy at the Bodleian Library, Oxford: "Oh I feele a hell already in my conscience, the number of my sinnes do muster before my eies, the poore mens plaints, that I have wronged, cries out in mine eares and saith, Robert Greene thou art damned . . . Now I do remember (though too late) I have read in the Scriptures, how neither adulterers, swearers, theeves nor murderers shall inherite the kingdome of Heaven. What hope then can I have of any grace, when *I exceeded all other in these kinde of sinnes?*"

1. In the first place Chettle's evidence must not be overlooked (in his preface to "Kind-heart's Dream," London, 1593), who says, that Greene at his death left "many papers in sundry booksellers hands." Cuthbert Burbie was most probably one of these, for he bought "The Third and Last Part of Connycatching" a few months before Greene's death. Indeed, we find his name figuring on the title-page of "Repentance,"[120] and he has left a description of that event.

2. No less strong a proof in favour of the authenticity of "Repentance" may be found in the opinions of Greene's contemporaries; for it never seems to have entered their heads to regard the work as a forgery. In 1596, four years after Greene's death, a certain T. B. (= Thomas Bowes), in the preface to his "French Academy," speaking of English atheists, refers to "the testimonie which one of that crew gave lately of himself, when the heavy hand of God by sickness summoned him to give an accompt of his dissolute life," and quotes an anecdote from Greene's "Repentance." Although T. B. does not give the name of the author of "Repentance," yet all who had read the "Groatsworth of Wit" (and who had not read that pamphlet, which created such a sensation in England at the time?) undoubtedly recognised who was meant.

3. In the preceding chapter we quoted Greene's last letter to his wife, in which he entreats her, in the name of the love and friendship that once united them, to pay his debts to his landlord, adding that, had it not

---

[120] [This note is superseded by the full title-page of the "Repentance" in Works, Vol. XII., p. 153.—G.]

been for this benevolent man, he would most probably have died in the streets. This truly pathetic letter was first printed in full in an appendix to "Repentance." Its authenticity is established by the evidence of Harvey, who saw Greene's autograph letter with his own eyes; and if his version of it is shorter than the other, this is easily explained by the fact that Harvey quoted from memory and endeavoured to reproduce it in as condensed a form as possible.

But perhaps the strongest evidence in proof of the authenticity of this work is the style and spirit in which it is written—that spirit of unaffected repentance, sincere contrition of heart and self-abasement with which it is impregnated. The reader will no doubt remember that signs of such a state of mind are evinced in other productions of Greene's; but in none in so great a degree as in his "Repentance," especially in the first part.

We have noticed above that "Repentance"[b*] consists of two parts. In the first, Greene gives a general review of his life, and breaks into bitter lamentations over his miserable fate. These laments, with which the first part is full, are the result of a boundless despair, which takes possession of the dying author whenever he fully realises the unfathomable abyss before him. These sobs of despair are interrupted by prayers to God and fits of tardy repentance. With

[b*] It seems superfluous pains on Storojenko's part to confute these German theorisers out of their own inner consciousness. Ill-informed and hasty, none are so grotesquely dogmatic. Of the authenticity of the "Repentance" there really cannot be a shadow of doubt.—G.

the exception of a single anecdote, quoted before (*vide* Note No. [41]), there is no autobiographical interest attached to this part. The second part contains a short autobiography of Greene, written with a view to turn others from following those pernicious paths through which his own life had passed. Greene's autobiography stands unique among works of the same kind. Usually autobiographies and memoirs are written by people for the purpose of defending themselves in the eyes of posterity, and showing their actions and motives in the best light possible. Greene's autobiography—the fruit of the exceptional state of mind he was in—is written for a diametrically opposite purpose. Having decided to lay bare the dissoluteness of his life for the instruction of his readers, Greene evidently took a morbid delight in representing himself, his actions, and all his motives, in the foulest and most repulsive colours. If we are to believe Greene, his whole life was an endless round of intoxication, debauch, and blasphemy. To what extent Greene's self-abusive tendency went, may be seen from the following examples.

In speaking of his tour in Italy he says nothing of the impressions made on him by Italian culture, learning, and art, and gives us to understand that all he learnt there was dissipation and depravity. Further, in speaking of his literary labours, he never mentions those in which he exposes some of the crying nuisances of London, and is perfectly silent as to the moral change in his character of which they were the fruits. Nevertheless we know that in these exposures he intended an atonement for the literary sins of his youth. In a word, he purposely conceals all that might, in his opinion, modify the sentence that he pronounces on his own life, for the edification of others. All this a biographer of Greene should keep in view, and, not content with the facts communicated by Greene himself, he should endeavour to supplement and illustrate them from other sources.

Having reviewed in chronological order the prose works of Greene, and having extracted from them the autobiographical material they contain,** let us endeavour to take a general view of Greene's literary work as a prose writer. The majority of Greene's works are so-called love-pamphlets, of almost every variety. Here, as we have seen, there are really pathetic love stories (such as "Mamillia," "Arbasto," etc.), pastoral romances ("Menaphon" for instance), moral tales ("Penelope's Web," "Alcida," etc.), and autobiographical novels ("Groatsworth of Wit" and "Repentance"). His principal Master—to whom Greene looked chiefly for inspiration—was Lylly, and his famous romance. But Greene, who knew several foreign languages well, shows besides a close acquaintance with a large mass of the productions of other literati—such as the novels of Boccaccio, that of Sannazzaro, the "Diana" of George de Montemayor, with Count Castiglione's ethical book entitled "Il Libro del Cortigiano," and with various collections of popular tales, chronicles, etc. From Boccaccio's

** Storojenko says he has extracted the autobiographical matter of the Works. A quick-eyed reader will easily treble, at least, such autobiographical matter, and often in unlikely places.—G.

"Decameron" he borrowed the concluding episode of his "Philomela,"[121] and several loose anecdotes of Catholic monks in his political pamphlet "The Spanish Masquerado." "Pandosto" is founded on a legend of the tragical fate of the wife of Duke Mazovius Zernovitus[122]; and the trial of female constancy in "Philomela" is probably taken from some collection of popular tales, where the subject is frequently met with, and from whence, no doubt, it found its way to the Italian novelists. A peculiarity, which at first sight seems original, of Greene's novels, is the alternation of prose and verse—an idea that he probably borrowed, either from the "Arcadia" of Sannazzaro or the "Diana" of Montemayor. The plan of introducing disputes on ideal subjects into the tale, and making the characters prove their arguments by telling

---

[121] In Dunlop's opinion the concluding episode of "Philomela" is borrowed from Boccaccio's "Titus and Giuseppa" (Dunlop, "Geschichte der Prosadichtungen," deutsch von Liebrecht, Berlin, 1851, p. 437). Might not Greene also be slightly indebted to Boccaccio for the fundamental idea of "Philomela" (see "Giomata Seconda, Novella Nona"), from which Shakspeare borrowed the plot for his *Cymbeline*?

[122] This legend, which has been chronicled by a contemporary, the Archbishop of Gnese, Tcharnkoffsky, may be found in the second volume of Sommersberg's "Rerum Silesiarum Scriptores" (Leipzig, 1729-32). *Vide* Karo's article in the *Magazin für die Literatur des Auslandes* for 1863, No. 33.

stories in exemplification, Greene might have borrowed from the Italian novelists. On the whole, Greene's prose works give evidence of their author's learning and scholarship. Without speaking of classical writers, Greene frequently quotes Dante, Ariosto, Guazzo, Erasmus, the historian Paulus Jovius, and many others.

Greene's love-pamphlets can neither be called novels nor romances, in the sense in which these words are used at the present day. They neither contain careful studies of contemporary events, historical colouring, nor analyses of the secrets of the human heart. They are simply moral tales; sometimes amusing and sometimes sad, but in either case reflecting the childhood of narrative literature. Their immense success gives us an insight into the tastes of the reading-public of those days, who asked of an author neither a representation of the spirit of the age, nor psychological correctness in the description of character and passions, but simply a flowing, interesting, and at the same time edifying narrative. These qualities Greene's pamphlets undoubtedly possess. They answered the requirements of the most heterogeneous public imaginable. They supplied a mass of interesting, pathetic, and occasionally bloodthirsty stories. They transported their readers from the narrow circle of sober fact to the bright world of romance and poetry. They familiarised them with the refined, intellectual pleasures of a higher state of civilisation. Young men studying at the universities liked them for their learning, ladies of fashion and professional beauties admired them for the exquisite mannerism of their style, respectable and solid citizens appreciated their moral tendency, and women in general were charmed by the exalted opinions of female perfection which they contained.[123] We may easily imagine with what interest the fair lady readers followed the adventures and trials that fell to the lot of the unfortunate Philomela; how they admired the talents and virtues of Penelope; how well they could estimate at its full value the peaceful attractions of a tranquil life such as that which Perimides the blacksmith and his wife led. What attaches no small value to Greene's stories is the fragmentary poems they contain, some of which are distinguished for their high order of poetical merit. Few of Greene's stories possess less than two or three such fragments, flowing, as it were, involuntarily from the author's exuberant heart at moments when prose seems to become dry and monotonous to

[123] According to Wood's testimony, given by Dyce (*vide* "Account of R. Greene," p. 37, note), Greene's works "were pleasing to men and women of his time; they made much sport, and were valued among schollars." A well-known admirer of Greene's expresses himself as follows on his art of moralising on amatory subjects:

> "His gadding Muse, although it run of love,
> Yet did he sweetly moralise his songs,
> Ne ever gave the looser cause to laugh,
> Ne men of judgment for to be offended."
> ("Greene's Funeralls," by R. B.: London, 1594.)

The only exceptions are two comical scenes in one of Greene's dramas, which savour strongly of the tavern. [See our Introduction.—G.]

him. Now he describes in glowing colours his mistress's charms [134]; now he sings of the fatal power of her passions, that demolish at one blow the promptings and arguments of reason [135]; now the excited imagination of the poet seeks rest in the contemplation of a fascinating picture of family happiness;—he conjures up a young and beautiful mother nursing her first-born, her joy, her pride, on her knee, and he hears her touching and poetical cradle song [136]; now he is carried away to the sunny south, the delights of which, alas! are unable to ease the pain of his aching heart [137]; now, after exhausting every form of poetical sensation, he turns to his sore point, his unsuccessful life, and complains bitterly of the heartless world, that has ruined

---

[134] See 'The Description of Silvestro's Lady' (in "Morando"), or 'Melicertus' Description of his Mistress' (in "Menaphon"), etc.

[135] See especially the lyric on love in "Menaphon," beginning "Some say love." [See Works, Vol. VI., pp. 41-2.—G.]

[136] See the exquisite cradle song of Sephestia in "Menaphon":

"Weepe not my wanton, smile upon my knee,
When thou art olde there's grief inough for thee, etc."

[Works, Vol. VI., pp. 43-4.—G.]

[137] "Faire fields, proud Flora's vaunt, why is't you smile,
When as I languish?
You golden meads, why strive you to beguile
My weeping anguish?"
(From "Menaphon.") [*Ibid.*, p. 105.]

him.[128] Although the subjects of these poems are always connected with the story into which they are introduced, and though the poet never speaks of himself, but puts his thoughts and feelings into the mouths of shepherds and shepherdesses, yet they all possess one common trait, and that is secret sorrow over blighted hopes and an unsuccessful career, which always haunted Greene.[d*] When one knows a little of Greene's life, and recollects in what society he moved, what an infected atmosphere he frequently had to breathe, his fondness for transferring himself to the world of reverie and dreams, and seeking oblivion in the melody of rhyme, will be easily understood.

[128] See the poem in the "Groatsworth of Wit" commencing:

> "Deceiving world, that with alluring toyes
> Hast made my life the subject of thy scorne, etc."

This beautiful poem has all the more significance, when we remember that it was written by Greene on his death-bed. The last verse is especially pathetic:

> "O that a yeare were graunted me to live,
> And for that yeare my former wits restorde!
> What rules of life, what counsell would I give?
> How should my sin with sorrow be deplorde.
> But I must die of every man abhorde:
> Time loosely spent will not againe be woonne;
> My time is loosely spent, and I undone."

[Works, Vol. XII., p. 138.—G.]

[d*] We have a present-day example of this (though without Greene's immorality) in Henri-Frédéric Amiel, whose "Journal Intime" has for note an abiding anguish over (imagined) failure.—G.

These dreams of a nobler life, relieved by attacks of sincere repentance, serve as good evidence to prove that the fire of idealism and poetry continually smouldered in his breast, and that, though the flame was occasionally choked by his passions, it was never entirely put out. Greene's personal disposition shows itself in the parts he assigns to women. In the years of his youth he loved to depict ideal women; to celebrate their obedience, faithfulness, modesty, and other virtues. His early love-pamphlets swarm with such ideal women: the reader will remember Mamillia, Myrania, Penelope, Fawnia, etc.; but afterwards, when, having been separated from his wife, he fell into the hands of London courtesans, his views underwent a change; the former "Homer of women," as Nashe called him, became their Zoilus. Ideal types of women become rarer and rarer in his later works (commencing with "Alcida")[e*]; and the heroines are all fascinating and dangerous syrens, who artfully draw inexperienced youths into their nets and pick them clean. Such are the three beautiful sisters in "The Mourning Garment," Infida in "Never too Late," Lamilia in "The Groatsworth of Wit," etc.

It now remains for us to devote a few words to the consideration of the style of Greene's love-pamphlets, which met with no small praise from his admirers.[129]

---

[129] Stapleton, in his preface to the second part of "Mamillia," calls Greene's diction a "sugred happy style." Elliot, in the French sonnet prefixed to

[e*] This must not be taken absolutely; for if there is Lamilia, there is also Isabel.—G.

Of Euphuism and the causes of its general acceptance in the higher circles of English society we have spoken at length elsewhere.[130] It is sufficient for our purpose here to say that this unnatural, stilted style, interlarded with antitheses and bristling with word-juggleries, classical allusions and similes, had found an able literary exponent in Lylly's "Euphues or the Anatomy of Wit" (1579).[131] This work had an immense success, and was soon found on the table of every man of fashion and every woman of quality in England.

In his love-pamphlets Greene appears as nothing more than a happy imitator of Lylly; and Harvey was to a certain extent right in calling him the "ape of Euphues." Indeed, these love-pamphlets are excellent patterns of Euphuism. All the characteristics of this style are found in abundance in these works of Greene, with the difference that their volume diminishes in the later pamphlets. The reaction in

---

"Perimides," compares the services rendered by Lylly and Greene to the English language to those Maro and Boccaccio respectively rendered the French and Italian, and calls them "*deux raffineurs de l'Anglois.*" [Works, Vol. VII., p. 10.—G.]

[130] "Predshestveniky Shakspeara," St. Petersburg, 1872, pp. 101-5.

[131] This opinion is given by the first editor of Lylly's comedies, Edward Blount. *Vide* "Six Court Comedies, written by the only rare poet of that time, the wittie, comical, facetiously-quick and unparalleled John Lilly" (London, 1632): Address to the Reader.

favour of simplicity of style—a very slight one, it must be confessed—is first noticeable in "Menaphon," and there is reason to believe that this change was due in great measure to the influence of Nashe.[133] [*] Whenever Greene applies himself to other subjects his style at once becomes simple and natural. Thus his political pamphlet "The Spanish Masquerado" (1589) bears few traces of Euphuism, while it is completely absent from his exposures of conycatching. Greene explains this alteration of style in "The Second and Last Part of Conny-Catching," when he replies to the attacks on the first part of this work for its poverty in those kinds of diction for which his other productions were famed, and informs his readers that he is acting in conformity with his theory of literary fitness. "Heere, by the way, give me leave to answer an objection, that some inferred against me, which was, that I shewed no eloquent phrases, nor

---

[133] In his preface to the "Menaphon" of Greene, and in his own "Anatomy of Absurditie," Nashe strongly protests against the artificial style of contemporary writers, and even throws a few stones at Lylly. When Harvey reproached him with imitating Greene's style, Nashe sarcastically replied: "Do I talke of any counterfeit birds or hearbs, or stones, or rake up any new-found poetry from under the wals of Troy?" ("Strange News," Collier's edition, p. 75.) [Our Works of Nashe, Vol. II., p. 267.—G.]

* Most improbable.—G.

fine figurative conveiance in my first book, as I had done in other of my workes," etc.[1*]

On the whole, Greene's satirical pamphlets form a distinct group, not only as regards the language in which they are written, but also as regards their character and contents. In strong contrast to his love-pamphlets, which give us none of the characteristics of contemporary society, they are full of realistic traits and hints and sketches of the times.

[1*] See Works, Vol. X., p. 71.—G.

CHAPTER III.

GREENE AS A DRAMATIST.

Greene's first attempts at play-writing: *King Alphonsus, Orlando,* and *A Looking Glass for England and London.*—Change of style in his dramatic works: *James IV.*—The peculiarities of Greene's more important plays: *Frier Bacon* and *The Pinner of Wakefield.*—Opinions of contemporary writers of Greene's powers as a dramatist.—Greene's place in the history of the English drama.

WITH what play and when Greene commenced his labours as a dramatist, and the order in which one play followed the other, are questions to which the attention of the student should be primarily directed. The satisfactory solution of these questions will alone give him a firm basis from which to calculate the development of Greene's dramatic gifts. Unfortunately these questions are answered in all those sources accessible to us, not even excluding Greene's own autobiographies, either by profound silence or by inaccurate and even contradictory information. From the "Repentance" we are unable to gather whether Greene commenced his literary career by composing love pamphlets or plays. In "Henslowe's Diary"[183] we find a record of the representation of several of Greene's plays, but as this diary commences in the February of 1591, it embraces a very short period of Greene's life. In view of these facts Dyce prophesied it would be impossible to determine the exact date of any one of Greene's plays from the present scanty information we possess.[184] But if it be impossible with the limited information at present accessible to us to give an exact chronology of Greene's plays, we may nevertheless endeavour to draw an approximately accurate line of demarcation between Greene's earlier works and his later and riper productions, guided as we shall be by the testimony of our authorities and the circumstantial evidence of the artistic merit of each individual play.

There is no doubt whatever that Greene turned towards the stage after he had already acquired a reputation as the author of love-pamphlets; and "Mamillia," "Morando," "Gwydonius," etc.,

---

[183] The Diary or rather Note-book of Henslowe, the proprietor of several private theatres, such as "The Rose," "Fortune," etc., was edited by Collier in 1845, for the Old Shakspere Society.

[184] Dyce's prophecy is justified by the hypothesis of Bernhardi, refuted by Simpson in the *Academy* for 24th March, 1874, and by the hypothetic chronology of Greene's plays proposed by Fleay in his "Shakespeare's Manual" (London, 1876), which will bear critical investigation perhaps as little as those of his predecessor.

were printed some time before we hear of any of Greene's plays.[185] What his first dramatic works were we are unable to say, but there is reason to believe that they were coldly received, and that Greene turned in disgust to prose again.[186] The success of Marlowe's *Tamburlaine*, which was put on the stage in 1586, piqued him and induced him to change his resolve. He wrote a play in imitation of *Tamburlaine*, also in blank verse; but his production was subjected to the most virulent attacks from two

[185] In "Repentance" Greene expresses himself so very vaguely that we might almost come to a contrary conclusion. "But after I had by degrees proceeded Maister of Arts, I left the University and away to London, where I became an author of plays and a penner of Love-Pamphlets, so that I soon grew famous in that quality, etc."

[186] In his preface to "Penelope's Web" (1587) Greene says that his "toys at the theatre of Rome (London) had been passed over in silence." In the preface to "Perimides," written a year later, he complains of two poets, who had ridiculed his piece, and says that he is now writing prose again (see note [77]). We give these personal announcements of Greene's more weight than the testimony of "Never too Late" and "Groatsworth of Wit" to the rapid success of Francesco and Roberto in their dramatic career. [Storojenko in this note ~~utterly~~ misreads and mistakes Greene's words. See ~~our~~ my Introduction for correction of this fundamental error—fundamental as colouring a good deal of his criticism.—G.]

unknown dramatists, who ridiculed Greene on the stage.[h*]

Both Ulrici and Simpson have very logically suggested that this unsuccessful play of Greene's was no other than *Alphonsus, King of Arragon*, which bears strong traces, as we shall presently see, of being an imitation of Marlowe's *Tamburlaine.* The title corresponding so ill with the contents, *The Comical History of Alphonsus, King of Arragon*, may be explained by the circumstance that the play, though abounding in bloodthirsty episodes, finishes, like a comedy, with the happy union of the lovers. In consideration of the above, we believe we are justified in commencing our review of Greene's plays with *Alphonsus*, as in all probability this is the earliest of those of his plays that have been handed down to us.

Carinus, king of Arragon, was dethroned by his cousin Flaminius. Forced to fly his country, he sought refuge, with his son Alphonsus, in some forest near Naples, where he lived many years. In the first scene, which may be called a sort of exposition of past events, we are introduced to a conversation between father and son. Ever since his father had first told him his misfortunes, Alphonsus had had no peace of mind. For a long time he silently and moodily brooded over what he had heard; at last he tells his father plainly that he can no longer endure his degradation, and has resolved either to acquire with the sword what belonged to him by

---

[h*] See Address to the Gentlemen Readers before "Perimedes" (Works, Vol. VII., pp. 7-8).—G.

right, or perish. The wise and experienced old man, dreading the loss of his only consolation, implores his son to give up his resolve, as it is madness to swim against the tide. He has recourse to an innocent deception, and assures his son he is quite resigned to his fate, and happy, and that a quiet and peaceful life is well worth a crown. But Alphonsus remains firm in his purpose. His father, seeing now that this is no fancy, but true heroism, blesses his son, and expresses his wish that he may come back as victorious as Cæsar. Alphonsus joins the army of Belinus, king of Naples, who found himself called upon to defend his country against an unexpected invasion of the hordes of Flaminius. The heroic appearance of Alphonsus makes so great an impression on Belinus, that he begs Alphonsus to join his army, promising in return to give him all he conquers, even though it be all Arragon. Alphonsus agrees, and succeeds in killing Flaminius in the first encounter. Belinus, true to his word, crowns him king of Arragon. But the throne of Arragon, which he had so passionately desired, can no longer satisfy his ambition. The kingdom of Naples was a fief of the crown of Arragon, and so Alphonsus insists that Belinus should declare himself Alphonsus' vassal, and come and do homage to his liege lord. Indignant at this insolence of an upstart, Belinus of course refuses, and accuses Alphonsus of ingratitude and cunning. A war ensues, in which Alphonsus, with the aid of his father's old generals, succeeds in completely routing Belinus and his ally the Duke of Milan. Belinus flies to Turkey and asks help of Sultan Amurack. Alphonsus, in the meantime, partitions out his possessions to his three generals, giving Naples to one, Milan to another, and Arragon to the third. On these protesting at his prodigality, and begging him to keep something for himself, he replies that Arragon is too small a field for his ambition, and that he is going to conquer Turkey. While Alphonsus is feasting with his generals, Belinus and Amurack approach the borders of Italy at the head of enormous armies. Alphonsus hastens to meet them, and first defeats Belinus and then discomfits Amurack. Belinus is killed in the fray, and Amurack is taken prisoner together with his wife and daughter. This latter Alphonsus had seen and admired before, but he had been refused. Circumstances are altered now, and she accepts him; but the Sultan will not hear of the alliance. Fortunately Alphonsus' old father arrives at this point, and by his tact and management conciliates all parties, and the marriage is thus agreed on, and the play brought to an end.

Greene's drama is divided into acts and scenes, and each act is preceded by a prologue, spoken by Venus, who descends from heaven and explains the contents of every act to the audience. Ulrici[187] considers it an original and poetical idea to supersede the old-

[187] "Shakspeares dramatische Kunst," dritte Auflage, 1 Theil, s. 171. We may state that the praises of the German critic are not quite disinterested. Ulrici thought Greene was acting with a purpose by so doing, that he wished to give a hint as to the fundamental idea of the play in his prologue; and it is

fashioned pantomime by a prologue in which Venus herself is introduced. Of course it would have been better still to have done without either pantomime or prologue, as Marlowe did in his *Tamburlaine*, but if Greene considered this innovation, for some reason or other, unseemly, he certainly chose the least of two evils.

Regarded from an æsthetic point of view, this play of Greene's is weak as a spectacle. In the stricter sense of the word it cannot be called a drama at all, for it contains neither a regularly-worked-out plot, nor dramatic action, nor the delineation of the passions of human nature, nor the development of a dramatic interest,—in a word, none of those things which we are accustomed to associate with the word drama. It is simply a fanciful history of King Alphonsus divided into acts and scenes, and the interest attached to it is of an epic rather than a dramatic nature. It cannot be denied that the play is lively, that some of the situations are effective, and that the *dénouement* is simple and clever. But when we have said this we have enumerated all its good points and said everything that can be said in its favour. It would be in vain to look for any well delineated characters, or a single carefully planned scene. Everything is sketchy, events come about accidentally, as it were, and in most cases unexpectedly. Its very unity is external rather than internal. The central figure evidently

---

well known that the finding of the fundamental idea (*Grundgedanke*), underlying every play is the weak side of that school of criticism to which Ulrici belongs.

should have been Alphonsus, but unfortunately his character is weakly drawn, and besides is void of that personal nobility and grandeur which should distinguish dramatic heroes. In our opinion his drama gives incontestable proof that when it was composed Greene's talents had as yet but entered on the first stage of their development. The subject offered several highly effective dramatic situations, of which he made no use, most likely because he did not appreciate their value: the relations of Alphonsus with Iphigenia, the Sultan's daughter, for instance. Without any centre of interest, and composed of faultily planned scenes, this play of Greene's presents to the contemporary reader a sort of phantasmagoria. This impression is deepened by a complete absence of historical colouring. Thus Greene makes Alphonsus, a Christian, and Amurack, a Mahometan, both recognise Jupiter as the supreme Divine Being. He transplants Medea to the Sultan's court, and then by magic spells raises Homer's Kalchas from the grave and makes him prophesy the result of the war between Amurack and Alphonsus![138] In enumerating

[138] Oddly enough, this strange conglomeration of epochs, depriving Greene's play, as it does, of every illusion, awakens the enthusiasm of some of his critics. "There is"—says an English critic—"a noble confusion of the associations of various religious systems, and the charms of Medea are grotesquely intermingled with the oracles of Mahomet" (Ward, "History of English Dramatic Literature," vol. i., p. 220).

the many faults of this piece we must not forget to mention a complete want of originality. A careful parallel study of *Alphonsus* and *Tamburlaine* will show beyond a doubt that the former is simply an imitation of the latter. Like Tamburlaine, Alphonsus rises from obscurity solely through greatness of spirit and exceptional heroism; like Tamburlaine, in a fit of rage and senseless pride he even dares Mahomet. Marlowe's influence may also be traced in the secondary characters and in several details of execution. Thus, for instance, the proud and unmanageable Amurat is evidently a copy of Bajazid in *Tamburlaine.* Marlowe's Tamburlaine drives on the stage in a chariot drawn by captive kings; Greene's Alphonsus goes greater lengths still,—he is discovered sitting on a throne, the canopy of which is ornamented with their heads; and finally, the first parts of *Tamburlaine* and *Alphonsus* both conclude with the marriage of the heroes with the daughters of defeated kings. Greene also intended to write a second part to his *Alphonsus*, in imitation of the second part of *Tamburlaine.*[130] In fact, from the

---

[130] In taking leave of the Muses, who had helped her in composing *Alphonsus,* Venus asks them, in the Epilogue :—

> "Meantime, deare Muses, wander you not farre
> Foorth of the path of high Pernassus hill,
> That, when I come to finish up his life,
> You may be ready for to succour me."

[Works, Vol. XIII., p. 414. See on this our Introduction to this Life.—G.]

dramatis personæ and situations down to the very blank verse, everything in Greene's *Alphonsus* bears the unmistakable sign of being imitated from Marlowe's *Tamburlaine*, and helps to confirm Ulrici's and Simpson's hypothesis, that it was this play and no other that called forth the cruel attacks of Marlowe's friends.[*]

After *Alphonsus* we may turn, with equal justice, towards the review either of *Orlando Furioso* or *A Looking Glasse for London and England*, as both these plays were probably written either at the close of 1588 or the beginning of 1589.[140] The idea of *Orlando* Greene borrowed from an episode in Ariosto's

[140] That *Orlando* could not have been written before the destruction of the Spanish Armada—that is, not before 1588—may be seen from the following passage:

"... And Spaniard tell, who mann'd with mighty fleets
Came to subdue my islands to their king,
Filling our seas with stately argosies, etc."

Bernhardi sets the date of *Orlando* at 1586, and bases his opinion on the fact that an old play called *Locrin*, written about 1586, certainly not later, contains two verses almost word for word borrowed from *Orlando*. This fact would settle the controversy if the lines mentioned could be found in the first edition of this *Locrin*; but the first edition has not

[*] In Introduction to this Life I show that if Greene did not write the promised "second part" of *Alphonsus*, we find in *Selimus* the same vein worked. Professor Storojenko did not know of *Selimus* at all. I question if the ridicule of the two poets had any influence one way or another.—G.

poem (Song 23), in which an account is given of Orlando's going mad out of jealousy for Angelica. Of course, Greene treated the subject with the greatest independence; he excluded much, changed a good deal, replanned several incidents, and added much of his own. Thus, he inserted scenes in which the actors were clowns of genuine English origin. The play begins like some old fairy tale. Having heard of the beauty of Angelica, the daughter of Marsillius, emperor of Africa, princes from all the countries in the world come to solicit her hand. All of them consecutively speak of the wonders and riches of their country and of the depth of their passion in gorgeous and high-flown language. Among the suitors there

---

been preserved, and the second is dated 1595, and is, as stated on the title-page, "*newly set forth, overseen and corrected.*" Who can guarantee that the anonymous "overseer" did not add these lines with the other "corrections," such as some lines from Greene's *Alphonsus* and some from a poem of Peele's on Drake's leaving England in 1589, with which he thought fit to adorn this old and somewhat hackneyed play. With regard to the *Looking Glass*, it is impossible to determine the exact date of its production, only it must have been written before the summer of 1589; for in the autumn of that year Lodge, the joint author with Greene, made a vow

—"To write no more of that, whence shame doth grow,
Or tie my pen to penny-knaves delight,
But live with fame, and so for fame to write."
"History of Glaucus and Scilla" (London, 1589).

are only two not of royal blood—namely, Orlando, the celebrated paladin of Charlemagne, and Sacripant, a Circassian count. After thanking the suitors for the honour they have conferred on him, Marsillius informs them that he leaves the choice of a husband entirely to his daughter, and that he will abide by her decision, and make the man she chooses heir to his throne. Angelica chooses Orlando. Offended at the preference thus shown to a subject, the princes menace Marsillius with war (the Sultan of Egypt excepted, who, remembering Menelaus, is of the opinion that so inconstant a creature as woman is not worth being fought for), and return to their various countries to collect armies to attack Marsillius from different points, and to fight for Angelica. Sacripant alone remains. Having no faith in violence, he has recourse to cunning: he devises a plan for causing a quarrel between Orlando and Angelica. At the court of Marsillius there lived one Medor who was much attached to Angelica, and accompanied her on her walks, etc. The relations between Medor and Angelica gave Sacripant a foundation for his crafty plan. Orlando was fond of walking in a certain wood, and there dreaming of his mistress. In this wood Sacripant carved the names of Medor and Angelica on nearly every tree. Besides this he hung symbolic devices and sonnets about, which Medor was supposed to have written in honour of Angelica. The diabolical plot succeeds admirably. Orlando goes mad with jealousy, and in a fit of rage tears off a leg of one of Sacripant's servants (this detail Greene borrowed from Ariosto), and, mistaking it for Hercules' club, rushes about with it in search of Angelica, whom he vows to kill. His page, Orgalio, fearing lest Orlando might really encounter and kill her, dresses up a clown, Tom, in woman's clothes, and hires him, for half a crown, to play the part of Angelica, assuring him that nothing serious will happen. This gives rise to a scene of very broad farce, probably much enjoyed by the audiences of those days.[1*]

Nevertheless it all ends happily. Melissa, an enchantress, cures Orlando by giving him some magic mixture; Orlando kills Sacripant, who confesses his guilt before he dies; and Orlando marries Angelica and takes her to the court of Charlemagne.

The text of *Orlando* has been handed down to us in a very mutilated condition. Even those versions Dyce gives us, taken from a copy of the play that belonged to the famous actor Edward Alleyne, do not help us much. It was evidently written for a court spectacle; and on the title-page of the first edition, which appeared in 1594, there is a notice to the effect that it was printed in the same form in which it was acted before the Queen. Ulrici justly observes that this circumstance accounts for the number of classical allusions and similes and Latin and Italian quotations in which it abounds. For though all Greene's works are remarkable for the profusion of their classical ornamentation, there is no doubt that Greene took special pains about this play, probably with a view towards outdoing his old master, Lylly, who, in the

---

[1*] Works, Vol. XIII., pp. 165-7.—G.

capacity of dramatist to the Queen, was most likely present at the performance. This affectation, this continual display of learning, strikes unpleasantly every one who takes the trouble to compare Greene's style with the beautiful simplicity of Ariosto's poem. Nevertheless there are passages in which Greene's true poetic turn of mind gets the better of his mannerism, and shines forth. In proof of this we quote the following monologue of Orlando's, addressed to the stars, which may be taken as a fair specimen of Greene's style, showing its defects as well as its excellencies :—

"Fair Queene of love." [k*]

As a drama *Orlando* is hardly many degrees removed from *Alphonsus* in point of excellence. Greene had evidently not made much progress in the art of dramatising since the composition of the latter. In delineation of character we notice some improvement in *Orlando*. The characters of Orlando and Angelica are not wholly void of individuality, which is reflected in their language. Orlando's madness comes over him gradually to some extent, and we are inclined to think that Greene profited much from Ariosto's mode of treatment here. Of the secondary characters, Greene has succeeded best in depicting the Circassian count, Sacripant, in creating whom he was less dependent on Ariosto. When we know the relation of Greene to Marlowe we may perhaps be excused for seeing a very transparent parody of Tamburlaine in this comical character,

---

[k*] Works, Vol. XIII., pp. 142-3.—G.

with his stupid self-satisfaction and childish longing for a crown.[141]

We pass over the remarkable play called *A Looking Glass for England and London*, a sort of mystery with interludes, as it was written conjointly by Greene and Lodge, and it is difficult to say how much of it and what part of it is to be ascribed to the one or to the other. Taking the penitent style and probable date (1589) of the play into consideration, and Greene's own hints,[142] we are inclined to think that

---

[141] We have but to compare the speech of Tamburlaine to Cosroe (Act II., scene vii.), that apotheosis of ambition, with Sacripant's dreams and yearnings after a crown, to be convinced that Greene represented the Circassian count in a comic light with a purpose. Might not Greene also have been the author of the parody of *Tamburlaine* which we find entered in the "Registers" under the 14th August, 1590, entitled "The True Comical Discourses of Tomberlein, the Scythian Shepparde"? [I doubt if this title justifies the supposition that this was a parody on Marlowe.—G.]

[142] In the dedication of the "Mourning Garment" (1590), to Lord Cumberland, Greene alludes to this play, [most] probably but recently put on the stage: "Having myself overweened with them of Nineveh in publishing sundry wanton pamphlets, and setting forth axioms of amorous philosophy, *tandem aliquando* taught with a feeling of my palpable follies, and hearing with the eares of my heart Jonas crying, *except thou repent*, as I have changed the inward affects of

Greene wrote the monologues of the prophets Hosea and Jonah, and the scenes from real life that are interspersed here and there. It is probably owing to these scenes, of which some are not without a certain strong, although rather coarse humour, that the play had so great a success,[143] and was afterwards reprinted several times in a separate form.

With *The Scottish History of James the Fourth* Greene takes a new departure in the field of dramatic composition, and makes a strong movement in favour of unaffectedness, simplicity, and nationality. Till now Greene's imagination had run riot in all the countries of the world—in Europe, Asia, and Africa, and had drawn subjects from all sorts of foreign sources (such as the Bible and Ariosto). From henceforth it was not to leave its native land; it was to thrive on native lore, and to reproduce none but native manners and customs. As this new tendency is first displayed in *James IV.*, it is very important to know at what time this play was written.

Unfortunately our authorities preserve a profound

---

my mind, so I have turned my wanton words to effectual labours, etc."

[143] Henslowe has entries in his Note-book of four representations of this piece in the interval between the 8th March and the 7th June, 1591. ("The Diary of Philip Henslowe," edited by Collier, pp. 23, 25, and 28.) [But on the first occasion it is not marked 'ne.' (=new), nor are the successive performances close to one another, as would have been the case had it been a 'new play.' The first is on the 8th, the next on

silence on this subject, and the opinions of modern scholars, unsupported by facts, will always partake of a hypothetical and personal character.[144] All that we have any right to affirm is, that *The Scottish History* was not written for Henslowe's company, otherwise we should doubtlessly have found an entry of it in his "Note-book." When it was written, and for what company,[145] are questions that are positively un-

---

the 27th March. I repeat that Henslowe's 'Diary' begins only in 1591.—G.]

[144] Fleay ("Shakspeare's Manual") argues that this play was written in 1589, from the fact of its bearing the motto "*Omne tulit punctum*," which Greene affixed to all the pamphlets he published in that year. Although readily admitting that the mottoes Greene used are important aids in determining the chronology of his pamphlets, we doubt whether that criterion can be justly adopted with regard to his dramatic works, for the simple reason that Greene did not publish his plays himself. Consequently the choice of a motto for *James IV.*, the earliest edition of which appeared two years after Greene's death, did not fall to Greene, but to the publisher, who either affixed it for no definite reason, or else was actuated by motives of which we know nothing. Collier, taking its decided tendency towards rhyme into consideration, is evidently inclined to accord an earlier date to this play, when Greene had not yet fully mastered blank verse, and occasionally made rhymes from habit.

[145] On the title-page of the edition of 1598 we find

answerable in the present state of our knowledge of Greene. It is extremely probable, however, that it was written subsequently to *Alphonsus* and *Orlando*, and that Greene, dissatisfied with his former plays, in which he had imitated the style of Lylly and the manner of Marlowe, decided on striking out a new and independent course. The earliest edition of *James IV.* which is entered in the "Registers," under 14th May, 1594, has not been handed down to us; but the edition of 1598, reprinted by Dyce, contains a note by the publisher, one Thomas Creede,[1*] to the effect that the text of the first edition had suffered such mutilation, that in many cases it was impossible to understand the thread of the discourse.

The title "History," that Greene thought fit to give his play, has been a snare to many scholars who have taken it seriously, and have zealously ransacked ancient Scottish chronicles to find the sources from whence they supposed Greene got his information. We need hardly add that they succeeded in finding nothing.[146] Had Greene really intended to write a

---

the words: "As it hath been sundrie times publikely plaide." [See Works, Vol. XIII., p. 201.—G.]

[146] "From what source," says Dyce, "our author derived the materials of this strange fiction, I have not been able to discover; nor could Mr. David Laing of Edinburgh, who is profoundly versed in the ancient literature of his country, point out to me any Scottish

[1*] The "one Thomas Creede" is excusable; but doubtless he was the well-known publisher of the play and others of Greene's writings.—G.

play in the style of those historical dramas so fashionable towards the close of the sixteenth century, he would doubtlessly have profited by all the historical information accessible to him; but the plot and construction of the play lead us to form a contrary opinion. It was not a dramatic chronicle of James IV.'s life that Greene wanted to write, but simply a romantic love drama, to which he put, for the enticement of the public, the fashionable title of "History." In reality there is as much history in his *History of James IV.* as there is of the comic element in the *Comical History of King Alphonsus.* Having taken three historical characters—namely, James IV., his wife Margaret (whom Greene calls Dorothea), and her father Henry VII. of England (of whom Greene only

---

chronicle or tract which might have afforded hints to the poet for its composition." Halliwell, in his "Dictionary of Old English Plays" (London, 1860, p. 131), speaks thus of Greene's play: "The design of this piece is taken from the history of that king, who lost his life in a battle with the English at Flodden Field, in the beginning of the sixteenth century, for further particulars of which see Buchanan and other Scottish historians." In pursuance of the advice of this venerable English bibliographer and archæologist, we have carefully searched the whole of the 23rd book of "Rerum Scoticarum Historia," and we have become convinced that this work had no influence whatever on Greene. Greene had only to glance at any Scottish or even English chronicle to discover that the events described in his drama could not have

speaks as the king of England, and whose name is never mentioned), Greene considered he had fulfilled his obligations to history. All the rest is solely the fruit of his imagination. He places these three characters in situations into which they were never brought in real life. In defiance of history he makes James attempt to murder his wife, and makes the latter fly from her husband to save her life. He mixes up two reigns, and confounds two historical epochs by making Henry VII. (who ought to have been dead) make war against James IV. on account of his daughter. We refuse to believe that so well

---

occurred in 1520, as is said in the prologue ("in the year fifteen hundred and twenty was in Scotland a king, overruled by parasites, misled by lust, etc."), for James IV. was killed at Flodden, as early as 1513. We believe that this drama would have gained much had it testified to even a superficial acquaintance with the facts of history. One of the weakest points in his drama is James's sudden and ill-planned love for Edith, which commences on the very day on which he is married to the beautiful English princess. Had Greene known that James's marriage with the daughter of the king of England was based on purely diplomatic considerations, and that the bride had hardly attained the age of twelve on her wedding day (Pinkerton's "History of Scotland," London, 1797, vol. ii., p. 40), he would certainly have made use of these circumstances to explain, and in a manner excuse, James's sudden passion for Edith. [See our Introduction for the actual source.—G.]

educated a man as Greene should not have known it was Henry VIII., the successor of Henry VII., who made war on James IV.; nor would he have been ignorant of the real name of James's wife, or have been unaware that she never dreamt of running away from her husband. These inaccuracies must have been intentional; they must have been made from dramatic considerations.

The play begins with the marriage of James IV. with the daughter of the king of England, Dorothea. Henry VII. brings his daughter to Edinburgh himself. In a few touching sentences he confides his daughter to his son-in-law's care, adding, that by loving her James will gain his affection for ever. James promises to love and cherish his wife, and crowns her on the spot amidst the clamorous cheering of the multitude. The king of England now prepares to take his departure, but considers it advisable to counsel his daughter how she is to behave in her new position and in a strange court. We quote the king's speech to show how much the dramatic diction has gained in simplicity and naturalness in *James IV.*[m*]

"But, *Dorothea*, since I must depart," etc.[n*]

Dorothea promises to impress her father's counsels on her heart, and the king bids farewell to James, and is escorted by his daughter to the vessel on which he is to embark. On the departure of the King of England, the audience involuntarily ask

[m*] On p. 182, ll. 15-18, one queries, What of the many lost Plays ?— G.

[n*] Works, Vol. XIII., pp. 213-14.—G.

themselves why James does not himself attend him to the ship? This riddle is solved in a monologue of the king's, wherein we discover that he has suddenly fallen in love with Edith, the daughter of the Countess of Arran, whom he has seen that day for the first time. He knows he is acting dishonourably, and he even reproaches himself with meanness. But, seeing the object of his passion in the crowd of courtiers, he takes her aside and whispers sweet tempting words into her ear, which the maiden adroitly parries. Their conversation is interrupted, just as it is getting unpleasant for Edith, by the return of the queen. The Countess of Arran and her daughter make their bow and leave. They are soon followed by the queen, whom James sends away under the pretext that he has important matters of state to consider, and the king is left alone with his passion and his rebellious thoughts. Now we see to what an extent this sudden feeling had gained power over him. For Edith he is ready to risk everything: the opinion of the world; his crown; his country. A certain Ateukin accidentally overhears his foolish speech, and immediately forms the plan of making the king's passion for Edith a stepping-stone to his own success. He assures James that his marriage is no barrier to his happiness with Edith; that the will of the king is law to all his subjects, even to the queen, and that Edith must become his; and he finishes by undertaking to mediate between her and the king. On hearing Ateukin's flattering speeches, James brightens up, and promises to give him gold enough if he only succeeds in arranging the matter. Ateukin sets off at once to the castle of the Countess of Arran, and informs Edith of the king's love for her. He assures her that she alone is able to bring peace and happiness to the king's disturbed mind, and, with rare impudence, formally asks her to become the king's mistress; promising honours and riches in case of consent, and suggesting that force might be used in case of refusal. Edith is revolted at the idea, and the modest and pious maiden indignantly rejects his offer. Ateukin, disappointed and angry, is obliged to return to the king and inform him of the failure of his embassy. In the meantime the love-sick king has neglected his duties, dismissed the former councillors of his father and surrounded himself with the friends and companions of Ateukin. At last the nobles, with the Bishop of St. Andrews at their head, think it their duty to inform the queen of the state of her husband's affections. But the queen will not believe her beloved husband false, and she thinks he is paying court to Edith only to put his wife to the test. The nobles, however, do not share her opinion, and consider it advisable to absent themselves from court, where the hateful influence of Ateukin grows stronger every day. The latter soon attains to the height of his ambition. Confident on the one hand of the power of his influence over the king, and on the other of the strength of the king's passion for Edith, he resolves to try the last expedient. He explains to the king that Edith's virtue is not to be shaken, and that the only means of possessing her is to marry her, after having previously put the queen out of the way. At first the idea of murdering the queen is abhorrent to James, but, blinded as he is by passion, he does not hesitate long, and permits Ateukin to get rid of Dorothea by any means in his power. Ateukin bribes a M. Jaques, a French traveller, to murder the queen, and promises to obtain for him the king's written order for the deed. But an old knight, Sir Bartram, who is attached to the queen, hears of this plot and informs her of it; and she decides on escaping. Disguised as a man, and attended by her faithful dwarf Nano, she wanders about the forests, in hiding from the pertinacious pursuit of her hired assassin. The latter succeeds in finding her, and wounds her, leaving her for dead. He hurries off to Ateukin, to inform him of his success and remind him of his engagements. The wounded queen is taken to a neighbouring castle belonging to a Sir Cuth. Anderson. The wound proves not to be dangerous, and the queen soon recovers. In the meantime the king, believing his wife dead, is attacked by remorse; nevertheless, he sends his favourite to Edith to say, that now the queen is dead there is nothing to prevent an honourable and happy union. Ateukin hastens to the castle of the Countess of Arran, and arrives just in time to witness the wedding of Edith to an English nobleman. Ateukin now loses courage; he sees the finger of God in the unexpected overthrow of all his plans, and begins to repent of the many misdeeds of which he has been guilty. Meanwhile the news of his daughter's death reaches the ears of the King of England, who collects a large army and marches to Scotland to avenge her. James also collects an army and marches against him.

On his way he meets one of Ateukin's messengers, who comes to inform him of Edith's marriage, and adds that Ateukin himself, dreading the king's anger, has fled from Scotland. The king is struck, as though with lightning, at this news, and curses the flatterers who have been the cause of Dorothea's death. He has Ateukin pursued; and, tormented by remorse and repentance, he continues his march. The English and Scottish armies stand already arrayed against each other, ready to begin the bloody fray, when the unexpected appearance of Dorothea, whom every one had supposed dead, rejoices the hearts of all and changes war into peace. Henry VII., in compliance with his daughter's entreaties, makes peace with his son-in-law, who begs forgiveness of the King of England, and of his wife, and solemnly promises to honour Henry as his father, and to love and cherish Dorothea as his true and faithful wife.

In this short account of the play, we have not touched on the numerous scenes of a humorous character, introduced by Greene in accordance with a custom prevalent among the dramatists of his time. These scenes had, generally, nothing whatever to do with the plot. They were inserted by the dramatists of the Elizabethan period for two reasons: they pleased the popular taste, which liked variety in an entertainment, and thus insured the success of the piece; and they were the means of conveying bitter and unpalatable truths in the sugared form of a jest. In those days there were neither newspapers nor periodical magazines in England [nor elsewhere—G.]. The dramatist had, therefore, to perform the functions of a leader writer as well, and to give his opinions on the various questions of the day through the mouths of his heroes. Thus Lylly, for instance, ridiculed several of the prejudices of society in his comedies, such as the belief in astrology and alchemy, the false notions of honour shown in duelling, and many other things.

In this play of Greene's there are several humorous scenes of this kind, and one in which he paints the morals of contemporary society in the most gloomy colours. This scene is decidedly interesting from a historical point of view, and it is remarkable that nobody has taken any notice of it. It is nothing less than a conversation held on the eve of the battle between England and Scotland by a lawyer, a merchant, and a clergyman, on the calamities and misfortunes of the time. The lawyer is of opinion that Scotland must soon perish owing to her internal disorder, her contempt for the law, her love of gain, and her extreme covetousness. The clergyman admits that these plagues are only too prevalent, but he considers they are chiefly due to the evil influence of the lawyer class. "Are you not those," etc.[**] The lawyer indignantly refutes the charge, and endeavours to show that the clergy are at the root of the evil: they have ignored their great mission, and have divided into numberless little sects, each hating the other, and each believing itself the only true representative of religion; they have become avaricious, and they have gradually lost all their influence over society.

** Works, Vol. XIII., p. 305, ll. 2282-3, and context.—G.

If we place this conversation side by side with a scene in the *Looking-Glass*, where a rogue of a pawnbroker, a venal judge, and a dishonest lawyer, who had conspired together to rob the poor, are introduced; and if we remember the courage with which Greene exposed the "Conny-catchers" and their snares, whereby he nearly lost his life, we are obliged to confess that Greene, dissolute and abandoned as he was, did his duty to society as a writer faithfully and honourably.[p*]

The principal actors in the humorous scenes in *James IV.* are Ateukin's servants, Andrew and Slipper, of whom the latter was long afterwards the most favourite character of the English popular stage.[q*]

He is the direct heir of the "Vice" of the old "Moralities" and "Mysteries"; he is a rogue, a drunkard, the personification of insolence and every wickedness under the sun; but also a witty, jolly fellow. He devises an original mode of advertising for a situation, and through it is taken into the service of Ateukin. He takes up his position on the high-road, holding a staff, with the following placard attached to it: "If any gentleman, etc."[r*] Ateukin,

---

[p*] The passage reads like a remembrance of the *Looking Glasse*, and is a guide to the Greene portions of the Play. His 'Roman hand' is supreme above Lodge's (*meo judicio*).—G.

[q*] No evidence is adduced; but Storojenko speaks generally that the 'wise fool' or wise fooling was popular—as exemplified by Slipper. See our Introduction on Slipper.—G.

[r*] Works, Vol. XIII., p. 226. Certainly it was not on the high road, nor was a staff used. It may have been in the market-place; but more likely Greene, accustomed to London

happening to pass by that way, is amused with so peculiar an announcement, and gets into conversation with Slipper.[15] He is so much struck by his witty and sharp answers, that he takes a fancy to him and engages him for himself. But he soon has reason to repent of his rashness. Slipper is but an unprofitable servant, and is always plotting and scheming how to get more sleep, more food, and how to do less work. He not infrequently familiarly "chaffs" his master, and finally robs Ateukin of some important documents, and sells them to Sir Bartram. In thus acting he never accuses himself of injuring his master's interests, and he does not even seem to understand that he is behaving dishonourably. As a specimen of his inimitable *naïveté*, and perfect absence of moral perception, which almost reaches cynicism, we quote the following :—

"*Bar*. Ho fellow, stay and let me speake with thee," etc.[16]

On receiving the money, Slipper does his very utmost to be a gentleman in appearance at least. He orders clothes of an "amorous cut," and fashionable boots, and even goes the length of buying a sword and dagger. But he is not fated to swagger long in his new finery. The Nemesis of fate overtakes him, and he falls by his own weapons, so to speak.

---

customs, meant it to be a place like St. Paul's, where bills were put up. See scene ii., p. 223, down to line 40, and note especially "as good lucke comes on the right hand, as on the left; heere's for me."—G.

[15] Ateukin clearly went of purpose to a known hiring place, as did those he hired.—G.

[16] Works, Vol. XIII., pp. 260-61.

His fellow-servant Andrew turns out as big a rogue as he is himself. Andrew is displeased at Slipper's succeeding in securing such solid comforts, so he engages three smart fellows to set upon poor Slipper and rob him.

But for one or two comic scenes, in which clowns and jesters are introduced, and which fit in badly with the others,[a*] Greene's *James IV.* would be considered a very humorous and correctly planned play, even by modern critics. It has a well-contrived plot, events follow one another in logical order, and some of the scenes are really artistic. On the other hand, we find an unequal distribution of light and shade in the characters depicted. Consequently the moral changes to which they are subjected under the influence of misfortunes are unexpected, and do not seem probable (Ateukin's sudden repentance, for instance). The gradual development of the passions is completely ignored (take, for example, James' love for Edith, which overtakes him like a tornado), and deeds are often decided on with too much precipitation (James consents to the murder of his wife with hardly a struggle). But these decided faults are amply atoned for by many really good qualities. The course of events is quick and vivid, the interest grows gradually, the diction is simple and unaffected; and, lastly, there are several really masterly drawn cha-

a* It is to be noted that the persons of the Introduction come personally into the Play, and that Oberon, a spectator of the Play, prophesies that one of the players shall be in danger of being hanged but for his intervention, though the player himself knows nothing of his danger!—G.

racters. The best of these is indisputably that of Dorothea. It is evident that Greene worked at this character with an artist's love, and that he threw into her all the better part of his own nature. She is the embodiment of his ideal of a virtuous and high-minded woman. Married, most likely for diplomatic and political reasons, to James, she appears from the first as a loving and generous wife. She has so high an opinion of her husband, she is so incapable of deceit and dissimulation, that she never observes, what every one else sees—namely, her husband's coldness towards her. When the nobles of James's court, incensed at his apathy and disgusted with his favourite, take upon themselves to inform the queen of the state of affairs, and even give her to understand that the king's apathy is due to his love for Edith, her faith in her husband's constancy remains as firm as ever. But there is still a greater trial in store for her. She discovers that the man in whom she had had such boundless faith, and whom she had loved so loyally, was not only untrue to her, but was even seeking her life. Sir Bartram and Lord Ross show her the order for her assassination, signed with the king's own hand. She refuses at first to read it.

"*Dor*. What should I reade? Perhappes he wrote it not." [*]

The queen follows the advice of Ross, disguises herself in man's clothes and hides in a forest. After being wounded by Jacques, she lives for some time at Sir C. Anderson's, *incognita*, without putting off her

---

[*] Works, Vol. XIII., p. 270.—G.

disguise. Here the rumour of a war between England and Scotland reaches her; she learns that the English have already marched into Scotland, and that the Scottish king, unprepared as he is for war, has completely lost his head. She is so overcome by this news that she nearly betrays her sex by fainting. On recovering a little, she sends off her trusted dwarf, Nano, to Edinburgh, to inform Sir Bartram and Lord Ross that she is still alive, and to entreat them, for he sake of the love they bear her, not to forsake her husband in his hour of need. Nano returns with bad news. The king of England had not only marched into Scotland, but was sending destruction and terror before him. He had caused seven thousand young men to be massacred, and had replied to James's solicitations for peace by a message to the effect that he would carry fire and sword all over the country till his daughter was restored to her former rights. James was consequently now marching at the head of an army to meet his father-in-law, and had ordered his queen to be searched for far and wide. Dorothea sees there is no time to lose. She reveals herself to Sir C. Anderson, and, accompanied by him, hastens to the spot where Scottish and English soon must meet, with a view to prevent bloodshed. She arrives just in time; places herself between the rival armies arrayed against each other, and lifting her veil, says: "I am the whelpe, bred by this Lyon up," etc.[**] At last James recognises the treasure of love and virtue sent him by heaven in the form of

[**] Works, Vol. XIII., pp. 319-20.—G.

Dorothea, and he sees how deeply he has wronged her. Mute with shame and penitence, he stands before her, not even daring to lift up his eyes into her face. Her revenge was to reassure and calm him: "Durst I presume to looke upon those eies? etc."[1*]

When Greene was drawing this exalted ideal of a Christian woman, thus nobly forgiving everything to the man to whom she was tied by the indissoluble bands of marriage, might he not have had the image of his wife before him, whom, perhaps, he once valued as little as James did Dorothea? If not, we fail to see why he should have given his wife's name to the daughter of Henry VII., who was called Margaret.[7*]

We now come to the most popular of all Greene's plays, *Friar Bacon*. Roger Bacon, the author of the "Opus Majus," was one of the earliest opponents of scholasticism, and at the same time the popular hero of many wild legends. Of course there is little in common between the all-powerful Bacon of folk-lore, and the real Bacon, who passed the greater portion of his life in prison for his opinions. Bacon, in popular legend, was a great magician, who was in league with evil spirits; the inventor of the magic looking-glass, in which all that was going on within a radius of forty miles could be clearly descried; the constructor of the famous brazen head, etc., etc. In the sixteenth century a collection of all the strange stories current

[1*] Works, Vol. XIII., pp. 320-1.—G.

[7*] See on this and other critical conclusions of Professor Storojenko, quotations from a masterly paper on Greene, by Professor J. M. Brown, of Canterbury College, Christchurch, New Zealand, in our Introduction to this Life.—G.

about Bacon and Bungay was published.[147] Greene made this book the basis of his play, adding to it a romantic episode of his own between the Prince of Wales, afterwards Edward I., and Margaret the daughter of a gamekeeper. Both subjects are artistically united, and Friar Bacon shows the prince in his magic mirror what his mistress is doing at the time; whereby the *dénouement* is materially advanced. The period to be assigned to the play no one has yet succeeded in accurately determining.[148] To go by the style, which has some of Marlowe's solemn figurativeness, but is not free from classical affectations,

---

[147] The earliest edition of this has not been preserved. In 1858 Thoms (in the first volume of his "Early English Prose Romances") reprinted "The Famous Historie of Fryer Bacon," placing it together with works of the beginning of the seventeenth century.

[148] It has not yet been discovered which play was the oldest, Greene's *Friar Bacon* or Marlowe's *Faustus*. Greene's continual desire to surpass Marlowe leads one to think that *Friar Bacon* was given to the world in consequence of the immense success of *Dr. Faustus*. Bernhardi ("Robert Greenes Leben und Schriften," p. 39,) in view of the following passage in Dr. Faustus' monologue:

> "Poring upon darke Hecats principles . . . . .
> And girt faire England with a wall of brasse,"

has concluded that Marlowe borrowed this detail from Greene, and that consequently *Bacon* was of earlier

it should be placed between *Orlando* and *James IV*. Judging from its internal qualities, however, and especially from its popular tone, we are inclined to place it in the last period of Greene's dramatic labours. From Henslowe's "Note-book" we learn that it was acted by his company on the 19th February, 1591; but that could hardly be the first time that it was put on the stage. Afterwards it was frequently acted,—a sign that it pleased the public. The earliest edition—in which it is not divided into acts, but only into scenes—was published in London in 1594.[149]

The plot runs as follows. Edward, Prince of Wales, engaged to Eleanor, daughter of the king of Spain, whilst hunting in the forest of Fresingfield with his suite, went into a gamekeeper's cottage to rest. The gamekeeper's captivating daughter, Margaret, not knowing who her guest was, received him unceremoniously, put before him plain simple food, and was yet so sweet and charming, that the prince went away madly in love with her. He was quite despondent, and his suite vainly tried to amuse him, though they suspected the real cause of his dejected state. At last his jester, Ralph, devised a plan

---

date than *Faustus*. To this of course we can reply that Marlowe had no need to borrow from Greene, seeing there is a whole chapter in the popular book on Bacon, on the way in which "Friar Bacon made a brasen head to speake, by the which he would have walled England about with brasse."

[149] [This note is superseded by the full title-page in Works, Vol. XIII., p. 3.—G.]

that gave the prince some hope, and slightly raised his spirits. The plan was this. One of the prince's friends, Lacy, Earl of Lincoln, was to disguise himself as a yeoman, and to see Margaret and give her a present in the name of the hunter whom she had entertained. At the same time Lacy was to watch her face and see whether she blushed or dropped her eyes at the mention of the prince. If she did so, it would show that a tender feeling had taken possession of her heart also, and there would be hope. In the meantime the prince and suite were to ride off to Oxford to solicit Bacon's aid in the matter. Lacy parted from the prince, disguised himself, and went off to Harleston fair, in the hope of meeting Margaret. Margaret was there with her friend Jane, and surrounded by a crowd of admirers. Lacy pretended to be a farmer's son, and joined the party[160] :—

"*Margaret.* Whence are you sir? of Suffolke?" etc.[**]

We need hardly say that Lacy felt the same feelings entering into his own breast. When he met Margaret again, he saw that he was not equal to the part of mediator, which he had voluntarily undertaken. An interior conflict took place in his soul, but it is needless to say what the result of that con-

[160] An allusion to Elizabeth's law against ruffs of an exaggerated height and long swords (*vide* "Curiosities of Literature," by Isaac D'Israeli—the curious article entitled "Anecdotes of Fashion"). [See ref. [**].—G.]

[**] Works, Vol. XIII., pp. 23-5.—G.

flict was. Lacy vainly accused himself of treachery to his prince and friend, and vainly endeavoured to retract. Love entangled his mind in sophisms; it craftily whispered him, that in affairs of the heart there were no friends; that all ranks were levelled. Lacy became gradually convinced that he was not acting dishonourably; that on the contrary his honour demanded that he should frustrate the prince in his designs on Margaret; for the prince only wanted to satisfy a passing fancy, whereas Lacy could not live without her. Wrapped in these profound considerations, Lacy did not observe that Margaret was nearing him, attended by Friar Bacon, who had already informed her who the supposed farmer's son really was.

"*Mar*. Come Frier I will shake him from his dumpes, etc."*†

The group is joined by a monk, who, wishing to expose Lacy, tells them the news, that the Earl of Lincoln had fled from Windsor, and that the king, fearing he might be planning a rebellion, had given orders to have him searched for far and wide, and had offered a reward to any one who would bring him back to Windsor. Lacy, seeing that further concealment is useless, discovers his rank to Margaret, solicits her hand in marriage, and seals her consent with a kiss. Prince Edward sees this scene in Bacon's looking-glass, and goes nearly beside himself with rage. He entreats Bacon to use all his magic and charms to prevent this marriage, and himself hastens to Fresingfield to punish his perfidious

*† Works, Vol. XIII., pp. 37-8.—G.

friend. He finds Lacy alone with Margaret; and this naturally excites him still more. Drawing his dagger, his eyes burning with passion, he charges Lacy with baseness and perfidy. Lacy gives him an accurate account of how matters had been brought about, and how his love for Margaret had gradually led him from his duty. He winds up by giving his opinion that it were better for Margaret to be his wife than a prince's mistress. But Edward is too excited to listen to reason, and so he replies,

"Lacie thou can'st not shroud thy traitrous thoughts, etc."[b†]

What a contrast to the simple and touching words of Margaret is the prince's gorgeous declaration of love, studded with the flowers of eloquence, and composed of the ingredients of Euphuism according to Lylly's recipe! Nevertheless, such a speech, however flowing it may be, is more in keeping with the classical education of a prince than with the simple surroundings of the poor village girl, whom Greene makes to answer in exactly the same style, using the same classical imagery.

"*Edward.* I tell thee Peggie I will haue thy loues, etc."[c†]

Refused by Margaret, the prince is as intent as ever on slaying Lacy; but Margaret stays his hand, and vows the sun will have illumined the east barely three times before she will have joined her loved one in heaven. Lacy now exclaims that he would not consent to live though the crown of England were offered him, and implores the prince to put an end to

---

b† Works, Vol. XIII., pp. 49-56.—G. c† *Ibid.*, p. 51.—G.

him. But Margaret will not allow her lover the right of dying. She is ready to purchase his life at the expense of her own.

"*Margaret.* Gentle Edward let me die, etc."[4†]

In view of the arrival of Edward's bride at Oxford, whom he has to join at once, Lacy's marriage with Margaret is postponed for a short time. The prince tells Margaret that he will take Lacy with him for a week or a fortnight at most, and that then they will become united for ever. Margaret replies that Lacy is free to do as he likes, but that he should remember that paces seem miles and minutes hours to lovers. The Prince hurries to Oxford, attended by Lacy. Here he finds his father, King Henry III., awaiting him, with his august guests, Frederic II., Emperor of Germany, and the King of Spain and his daughter. In the presence of all these assembled potentates, a great trial of skill takes place between Bungay and the German magician Vandermast, and when the latter overcomes Bungay, a contention takes place between him and Bacon. The idea of this contention is borrowed from the popular legends already referred to. After vanquishing Vandermast, Bacon orders the devil to carry him back again to Germany, and then invites the crowned heads to his cell, where he entertains them in true Lucullian style, not of course without the valuable assistance of his devil.

While all this is going on at Oxford, events of some interest are occurring in the humble cottage of the

---

4† Works, Vol. XIII., p. 52.—G.

forester of Fresingfield. Two squires, Lambert and Serlby, come to solicit Margaret's hand in marriage. As the old forester is ignorant of Margaret's engagement, he thanks the squires for the honour thus done him; but tells them he will leave the choice to Margaret, and not thwart her in any way. Margaret is called, and the squires forthwith proceed to pay their court, each in his own fashion. Lambert, who has some pretensions in education, speaks somewhat eloquently, adroitly making a few classical allusions, and evidently trusting to his powers of speech. His rival, a matter-of-fact, well fed country yokel, probably presupposing an equally prosaic disposition in Margaret, urges his suit with commendable common sense. He tells her what his income is, and dwells fondly on the excellence of his pasture lands and the fine wool of his sheep. Not wishing to betray her secret, Margaret gets rid of her suitors by begging them to return in ten days for a definite answer; for by that time she hopes Lacy will have returned. The rival squires go away, but before leaving they interchange a few invectives, and determine on settling the matter by single-combat. Immediately after the departure of the squires, a messenger arrives with a letter from Lacy, who is still at Oxford. In this letter Lacy informs his betrothed, in the most approved Euphuistic language, that his love for her has faded like the blossoms on an almond tree, which bloom in the morning and wither at night, and that he is going to marry a Spanish lady in the suite of Princess Eleanor. With this letter is sent the sum of ten pounds as a dowry for Margaret in case of her marrying some one else. Margaret is so overcome by this unexpected news, thus suddenly crushing all her hopes of happiness at one blow, that even the messenger feels sorry for her.

"*Post.* It grieues me damsell, but the Earle is forst, etc."*†

We are fully convinced that no present-day reader would suppose this letter, which is such an afflicting blow to Margaret's heart, could be a cruel jest on the part of Lacy—a so-called "trial of female faithfulness." No dramatist would dare nowadays to use so barbarous a device, from the fear of outraging the moral sense of his audience. But the public of Greene's time looked on the matter very differently. Testing woman's love and faithfulness by all sorts of possible and impossible means was one of the most favourite subjects of the literature of that time, and the introduction of this subject into a drama would certainly not rouse the indignation of the patrons of Henslowe's theatre, especially as they knew beforehand that it would all end happily. Greene's mistake did not lie so much in using this device as in the fact that there was no necessity for it in the contrivance of the plot. [Cf. Dekker's *Patient Grissil* in "Non-dramatic Works," Vol. V., in HUTH LIBRARY.—G.] After Margaret had shown her love for Lacy three days before by preferring him to a prince of the blood, and had assured the latter of her firm resolve not to survive her lover, to demand further proof of the sincerity and constancy of her affection seems superfluous, to say the least, and

*† Works, Vol. XIII., pp. 75-6.—G.

harmonises ill with Lacy's character, who has not, until now, evinced any signs of a morbidly suspicious disposition. However this may be, Margaret was far from thinking that her beloved was going to put her love to so severe a test. Having given up all hopes, she resolves to immure herself in a convent and to take the veil. It is useless for her father to try to persuade her to change her mind; she remains firm to her purpose:

"*Mar.* I loued once, lord Lacie was my loue, etc."[f†]

Margaret has scarcely pronounced these words, when Lacy appears, attended by two friends of his, Ermsby and Warren. He tells her that his letter was but meant to prove her, easily succeeds in persuading her to change her mind about the convent, and carries her off to Windsor, where two marriages are simultaneously celebrated—namely, that of Prince Edward with Eleanor, and that of Lacy with Margaret. Notwithstanding this happy termination and the union of the lovers, the brutality of this scene produces an unpleasant impression on a modern reader, although it could hardly have had that effect on the public of that day. Lacy comes up to the forester's cottage as though nothing had happened, conversing easily and unconcernedly with his companions. He never bestows a thought on the agony that Margaret must be suffering all this time. Seeing his betrothed habited as a nun, he expresses the greatest surprise at her costume and her melancholy countenance. He does not even ask her pardon for having thus trifled

[f†] Works, Vol. XIII., pp. 92-3.—G.

with her feelings, but serenely informs her he had written the letter to prove her love, and asks her to make haste and get ready, as the bridal dress was already ordered. When Margaret does not at once recover at so wonderful a change of fortune, and wavers, Ermsby coarsely puts the following dilemma to her:—

"*Erms.* Choose you faire damsell, yet, the choise is yours,
Either a solemne Nunnerie, or the court,
God, or Lord Lacie; which contents you best,
To be a Nun, or els Lord Lacies wife?

. . . . . .

Mar. The flesh is frayle; my Lord doth know it well,
That when he comes with his inchanting face,
What so ere betyde I cannot say him nay." g†

At this reply, Warren, with some irony, remarks to Ermsby:—

"To see the nature of women, that be they never so neare God, yet they love to die in a mans armes." h†

Lacy takes Margaret off to Windsor, and the scene again carries us to Oxford, to the cell of Friar Bacon. He had made a brazen head, which was to say "strange and wonderful aphorisms," and to surround England with a wall of brass. That these wonders might be accomplished, it was necessary to wait till the head spoke, and then the opportunity was to be seized. With this end in view Bacon had watched it for sixty-eight consecutive days and nights. At the end of this period he was so fatigued that he was obliged to appoint Miles, his idiotic familiar, to relieve

g† Works, Vol. XIII., pp. 95-6.—G.
h† *Ibid.*, p. 96.—G.

him. Miles, however, whose stupidity is insurpassable, wakes his master too late, and the work of seven years is wasted. In addition to this misfortune, a circumstance occurs which causes Bacon to reflect seriously on his past career, and to forsake it for ever. Two students come to ask him to let them look into his magic mirror, to find out how things are going on at their respective homes. These students are the sons of those squires who had solicited Margaret's hand in marriage, and had quarrelled on being sent away. The young men, seeing their fathers fighting in the glass, draw their daggers, stab each other, and simultaneously fall down dead at the monk's feet. Poor Bacon is so agitated by this untoward event that he smashes his mirror, abjures magic, and penitently prays forgiveness of his sins. He declares his new resolve in the presence of King Henry and his august guests, and becomes a hermit. The play finishes with a very adroit compliment to Queen Elizabeth, which Greene puts into the mouth of the repentant magician:—

"I finde by deep præscience of mine Art, etc." ♃

The similarity of subjects and the nearly simultaneous appearance of Marlowe's *Faustus* and Greene's *Bacon*, involuntarily lead us to compare these two plays. The result of such a comparison, as far as the characters of the plays go, will prove far from favourable to Greene. While Greene was satisfied with dramatising the simple popular tales of Bacon, his more gifted and profounder rival has given

♃ Works, Vol. XIII., pp. 102-3.—G.

a philosophical and psychological interest to the legend of "Faust." Marlowe saw at once that the centre of gravity of the legend lay in Faustus' compact with the devil, and represented this compact as the result of the unsatisfactory state of learning in the Middle Ages and a passionate thirst for the pleasures of life. In the contention of the two good and bad angels over Faustus, he gives us a symbolical representation of the combat that went on in Faustus' own breast preliminary to his signing the compact. Finally, the last act of Faustus' earthly life, his repentance, is beautifully explained by Marlowe by the sudden awakening of religious feeling and the dread of eternal punishment. Thanks to this truly artistic treatment, the story of Faustus receives a deep significance, and the enigmatical old magician becomes a typical character of the period. We shall find nothing of the sort in Greene's play. When and at what price Bacon obtained his power over the dark powers of hell, whether the conclusion of a compact with the devil cost him any internal struggle, or whether there was any compact signed at all, are questions to which Greene's play will give us no answer. We only learn that Bacon had a magic book, by the aid of which he composed his all-powerful spells; that he possessed a magic mirror, which reflected objects within forty miles of it; that he constructed a brazen head with the aid of his charms, which head was to speak "wonderful aphorisms" and encompass England with a brazen wall. When all Bacon's grand schemes had miscarried through the stupidity of Miles, when two students murdered each other before his eyes, thanks to his magic mirror, then Bacon saw that magic was an unjustifiable, godless employment; then he smashed his mirror, took leave of magic, and sought to do penance for his former wickednesses by turning hermit. We see at once that the deep significance of the union of the devil with man had escaped Greene; that the psychological problems that Marlowe had undertaken to solve were completely foreign to him. But though philosophically and psychologically insignificant, Greene's play is far superior to Marlowe's from a dramatic point of view. The interest of Marlowe's play is centred in the description, in beautiful verses, of the various states of mind that Faustus experiences. Its merit has more of a lyrical than a dramatic nature. The only woman that appears in *Faustus* is Helen of Troy,—not a living person, but the personification of ancient Grecian beauty and graces. She only appears that Faustus may pronounce his celebrated monologue, and then vanishes like a vision. Owing to the lyrical character of the play the action is slow, and drags on monotonously. Not so with Greene. On the contrary, his play, especially the part in which Margaret appears, is full of life and activity. The connection between the two plots is certainly merely external, but in condemning Greene for this dramatic error, we must remember it was only given to a genius like Goethe to succeed in merging two dramas in one artistic whole, thus making Faustus play the fatal part in the tragedy of Gretchen. No small portion of the liveliness of some of Greene's scenes is due to Miles, Bacon's simple, stupid, but highly amusing familiar. Without him the scenes in which Bacon is introduced would be extremely tedious; he alone enlivens them by his boundless and irrepressible animal spirits. On the whole, Miles is one of the most happy comic characters that Greene has created. We say created advisedly, for the legendary Miles is a decidedly vapid and uninteresting personage. Greene's Miles is a generous liver, who is incapable of taking a serious view of anything; who has always a joke or a mutilated Latin quotation ready which can set even the austere Oxford dons laughing. However difficult a situation he may be placed in, he never loses either his presence of mind or his *naïve* humour. He can even meet the devil, who is commissioned by Bacon to convey him to the lower regions, with a merry laugh and an appropriate joke:

"*Devil.* Doost thou know me, etc.?" ✝

We now come to the last of Greene's plays that have been handed down to us, *The Pinner of Wakefield.* Most likely this was the last play Greene wrote; for the evidence we possess of its having been performed at Henslowe's theatre refers to the latter part of 1593, when Greene had already breathed his last.[2]✝ The style is simple and natural, free from classical ornamentation and Euphuism, and resembles that of *James IV.* The earliest edition of which

✝ Works, Vol. XIII., pp. 98-9.—G.

[2]✝ It may have been; but that it was played after his death is no evidence. We know it was 'played' during his lifetime, and that he himself took the part of the 'Pinner' (see facsimile of title page *in loco*). We know not how far Greene was connected with the theatre. Perhaps we shall not err if we

copies have been preserved is a London one of 1599,[151] which does not bear the author's name, and this has given rise to a doubt as to whether he wrote it at all.[152] At the present day the question of its authenticity, thanks to the discovery of fresh contemporary evidence,[153] has been finally settled; and the majority of critics, with Dyce at their head, acknowledge it to be indisputably a production of Greene's. The play is founded on popular tales and ballads about George-a-Greene, the pinner of Wake-

---

[151] [The first part of this note is superseded by the full title-page in Works, Vol. XIV., p. 117.—G.] Under the 1st April, 1595, we find an entry in the "Registers" of "An Enterlude called the Pinner of Wakefielde," but this edition has not been preserved. The publisher was also Cuthbert Burbie.

[152] Thus, for instance, Ludwig Tieck, who has translated "The Pinner of Wakefield" in the first part of his "Alt-Englisches Theater" (Berlin, 1811), considered it one of Shakspeare's juvenile productions; but later on he changed his opinion, and, in the preface to his "Shakspeares Vorschule," he expresses himself decidedly in favour of Greene.

[153] [The earlier portion of this note is superseded by the facsimile full title-page in Works, Vol. XIV., p. 7.—G.] Dyce, who, as we have seen before (*vide* note No. [4]), tries to identify Robert Greene, the dramatist, with the court chaplain of Elizabeth, thinks

conclude that his acting suggests extremity of need, albeit he may have been 'actor' as well as author; and in actual life he did 'play' many parts—*e.g.*, 'student' of physic, and a clergyman.—G.

field; who, like Robin Hood, was one of the most popular heroes of old "merry England." That Greene also made use of a popular book on the pinner of Wakefield (as Dyce states), we consider doubtful, as this book has reference to a much later period.[164]

The plot is based on the rebellion of Henry

---

that the *minister* is in apposition to the name of Robert Greene, which has been effaced by time. But if the name of the dramatist Robert Greene had stood before the word *minister*, the second note would be superfluous. Consequently it is more probable that there were two opinions held at the time as to who was the author of the *Pinner of Wakefield*. Some attributed it, owing to the similarity of name, to Robert Greene the chaplain, who was believed to have played the principal part, and gave Shakspeare as their authority. Others, on the contrary, maintained, on the testimony of Edward Juby, a contemporary actor and dramatist of Greene's, that it had been written by the author of *Bacon* and *James IV*. If we accept this interpretation, the second note has its *raison d'être*, as a correction of the first. Another circumstance is also in favour of Greene, and this is that the copyright of *The Pinner of Wakefield* belonged to the same bookseller who published "Repentance" and *Orlando Furioso*. [Again Professor Storojenko strangely misreads his authority. See our Introduction for correction.—G.]

[164] It is reprinted by Thoms in the second volume of his "Early English Prose Romances" (London, 1858), from an eighteenth-century copy. Dyce bases his

Momford, Earl of Kendal, and other nobles in league with the King of Scotland against Edward III. Although the Earl of Kendal and his supporters give out that they are rising to reserve the rights of the people, and are drawing their swords in defence of the oppressed, their aims are in reality purely selfish :

"My friends, you see what we have to winne," etc. ♃

---

supposition on the universally known fact that the dramatists of the sixteenth century generally borrowed their plots from novels and popular legends. No one will dispute this, especially as Greene—as we have seen—undoubtedly borrowed the plot of his *Bacon* from popular legends. But the tale of the "Pinner of Wakefield," edited by Thoms, which Dyce considers the source of Greene's play, resembles a popular legend but little in language and mode of treatment. It may more justly be called a critical account of the legends of George Greene; for the author frequently compares them with the chronicles and refers to history, etc. Greene's play does certainly present a surprising similarity in many places to the tale that Thoms has edited; but this can be explained by the fact that both Greene and the author of this tale were indebted to the same sources, or, still more likely, that the latter was acquainted with Greene's play, as Ritson suggests. [If this prose book has reference "to a much later period" than does Greene's Play, that is no argument against the Play being taken from it. If it refers to a later period than 1592 it is an argument.—G.]

♃ Works, Vol. XIV., pp. 122-3.—G.

The rebels succeed in collecting a large army, but find themselves growing short of provisions. To get these Kendal sends Sir John Mannering to the neighbouring town of Wakefield. But neither solicitations, demands, nor threats have any effect on the loyal citizens of that town, who remain true to their king, and refuse to have any dealings with the rebels. It is during the negotiations between these citizens and the envoys of Kendal, held before the walls of Wakefield, that the grand character of the dauntless pinner, George-a-Greene, first appears on the scene.

"*Mannering.* See you these seales, etc." [m†]

Mannering returns to Kendal empty-handed, gives him a full account of his reception, and is despatched at the head of an army, to punish the insolent inhabitants of Wakefield. But Kendal's curiosity is excited with regard to Greene, and he orders Bonfield and Armstrong to disguise themselves, and, attended by a small escort, he goes off in search of this pinner of Wakefield, to see whether he is really so brave and dauntless as he is made out to be. On approaching Wakefield the nobles dismount, let their horses loose in the cornfields, send their escort away, and patiently await the course of events. On hearing that the horses of strangers are pasturing in the Wakefield cornfields, George immediately sends his subordinate, Jenkin, to drive them into the town.[n†] On Jenkin's declining to execute this order, from fear of being

[m†] Works, Vol. XIV., pp. 126-29.—G.

[n†] *Ibid.*, p. 142, etc. Storojenko inadvertently places them in the 'forest' and on the 'commons'—corrected above.—G.

well thrashed by the three strangers, George himself goes out. A tussle ensues, in which George fells the Earl of Kendal to the ground with one blow. At this moment a signal is given, the escort come up and surround George, who now discovers he has fallen into the hands of the rebels. Seeing things are looking bad, George has recourse to cunning. After listening to Kendal, who explains the object of the rebellion, he declares his willingness to join the rebels, cudgelling his brain in the meantime for a plan to take the leaders alive. He assures Kendal, who is very superstitious, that there is a hermit residing in the neighbourhood of Wakefield famed for his gifts of prophecy and soothsaying.

"Nowe list to me: etc."[o†]

Kendal agrees to the plan, not so much from superstition as from a desire to win over the dauntless pinner to his side at all hazards. On the following day the three nobles, under the guidance of Jenkin, go to consult the hermit, who is no other than George-a-Greene in disguise. We think it perhaps as well to refer in full to this fine and effective scene.

"*Jen.* Come, olde man, etc."[p†]

On feeling his staff in his powerful hands, George-a-Greene throws off his hood and cowl and shows his visitors who he really is. In the struggle that follows he kills one of his opponents, Sir Gilbert Armstrong, and takes the other two prisoners, and delivers them into the hands of the magistrates to be sent to the

---

[o†] Works, Vol. XIV., pp. 148-9.—G.

[p†] *Ibid.*, pp. 152-56.—G.

king. On hearing that their leaders are taken prisoners, the rebel army disperse. King James is also defeated and taken prisoner at nearly the same time, by the venerable century-old hero, Musgrove, and thus the rebellion, that had threatened to endanger the throne of King Edward, is completely put down. Hearing that the most dangerous of his enemies, the Earl of Kendal, was taken prisoner by George-a-Greene, the King goes in person to Wakefield in order himself to see the brave pinner. After thanking him for his daring exploit, the King promises to grant any boon Greene may ask him. Now, George-a-Greene has long had a wish at heart. He loves Beatrice, the charming daughter of old master Grimes, and is loved by her in return; but her father will not let his daughter marry a needy pinner. This is the only grievance George has. The King graciously listens to his love-story, and undertakes to be his mediator with the squire. It is needless to say that he is successful. But the King wishes to reward George in some other way besides, for the great services he has rendered the state.

"*Edward.* But ere I go, etc." *†

He will not be rewarded.

Astonished at such high-mindedness, and at a loss how to reward this disinterested son of nature, the King asks George to state the ransom he thinks King James ought to pay. It is useless for Greene to protest that such matters are too abstruse for his mind, and that he is not worthy of such an honour. The

*† Works, Vol. XIV., pp. 176-7.—G.

King insists on it. Then George-a-Greene suggests that James of Scotland, instead of paying a ransom, should be made to rebuild the towns he had destroyed on the English border, and to make some provision for the children of the unfortunate soldiers who had fallen in the war through his fault.

This is the plot of the play. Greene has added to the central story, as was his wont, a few scenes and incidents that have perhaps little to do with the plot, but that help, nevertheless, to acquaint us with the characters of some of the principal actors, and which carry us back to the England of the Middle Ages. Such, for instance, are the scenes relating to James's passion for Jane-a-Barley; the flight of Beatrice from her father's house—a scene in which we are brought face to face with the popular idol, Robin Hood; and another scene in which we are made acquainted with same of the peculiar customs of the corporation of shoemakers of Bradford. The brave pinner is undoubtedly the best of Greene's male characters. He is the real centre of interest of the play, giving it internal unity. From beginning to end the attention both of the audience and the other actors is fixed on him. The fame of his strength and prowess goes over all England: not only do the Earl of Kendal and King Edward come to see him, but even Robin Hood comes to Wakefield on purpose to make the acquaintance of the celebrated pinner. In opposition to his usual custom of drawing his *dramatis personæ* only in profile, and of showing them to us from only one point of view, Greene has treated us this time to a complete and real portraiture. The author has put his hero in all kinds of different situations, to show his character from every side. We first become acquainted with George-a-Greene when he appears as so faithful an exponent of the public spirit of his town, and sends Sir John Mannering ignominiously away. He fulfils his duty honourably and stands up boldly for the interests of his town when Kendal lets his horses loose to pasture in George's wheat close, and bluntly tells him that if he were to meet the horses of the king himself trampling on the corn of his fellow-citizens, he would drive them into the pound like those of any one else. When he knocks down Kendal, and Lord Bonfield exclaims "Villaine, what hast thou done? Thou hast stroke an Earl, etc.," George answers, with a just appreciation of his own worth,

> "Why, what care I? A poore man that is true
> Is better then an Earle, if he be false." '†

After having foiled the plans of the rebels and taken their ringleaders prisoners, he gives over Kendal and Bonfield to the magistrates, and himself quietly remains at home, never thinking to be rewarded for his exploit, and hardly even giving it any importance. He has only to ask the King (through a courtier) to spare the life of Kendal, and his prayer is granted, the King saying that he would not have spared him for any other man in England. In the last scene we have an astounding instance of his high-mindedness. when he declines knighthood and riches, and begs the King, as a favour, to be allowed to remain the

'† Works, Vol. XIV., p. 145. Note that our text has inadvertently 'he he' for 'he be.'—G.

simple yeoman he had been before. Remembering Greene's democratic predilections, as manifested in his pamphlet against Harvey, we have some right in saying that Greene has represented to his countrymen, in the person of the pinner of Wakefield, his ideal of an English yeoman, proud of his honourable poverty, of his simple standing, and of his consciousness of having done his duty. How insignificant and small all those Earls of Kendal and Lords Bonfield become, who have risen ostensibly for the defence of the rights of the people but really for the attainment of their own selfish ends! How they lose by comparison with this true son of the people, this embodiment of old English valour, grand and simple, like one of Homer's heroes! Among the other characters of the piece we must not forget to mention the fine old hero Musgrove; George's subordinate, Jenkin, a comic character; and the sharp-witted little son of Lady Barley, Neddy. Notwithstanding the numerous episodes with which the play is crowded, this drama gives the impression of an artistic whole, and the plot is the best constructed of any of Greene's plays. Some of the actions are perhaps too naïvely contrived; disguise plays too important a part; state affairs are managed a little too patriarchally: thus the King himself goes down to make George-a-Greene's acquaintance, etc. But then these are faults common to all the ancient English dramatists, Shakspeare himself included.

Having thus passed in review those of Greene's plays handed down to us, we return to the opinion expressed at the commencement of this chapter, that it is possible to draw a comparatively accurate line separating the two periods of Greene's dramatic labours, after duly studying the authorities we possess, and after taking the artistic merits of each play into consideration. How far we have succeeded in accomplishing this task, how far our critical remarks agree with the very defective data accessible to us, it is of course not for us to say. It is extremely probable that we may not have put the plays in exact chronological order; we may have assigned too early a date for one play, and too late a date for another; but we maintain, that nobody reading Greene's dramatic works in the order in which we have placed them will ever assign *Orlando* or *Alphonsus* to the same period as *James IV.* and *The Pinner of Wakefield.* To deny a decided distinction between the spirit and conception of these two groups would in our opinion amount to a denial of the natural development of Greene's dramatic genius.

His contemporaries had a high opinion of Greene's abilities as a dramatist. In that circle of eminent dramatists which counted amongst its members Peele, Lodge, Nashe, and subsequently Lylly and Marlowe, Greene played a leading part, if not so much for his talents, certainly for his exceptional productiveness.[155] Harvey calls him, sarcastically, the "King of the paper stage,"[156] Meres enumerates him with

---

[155] Nashe, in his preface to "Strange News" (London, 1592), calls Greene "chief agent for the companie, for he writ more than four others."

[156] "I was certified," says Harvey in his "Four

Shakspeare and Lylly as a comic writer,[157] and Nashe, not much given to praising others, confesses that Greene, though behind him in everything else, surpassed his friend in "plotting plaies, wherein he was his craft's master."[158] Chettle places him higher still, and unhesitatingly calls him "the only comedian, of a vulgar writer in this country."[159] In these words we find the best definition possible of the place Greene occupies in the history of the English drama. And certainly the title of "a vulgar writer" suits no one so well as Greene; for in the works of no other dramatist of his day shall we find so many scenes taken bodily, so to speak, out of English real life, and put into so pure and popular a language, free from all euphuistic admixture and florid classical figurativeness. Exactly half of those plays of Greene's which we still possess are devoted to the representation of the life of the people. For Chettle,

---

Letters," "that the King of the paper stage had played his last part and was gone to Tarltone."

[157] "Palladis Tamia, Wit's Treasury" (London, 1598).

[158] "He (*i.e.* Greene) subscribing to me in anything, but plotting plaies, wherein he was his craft's master" ("Have with you to Saffron Walden," London, 1596). We may add that Roberto, in the "Groatsworth of Wit," was "now famoused for an arch-playmaking poet."

[159] "He was of singular pleasaunce the verye supporter, and to no man's disgrace be this intended, the only comedian of a vulgar writer in this country" ("Kind Heart's Dreame," Chettle, London, 1593).

who knew all Greene's plays, affirms that the percentage of the popular was considerably greater. Even in Greene's earlier dramatic attempts,—in which he imitated Marlowe's gorgeous manner and Lylly's euphuistic style,—we shall always find two or three scenes of popular life, which are so witty, lively and fresh, that they leave nothing to be desired. But another circumstance contributed not a little to Greene's popularity as a dramatist. His plays, with their fantastical characters and their numerous unexpected adventures, reminded the public of their favourite novels, tales of chivalry, and wonderful romances. In appraising Greene's dramatic works, we must not lose sight of the stories they were based on,—all the more so as Greene, before being a dramatist, was a romance writer. The novel, romance, pastoral and legend—all these forms of the literature of that day, notwithstanding the difference in the subjects they treated of—had one common trait, and this was the preponderance of the stirring, exciting, unexpected, and adventurous element over the psychological. Authors tried then to make their stories as sensational as possible, to excite the interest of their readers by a series of wild intrigues and a continual supply of every kind of adventure. This was their principal aim, and for this object they not only readily sacrificed all psychological accuracy and development of character, but even overstepped the bounds of common probability. Hence the imaginative colouring of all Renaissance literature. The English dramatists early recognised the value of such material for dramatic purposes, and flooded the stage with plays borrowed from romantic literature long before Greene's time.[160] These plays, though rude and uncouth, and void of all artistic merit, were liked by the people for their liveliness, variety of action, and abundance of surprises. Marlowe himself adopted this style, but he adopted it that he might reform the tendency. In conformity with the bent of his genius, he confined himself to purely tragic subjects, to passions that ignored probability. In his *Dr. Faustus* and *The Jew of Malta* he first attempted artistic tragedy, with more or less of psychological treatment, and with clearly delineated characters. After two or three unsuccessful attempts, Greene discovered himself unable to cope with Marlowe in that field, and found a course more suited to his faculty. Without forsaking the old romantic dramas, which left the imagination so wide a range, he introduced the love element into them. In his hands this chaotic and irregular form of drama first obtained artistic organisation, first received more or less well-planned scenes, and was first filled with artistically delineated charac-

[160] The well-known enemy of theatres, the Puritan Gosson, who had at one time himself been a dramatist, complains in his "Playes Confuted" (London, 1582), that the "Palace of Pleasure" (a collection of Italian novels translated into English and edited by Panter in 1566), "The Golden Ass," the "Æthiopian History" (a pastoral of Heliodorus translated into English in 1577), "Amadis of Fraunce," and the "Round Table," etc., have been thoroughly ransacked to furnish the playhouses in London.

ters. Of these latter, his female characters have a charm and moral altitude to which no contemporary dramatist, Shakspeare alone excepted, attained. It cannot be denied that the relationship between even the last of Greene's plays and their originals is easily discernible; that there are too many surprises, too many unexpected and badly contrived occurrences; that too much prominence is given to disguises and such ingenious devices; yet, if we compare Greene's dramas with those of his predecessors and contemporaries of the same tendency, we shall discover a marked difference. We shall then be obliged to confess that Greene did for the "romantic drama" what Marlowe had done for tragedy and the "historical drama"; and we shall see that the labours of these two writers form an indispensable step in the development of the old English stage.

CHAPTER IV.

GREENE AND SHAKSPEARE.

Greene's allusions to Shakspeare, and their explanation.—Argument of Simpson's hypothesis regarding the relations between Greene and Shakspeare.—Who was the author of *Fair Emm*, which Greene ridiculed?—Traces of Greene's influence on Shakspeare.—Greene's ideal female characters and Shakspeare's Imogen.—Bohan, in the prologue to *James IV.*, and Shakspeare's *Timon of Athens.* —Greene's "Pandosto" the source of the *Winter's Tale.*[*]†

IN the interesting after-words to his "Groatsworth of Wit" (the greater part of which is quoted in the first chapter of this work), Greene, turning to his professional brethren, Marlowe, Nashe, and Peele, holds himself up as a warning to them to leave off writing for the stage and for thankless actors, and to devote their energies to some other and more useful labour: "Al three of you . . . Shake-scene in a countrie, etc." [Works, Vol. XII., pp. 142-4.—G.]. These last words, in which Greene parodies Shakspeare's name, leave no doubt behind them that it was Shakspeare at whom

---

*† See our Introduction on various points of this chapter, with quotations from Professor J. M. Brown's paper on Greene.—G.

he was aiming. Should any one, however, be inclined to waver before accepting this explanation of Greene's words, he will be thoroughly convinced by the confession of Chettle, the editor of the "Groatsworth of Wit," who, having afterwards heard much good of Shakspeare, lamented he had not omitted this passage.[161] [†] To understand Greene's abuse of Shakspeare, we must recollect that the latter was a member of the corporation of actors, whom Greene so much detested, and whom he has accused of such ingratitude. Besides, Greene was justified to a certain extent in looking on Shakspeare as a plagiarist. When Shakspeare came to London, in 1585, or more likely in 1586, and joined the Lord Chamberlain's company, he began his career as a dramatist by rewriting and altering old plays to suit his company. We shall find the original of nearly every one of Shakspeare's juvenile productions in the dramatic literature of the early part of that period. So long as he was content with writing for his own company he could not have occasioned any severe loss to Greene and his friends, who wrote for other companies. But when, in the course of time, he began to widen his sphere of action and to offer his services to

---

[161] *Vide* Chettle's preface (To the Gentlemen Readers) to "Kind-heart's Dreame."

[†] But surely the quotation from Greene and his use therein of "Shake-scene" are far more decisive than Chettle's, who, indeed, gives no clue to the name of any save as they confirm the intended reference of "Shake-scene." Without that term Chettle's reference could only have been conjectured or thought probable.—G.

other companies[168] [a]†; when he became a regular factotum, threatening to flood the theatres of London with his productions, then all Greene's clique were up in arms against him, with Greene himself at their head, the loudest and foremost in the fray. The indignation of Greene's circle increased when Shakspeare began rewriting plays composed by them, and altering them so that they became utterly unrecognisable. Malone, Dyce, Ingleby, and others are of opinion that the old plays *The First Part of the Contention* and *The true Tragedie of Richard Duke of York* (in the latter piece the words occur "Oh, tiger's heart wrapped in a woman's hide!" which Greene so cleverly parodies), was written by one of Greene's set, and then introduced by Shakspeare into *Henry VI.* If we accept so very probable a supposition, Greene's anger will become thoroughly intelligible. Greene saw in Shakspeare, not only a successful rival, but an enemy, who beat the established dramatists with their own weapons, which he had stolen from them. Greene's anxiety at Shakspeare's growing popularity, manifested in his advice

[168] Under the 7th March, 1591, Henslowe has an entry of the representation of *Henry VI.* by the company of Lord Strange ("The Diary of Philip Henslowe," edited by Collier; London, 1845, p. 22).

[a]† It never has been established that Shakspeare wrote for "other companies," albeit it is not impossible that in the earlier part of his career he wrote "purple patches" for any play submitted to him. It was indeed sufficient that Shakspeare's superior productions drew, and argal drew away the audiences of other theatres.—G.

to his friends to give up the thankless profession of play-writing, was justified by subsequent events. In a few years' time Shakspeare was to out-distance all the "university pens" of his day, Ben Jonson not excepted.[163]

Greene's dying mention of Shakspeare, the last act in the drama of their mutual relations, involuntarily leads us to conclude that this last act was preceded by innumerable disagreeables and jostlings, of which traces must have been left in their works. Hence the desire to lift the veil hiding Shakspeare's relations with one of the most gifted of his predecessors, has naturally arisen. Greene's sad allusions to his secret enemies, with which his pamphlets are filled, would act as guides in this attempt and encourage further investigations. An attempt of this kind has been published in a posthumous work of Simpson's [164]— one of the best Shakspearian scholars of England.[v†]

[163] In *The Return from Pernassus*, a play first printed in 1606, but performed by the students of Cambridge University in the lifetime of Queen Elizabeth, the celebrated actor, Kemp, is made to say: "Few of the university pen plaies well; they smell too much of that writer Ovid, and talke too much of Proserpina and Jupiter. Why here's our fellow Shakspeare puts them all downe, and Ben Jonson too."

[164] "The School of Shakspeare, edited, with Intro-

v† Very doubtful;—sifted, his entire writings yield a mere palmful of real grain out of enormous chaff. He had no "critical" faculty, and extreme dogmatism. But *certes* Simpson nowhere calls *gentle* Shakspeare malignant or even implacable.—G.

We have seen that Greene frequently complains, in the prefaces and dedications affixed to his love-pamphlets, of his literary enemies, who persecuted him with their malignant slanders, sneered at his blank verse, were sceptical as to the sincerity of his repentance, and to whom he gave no quarter in return. Simpson turns all these innumerable enemies into one powerful opponent, malignant, implacable and omnipresent; and avers that this enemy was no other than Shakspeare. To prove this hypothesis, Simpson has spent a considerable amount of labour and wit. He supports it with the obstinate casuistry of a lawyer, who wishes at all hazards to prove the guilt of the accused, and who can subtly use every hint, every vague expression, every suspicious circumstance, as corroborative evidence in favour of his case. By means of such special-pleading Simpson succeeded, after bringing his undisputed erudition and ingeniousness to bear upon the subject, in weaving a skilful logical net, wherein to entrap his victim. Unfortunately for him, however, this net is not woven of threads of good stout facts, but made of the fragile materials of cobweb allusions, suppositions, and fictitious allegories, which fall to pieces as soon as they are brought in contact with critical analysis.

We shall give a few illustrations in support of this statement. In "Planetomachia" Greene describes a

---

duction and notes, and an account of R. Greene, his prose works and his Quarrels with Shakspeare." London, 1878. 2 vols.

revengeful and crafty hypocrite, Valdracko, who hires an assassin to murder his son-in-law and that son-in-law's father, Count Celio. In this character we find the embodiment of everything evil and low in human nature. Simpson at once draws our attention to the fact that "Planetomachia" was issued in 1585—namely, at exactly the same time at which, in his opinion, Shakspeare first began to write for the stage. He goes on to show, that Valdracko has all those bad qualities which Greene so frequently ascribes to his unknown enemy, who combined the functions of actor and dramatist in one; and he triumphantly points to Shakspeare as the original of Valdracko. Such conclusions—however strange they may be—would have some standing-ground if we knew, and knew for certain, when Shakspeare came to London and commenced writing for the theatres, and when he first met Greene. But we have no reliable information on the subject, and it is very probable that Shakspeare had not yet taken up his abode in London in 1585, at the time of the publication of "Planetomachia"; for we have documentary evidence to the effect that he had twins, Hamnet and Judith, borne him in that year [at Stratford-on-Avon.—G.] We are equally unable to say whether Greene himself was in London then, for his marriage took place at the end of that year; after which he lived in the country until his separation from his wife, a little over a year; *† and we may thus state, almost con-

*† It must be kept in mind that Greene was vicar of Tollesbury in 1585. See our Introduction.—G.

fidently, that Greene could not have met Shakspeare before the end of 1586 or the commencement of 1587. Let us go a little further. When Greene commenced his dramatical labours, his first productions were satirised by two unknown dramatists (note [77]), one of whom was Marlowe.[1]† If Simpson could have succeeded in proving the other to have been Shakspeare, all his subsequent conjectures regarding Greene's and Nashe's enmity with Shakspeare would have received material support. But until this is done, we have no right to suppose that Nashe had Shakspeare in view when attacking "lack-latins" and conceited actors, or that it was Shakspeare whom Greene represented in his "Menaphon" as Doron, the rude and ignorant shepherd. To what an extent a cherished crotchet can obscure the critical perspicacity of the investigator may be seen from the following. Our readers will remember that Greene condemns in his preface to "Farewell to Follie" a certain contemporary play, the author of which makes his hero and heroine interlard their declarations of love with passages from the Scriptures. Bernhardi has shown that this play is *Fair Emm*, and that it is evidently an imitation of Greene's *Bacon*. *Fair Emm* was well known to the admirers of old English plays, and has been attributed by some to

---

[1]† I should qualify by reading was 'possibly' Marlowe. This is the utmost that can safely be said. Greene would hardly have spoken of "two Gentlemen Poets" without naming Marlowe, and then have given in the way he does that *Atheist* Tamburlan's name.—G.

Shakspeare,[105] and by others to Greene.[106] Tieck has translated it into German, and published it in the second volume of his "Shakspeare's Vorschule" as a juvenile production of Shakspeare's. It was only necessary to prove that this play had really been written by Shakspeare, and the hypothesis of the strange enmity between Shakspeare and Greene would receive substantial corroborative support. The temptation was too great for a man of Simpson's intellectual temperament to withstand. We thus find him proving *Fair Emm*, from its style, moral tone, diction, and dramatic effect, fully worthy to be called a work of Shakspeare's. It had yet to be discovered why this play should have roused Greene's indignation. Even this mystery has not been hidden from Simpson. An attentive perusal of the play has revealed to him its interior, hidden meaning. The more he read it, the more convinced he became that this was not the simple drama it purported to be, but an allegorical satire; that Maundeville, who wavers

---

[105] This tradition takes its origin, as Malone says, from the fact that the librarian of Charles II. had *Fair Emm* bound up with several other plays, and labelled "Shakspeare, vol. i."

[106] Philipps, in his "Theatrum Poetarum" (London, 1675), includes *Fair Emm*, together with several other plays rejected by modern critics, among the works of Greene. In Delius' preface to his edition of *Fair Emm* ("Pseudo Shakspearische Dramen, fünftes Heft"), the entire history of the *Fair Emm* controversy, up to 1874, is given.

between two mistresses and is finally refused by both, is meant for Greene, wavering between romance and drama, and successful in neither. Greene, of course, at once recognised his own portrait in the unsuccessful Maundeville, and hence his indignation against the author of *Fair Emm*. *Habent sua fata libelli!* While Simpson was thus, with unexampled patience, seeking out one proof after another in corroboration of his hypothesis, he little thought there existed a reply by the real author of this piece to Greene's attacks, a reply which was destined to sweep his carefully erected house of cards from off the face of the earth. We will now proceed to consider this reply. It will be found in the preface to a puritanical pamphlet[7†] entitled "Martin Mar-Sixtus," which appeared in the beginning of 1592 (in the "Registers" it is entered under the 8th November, 1591)—a few months, therefore, after the publication of "Farewell to Follie." [167] It runs thus :—

"Loath I was to display my selfe to the world, but for that I hope to daunce vnder a maske, and bluster out like the winde, which, though every man heareth, yet none can in sight descrie, I was content for once to become odious, that is, to speake in print, that such as vse to carpe at they know not what, may

[167] This pamphlet is a bibliographical rarity. It is not to be found even in the library of the British Museum. However, the preface to it is reprinted in the "British Bibliographer," vol. i., pp. 39—41. [Now in B. M.—G].

[7†] See our Introduction. It is not 'puritanical.'—G.

for once likewise condemne they know not whome, and yet I doo not so accuse the readers, as if all writers were faultles, for why? We liue in a printing age, wherein there is no man either so vainely, or factiously, or filthily disposed, but there are crept out of all sorts vnauthorised authors, to fill and fit his humor, and if a mans deuotion serve him not to goe to the Church of GOD, he neede but repayre to a stationers shop and reade a sermon of the diuels; I loath to speake it, euery red-nosed minister is an author, euery drunken mans dreame is a booke,[168] and he whose talent of little wit is hardly worth a farthing, yet layeth about him so outragiously *as if all* Helicon *had run through his pen*, in a word, scarce a cat can looke out of a gutter, but out starts a halfpeny Chronicler, *and presently* A propper new ballet of a strange sight *is endited*; what publishing of friuolous and scurrilous Prognostications? *as if* Will Sommers[169] were againe reuiued: what counterfeiting and cogging of prodigious and fabulous monsters? as if they labored to *exceede the Poet in his* Metamorphosis; what lasciuious, vnhonest, and amorous discourses, *such as* Augustus in a heathen common

---

[168] An allusion to a poem of Greene's published in 1591, entitled "A Maiden's Dream, upon the death of Sir Christopher Hatton." This poem may be found in Dyce's edition of Greene's works. [See Works, Vol. XIV., pp. 293—317.—G.]

[169] Will Somers was the famous fool of King Henry VIII., celebrated for his witty, though rather broad and coarse repartees.

wealth could neuer tolerate? and yet they shame not *to subscribe*, By a graduate in Cambridge; In Artibus Magister; *as if* men should iudge of the fruites of Art by the ragges and parings of wit, *and endite* [= indict.—G.] *the* Vniuersities, *as not onely* accessary to their vanitie, but nurses of bawdry; we would the world should know, that howsoeuer those places have power to create a Master of Artes, yet the art of loue is none of the seauen; and be *it true that* Honos alit artes, yet *small* honor is it to be honored for such artes, nor shal he carry the price [= prize.—G.] that seasoneth his profit with such a sweete; it is the complaint of our age, that men are wanton and sick of wit, with which (as with a loathsome potion in the stomack) they are neuer well till all be out. *They are the* Pharisees *of our time*, they write al, & speak al, *and do al*, vt audiantur ab hominibus; *or to tel a plaine truth* plainely, it is with our hackney authors, as with Oyster-wiues, they care not how sweetely but how loudely they cry, and cōming abroad, they are receaued as vnsauory wares, men are faine to stop their noses, and crie: Fie vpon this wit; thus affecting to be famous, they become notorious, that it may be saide of them *as of the* Sophisters *at* Athens: dum volunt haberi celebriter docti innotescunt insigniter asinini, *and when with shame* they see their folly, they are faine to put on a mourning garment, and crie, Far well [to Folly.]"[2†]

[2†] The following is the full and accurate title of the book: "MARTINE MAR-SIXTUS / A second replie against / *the defensory and Apology of* Sixtus *the* / fift, late Pope of *Rome*,

There can be little doubt that we have here to deal with an author's outraged self-respect. Personal irritation can be detected in almost every line, and shows itself in the allusions to Greene's intemperate habits, his red nose, etc. Greene cruelly cut up *Fair Emm*,[170] and was especially severe on the author for his blasphemous introduction of quotations from the Bible into his love-passages. The author revengefully attacked Greene's own works in return, and called them "lascivious, inhonest, amorous discourses."

Who then was this most mysterious, malignant, and perhaps wittiest of Greene's enemies? We should never have discovered his name had he not himself accidentally given us the clue by putting his

[170] Halliwell, "A Dictionary of Old English Plays" (London, 1860), *sub voce.*

defending the exe / crable fact of the Jacobine Frier, vpon the per / son of *Henry* the third, late King of *France*, / *to be both commendable, admirable*, / *and meritorous.* / [A few words as to the translation of Sixtus speech from the French, and a text from Scripture, a printer's device, and] AT LONDON / Printed for *Thomas Woodcock*, and are to be sold at his shop in Paules / Church-yard, at the signe of the Black Beare, 1591./ The writer giues his initials at the end of the Dedication—"Your Worships in / all duety, R. W." In the prior part of his Dedication he says, "this short treatise, the fruites of a Schollers Study." Then follows the quotation *ut supra*—kindly copied for me from the original in the British Museum in preference to the retranslation of Professor Storojenko's translation into Russian. See our Introduction on the assignation of *Fair Emm* to this R[obert] W[ilson] and on the relation of the above tractate to others.—G.

initials R. W. at the end of his Dedication. We know that two pamphlets, "Three Ladies of London" and "Three Lords and Ladies of London," the first published in 1584 and the other in 1590, had these same initials affixed to them.*‡ Now all authorities on the subject are agreed that these two pamphlets were written by Robert Wilson, senior,[171] an actor in Leicester's company, a celebrated comedian, second to Tarlton alone in comic power. According to Collier, he was not only an excellent performer, but also a talented dramatist, especially renowned for his ready repartees and quickness of wit.[172] Like Gosson, Wilson was a Puritan by religion (Furnivall calls him a "Puritanical writer"), which, however, by no means interfered with his acting, nor prevented him from being a dramatist and having a fondness for the stage; which latter he defended, though but faintly, it must be confessed, from the attacks by Puritan

[171] We shall call him so to distinguish him from another Robert Wilson, his son (1579—1610), also a dramatist, who wrote plays conjointly with Drayton, Hethaway, and others, and of whom Meres speaks in the following terms: "Our worthy Wilson, for learning and extemporal wit without compare or compeer."

[172] *Vide* Collier's "Introduction" to the five plays he edited in 1851 for the "Roxburghe Club." It is reprinted by Hazlitt, in the sixth volume of his edition of Dodsley, "Old English Plays" (London, 1874).

*‡ There are two Plays—one called "A right excellent and famous Comodey," the other "The pleasant and stately Morall of, etc." See Hazlitt's Dodsley, vol. vi.—G.

brethren.[173] In support of our belief that Robert Wilson, senior, was the author of "Martin Mar-Sixtus," and consequently of the *Fair Emm* Greene ridiculed, we may give the following arguments:—

1. Like the author of "Martin Mar-Sixtus," who did not like to see his name printed in full, but preferred writing under the mask of his initials, Robert Wilson did not appear in print, and preferred signing his productions with the initial letters of his name, R. W. As far as we are aware, only one of his plays ever bore his name in full, and that was *The Cobbler's Prophecy.*

2. If we read the dedication of the "Farewell to Follie" in connection with Greene's address to the students of Oxford and Cambridge, where the attack on *Fair Emm* is to be found, we shall see that in both cases Greene is speaking really of only one person, whom he calls a Puritanical Pharisee, and whose satirical sneers Greene was fully prepared for, as they had been directed against him before. The

[173] Gosson, in "Plays Confuted," speaks thus of Wilson: "Whether this be the practise of Poets in these dayes, you may perceive by the drift of him that wrote the play termed the *Three Ladies of London*, which in the catastrophe maketh Love and Conscience to be examined how their good ladyshippes like of playes? Love answeres that she detesteth them, because her guttes are tourned outward and all her secret conveighaunce is blazed with colours to the peoples-eye. Conscience, like a kind-hearted gentlewoman, doth allow them." [Can't find this.—G.]

shaft evidently hit its mark. The author of "Martin Mar-Sixtus" insulted, not only as an author, but as a man of certain religious convictions, attacks Greene with his own weapons, replying to the effect that real Pharisees, in his opinion, were those who, like Greene, ostentatiously trumpeted their repentance to the whole world.

3. Greene alludes to some connection between the author of *Fair Emm* and the parish of St. Giles, Cripplegate (the sexton of which he supposes assisted the author in writing this play).[b‡] Now, we know that Robert Wilson was buried in the grounds of this church,[174] probably because he had always lived in the parish of St. Giles.

On the face of these considerations we affirm that the author of "Martin Mar-Sixtus" and of the drama of *Fair Emm* were one and the same person, and that this person was no other than Robert Wilson, senior, an old enemy of Greene's; and that consequently it is to him and Marlowe that most of the allusions and venomous attacks found in Greene's love-pamphlets relate, and not to Shakspeare.

---

[174] In the parish register of St. Giles, Cripplegate, we read: "Buried, Robert Wilson, yoman, a player 20 Nov. 1600." (Collier's "Memoirs of the Principal Actors." London, 1846. Introduction, p. xviii.)

[b‡] The argument is not really altered by Greene's actual statement, but see it in Vol. IX. p. 233—*i.e.* "Clearkes of parish churches," not the "sexton," the latter being only pronounced one who would have been ashamed of such "blasphemous rhetoricke."—G.

We now proceed, from the misty realms of speculation and guesses as to the relations of Greene with Shakspeare and other contemporaries, where even such experts as Simpson are apt to lose their way, to the domain of sober fact, and will endeavour to show what were the literary relations between Greene and Shakspeare, and to determine the degree of influence exercised by the former over the latter. It stands to reason that we shall confine ourselves to those aspects of this question which have, in our opinion, been either not sufficiently explained, or else completely ignored by Shakspearean critics.

There is a whole group of Shakspeare's plays, principally borrowed from novels and pastoral romances, which, from their fantastical character, inherited from the originals, do not fall in with the usual division either of comedies, tragedies, or historical dramas. Such, for instance, are *Cymbeline*, *Winter's Tale*, *Midsummer Night's Dream*, *As You Like it*, etc. Their distinguishing features are an intricacy of plot, often branching off into independent little bye-plots; an irregular development and movement of actions, attended by admirably drawn characters; an abundance of all sorts of unexpected occurrences, disguises, mysterious disappearances, elopements; and, as the necessary consequence of all this, much of *fantastique*.

English critics of the present day call this peculiar genus "romantic comedies." Gervinus calls one of these plays, owing to the predominance of the epic element in it, "Episches Drama" and "Dramatisches Epos"; and Mezierre, a French critic, proposes to christen them "drame romanesque," and suggests ironically that the old classification of plays should be changed into moods and genders on their account. In consequence of their strange construction and fantastical action, these plays have sometimes called down on themselves the severe censure of critics brought up in the stern simplicity of the classic school.

Dr. Johnson's opinion of *Cymbeline* is well known. He considered it simply absurd, found fault with the subject and plot, proved that the events described could never have happened anywhere, and reproached Shakspeare for mixing up persons and customs belonging to different epochs.c‡ Schlegel, on the other hand, who belonged to the romantic school, thinks *Cymbeline* the pearl of Shakspeare's plays for the very same reasons. He is struck with the art with which Shakspeare blends Boccaccio's novel with the ancient British traditions; the manners and customs of his own more modern day with those of the heroic period. This original type of drama Greene inherited, as it were, from his predecessors, and as Greene was the principal representative of this type, as he was the first to endow this type with some amount of artistic organisation, Shakspeare's obligations to Greene, in this respect, are beyond dispute. In Greene's works (especially in *Bacon*), Shakspeare could find that mode of treatment which he afterwards showed so much partiality for, and made so famous—namely, of carrying on two parallel

c‡ Variorum edition, 1821, Vol. XIII., p. 229.—G.

plots and connecting them with each other, either at the commencement or else at the end of the play. This plan was also adopted by the author of *Fair Emm*; but this drama, as Bernhardi has already pointed out, bears such evident traces of being an imitation of Greene's play, that there can be no question of supremacy between the two authors. It is also from Greene that Shakspeare might have borrowed the art of introducing humorous episodes into the course of his plays. Humorous scenes had long been indispensable attributes of the old English theatre. We find them already in a sufficiently developed form in the *Mysteries*. Rarely did a play, however serious it might be, get on without them. But up to Greene's time these comic episodes were simply introduced "to make pastime" (as an old dramatist, T[homas] Preston, says in the preface to his *Cambyses*, a play published about 1570). Clowns came on the stage and departed, after duly amusing the audience by their wit and drollery, but the course of the play was not helped on one jot by them. The plot was kept at a standstill, for, properly speaking, they were outside the plot. As far as we know, Greene was the first to bring these comic episodes in closer union with the play. In *Bacon* and in *James IV.* the humorous scenes have a great deal to do with the main plot. The stupidity of Miles is one of the principal causes that lead to Bacon's rupture with the devil. Slipper's selling the king's order to murder his queen to Sir Bartram constitutes the crisis of the plot, for it is only on seeing this document that the queen decides on flying, and saves her life. Finally, notwithstanding the inferiority of Greene's genius as compared with that of Shakspeare, the former could have acted as a model to the latter in yet another respect. In Greene's works Shakspeare would find numerous pictures of life among the lower classes, filled with a strong love for the people, and for country-life and scenery, and breathing such freshness and such moral health, that they are second to none of the same kind, those alone excepted which we come across in Shakspeare's own plays.

Having indicated the influence Greene's works had on Shakspeare's fantastical or romantic dramas in general, we can now proceed to discuss details. We have stated above that Greene's originality manifested itself particularly in the creation of ideal female characters. We meet with no parallel to them in all the dramatic literature of England until we come to Shakspeare. All Greene's ideal women have a family likeness, so to speak. They all belong to a family of loving and devoted martyrs, who endure the trials they are subjected to with grateful submissiveness, never losing their faith in a supreme justice, and seemingly drawing fresh power to love from these very trials.[a]‡ In their love there is neither passion nor egotism. They love ideally. Their devotion is an uninterrupted self-sacrifice. This beautiful feminine principle, this boundless devotion, love, long-suffering, and open-heartedness, which we find in Shakspeare's Imogen, Greene has infused into three of his ideal female characters—Philomela, Margaret, and Doro-

[a]‡ All were probably modelled on his Dorothea. See our Introduction for Prof. Brown on 'Dorothea.'—G.

thea. Hazlitt's well-known saying that Shakspeare's heroines lived only through their devotion to other people, may be applied with equal justice to those of Greene. We once had occasion to read the *Cymbeline* of Shakspeare immediately after Greene's "Philomela," and we were struck with the astounding resemblance there exists between the characters of Philomela and Imogen. A more careful perusal of these two productions confirmed the accuracy of our first impression, and implanted in us a strong conviction that the character of Philomela had its influence on Shakspeare,—the more so as the fortunes of the two heroines have several points of similarity. Both were famous for their beauty and mental endowments; both had to suffer at the hands of those they loved; their love and fidelity were subjected to the most cruel and insulting tests by their husbands; both came through the ordeal, though broken-hearted, yet with unstained honour. But there is a difference here. Imogen's husband, believing himself deceived by her, orders his servant to kill her. Philomela's suspicious husband, on the other hand, invents a means of killing her morally. He has her prosecuted, hires false witnesses and succeeds in getting her banished the country. At first, like Imogen, she succumbs to the natural feeling of indignation at her treatment, and broods over her revenge. But this does not last long. Philomela remembers that the word "husband" is a great word, easily spoken, but not so easily torn from the heart. She even tries to find an excuse for her husband, and persuades herself that his jealousy and suspicion arise from his great love for her. On learning that he is in prison, under trial for murder, she appears before the court and accuses herself of the crime, to save his life. This angelic act so touches her husband's heart, so agitates him, that he dies the same day. After he has breathed his last in her arms, Philomela returns to Venice, to pass the rest of her life in mourning his death.[175]

One of the later English critics (Fletcher, if we are not mistaken), in analysing the character of Imogen, insists on her moral relationship to Juliet. He is of opinion that Juliet is a bud, capable of blossoming forth into a full-blown flower like Imogen. With this conclusion we find it difficult to agree, for the natures of these two heroines are as different as possible. In the enthusiastic and ardent temperament of Juliet passion and imagination predominate. The basis to Imogen's more equally balanced mind, on the other hand, is that cordial simplicity of heart which the Germans call *Gemüth*. The difference in their character may be best seen from their attitude towards their husbands. Juliet loves with the impetuosity of an Italian. Her love, kindled by her ardent imagination, makes her form heroic resolutions; Imogen's love is unselfish devotion and a complete abnegation of self. On the side of Juliet

---

[175] Not having Greene's "Philomela" at hand, we give the plot according to Dunlop, who, it may be added, gives a very careful account of this tale. [See "Philomela" itself, in Works, Vol. XI., pp. 104—211. Page 244, ll. 23-5, one queries "Promos and Cassandra" (1578).—G.]

we find impulse and passion, on that of Imogen depth and constancy. For these reasons we think the observations of the English critic may be applied with better justice to Philomela than to Juliet. If we analyse the character of Imogen we shall find in it the same fundamental qualities of which that of Philomela is composed—namely, depth of feeling, complete devotion to the man of her choice, energy and self-control; only in a much higher degree, and surrounded by an aureola of poetry that makes her, perhaps, the most attractive of all the female characters Shakspeare's genius has created.

In view of the fact that Shakspeare always took a great interest in the type of misanthrope during his dramatic labours, and has shown us this type from various points of view and in various degrees of development in the melancholy Jacques, Hamlet, and Timon of Athens, we think it as well to point out that a sketch of such a character will be first found in Greene's works.*‡ In the prologue to *James IV.* Greene treats us to an original in the character of Bohan, a Scottish misanthrope. This prologue is, in fact, a dialogue between this individual and Oberon, the king of the elves. Oberon, wishing to amuse the hermit, sends his elves to dance round the grave, where he has buried himself alive. Irritated by the sounds of merriment and music, Bohan rushes out of

*‡ See our Introduction on this. For myself I would hardly go so far, albeit 'sketch' is not a very large claim. Besides, there was a 'Hamlet' before Shakspeare's 'Hamlet,' and a 'Timon' before his 'Timon.' The pity is we don't know how they were drawn.—G.

his vault, and so frightens the elves by his uncouth appearance that they take to flight. Oberon thus finds himself alone confronted with him :—

"*Bohan.* Ay say, what's thou ?" [f‡]

But as this moving appeal has no effect on Oberon, who does not budge a step, Bohan tries to draw his sword to run him through. Oberon, however, has charmed the sword, and all Bohan's endeavours to draw it from its scabbard prove fruitless. Amused at the odd old fellow's rage, Oberon asks to be told the story of his life. Bohan agrees, for he wishes to vent his bile on some one. From Bohan's narrative we learn that he belonged to one of the best and oldest Scottish families ; that he had served with distinction at court, and taken part in numerous battles, but his services were not appreciated, and on a post of importance becoming vacant, another was preferred before him. He then became convinced that only intriguers and flatterers could succeed at court, and so he retired to the country.

"*Oberon.* To what life didst thou then betake thee ? etc." [g‡]

To prove to Oberon the emptiness of the world and the vanity of human beings, Bohan hires[h‡] a

---

[f‡] Works, Vol. XIII., p. 205.—G.

[g‡] *Ibid.*, p. 208.—G.

[h‡] The text is, "That story haue I set down : gang with me to the gallery and Ile shew thee the same in Action by guid fellowes of our country men." No word of 'hiring.' The mention of 'gallery' taken with Slipper, Nano, and others coming in personally (as noted before), suggests that Greene wrote in haste and not improbably when drinking a good deal.—G.

company of actors to perform the play of *James IV.*, and accompanies every act with sardonic comments and caustic remarks on the perverseness of mankind.

Does not this disappointed and irritable old man, living in a vault, and sending out from thence his anathemas against a deceitful world, remind us of Timon of Athens? Is not he the first, though certainly an incomplete and rough sketch of this immortal type? We do not wish to say dogmatically that Greene was the immediate source of *Timon of Athens*, but why should it not be admitted that the character of this morose Scotchman, as described by Greene, might have interested Shakspeare and awakened in him a desire to work it out more fully, especially after meeting a similar type in Plutarch?[1‡]

We now turn to Greene's "Pandosto, or Dorastus and Faunia," whence Shakspeare borrowed the plot of his *Winter's Tale*. Much has been said already on Shakspeare's attitude towards his original, in special works on Shakspeare's plays. We shall therefore, to avoid unnecessary repetition, limit ourselves to as few critical remarks as possible.

"Dorastus and Faunia" belongs to the central period of Greene's literary labours, when he was still under the influence of Lylly. The pamphlet is written in language so euphuistic as to be inferior in nothing to the "Euphues" of the great Lylly himself. The story does not stand out from among the

---

[1‡] Of course Storojenko thinks of Shakspeare's 'Timon,' not the historical man-hater of the time of Alcibiades. See our Introduction on these dim preludes of Shakspearean characters.—G.

rest of Greene's love-pamphlets. We find in it no delineation of character, no psychological analysis of the human heart. We are made acquainted with the emotions of some of the characters by the lyrical effusions alone to which they occasionally give way; but even these effusions have more of euphuism than of real passion in them. The plot, however, is rather interesting; but here Greene has, as usual, mixed up all sorts of periods and transgressed the laws of probability. He bestows a sea-coast on Bohemia, and makes the kings of that country and Sicily the contemporaries of the oracle of Delphi. It has been remarked that Shakspeare treated the English translations of Italian novels very differently from original works bearing such celebrated names as Greene and Lodge.[176] With the former he made no ceremony, and, after borrowing the plot and general story, created his own characters and made his own scenes. The latter, speaking generally, he treated more respectfully, kept himself more strictly to the original plot, changing only a few details here and there to suit stage effect, and leaving all the original characters, endeavouring merely to make them stand out in better relief, and occasionally venturing to add a few new ones of his own.[J‡]

---

[176] *Vide* Delius's article, "Lodge's Rosalynd und Shakspeare's *As you Like it*," in the sixth volume of the "Jahrbuch der deutschen Shakspeare-Gesellschaft."

[J‡] Because these stories were known to the public, and one was more apt to wish to see a known story dramatised

Let us now see what changes Shakspeare made in Greene's novel. In transforming it into a drama he first of all altered the name, and instead of calling it "Pandosto, or Dorastus and Faunia," he entitled it *A Winter's Tale*, as though to indicate the fairy-like and imaginative character of the piece. Further, for reasons unknown to us, he re-christened all the *dramatis personæ*. The king of Bohemia, Pandosto, he called Leontes, and removed to Sicily; and Egistus, the king of Sicily, he called Polixenes, and transplanted to Bohemia. With Greene Egistus is married to the daughter of the Tsar of Russia,[177] and this circumstance is one of the reasons why Pandosto postpones his plan of revenge against Egistus, and determines on reeking his vengeance on Bellaria (in

---

[177] Greene makes Egistus marry the daughter of the Tsar of Russia. Probably because towards the close of the sixteenth century Russia was already beginning to excite the interest of Englishmen. Besides the active diplomatic relations that commenced between the two countries at about this time, commercial relations were also entered on. Englishmen, who had been in Russia, told their countrymen strange stories on their return, and taught them a few Russian phrases. Thomas Nashe, in his pamphlet against Harvey ("Have with you to Saffron Walden," London, 1596), says of his enemies: "I will compel them to fall down and worship me ere I cease or make an

than an unknown; just as they went to see *Henry V.* or other histories. Moreover, people don't like seeing known stories so altered as to jar with their recollections.—G.

Shakspeare Hermione); Shakspeare, on the other hand, makes Hermione declare herself the daughter of the Tsar before the court of judicature, and deplore that he is unable to help her. In the first three acts Shakspeare closely follows the novel, departing from it only in cases when this was necessary for dramatic purposes. In one instance, however, a departure from the original, called forth undoubtedly by scenic considerations, does not improve the drama. With Shakspeare the jealousy of Leontes is not probable. Leontes grows jealous of his wife and begins to suspect her because she asked Polixenes, in compliance with her husband's wishes, to prolong his stay for some days. The recollection of the animation with which she spoke to the guest serves to confirm him in his suspicion. With Greene Pandosto's jealousy is far better contrived. We read in his novel

---

end, crying upon their knees *Pomiloi nashe.*" He informs us in another passage of a curious office, that was supposed to exist in Russia: "Then gather yourselves together in a ring and grand Consiliadoro be you the grand commander of Silence, which is a chiefe office in the Emperour of Russia's court." The following extract from a letter of John Chamberlain's, dated 4th November, 1602, may be not uninteresting: "We have here foure youths come from Moscovie to learne our language and latin, and are to be dispersed to divers schools at Westminster, Eaton, Cambridge, and Oxford." ("J. Chamberlain's Letters during the reign of Elizabeth, edited by Sarah Williams for the Camden Society." London, 1861.)

that Bellaria and Egistus were fond of being together, that they often took long walks, liked being alone, and that they were melancholy without each other's company. Thus Pandosto's jealousy, although there is no cause for it, is at all events comprehensible; besides, time is given for it to develop. This slip[k‡] Shakspeare atones for by numerous charming scenes, for which we may search in vain in Greene. In the novel the jealous king simply orders his wife to be put in prison, and has her unfaithfulness proclaimed to his subjects. In the place of this official announcement, Shakspeare gives us a beautiful scene, wherein Hermione refutes, in the presence of the whole court, the charge brought against her, with unequalled dignity. Following this, we have two more scenes, in which Antigonus and Paulina successively plead for Hermione. These two characters Greene has not got at all. The birth of a daughter to the queen, the queen's trial, the reply of the oracle, the lethargy into which the queen falls when the news of her son's death is suddenly brought her,—all these events are taken wholesale from Greene, with one essential difference, however; for Shakspeare makes Hermione, whom every one thinks dead, awaken, and hide for sixteen years at Paulina's, whereas Bellaria dies.

The chief difference between the drama and the novel commences at the fourth act. In Greene's tale the interest is centred on the love of Dorastus, son of Egistus, for Pandosto's daughter, Faunia. Nearly

[k‡] No 'slip,' but intentional, probably through the exigencies of a dramatic representation.—G.

half of the novel is taken up with this love episode. Shakspeare, on the contrary, centres the interest on the jealousy of the king and the evil consequences that ensue from it. The love-passages between Florizel and Perdita only constitute a captivating episode, and take up the fourth act, where Autolycus appears, a most amusing character, whom we do not find in Greene. The tale finishes by Pandosto's falling in love with the wife of ~~Florizel~~. On his discovering Dorastus
that she is his daughter, he falls into a fit of melancholy and commits suicide. Shakspeare justly considered such a conclusion too gloomy, and not in harmony with the light and imaginative character of the story. With him Hermione proves to be alive, and Leontes, sufficiently punished by the pangs of remorse, and by a separation from his wife of sixteen years, implores her forgiveness, is pardoned, and the play finishes with the happiness of all concerned.

It would be interesting to investigate in detail the influence exercised by Greene on every single one of his contemporary dramatists; but the study of this question would lead us beyond the precincts of the task we have set ourselves to perform. Besides, there is no great difference of opinion on that subject among critics. The majority of these acknowledge the influence of Marlowe and Greene more or less on the whole drama of the period, with the exception only of Shakspeare. Ulrici, for instance, does not deny the influence of Marlowe and Greene on Chettle, Thomas Heywood, etc., but he draws a hard and fast line between the Marlowe-Greene school on the one hand, and Shakspeare on the other. Some time ago

Elze[178] partially corrected this error, and proved that *The Jew of Malta* served as a prototype for the *Merchant of Venice*. We wished to render a similar service to Greene. It is not for us, of course, to say how far we have succeeded in attaining our object, but we shall consider ourselves fortunate if the readers of this book carry away with them the firm conviction that the labours of his forgotten contemporary left some impression on Shakspeare.

---

[178] In his article "Zum Kaufmann von Vendig," in the "Jahrbuch der deutschen Shakspeare Gesellschaft," vol. vi. With regard to the influence of Marlowe's *Edward II.* on Shakspeare's *Richard II.*, *vide* "Predshestveniky Shakspeara," pp. 287-8.

APPENDIX.

A. Page 26.

The following are Greene's two Epistles from "Euphues Shadow":—

To the right Honourable, Robert
Ratcliffe, *Viscount* Fitzwaters: *Robert Greene*,
wisheth increase of honour
and vertue.

EVer desirous (right honorable) to shew my affectionate duty to your Lordship, as well for the generall report of your vertue vniuersally conceipted in the opinion of all men, as for the natiue place of my birth, whereby I am bounde to affect your honourable father and you for him aboue others, in suspence of this dutifull desire, it fortuned that one M. *Thomas Lodge*, who nowe is gone to sea with Mayster *Candish*, had bestowed some serious labour, in penning of a booke called *Euphues Shadowe*: and by his last letters gaue straight charge, that I should not onely haue the care for his sake of the impression thereof, but also in his absence to bestowe it on some man of Honor, whose worthye vertues might bee a patronage to his worke, where vpon taking aduice with my selfe, I thought none more fit then your Honour, seeing your Lordships disposition was wholy giuen to the studie of good letters, to be a Mecenas to the well imployed laboures of the absent Gentleman: may therfore your lordship fauourably censure of my good meaning, in presenting your honour with this Pamphlet, and courteouslye graunt acceptance of his workes and my good will, his labour hath his end, and my desire in dutie rests satisfied, and so humbly praying for your Lordships health and welfare I take my leaue.

Your honors humbly
to commaund. *Rob. Greene.*
Norfolciensis.

To the Gentlemen Readers,
Health.

GEntlemen, after many of mine owne labours that you haue courteouslie accepted, I present you with *Euphues shadowe*, in the behalfe of my absent friend M. *Thomas Lodge*, who at his departure to sea vpon a long voyage, was willing, as a generall farewell to all courteous Gentlemen, to leaue this his worke to the view, which if you grace with your fauours eyther as his affected meaning, or the worthe of the worke requires, not onely I for him shall rest yours, but what laboures his sea studies affords, shall be I dare promise, offered to your sight, to gratifie your courtesies, and his pen as himselfe, euery waye yours for euer Farewell.

Yours to commaund,
Rob. Greene.

B. Page 44.

I. CONDEMNATION OF FRANCIS KETT FOR AN HERETICK.

(*Brit. Mus. Lansd. MSS. N.* 982, *fol.* 102.)

Articles of heretical Pravity objected by Edmund Scambler, Bishop of Norwich against Francis Kett, Master of Arts, late of Wymondham in the Dioc. of Norwich. A. D. 1588.

1. That the new Covenant promised is not yet established, and that the Covenant, which you mean, is the Lawe of God written in our hearts and the forgiveness of our sinnes.

2. That there is no sufficient sacrifice past for the sinnes of the worlde, but that Christ shall offer it at the ende of the worlde.

3. That the Christ hath suffered only as Jesus allready and shall suffer hereafter as Jesus Chryste.

4. That Chryste is now in his human nature gathering a church here in earth in Judea.

5. That this yeare of our Lord 1588 dyvers and fewes shall be sent into dyvers countryes to publishe the new covenant.

6. That Chryste shall againe suffer and gyve his soule for the synne of the worlde before the last daye.

7. That Chryste shall comme before the ende of the world, before the last daye.

II. BLASPHEMOUS HERESYES OF ONE KETT.

(*MSS. State Paper Office, vol. CCXVII., fol.* 11.)

1. That there is no churche in England, neither have the ministers any power or aucthoritie to excommunicate, to bind or to lowse.

2. That Christ was not High Priest until his Assention into Heaven.

3. That the Holie Goste is not god, but an Holyspirite.

4. That there is no such persone and that God is no person.

5. That Christ is only man and synfull as other men are.

6. That Christ shall come before the last daie and raigne as materiall Kynge uppon Mounte Syon at Jerusalem.

7. That he shall suffer there again as Jesus Christ and then to be without Synne.

8. That there shalbe two Resurrections one before the Judgement daie and an other at that daie.

9. That the soules of all men are reserved in a sweete sleape untill the revelation of joye, when Christ comes unto his materiall kingdom at Jerusalem.

10. That there is no hell until that tyme shall come, specified of before.

11. That no Children ought to be baptized before their full age and to knowe what they should beleave.

12. That no man ought to be put to death for heresies, but that the wheate and tares should both growe together.

13. That no man as yeat doth preach the trewe Gospel of Christ.

14. That Christ, when he comes to be a materiall Kynge at Jerusalem, then and there will he make a new Covenante with his people.

15. That he is even gatheringe his people togeyther at Ierusalem in his owne personne.

III. KETT'S BOOK.

VIVAT ELIZABETHA / REGINA, the Royal Arms beneath, surmounted by a crown, with E [= Elizabeth] on one side of the Arms, and R [= Regina] on the other: all placed on a page preceding and opposite to title-page. The title-page, "by FRAVNCIS KETT / Doctor of Phisick : / . . . 1585." A dedication to her Majesty is very high-flown and panegyrical. In it we find:—"As the glory of the last house or testament of God, was greater than the first : so is it, in the manner of the two commings of Christ : for first hee came in the humilitie of the fleshe, to be to vs a sauing health: beeing borne of the Virgin Mary by the working of the holy Ghoste, very man and mortall and yet the same very GOD and immortall, in whome dwelleth all the fulness of the Godhead bodyly: yet did he neuerthelesse make himself of no reputation, takeing vpon him the shape of a seruant, and became lyke vnto men, . . . : for though hee were God's sonne yet learned hee obedyence, by those things which hee suffered, and was made perfect, and the cause of eternall saluation vnto al that obey him, according to John. In the beginning was the word, and the word was with God, and the word was God, and this worde was made fleshe, beeing the lyfe and light of men, giuing power to all that belieue in him to be the sonnes of God: for it pleased the father to send his sonne in the sinfull fleshe (being without sinne) and by sinne dampned sinne in the fleshe, and loused the workes of the deuil" [Rom. ii., margin], and he goes on quoting Heb. i., ending "that hee [Christ] might be all in all."

Other evidence of his then orthodoxy is in his Dedication.

"Your God and Sauiour Jesus Christ."

Ch. I. "So that wee haue such an Aduocate with the Father . . . as hath put down through his death and passion the deuill that hath the Lordship ouer death," &c.

"And besides seeing wee are made perfect with one only offering made by Christe him selfe through the spirit that sanctifieth." Also we have in Ch. I. the following repetition of the Dedication words:—"for first hee [Christ] came in the humilitie of the flesh, to be to vs a sauing health: beeing borne of the Virgin Mary by the working of the holy Ghoste, very man and mortall and yet the same very GOD and immortall, who beeing in the shape of God an equall with God, in whome dwelleth all the fulnes of the Godhead bodyly: yet did he neuerthelesse make him self of no reputation," etc.

The headings of the other chapters have:—

Ch. II. "How man shall bee chaunged at the sounde of laste troump from mortalitie to immortality and appeare before the judgement seat of Christ, . . .

Ch. III. "The mysterie of the glorious comming of Christ at the end of the worlde, and howe he shall sit in his glittering seate of Maiestie in all brightnesse of glorie, power, and dominion. And where, and howe all thinges both in heauen and earth shall be gathered together in Christ, and see his glorie and in him our glorification.

Ch. IV. "Of the euerlasting ioy of our glorification . . . and new glorious Ierusalem in which wee shall dwell the Sonnes and Saincts of GOD for euer.

Ch. V. "Of the pure Christall and glassie Sea, on which the Elect shall stand before Christ, . . . "

It will thus be seen that at the date Kett was ultra-orthodox. He must not be confounded with the Ket or Kett of the Norfolk rebellion, much earlier.—G.

END OF VOL. I.

Printed by Hasell, Watson, & Viney, Ld., London and Aylesbury.